'It seems to me that I was as much my father's property as Atwood Mine.'

'But a more desirable property,' Marcus smiled.

'Am I?' she remarked coldly. 'I'm glad you think so, Mr Fitzalan, but that does not alter the fact that you cannot have one without the other—or, at least, you cannot have the mine without me, whereas you would not have me without the mine by choice.'

'You do me an injustice, Miss Somerville. I am not nearly as mercenary as you make me out to be.'

'And I have every reason to think you are,' she shot back at him.

Helen Dickson was born and still lives in South Yorkshire with her husband, on a busy arable farm where she combines writing with keeping a chaotic farmhouse. An incurable romantic, she writes for pleasure, owing much of her inspiration to the beauty of the surrounding countryside. She enjoys reading and music. History has always captivated her, and she likes travel and visiting ancient buildings.

Recent titles by the same author:

AN UNPREDICTABLE BRIDE
AN ILLUSTRIOUS LORD

THE PROPERTY OF A GENTLEMAN

Helen Dickson

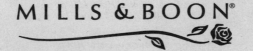

MILLS & BOON®

First published in Great Britain 1998
Harlequin Mills & Boon Limited,
Eton House, 18-24 Paradise Road, Richmond, Surrey TW9 1SR

© Helen Dickson 1998

ISBN 0 263 81154 9

Set in Times Roman 10 on 11¼ pt.
04-9809-93573 C1

Printed and bound in Great Britain
by Caledonian International Book Manufacturing Ltd, Glasgow

Chapter One

1800

Born into the private establishment of privilege and exclusivity, Eve Somerville was every bit as beautiful as she was rich.

She was passionate and feckless and subject to all the moods and contradictions of a high-spirited girl. The only daughter of parents who adored her and cosseted and indulged her every whim, she knew exactly what the future would be. She would marry well and be happy and secure for the rest of her life.

But when she was seventeen years old she discovered that nothing is that certain, for when her mother died from consumption, her father was also struck down by a terrible illness—the doctors he consulted telling him he could not hope to live beyond the next three years. Sadly, he did not even have that because he was killed in a carriage accident shortly after Eve's twentieth birthday.

The funeral of Sir John Somerville was attended by a few distant relatives, friends and acquaintances, having come from north and south, east and west to the steadily thriving, coal-mining market town of Atwood in the West Riding of Yorkshire, a manor in the ancient and extensive parish of Leeds. It was attractively situated in an area of contrasts, with beautiful hills and valleys lying between Atwood and the pleasant and equally prosperous market town of Netherley five miles to the north.

The narrow, tree-shaded lane from Burntwood Hall to the church, set away from the town and adjacent to the grounds of the great house, with its beautiful slender cream spire soaring high above the trees, was fringed with a silent line of estate workers and coal miners alike—men and women who, like their ancestors before them, had helped make the Somervilles what they were today.

The estate, which, unfortunately for Eve, was entailed in default of male heirs—the next in line being a cousin of her father's, Gerald Somerville—was causing some speculation as to what would happen to it when the new owner took up residence, and to Eve, although it was certain she would be well taken care of.

The cortège was quite magnificent: the elegant carriages carrying the many mourners leaving Burntwood Hall, the splendour of the black hearse which was drawn by six plumed black horses with their coats highly polished, carrying Sir John Somerville's coffin, depicting everything he had attained in life.

Shrouded in black silk with a black lace veil attached to her bonnet and covering her pale face, Eve sat beside her maternal grandmother, the formidable Lady Abigail Pemberton, both in the carriage and in the church, taking strength from the older woman's stiff, straightbacked figure, whose gloved hand clutched the gold knob of her walking cane so hard that her knuckles stood out sharply.

Her face behind her veil was grim, her thin mouth pressed in a hard line as she looked straight ahead, giving no indication of her thoughts or emotions, for she had been brought up in an age and society that had taught her it was not done to show one's feelings in public, not even grief for the death of a dear son-in-law. Eve accepted the condolences of those who came to pay their respects graciously, sadly contemplating on what her future would be like without her father.

When the funeral was over they returned to Burntwood Hall, a large, stately Tudor manor house set in a wooded hamlet on the south side of Atwood, a prosperous and populous township where the Somervilles had lived from the sixteenth century. The mining of coal was anciently established in the area, the Somervilles one of several families dominating its production.

Apart from Mr Alex Soames, Eve's father's lawyer, sitting at the big, highly polished table, his elderly grey head bowed over her father's last will and testament, few people were present for the reading, just a few important members of the household, Gerald Somerville, her grandmother and herself—and Mr Marcus Fitzalan from Netherley.

Marcus Fitzalan was tall and lean with strong muscled shoulders. His sharp, distinguished good looks and bearing demanded a second look—and, indeed, with his reputation for being an astute businessman with an inbred iron toughness, he was not a man who could be ignored. There was an authoritative, brisk, no-nonsense air about him and he had an easy, confident way of moving and a haughty way of holding his head. His hair, thick and jet black, was brushed back from his forehead, his cheek bones high and angular, making his face look severe.

Thirty years old, he was a striking-looking man with an enormous presence—a man Eve had met three years ago and had not seen since. It was an encounter which had been most unpleasant, one she did not wish to recall, for anger and the humiliation she had suffered at his hands still festered like a raw wound deep inside her. It was an encounter that had left a stain on her reputation and lost her the man she might have married.

From the moment Eve had seen Marcus Fitzalan in the church she had been unprepared for the uncontrollable tremor that shot through her. During the three years since she had last laid eyes on him, she thought she had remembered exactly what he looked like, but now she realised she was mistaken as her eyes refused to tear themselves away from the sheer male beauty of him.

He seemed to radiate a compelling magnetism, everything about him exuding a ruthless sensuality. He had a straight, aquiline nose which suggested arrogance, and his firm lips, which she knew to her cost, could be cynical or sensuous. His stark black brows were slashed across his forehead and his eyes were compelling, pale blue and clear. Hidden deep in their depths was humour, but also a watchfulness that made one wary. Eve found it hard to believe this was the same man who had kissed her so seductively and passionately three years ago.

When he had taken his seat across from her at the other side of the church in one of the tall box pews, he seemed to sense her watching him and had turned slowly. As their eyes met his dark brows lifted in bland enquiry. Eve caught her breath and felt heat scorch through her body before hastily looking away, ashamed that his look made her legs begin to quake and her treacherous heart to race, as it had on that other occasion when he had kissed her so devastatingly and sent her young, innocent heart soaring heavenwards.

His presence made her feel uneasy and she did her best to evade him, having no desire to come face to face with the man for whom she felt resentment heavy in her breast.

But her grandmother, always keen to meet the local gentry and, unlike her granddaughter, impressed by Mr Fitzalan's importance and air of distinction, lost no time in acquainting herself once they were back at the house. She made sure that her granddaughter was introduced afterwards, ignorant of the fact that he was the man responsible for her ruin and disgrace, even though her father had packed Eve off to Cumbria to stay with her immediately after the unfortunate affair, the explanation being that a visit to her grandmother was long overdue.

Fortunately, her reputation had not been ruined beyond recall, the incident had soon passed over and she had returned home, but Marcus Fitzalan's conduct towards her had left her with a deep sense of loathing and bitter humiliation.

He had left for a lengthy stay in London the following day, blissfully unaware of the furore he had left behind, thinking her nothing more than a promiscuous little flirt whom he had taught a harsh, yet valuable, lesson in life, and she had been too proud to let him think anything else—and it was that same pride that refused to let him see how deeply his callous behaviour towards her had hurt her.

'Let me take you over to meet Mr Fitzalan, Eve. I find it difficult to believe you have never been properly introduced, considering he and your father were such good friends and partners in several business concerns,' said her grandmother.

Panic gripped Eve as her grandmother began steering her in Mr Fitzalan's direction. 'I would really rather not, Grandmother. Besides—see—he is engaged in conversation with Mr and Mrs Lister. I would not wish to interrupt.'

Unfortunately, her grandmother was not to be put off. 'Nonsense, Eve. Come along. Mr Fitzalan will not eat you, you know.'

Marcus turned as they approached, Mr and Mrs Lister moving on to speak to someone else. With Eve's veil turned back over her bonnet, Marcus was able to look down into her white face, framed by hair of sable blackness, and their eyes met, frozen by time and memory. He thought how young she looked, more beautiful than he remembered, and he noticed how her soft lips trembled as she tilted her head back a little to look up at him.

With a warmth flooding and throbbing through his veins he remembered how it had felt to hold her, how soft and yielding her lips had been when she had kissed him with such tender passion, and how her body had moulded itself innocently into his own. He was seized by the same uncontrollable compulsion to repeat the pleasurable incident that had left a deep and lasting impression on him three years ago when she had sought him out at Atwood Fair.

A poignant memory came back to him of that time, of a bewitchingly beautiful young girl who had brazenly approached him and foolishly made an immature and improper attempt to seduce him—he later discovered for some mischievous prank concocted by her and her friends for their own amusement. But it was unfortunate that the man she had hoped to marry had found out about her indiscretion and spurned her because of it.

At the time he had regarded the incident with amusement, remembering how surprised she had been when he had turned the tables on her with an expert subtlety and started to play her at her own game. Because of her inexperience and ignorance of the rules of nature he had soon had her at his mercy. In no time at all she had been unable to prevent herself from becoming his victim—and he retained a poignant memory of how willingly she had melted in his arms.

But the incident had not turned out as either of them had intended, for he had continued to think of her. For a long time afterwards he had been unable to get her out of his mind. She had done something to him, aroused feelings he had not experienced before.

'Mr Fitzalan, I would like to introduce you to my granddaughter, Eve Somerville—although I have just been saying to her how odd it is that the two of you have not been formaly introduced before, considering your close friendship with Sir John.'

Bowing his dark head slightly, Marcus looked at Eve with a gaze that seemed to look straight into her heart, seeing that her lovely eyes were shuttered, giving no insight as to what her feelings might be. With the exception of a muscle that tightened at the corner of his mouth his expression was impassive, his voice coolly polite when he spoke.

'On the contrary, Lady Pemberton, we have met briefly, several years ago—although we were not properly introduced at the time,' he said, without any hint of implications, for he was gravely conscious of the solemnity of the occasion and had no wish to embarrass Eve or cause any constraint between them. But Eve knew exactly to what he was referring. It was a meeting she would prefer to forget and she was angry that he had the audacity to allude to it now.

'It's a pleasure to meet you again, Miss Somerville,' he continued. 'However, had it not been for your father's untimely death, I believe he was about to bring you over to Brooklands shortly,' he told her, referring to his home. Taking her hand, he felt it tremble slightly. 'May I offer you my condolences. What happened to your father was a tragedy. He will be sadly missed.'

With cool disdain she lifted her chin and smiled politely, trying to ignore the tightness at the base of her throat. 'Thank you.'

'Your grandmother has only recently returned from London, I believe,' he said by way of conversation, as the aforesaid lady turned to speak to an acquaintance.

'Yes,' she replied stiffly, wishing he would go away and speak to someone else—anyone, just so long as she did not have to suffer his odious presence. 'She has been visiting my Aunt Shona—my mother's sister who lives in Bloomsbury with her family. She is travelling back to her home in Cumbria and thought she would break her journey to spend some time with me and my father here at Burntwood Hall. Sadly, it has not turned out as she expected. I am only thankful she arrived to see my father before the terrible accident happened.'

'I am surprised you did not travel with her to London to visit your aunt.'

'Had my father been in better health I might have—but as it was I did not wish to be away from home in—in case…'

'I understand,' he said quietly when she faltered, her tight façade of dignity slipping slightly, and for a brief moment she looked like a forlorn child. 'Your father spoke of you often. Indeed, he told me so much about you that I feel I have known you all my life.'

'Really!' she retorted crisply, the shutters up once more. 'You surprise me, Mr Fitzalan. So much of my father's time was spent away from home, despite his illness, that I am flattered to learn he could find the time even to think of me, let alone to discuss me with a total stranger.'

'Your father and I were hardly strangers, Miss Somerville. And,' he said with a gentle lift to his eyebrows, holding her gaze steadily, 'neither are we, come to think of it.'

'Despite what took place between us on our previous encounter you are to me,' Eve replied directly, her voice cool, finding it difficult to conceal her dislike. 'However, when he was at home it may interest you to know that he always spoke of you a great deal, too, Mr Fitzalan,' she said pointedly. 'In fact, there was never a day went by when he did not sing your praises.' Her voice held a faint trace of sarcasm and was cold, which she knew was reflected in her eyes.

'I myself would hardly deem our meeting a pleasure,' she continued, the impressionable, ignorant girl she had been when he had last seen her having fled away, although the remembrance of their encounter and the resulting chaos knifed through her as it had then.

Marcus frowned. 'What happened between us was a long time ago. Surely now—especially at this time with your father so recently laid to rest—we can at least be friends.'

'I doubt we can be friends now or in the future, Mr Fitzalan. After today it is most unlikely that our paths will cross again.'

His eyes became probing, penetrating hers like dagger thrusts, his face a hard, expressionless mask. 'Don't be too sure about that, Miss Somerville,' he said quietly. 'Atwood and Netherley are not so far apart—and your father and I were business partners as well as friends. I would say it is inevitable that we meet at some social event or other.'

'We do not mix in the same society, Mr Fitzalan, but if we do chance to meet you will forgive me if I seem to avoid you.'

'Come now, you were not so ill disposed towards me the last time we met,' he said, his tone silky, easy, his eyes regarding her with fascinated amusement. 'In fact, you were rather amiable, as I remember.'

'You remember too much,' Eve snapped, two sparks of anger showing briefly beneath her lowered lids. 'It was an incident which I have had cause to reproach myself for many times.'

Undeterred by her show of anger Marcus chuckled softly, a glint of white teeth showing from between his parted lips. 'I recall how you went off in an extremely disagreeable mood.'

'I am still disagreeable and will remain so while ever I am in your company, Mr Fitzalan. Now you must excuse me. There are several people I must speak to before they depart.'

Before Marcus could reply and uncaring that her words might have given offence, Eve turned from him, seeing her friend Emma Parkinson moving towards her. Quickly she moved on, leaving her grandmother to carry on the conversation, determined not to give Mr Fitzalan another thought.

But it was not possible for her to dismiss a man of Marcus Fitzalan's calibre from her mind—in fact, she thought with bitter irony, she doubted that anyone would be able to. Once met, he was not the kind of man who could be forgotten. When he had taken her hand he had kept it far too long in his hard grasp for her liking, and the fact that she had to look up at him had annoyed her, causing fresh resentment to flare up inside her, but she had been unable to take her eyes off his handsome features, which had caused him to arch his clearly defined eyebrows and a half-smile to curve his infuriatingly arrogant lips.

When he spoke, his voice was of a depth and timbre that was like a caress, causing a faint stroke of colour to sweep over her creamy skin, bringing a smile to his lips, for he knew exactly the effect he was having on her.

Despite the solemnity of the occasion, as she moved among the mourners who congregated at Burntwood Hall after the funeral, she was conscious of Marcus Fitzalan's presence throughout, becoming annoyed with herself as she found her eyes unconsciously seeking him out, and she would find herself studying him when she thought he was not looking. But several times their eyes would meet and he made no attempt to hide the gleam of interest that entered his eyes as she felt herself undergoing the selfsame scrutiny.

Eve was not used to men of the world like Marcus Fitzalan, and for the first time in her life realised she was in danger of stepping out of her depth. He had a reputation as being one for the ladies, although he was always discreet in his affairs. By all accounts he was arrogant, conceited and ruthless—in fact, he was everything Eve hated. She had every reason to dislike him and, seeing him again for the first time in three years, she was determined that nothing would sway her from her opinion.

Waiting for Mr Soames to begin reading the will, Eve could feel Marcus's eyes on her yet again, vibrant, alarmingly alive, assessing her in a way she found offensive as he stood by the window, looking for all the world as if he owned the place.

He was a neighbour and an associate in several of her father's business concerns, a man her father had been extremely fond of, as well as being a wealthy land and mine owner in his own right, so there was nothing unusual about his presence for the reading of the will.

The Fitzalans had had to struggle to achieve prosperity as opposed to the Somervilles, who were rich not only in wealth but also in lineage. Marcus's grandfather had been an astute, self-made man, seizing on the opportunities to be achieved by the mining of coal, knowing it was fuel for a whole range of industrial processes and for the new generation of industrial workers—and also knowing there was no shortage of it beneath the soil of Britain.

Reaching some degree of financial ability, he had bought

fifty acres of land adjacent to the Somerville estate and opened his own mine—Atwood Mine. Coal had enabled him to sink more mines and given him the means to build Brooklands— a house to be envied and admired—but after a series of serious mishaps Atwood Mine had fallen into the hands of John Somerville.

Marcus's handsome eyes raked the face of the girl sitting primly at the table across the room without her bonnet. His eyes dwelt on her hair, as ebony black and shiny like his own, her eyebrows arched and sleek, her neck rising graceful and swanlike from her slender shoulders. There was a creamy smoothness to her skin with a soft blush on her angular cheeks, giving a slant to her large and mysterious violet-coloured eyes that held his like magnets. Her lips were luscious, her chin pert with a stubborn thrust, and all these attractive features were encompassed in a perfect, heart-shaped face.

She was beautiful, slim and vibrant, the gentle curve of her young breasts straining beneath the bodice of her black dress. She still had the looks of a child, but there was something bold and defiant in the way her eyes locked on to his, which told him she was no innocent and that she possessed a spirit as strong and rebellious as his own, giving him the feeling that in this seemingly fragile girl he might have met his match.

After Mr Soames had read out the generous bequests Sir John Somerville had made to his loyal retainers and they had quietly left the room, everyone waited for him to continue as he licked his lips nervously, focusing his gaze on Eve.

With growing impatience Gerald Somerville was sitting with bated breath for Sir John's will to be read out, finding it difficult to control his excitement. It was like finding a treasure chest just waiting to be opened. His hooded eyes were transfixed on Mr Soames, knowing he was about to inherit the title and complete control over his cousin's property, which would elevate him at last from the penury and insecurity that had bedevilled him for far too long. It was a moment he had waited for, a moment which had come sooner rather than later owing

to the tragic, but fortuitous, carriage accident which had killed
Sir John.

Always the poor relation, all his life Gerald had hated pov-
erty and dreamed of being rich and enjoying all that money
could buy. He had loathed his respectable home and his parents' dull existence. Aware that he was heir to Sir John's estate
he was impatient, knowing that it could be years before he
came into his inheritance, but on learning of his cousin's increasing ill health he had quietly rubbed his hands with hope-
ful anticipation, suspecting he would not have too long to wait
after all. He bided his time, enjoying the adventures and excitement in the gaming rooms of London, which had become
his haunts on the death of his parents, seeing gambling as a
chance to become rich and powerful, which he craved.

'What I am about to disclose will come as something of a
shock, Eve, and you must understand that the will was written
at a very difficult time of your father's life,' said Mr Soames
gently, looking at her in a kind and sympathetic way, having
known her from birth.

Her parents had spoilt and cosseted her to excess from the
moment she was born, sheltering and allowing her to go her
own wilful way—until three years ago, when, by her own
foolishness, she had suffered a lapse from grace and her
mother had died, causing her much grief. Her sorrow had increased in intensity when Sir John had become ill soon afterwards with a cancer that had slowly begun to eat its way
through his wretched body.

Sitting perched on the edge of her seat as if her backbone
was made of hard steel, Eve tried to fight off her growing
alarm. Until now she had believed that the reading of the will
was to be a mere formality, confident that she knew exactly
what it contained and having no reason to be concerned—that
even though the estate was in entailment and that no part of
it could be sold to provide for her, her father would have seen
to it that she would be well taken care of.

But suddenly she felt herself grow tense and anxious, sensing instinctively by the tone of Mr Soames's voice that all was not as it should be. Her throat went dry and she spoke with difficulty.

'A shock? But why should it be a shock? What precisely do you mean, Mr Soames? My father has left me well taken care of, hasn't he?'

'Yes—that is so, but it may not be what you are expecting.' He focused his eyes on Gerald, who was watching him intently, every muscle in his face tense. 'The entire estate—that is, the land, the house and other properties—both here and in London, are to go to you, sir.'

Eve waited, going colder by the second, trying not to look at Gerald as he tried to conceal his triumph, knowing there was little left to come her way but expecting her father to have made a substantial sum over to her.

'You, Eve,' Mr Soames went on, shifting his gaze once more to her, 'are to receive an annuity in the sum of two thousand pounds a year.'

When he fell silent she waited in expectant anticipation, expecting him to continue, to tell her there was more, until she realised there was nothing more. Her heart rose up to choke her and she stared at him in absolute confusion and astonishment.

'But—but that's not possible. There must be some mistake. There has to be. My father's assets—he—he was an extremely wealthy man. It has to be more than this.'

'There is no mistake,' he said quietly, his voice penetrating the mist of Eve's bemused senses. 'His main assets are private matters and have nothing to do with the estate—namely, his shares in several coal mines and interests in various industrial concerns and so forth, several of them in which he and Mr Fitzalan were partners and which he made over to him before he died.'

All the colour drained out of Eve's face and her hand rose and clasped the collar of her black mourning dress. She was stunned, unable to believe what he had told her. A silence fell upon the room which seemed to last an age, the small assembly around her becoming shadowy, faceless figures, all staring at her, until Gerald, acknowledging his good fortune in inheriting the estate—and yet beginning to feel a trifle perplexed that not all Sir John's property had passed on to him as he had expected it would—began talking animatedly to Mr Soames about what it would mean to him, with little regard for the pain and disappointment that was tearing Eve apart.

The still, quiet figure of Lady Pemberton sat rigidly on her chair towards the back of the room, neither shock nor surprise disturbing the marble severity of her face, but her eyes and ears missed nothing. Only the hand cupping the gold knob of her cane gave any indication of the way she felt, for it gripped the knob hard, so hard that her knuckle bones nearly punctured the thin white skin covering them.

Only Marcus seemed to be aware of the pain Eve was suffering. She was young and unable to deal with the dilemma in which she found herself. As he looked at her his gaze was secretive and seemed to probe beneath the surface, but he could see by the terror in her eyes, how her face had become drained of blood and the way her fingers clutched her throat, that this unexpected blow from her father had hit her hard.

From what Sir John had told him he knew she was a strong-minded girl who would know how to take care of herself well enough, but it was only a girl who was behind the artificial ageing of bereavement, and it would not be easy for her to get over something like this.

Something in the region of his heart softened and he wanted to go to her and offer some words of comfort, wishing he could erase the sad, stricken look from her face, but he knew by the cold hostility she had not attempted to conceal when they had been introduced after the funeral, and in her eyes when she looked at him, that by his own fault she would not welcome his sympathy.

'Is that it? Am I to get nothing else?' she asked, her voice surprisingly calm, but so quiet Mr Soames had difficulty hearing her. 'With all his wealth, did my father make no other financial provision for me? Am I to be reduced to such dire straits that I must starve?'

Mr Soames was beginning to feel distinctly uncomfortable before Eve's hard gaze and his eyes wavered as he looked down at the papers in front of him, coughing nervously. 'No— it is not quite as bad as that.'

'Then please tell me. And where am I to live?'

'Perhaps when I have explained everything to you it will be much clearer. Your father did not leave you as destitute as it would seem—for, as you know, he always had your best interests at heart. But there are certain conditions to be adhered to—certain clauses that may seem strange to you.'

'Conditions? What kind of conditions?'

'That you and Mr Marcus Fitzalan marry within six months of his death.'

Eve was so stunned she was unable to speak.

'Should this be agreeable to you both,' Mr Soames went on hurriedly, wanting to get this unpleasant part of reading the will over and done with as quickly as possible, 'Atwood Mine—of which your father was the sole owner—will become yours jointly.'

The words came as a shattering blow to Gerald, whose face became as white as his frothing lace cravat, bringing an angry exclamation to his lips and jolting him to his feet, causing all heads to turn in his direction. 'No, sir. It will not do. This I cannot accept. Atwood Mine is Sir John's main asset and is surely entailed with the rest of his estate.'

'That is not the case. Sir John purchased the lease, not the land. As everyone is aware Atwood Mine—which is the largest and most profitable mine in the area—was sunk by Mr Fitzalan's grandfather and the lease sold by Mrs Fitzalan to Sir John privately on the death of her husband. The lease has another fifteen years to run—with the rent arranged annually on a scale related to the amount of coal mined. You are correct in saying it was Sir John's greatest asset, and it was his wish that the lease be returned to the Fitzalan family—providing Mr Marcus Fitzalan marries his daughter Eve.'

Eve looked at Gerald properly for the first time that day. Both his parents were dead, and his home, where his younger brother Matthew—a quiet, gentle young man whom she knew well and had a strong liking for—still lived, was three miles from Burntwood Hall, but for most of the time he resided in London and she had not seen him for several months.

He had been a frequent visitor to Burntwood Hall in the past, and both she and her father had shared a very low opinion of him. On his last visit she noticed how changed he was towards her, as if he noticed for the first time that she was no longer a child but a young woman. She hadn't liked the way he looked at her—too long and too hard, and not in the least like a relation who should know better than to lust after his cousin's daughter.

Seeing him now, she liked him even less. At one time she had thought him to be as handsome as a Greek god, with hair the colour of spun gold and looks that made every woman he came into contact with swoon and fall at his feet. He was more corpulent than when she had last seen him, but he was a handsome figure still, though soft living and overindulgence had blurred him somewhat and there was a seediness creeping through.

At twenty-eight he had been spoilt by an adoring mother and fawned over and adored by countless women. He thought he had only to wink an eye to have any one of them tumble into his bed; if all the stories about him were to be believed, then there was an army of women he had enjoyed and then grown tired of, casting them aside as one would discard a worn-out toy. In the past he had been involved in one scandal after another, causing her father acute embarrassment.

As her gaze focused on his face she saw his expression was closed as he watched, his brown eyes, glittering with menace, darting from her to Marcus Fitzalan. They were filled with such hatred that her heart skipped a beat. His slack lips were

set in a slight smile that was not pleasant; in fact, there was
something about him that reminded her of something sinister
and evil.

Her eyes shifted from Gerald and travelled across the room
to meet the cold, pale-blue implacable stare of Marcus
Fitzalan, where he still stood with what she could only describe as lounging insolence. He seemed so cool, so self-
assured, while she felt as if she were falling apart.

Chapter Two

Marcus Fitzalan's expression was unreadable, but Eve suspected he must be feeling every bit as shocked and horrified as she was. Or was he? she asked herself. It was no secret that her father had been an ill man, whose health had deteriorated rapidly over the last few months. The doctor had given him another twelve months to live at the most, and being such close friends, was it possible that this had been contrived by Mr Fitzalan in order to get his hands on Atwood Mine? After all, there wasn't a man or woman in the whole of Atwood or Netherley who didn't know how much he wanted it returned once more to his family. A wave of sick disgust swept over her.

'Did you know about this?' she demanded, having to fight to keep her anger in check, the horror of that first dreadful shock having left her eyes. 'Did my father discuss this with you?'

'No, he did not,' he said crisply, giving no indication of the initial rush of gratitude that had washed over him towards Sir John for making it possible for him to own his father's mine once more, for sentimental reasons rather than profit—the enormous wealth he accumulated from his other mines and business ventures provided him with more than adequate profit to enable him to maintain Brooklands and live comfortably.

The condition that he marry Sir John's daughter did not pose a problem—providing she was agreeable. He was confident that despite the hostility she so clearly felt towards him she could be persuaded, for he seemed to have a power over women that often puzzled him. They had a way of retaining him in their minds and once met he was never forgotten, but no woman had ever managed to push him over the edge and into marriage—the love of his life being his work. But with Atwood Mine being offered to him he was prepared to adhere to any conditions Sir John had made.

Eve stared at him with angry, bewildered eyes. This was too much. Her father should have called Marcus Fitzalan out and shot him over his disgraceful behaviour towards her, after he had degraded and humiliated her so shockingly. How could he have been so audacious as to arrange a marriage for her with him when he had almost ruined her? The very idea was unthinkable—impossible.

'I cannot possibly agree to this,' she said furiously, beginning to lose control of her precariously held temper. 'What can my father have been thinking of to ask this of me? He should not have done it. Why did he not tell me what he intended?'

'Perhaps he would have—but for the accident,' said Mr Soames. 'It was very sudden.'

'Nevertheless it is quite preposterous. Let me make it quite plain here and now that I will *never* agree to conditions such as these.'

Marcus remained silent, but roused from his complacent stance by the window he moved towards the table.

'Shouldn't you at least consider it?' said Mr Soames. 'When you get over the shock and weigh up what it will mean to you both—is it really so preposterous as all that?'

'Yes, it is—to me. It was quite outrageous of my father to expect me to marry on these terms. I have been troublesome in the past, I know, but I have done nothing to contribute to his decision to treat me so shockingly. Clearly he was sick in mind as well as body—or it was done for some malicious reason of his own. He seems to have thought of everything.'

Marcus shot her an angry look. 'Hasn't he just. But your father was not insane and nor was he a malicious man, Miss Somerville—and you do him a grave injustice by accusing him of such. Being a man of honour and integrity, a man who considered the well being of others before his own throughout his life, I am sure he thought this over very carefully before laying down conditions that are clearly so abhorrent to you,' he said coolly, in defence of her father, fixing her with an icy, hard stare.

Eve's own eyes snapped back at him, angered that he of all people should have the temerity to reproach her like a naughty child, although she did regret using the word 'malicious', which was spoken unintentionally and in the heat of the moment. Mr Fitzalan was right. Her father had been a caring and gentle man and as honest as the day is long, and could not be accused of being 'malicious', but she did not need the likes of Marcus Fitzalan to tell her so.

'And you would know, wouldn't you, Mr Fitzalan?' she said heatedly, accusingly, blinded with wrath, standing up and lifting her head imperiously, meeting his gaze boldly and squaring her chin in her proud challenge to his authority.

'From the amount of time the two of you spent together you must have got to know my father very well. Knowing what little time he had left, was it your intention to wheedle your way into his good graces in an attempt to persuade him to transfer the lease of Atwood Mine back to you? After all, everyone knows how keen you are to get your hands on it once more.'

Her accusation bit deep, causing Marcus's own temper to rise. His lean face darkened and his metallic eyes narrowed furiously, warningly, and Eve felt the effort it was costing him to keep his rage under control.

'I refute that. I have been accused of many things, Miss Somerville, and have been the subject of much gossip and speculation over the years, but let me make it clear that, contrary to what you might think of me, it is not in my nature to stoop so low as to acquire anything by flattery or guile. I held your father in the highest regard and knew he was a very sick man—but not how sick. We were friends, good friends, and I thought—and hoped—him fit for a good many years to come.'

His lip curled scornfully across his even white teeth as he spoke softly and with a menacing calm. 'At any other time— and if you were a man—I would take you to task for such an insult, but this is neither the time nor the occasion for doing so.'

'That is extremely civil of you, Mr Fitzalan. But I do not retract what I said,' Eve retorted, trying to speak with the utmost composure while growing more and more angry by the second.

'That is your prerogative. I understand that you have justifiable reason to be shocked by the contents of your father's will and that you are naturally quite distraught by your tragic loss—which I shall put down to being the reason for your outburst—so I shall take no offence and will ignore the affront to my character.'

His voice sounded calm, giving everyone the impression that he was not in the least put out by her insulting remark, but Eve was not deceived for his mouth hardened and his eyes flared like molten quicksilver, daring her to say more. But she refused to cower before him. Her eyes flashed defiance and her face assumed an expression of hardened resentment.

She opened her mouth to challenge his statement but the expression in his eyes made her close it quickly. With her lips clamped together she averted her gaze, considering it prudent to let the matter rest—for now.

Everyone present had listened to the angry altercation between them in astonishment and silence, amazed that Eve could have been so outspoken and unable to think of anything that could justify such behaviour, but, like Marcus, they put it down to her being overwrought and her dispirited and anxious state of mind. Only Gerald remained watchful, a ruthless gleam lighting up his eyes.

Marcus chose to put the matter from his mind—hoping that everyone else would do the same—but it was not forgotten.

'What happens to the bequest if we do not marry?' he asked, prising his eyes away from Eve's stony expression and fixing them on Mr Soames, trying hard to ignore the burning hatred in Gerald Somerville's eyes as they bored into him. He knew how Gerald had coveted Atwood Mine and how cheated he must be feeling on discovering that the estate had been creamed of its most lucrative asset—an asset Gerald had been depending on to help clear an outstanding debt of thousands of pounds he had acquired through gambling, having borrowed the money to settle his debt from ruthless moneylenders who would stop at nothing until it was repaid with extortionate interest.

But Marcus also knew how hard Sir John had worked to achieve success where Atwood Mine was concerned, and how much he had wanted it kept out of the hands of his cousin, who would have little interest in the mine itself, only the wealth it would bring to him.

'You get nothing,' said Mr Soames in answer to his question.

'Nothing!' whispered Eve, deeply shocked, turning her attention to her father's lawyer. 'But what will I do? Where am I to live.'

'Should a marriage between you and Mr Fitzalan not take place you will get your annuity, of course, and he has made provisions for you to live with your grandmother in Cumbria.'

'And the mine?' asked Marcus abruptly.

'Will revert to Mr Gerald Somerville and his heirs until the lease has run out, at which time it will be up to you or your heir—should you not be alive at the time—to decide whether or not it is renewed.'

A cold and calculating gleam entered Gerald's eyes when he realised all might not be lost after all. It would appear that all he had to do was prevent Eve from entering into a marriage with Marcus Fitzalan, and if he wasn't mistaken that shouldn't prove too difficult—not when he observed that every time she looked at him or spoke to him, she did so with unconcealed hostility.

'I realise that no one can force you to marry,' Mr Soames went on, 'that is for you to choose—but I ask you to give very serious thought to the matter.'

Marcus nodded, his face grim. 'You can count on it.'

Eve scowled at him. 'The day I marry you, Mr Fitzalan, will be the day hell freezes over. We do not suit.' She returned her attention once more to Mr Soames, ignoring Marcus's black look. 'Did my father give no explanation when he laid down these conditions?'

'I'm afraid not. Whatever it was that prompted him to do it I cannot say—and indeed, we may never know. I think, perhaps, that if he had lived a little longer, he might have explained everything to you. As you know, your father and I were friends for a good many years, and I knew him well enough to know he would not have set down these conditions without good reason. Knowing his death was imminent sharpened his anxiety to procure a suitable match for you.'

'But what if Mr Fitzalan had decided to marry someone else before my father died?' asked Eve, wishing he had.

'Your father knew Mr Fitzalan had no one in mind—and, considering your father had only a few months left to live— a year at the most—he thought it unlikely that Mr Fitzalan would do so before his death.'

Eve looked at Marcus Fitzalan and could see that he was contemplating what the loss of the mine would mean to him— and to her. Then she saw herself living in the harsh, craggy wilderness of Cumbria with her grandmother, where everyday life can be particularly severe and so remote she would see no one from one day's end to the next. The thought was not pleasant.

Turning his gaze on Eve once more, Marcus's black brows

drew together in a deep frown. He seemed to sense what was going through her mind.

Feeling betrayed, abandoned and unable to think clearly because of the shock all this had been to her, Eve rose suddenly, clenching her fists in the folds of her dress to stop them from shaking.

'Please, excuse me,' she said, turning and crossing to the door with a quiet dignity, having no wish to stay and hear more, only a strong desire to be by herself.

Not wanting to leave the matter in suspension indefinitely—which, he suspected, was what Miss Somerville intended doing—with long strides Marcus followed her out of the room into the large dark panelled hall, closing the door behind them. Two sleek liver and white hounds lay curled up in front of a huge stone hearth where a fire burned bright in an iron grate, despite the heat of the summer's day. They stretched languidly, each cocking an uninterested eye in the direction of the intruders before resuming their doze in a state of blissful lassitude, ignoring the disturbance.

'Wait,' Marcus commanded. 'We cannot leave matters like this.'

Eve paused at the sound of his voice and turned and faced him, extremely conscious of his towering, masculine presence. The immaculate cut of his coat was without a crease, moulding his strong shoulders. As his ice blue eyes swept over her his expression was grim and Eve felt extremely uncomfortable at the way he was regarding her—no doubt assessing her suitability as a possible wife, she thought wryly.

Having recovered some of her self-possession, she threw back her shoulders and lifted her head, the action meaning to tell him she was in control of herself. He felt a stirring of admiration for the way in which she conducted herself, but looking into her lovely violet eyes he could see they were as turbulent as storm clouds and that she had withdrawn inside herself to a place where she could not be reached.

'This has come as a shock to you, I can see,' he said, glad to be out of earshot of the others.

'Yes. I am both shocked and disappointed. I cannot imagine what prompted my father to do this,' she said, trying to keep a stranglehold on her emotions, 'unless, of course, he had a momentary lapse of his senses when he saw fit to make these conditions in his will in the first place. But the last thing I want right now, Mr Fitzalan, is a husband—and when I do I would prefer to choose my own.'

Faced with her anger, Marcus paled and his eyes glittered like steel flints as he tried, with great difficulty, to keep his own anger in check, knowing exactly why she was doing her utmost to make matters as difficult as possible between them. She was still embittered by what had happened between them three years ago—although why she should continue to be so baffled him, for she had no one to blame but herself. Was it usual that the moment her will was crossed she started the sparks flying and spitting fire?

'And I have no more need of a wife than you a husband, Miss Somerville,' he replied, his voice carrying anger. 'However, if we want to hold on to the mine then we have no choice but to heed your father's wishes and make the best of it.'

'And how do you know that is what I want? How can you possibly know?' she said, her voice as cold as her face, whilst inside her stomach was churning. 'As far as I am concerned the mine is the last thing on my mind at this moment. Marriage to me is important and I am hardly likely to walk into it blindly with a man who has treated me so abominably—to put my trust and myself completely in your power for the whole of my life. Besides, it is hardly flattering to know you would only be marrying me for what I could bring, Mr Fitzalan.'

'The same could be said of yourself, Miss Somerville,' he replied coldly. He gave her a hard look, his mouth tightening as he stared down at her. 'Are you always so difficult?'

'I can be as impossible as I like when something—or someone—upsets me,' she answered.

He arched an eyebrow. 'Really?'

'Yes.'

'Then I suppose that is something I shall have to get used to if we are to make anything of your father's will. Tell me, are you well acquainted with Gerald Somerville?'

'No. I believe he has been in London himself and has only returned to the north this last week. We have met frequently over the years, but I cannot say that I know him at all well. My grandmother does not hold him in high regard and saw nothing of him while she was in town.'

Marcus's lips twisted with slight scorn. 'How could she? The kind of world your father's cousin inhabits is a night-time world of gambling and high living. There is no polite way to describe him. He is a slippery character and he has only one motive in life: to serve himself. He'd be considered a joke if he were not so ruthless in everything he does. He is to be found anywhere the *beau monde* chooses to congregate, and has an inability to resist the gambling halls and social whirl of London.'

'That I am already aware of.'

'His own estate is falling apart and bankruptcy is staring him in the face. He has lived in penury for most of his life and Sir John's death has suddenly elevated him to an attainable position. I do not believe it will be too long before the estate shows signs of neglect as he uses it as a means to pay off his debts—which, I know for a fact, are astronomical.'

Wanting desperately to escape the threat she imagined this overbearing man suddenly posed to her life, Eve stepped back from him abruptly. 'Do you think I haven't worked that out for myself? It's what I have always known. But it would seem you know Gerald well, Mr Fitzalan. Perhaps he frequents the same seedy establishments as yourself—is that it?'

'I am very particular in choosing my friends, Miss Somerville,' Marcus replied scathingly, choosing to ignore her outspoken attack on his social habits. 'Your father's cousin has a reputation for spending far more than his own father could support when he was alive. It is my misfortune to be a member of the same club—White's in St James's—and I was witness to him squandering his entire fortune at the card tables at a single sitting.'

Eve stared at him in astonishment. 'Might I ask how much?'

'If you are interested. It was thirty-five thousand pounds.'

She was stunned, unable to believe anybody could lose so much money, although her Aunt Shona had told her on one of her visits to London, that the rattling of a dice box or ill luck at cards, could well result in many a gentleman's country estate being lost, and that as a result suicides were not uncommon.

'But that is an enormous sum of money.'

'Indeed it is. It is not something that can be dismissed with a flick of the wrist.'

'And what did he do? Could he pay?'

Marcus smiled indulgently at her naïvety. 'No. His estate was already mortgaged up to the hilt. Facing ruination, anyone else would have shot himself—but not Gerald Somerville. He took the only option and borrowed the money from unscrupulous moneylenders—who, on learning of your father's death and knowing Gerald was his heir, have called in the loan…with astronomical interest. These men are ruthless and show no mercy to those who cannot pay. I have heard that they are exerting enormous pressure on him, so I don't wonder at his anger on finding Atwood Mine is not his by right. He is in deep water. He needs it desperately to pay off his loan and get the these men off his back.'

Eve was astounded to learn all this. 'I—I had no idea Gerald's situation was so serious.'

'Yes, it is. Inheriting your father's estate will have come as a godsend to him—but your father has seen to it that he has not come into a fortune. Through his own hard work and good management the estate has never been so prosperous, and if Gerald is sensible and takes legal advice on how to settle his loan, then it will continue to be so—but if he does not mend his ways then I am afraid that in no time at all you will begin to see signs of its decline. Everything your father has worked so hard to achieve will be eradicated in one fell swoop.'

Eve winced, the very idea of her beloved home being mortgaged to pay off Gerald's gambling debts and falling into the greedy hands of moneylenders and suchlike angering her beyond words. But there was nothing she could do.

'Which is why your father made quite sure his financial affairs were put in order before he died.'

'It's a pity he did not consider putting me before his financial affairs,' Eve remarked bitterly. 'It seems to me that I was as much his property as Atwood Mine.'

'But a more desirable property,' Marcus smiled, his expression softening.

'Am I?' she remarked coldly. 'I'm glad you think so, Mr Fitzalan, but that does not alter the fact that you cannot have one without the other—or, at least, you cannot have the mine without me, whereas you would not have me without the mine by choice.'

Marcus frowned with annoyance. 'You do me an injustice, Miss Somerville. I am not nearly as mercenary as you make me out to be.'

'And I have every reason to think you are,' she shot back at him, referring to their encounter three years ago. 'But what if I do not agree to marry you? And if my father thought so highly of you, why did he not leave Atwood Mine to you outright, knowing how important it is to you? It would certainly have avoided all these complications and I would not be faced with the daunting prospect of marrying a man not of my choosing—a man I have every reason in the world to despise. I could as easily have gone to Cumbria to live with my grandmother—or to London to my Aunt Shona.'

'He knew that—just like he knew you would see the sense in what he was asking of you. I tend to share Mr Soames's view.'

'And that is?'

'That, if it were not for his untimely death, he would have explained it to you himself—and to me. He probably believed you would fall prey to all manner of fortune hunters if you were left alone.'

'What? Two thousand pounds is hardly a fortune, Mr Fitzalan.'

'Two thousand pounds is a great deal of money to men who have nothing, Miss Somerville. Perhaps the conditions he laid down were his way of making sure you would be taken care of. Do not forget that your father desired only your peace of mind and future happiness. You must believe that.'

'Which is why he has suggested making you my keeper, is that not so, Mr Fitzalan?' she said scathingly. 'However, I do not need you or anyone else to tell me what my own father desired for me,' she said, lowering her head so he would not see the tears collecting her eyes.

'Your husband—not your keeper,' Marcus contradicted in a low voice.

'Nevertheless, I confess I am bewildered by all this. It's a riddle I cannot begin to comprehend. I always believed I knew how his mind worked—but it seems I was wrong. I would like to know why, knowing how I feel about you, he has used what can only be described as emotional blackmail to virtually force me into marriage with you. If I decide not to abide by his wishes, and I am sorely tempted not to,' she said rebelliously, 'then Gerald will stand to benefit enormously.'

'That is true—and I implore you to consider his wishes seriously.'

Eve sighed deeply, so confused her head was spinning. Since her mother's death and the onset of her father's illness, she had stubbornly refused to consider the future and what it would mean to her when the inevitable happened, but now the future was with her and she was unprepared for the life that was being thrust at her. When she spoke a touch of anger had come to add to the bitterness of her disappointment.

'Oh, I shall. I always knew how much my father's work

meant to him—Atwood Mine and all his other concerns—but it did not occur to me until now that he would allow his loyalty to all that, and to you, to affect his dealings with me, his daughter. Please—you must excuse me,' she said quickly. 'All this has come as something of a shock. I need some time to myself.'

'Of course. I fully understand. I am leaving myself presently. I realise that you are your own mistress—but anger is a bad counsellor. Do not allow it to influence your decision, and do not foolishly refuse what is your due.' He sighed. 'We both have much to think about. I shall return to Burntwood Hall when you've had time to recover from today and we can talk seriously about what is to be done,' he said, standing aside to let her pass.

'Yes—thank you,' she said stiffly. 'Goodbye, Mr Fitzalan.'

Marcus watched her go, staring thoughtfully after her. Meeting Eve Somerville for the first time in three years had been like being a contestant in the first round of a boxing match. She was possessed of the most formidable temper he'd ever witnessed in a woman, having a tongue that could flay the meanest man, gladly stamping on his pieces of lacerated flesh before finally pulverising them into dust with the heel of her pretty foot.

He realised that the lady was a termagant, but he sensed she had a magic quality—if she chose to use it. Troubled, he turned to go back to Alex Soames, his expression tightening, his brows drawn together in an ominous black line when he continued to think of her.

He had felt a slight sense of shock the first time she had looked at him fully, when her grandmother had brought her to be introduced to him after the funeral. There was something in her eyes that set his pulse racing and he felt a great sense of excitement—as he had on that other occasion when he had had her at his mercy three years ago. She looked very young— almost a child—yet he already knew that behind the childlike exterior there was a ripe sensuality just bursting to be set free.

Instinctively, he knew that no matter how in control and confident she might conceivably be, she had that bewitching quality that could well captivate a man and enslave him for life—a burgeoning femme fatale. Yet, when he recollected how outspoken she had been at the reading of the will, of the insult she had thrown at him and how quick she was to anger, then he would make damned sure she curbed that temper of hers if she became his wife; if she did not come to heel, she would feel more than the length of his tongue.

When he entered the room once more, his eyes were cold and without expression as he took stock of Gerald Somerville and observed the unconcealed greed glittering in his eyes, knowing it would be exceedingly profitable for him if Marcus did not marry Eve. But there was something else lurking in their depths, something unpleasantly sinister and unconcealed as their eyes locked—a moment in which each of them knew they were mortal enemies.

Marcus had meant what he said when he had told Eve that Gerald Somerville was not unknown to him. He was a notorious rake about town, a man with a sordid reputation, and he was well acquainted with his depraved and corrupt ways, that differed greatly from the accepted standards of behaviour.

He remembered well the night Gerald had faced ruination, and the card game which he himself had been privy to. He'd been at White's, seen with his own eyes the money Gerald had lost—and Gerald was aware that he knew and hated him for knowing. He recalled seeing his fellow players sitting intently round the the table watching Gerald lose, and not even wearing his loose frieze greatcoat inside out—which was often the case by those hoping to win—had brought Gerald luck.

He'd heard it rumoured the following day that in desperation Gerald had borrowed the money to pay off his debt from moneylenders—men without scruples who would resort to any foul and violent means to reclaim loans—digging himself deeper into the mire.

Gerald's expression became set and grim, his eyes shining with a deadly glitter as his gaze became fixed, his feelings for Marcus clearly beyond words. He was filled with an impotent, cold black fury on finding himself cheated by Marcus Fitzalan out of something that he coveted.

Gerald was the kind of man Marcus despised and went out of his way to avoid. Because he knew that nothing was beneath Gerald, that he might even attempt persuading—or, even worse, compromising—Eve into marrying him in order to revert Atwood Mine to him, Marcus was even more determined to return to Burntwood Hall very soon to save Eve from herself in securing her hand in marriage.

Later, slipping out of the house unseen by the few remaining mourners who still lingered on, content to partake of the late Sir John's liquor and to talk and rekindle old memories and dwell on times they had shared, in the falling dusk Eve took the path towards the church, glad there was no one about so that she could be alone, to pay one last visit to her parents' grave before the day that had heralded such a change to her life ended.

She opened the gate into the churchyard, which was enclosed by a high stone wall covered by a wild tangle of weeds and ivy. A mass of ancient yew trees, black in the gathering gloom, were in stark contrast to the creamy sandstone church. All around her was silence, a sudden stillness, as drifting clouds passed over the moon just beginning to appear.

The churchyard was a sad and sorrowful place and Eve moved along the paths in sympathy to nature's silence, the huge, cold grey gravestones covered in lichen and casting looming, grotesque shadows in the gathering gloom. Coming to a halt, she stood looking down at the mound of newly dug earth and clay strewn with flowers, noticing how they were already beginning to wilt and to lose all their frail beauty. Tomorrow they too would be dead. She felt a terrible pain wrench her heart when she contemplated the lifeless forms of her parents lying side by side beneath the soil.

Unlike their ancestors before them who had been interred inside the church, her parents had long since chosen to be buried side by side in the churchyard. Unable to contain the grief that had been accumulating in her heart since her father's accident, tears started in her eyes and streamed down her face.

She fell to her knees and bowed her head as she finally gave way under the long strain that possessed her. All her reserve was gone and she began to cry dementedly, her body shaking with an uncontrollable reservoir of grief, bewilderment and betrayal—unable to understand why her father, who had loved her, had treated her so harshly, unaware as she wept of the tall, silent figure that stood watching her from the gate.

Having taken longer to depart from Burntwood Hall than he had intended, Marcus had come to the churchyard to pay his final respects to the man who had become more than a friend to him over the few years he had known him, a man to whom he owed so much. He paused at the gate on seeing the kneeling, sorrowing figure beside the grave, only just able to make out in the dusk the profile of Eve Somerville, her slender form racked with grief.

His heart contracted with pain and pity, for never had he seen or heard so much desolation in anyone before. He took a step, intending to go to her, but checked himself, thinking it would be best to leave her, that it would do her good to cry, for he suspected there was no one in that great house to offer her comfort. He had to fight the urge to go to her, to take her in his arms and hold her, to caress the soft cloud of hair that had tumbled loose from its pins and fell in wanton disarray about her lovely face.

Aware of his own inadequacy he cursed softly, knowing that Eve Somerville had made a deep and lasting impression on him, penetrating his tough exterior and finding a way into his heart as no other woman had done before. It took all his willpower to tear his eyes from her forlorn figure, to turn and walk away—but it was a picture he knew would never leave him.

Chapter Three

Later, feeling drained of all emotion and extremely tired, Eve sought the sanctuary of her room, curling up in the large winged chair by the fire and closing her eyes, unable to cast Marcus Fitzalan from her mind. Falling into a fitful doze, she found her mind drifting back over the years to the time of Atwood Fair, when she had been seventeen years old, amazed that she should remember every detail and all the words he had said to her, which, because of the humiliation it never failed to evoke, she always refused to do.

She remembered that it had all begun as a silly, girlish prank on the day of the fair—although it could be said that the nature of the prank was not the kind any respectable, well brought-up young lady would have indulged in.

Knowing how much the townspeople looked forward to seeing them, normally her parents showed their faces for just a little while, allowing Eve to accompany them, but this time her mother was not feeling well so was unable to attend. However, knowing how much Eve loved the fair and not wishing to disappoint her, she allowed her to go in the company of Mrs Parkinson, a good friend and the wife of a reputable local squire, whose own daughter Emma was Eve's closest friend. She was confident that she would be well chaperoned and that Mrs Parkinson would see that she did not get up to any mischief.

Atwood Fair was a tremendous social event and the highlight of the year, when the close-knit families of Atwood and the surrounding countryside came together to enjoy and revel in the two days of festivities. It was also of economic importance, for livestock and farm produce were brought in from nearby farms and villages to be sold. Drovers also brought in flocks of sheep and cattle from considerable distances, and wandering gypsies came in gaily painted caravans, positioning them in fields adjacent to the fairground.

There was always so much variety, with so many delightful attractions such as puppet shows, waxworks, shooting galleries and bowling, but also what Eve considered the less attractive events, such as bear baitings, cockfights and prize fights, which always attracted large crowds but which she never went near, finding such spectacles quite revolting.

Traders and merchants had set up stalls to try to tempt visitors to part with their money, and children romped about while lovers strolled hand in hand among the many colourful booths. The appetising aroma of cooking food filled the air, and Eve's father always donated an ox to be roasted on a spit above an open fire, the fat sizzling noisily as it dripped into the hot charcoal embers.

It was mid-afternoon when Eve arrived with her friends Emma Parkinson and Angela Lambert. Eve and Emma were friends of long standing, but she had never got on really well with Angela, who rarely lost an opportunity to embarrass her. She was single minded and forever in pursuit of her own interests. Normally Eve would ignore her, although it did not occur to her that Angela might be jealous of her family's wealth and superior standing in the district, and envious of her popularity with the local young men, selfishly wanting all their attention focused on herself.

Angela and Emma were so very different. Emma was as slender as a wand and had nut-brown hair with eyes to match, and while she was of a gentle disposition with a placid indolence, Angela, with auburn hair and hazel eyes, was quite the opposite, being rather voluptuous, lively and full of energies she found hard to repress. There was also a jealous, malicious streak to her nature that often challenged Eve's own.

Sitting on the grass on the edge of the crowd beneath a warm July sun—where they were being watched over by a sharp-eyed Mrs Parkinson as she conversed with a group of ladies—they were discussing Eve's imminent betrothal to Leslie Stephenson, the good-looking eldest son of a baronet who lived in the area, who had taken little persuading to come to the fair, although he had soon taken himself off to watch the wrestling and boxing matches in progress.

Leslie seemed to find Eve quite enchanting and she couldn't believe her good fortune that she had made such a conquest, although he did seem to be taking an awfully long time in applying to her father for her hand in marriage, which was secretly beginning to worry and vex her.

Eve and Emma sat listening as Angela enthused at length about a young man from her home town of Little Bolton, which was situated halfway between Atwood and Netherley. She considered herself an authority on everything—especially men, positively thriving on their attentions; she was already an expert at knowing how to attract them.

'There are more important things in life,' Eve commented, bored by the fervour with which Angela insisted they know all about a young man they had not met.

Angela scowled crossly. 'You can say that when you're almost betrothed to one of the most eligible men in the north, Eve,' she said, reaching into a box of bonbons Leslie had brought them before disappearing.

'And you will find as big a catch one day, Angela. Men flock round you in droves. You know how to flirt, how to say what pleases them. You'll soon have yourself a husband— although if you carry on eating those bonbons like that you'll become so plump you'll put them off,' she said as Angela popped another into her mouth. She watched as Angela's soft pink lips closed around the sugary sweet, beginning to feel distinctly uneasy about the way Angela always attached herself to Leslie, who, to her anger and dismay, seemed flattered by it and not to mind in the slightest.

'If he's half as rich and good looking as Leslie, then I'll be well satisfied,' Angela replied, softly and serenely, licking each sticky finger, her mouth as pink as a rosebud and her eyes lighting with sudden interest when they came to rest on a man riding by on a powerfully built chestnut stallion, the man in the saddle exuding virility and a lazy confidence.

His head was bare, the sunlight shining on his hair, which was as black as ebony, his body in complete proportion as he moved as one with his horse. His shoulders and hips were firm, his booted legs long and his thighs powerful as they gripped his horse.

'Good Lord,' gasped Angela, agog with excitement. 'It's Marcus Fitzalan.'

As he rode past Angela and Emma stole long, lingering looks at him—but not so much Eve, who remained unimpressed. He was well-known and people moved out of the way to let him pass. Eve merely glanced at him with idle curiosity, because although they had never met—she had caught only a brief glimpse of him when he had called at Burntwood Hall once—she knew him to be a business associate and close friend of her father's.

He seemed oblivious to the mayhem he caused within the breasts of two of the young ladies, his mind being on other things, but on hearing Angela's unrestrained girlish giggles he condescended to look their way. The blast from his eyes acted like a douche of cold air as they swept over the group with little interest.

'Goodness! What a handsome man,' Emma exclaimed, sighing ecstatically as her eyes followed the delectable Mr Fitzalan, watching him become swallowed up by the crowd.

'And he knows it,' said Angela.

'I wonder what he's doing here.'

Eve shrugged. 'I really do not care,' she said, trying to sound indifferent, although the wave of excitement that had swept over her when she had watched him ride by told her she was not as indifferent to his masculine allure as she appeared.

'I wonder if he's staying for the dancing later,' said Emma.

'Maybe he will—although I'm sure he won't dance,' said Eve. 'He's far too superior—and I'm sure he wouldn't be seen dead dancing with any of the local girls.'

Angela's eyes narrowed, suddenly filling with mischief as an outlandish scheme came to mind. 'But we're not local girls, are we? At least not in the sense you mean, Eve—and I think we should have some fun with Mr Fitzalan—see if we can't melt that ice-sculptured exterior he's so fond of portraying to the world.'

'What do you suggest?'

'That one of us should ask him to dance.'

'Angela! That's quite outrageous,' gasped Emma.

'Yes—but it's fun—and I think it should be you, Eve,' she said decisively, her eyes coming to rest with a sly, faint challenge on her friend.

Eve sat up with a jolt and stared at her in disbelief. Normally nothing Angela suggested either shocked or amazed her, but this was something quite outrageous—even by Angela's standards.

'Oh, no. I couldn't,' she whispered. 'What you suggest is preposterous, Angela—and besides, if I am to dance at all— should Mrs Parkinson permit it—then I shall be dancing with Leslie.'

'That's if Leslie feels inclined to dance,' Angela commented flatly, piqued. On seeing Eve shoot her a cross look she sighed, not to be deterred. 'Oh, Eve—think about it. Leslie has paid you such scant attention today that I shall be surprised if he finds the time to seek you out at all—and he seems to be in no hurry to approach your father to ask his permission to marry you. He's been dithering for weeks and you know it.'

'That's not true, Angela,' Eve replied hotly, hating it when Angela took her to task over anything, but she could not deny that what she said was true. The manner in which he was dragging his feet in making any kind of commitment to her was being noticed by everyone.

'Just think, Eve,' Angela went on, smiling with enthusiasm, her eyes regarding her sardonically, 'if he sees a man of Mr Fitzalan's distinction paying you particular attention by asking you to dance, it's bound to make him jealous and increase his intention to marry you.'

'But if I am to do as you say, it will be *me* asking Mr Fitzalan to dance, not the other way round,' she said drily.

'Nevertheless, it could be just what Leslie needs to sharpen him up a bit. Mark my words, if he thinks Marcus Fitzalan is interested in you he'll insist on seeking your father out immediately to ask for your hand in marriage.'

Eve frowned, uncertain. 'Do you think so?'

'Of course he will.'

'But I could just as easily make him jealous by dancing with someone else. It doesn't have to be Mr Fitzalan,' she said, the very thought of approaching the formidable Mr Fitzalan making her stomach churn and her spirits sink.

'But that wouldn't have the same effect. Besides, everyone knows what good friends he and your father are. You're far more likely to succeed with him than Emma or I. Unless, of course, you don't think you can charm him into dancing with you—or anything else, for that matter,' she said, in a deceptively casual way, lying back on the grass and closing her eyes with a sigh, giving the impression that she wasn't really interested one way or the other.

But Eve was not deceived. The challenge had been tossed down and unless she wanted to look a fool she had no alternative but to take her up on it—but she had the uneasy sensation of being the victim of some secret plot. Goaded into action, she was determined to prove Angela wrong.

When a group of fiddlers started to play and the dancing began, that was the moment when Eve, having escaped the watchful eye of Mrs Parkinson, found herself walking in the direction of Marcus Fitzalan, unaware as she did so of the smug, self-satisfied smile curling Angela's lips, and the malicious, ruthless gleam in her slanting eyes as she watched her go—like a lamb to the slaughter.

Observing the scene with his brooding gaze, Mr Fitzalan stood where a large crowd of spectators gathered. Dressed all in black, apart from his startlingly white neckcloth, he reminded Eve of a predatory hawk. She stopped short, becoming nervous suddenly, for what had started out as a silly prank no longer seemed like fun and already she was beginning to regret her silly impulse to call Angela's bluff.

She was tempted to walk past Mr Fitzalan but, aware of Angela's watchful gaze and the challenge she had thrown down, her pride forbade it, despite being intensely conscious of the impropriety of her actions and that her parents would be furious and deeply shocked if they were to find out.

And so it was that against the dictates of her better judgement she hesitantly stepped into the arena, feeling rather like Daniel stepping into the lions' den, blessedly unaware as she did so that the situation she was about to get herself into would alter the entire course of her life.

She looked up at Mr Fitzalan with her heart in confusion, gazing into a pair of ice blue eyes, having no idea of the bright-eyed picture she presented to Marcus Fitzalan—a dainty, lovely image of fragility. He observed the healthy glow of her skin, how demure she looked in her high-waisted pale pink sprigged dress with its scoop neck, the delectable mounds of her young breasts peeping tantalisingly over the top.

He had seen her with her friends when he arrived, all of them in high spirits. Taking her for one of the country girls who had come to enjoy the fair—for no properly brought-up young lady would be seen watching what was about to take place—his eyes raked over her.

Eve looked up at him, taking the bull by the horns, for she would have to speak to him now. He would think it odd if she just walked away. 'Have you only just arrived at the fair, Mr Fitzalan?' she found herself asking.

He stared down at her in fascination, both repelled by the cool manner in which she had approached him and attracted by her physical beauty.

'Yes. And you? Are you enjoying the fair?' he asked politely.

She smiled. 'Very much, thank you.'

Marcus was the kind of man who understood flirting and always found it distasteful—except when it happened to be from the right woman. But this was not a woman, this was a girl, and if she had not chosen that moment to smile he would have moved on, but it melted his bones to water and he found himself wanting to know more about her and enjoy her company a little longer. He was intrigued. Perhaps a little dalliance wouldn't go amiss before he had to return to Netherley.

Eve felt herself begin to relax, turning to observe the event that was about to start. 'What is going to happen?' she asked innocently.

'Another prize fight,' he answered, his attention drawn to a brute of a man with a bare chest and massive shoulders prowling in the ring before them.

Eve paled suddenly when she realised she was close to the ring where pugilists were displaying their skills, accepting bets from amateurs who fancied their chances in fighting them. If she had known this was to be the attraction, she would have waited until Mr Fitzalan had moved away. Her eyes became riveted on the fighter awaiting another challenger. His fists were clenched and bloodied, his last challenger having retired with a broken jaw and bloody nose. He was powerfully built, rippling with muscles, his head covered with black patches to hide his scars.

Eve turned to speak to her companion, about to move further away, but the excited crowd closed in around them, forcing her to remain where she was, the roar that rose from a hundred throats as another challenger stepped into the ring rendering her speechless. She became dismayed and nauseated when she realised she would have to stay and watch the brutal slaughter.

Swallowing hard, she was determined not to waver, remembering Angela would be watching her mercilessly. 'Oh—on whom do you place your money, Mr Fitzalan?' she heard herself asking tentatively, wondering if he approved of this crude and violent sport. 'Will it be the reigning champion, do you think, whose last opponent looks to be in a sorry state,' she said, indicating the poor man holding his broken jaw and having a wound on his cheek sewn up at the ringside, 'or the challenger?'

'Neither. I'm not a gambling man. I would never bet on the obvious for I fear the challenger is destined to be the loser.'

'I disagree,' said Eve, studying the man who had stepped into the ring to try his luck. 'I suspect the challenger is about to make his reputation. The champion is strong and lithe, I grant you, while his opponent is stout and not so great in stature—but he is full of fire which will give him added strength.'

Marcus looked down at her with slight amusement. 'You speak like an expert. Do you enjoy prize fights?'

'No,' she replied, wincing, unable to hide her repugnance as the two men began hitting each other with their bare fists, a man holding a long staff standing by ready to separate them should blood flow. 'I confess it is the first time I have seen one at close range. It's horrible.'

'My feelings entirely. The public taste for violence always appals me. Come, we don't have to stay and watch two men knock the sense out of each other—if they had any in the first place for believing it wise to indulge in such brutality,' he said, taking her arm and drawing her back, the crowd parting to let them through. He paused where his horse was tethered to a tree, beginning to loosen the reins.

Free of the constriction of the crowd, Eve breathed a sigh of relief. 'Thank you. I don't believe I could have watched them fight to the bitter end. What a magnificent horse,' she said, her attention caught as always when she recognised good horseflesh, reaching up to slide her hand along its silken neck.

'Yes. He's very special. You like horses?'

She nodded, about to tell him her father had a stable full of superb horseflesh, but thought better of it. Better that he didn't know who she was. She became alarmed when she suspected he was about to leave.

'You—you're not leaving?'

'I must. It's a long ride back to Netherley.'

Panic washed over her as she turned briefly, seeing Angela with a smug expression on her face, watching her like a cat watches a mouse, reminding her what it was she had to do. 'Oh—but—but I...' she faltered, acutely embarrassed and unable to go on.

Marcus raised his eyebrows in question, waiting for her to continue, enjoying her confusion.

Eve looked towards the fiddlers and the laughing, dancing swirl of people, acutely conscience of Angela's challenge and knowing she would have to ask him now. 'I—I—thought you might like to dance.'

Unable to believe that she had said those words she watched him, unconscious that she was holding her breath or that her eyes were wide open as she waited expectantly for him to reply, seeing neither shock nor surprise register on his carefully schooled features at her bold request.

'No.'

'Oh—I see.'

Eve stepped back, ashamed and filled with mortification by his blunt rebuff, wanting to extricate herself from the awful embarrassment of the predicament she had created in the first place as quickly as possible, but she felt a stab of anger that he could have been so rude as to refuse her in such a brusque manner, and a dull ache of disappointment in her chest that Angela would crow with delight at her inability to tempt the high and mighty Mr Fitzalan to dance with her. Making a conscious effort to escape from the situation with as much dignity as she could muster, she stepped away from him.

'Very well, Mr Fitzalan. Since you seem averse to my company I will bid you good day. Please forgive me for troubling you.'

Marcus's hand shot out and gripped her arm. Out of the corner of his eye he saw her friends not twenty yards away watching expectantly, giggling and nudging each other in anticipation of what might happen next. His eyes narrowed and he nodded slightly, looking down at his delightful companion whose face was flushed with indignation.

He was no fool. He knew exactly what she was up to. For some reason known only to her and her friends she was playing some kind of game. He smiled slightly with bland amusement, determined to give little Miss Whoever-she-was a shade more than she had bargained for. But not here—he had no mind to be watched by two giggling girls.

'I did not say that. On the contrary, I find your presence pleasing. Come—it's just that I am not inclined to dance, I never do at these occasions. But perhaps you will take a walk with me along the path by the river?'

Eve stared at him, feeling her heart turn over at his unexpected request. His voice was incredibly seductive, his eyes smiling and compelling her to say yes. She felt a warmth creeping throughout her body which made her doubt her earlier conviction that she was not attracted by him. How could she not be when he looked at her like this? She was confused, the situation having become one she had not anticipated—one she was unsure how to deal with, not being experienced or worldly enough to grasp the type of man Marcus Fitzalan was.

'Why—I—I shouldn't—I...'

He smiled invitingly, his voice low and persuasive.

'Come—you must say yes. It's rather like the enticer becoming the enticed, is it not?' he said softly, lifting a knowing eyebrow.

Eve expelled her breath in a rush, her eyes registering shock, horror and disbelief, for his look told her that he knew exactly what she had been about. 'Oh—I wasn't—I mean—'

He laughed softly, his teeth gleaming white from between his parted lips. 'Does it matter?' and he sensed victory when she began to follow him as he led his horse along the path by the side of the river, long before she realised she had been defeated.

The fact that Eve's absence might have been noted by Mrs Parkinson, and that Leslie had returned to the group, was the last thing on her mind just then. As they walked the sun, warm and benign to lovers—and yet they weren't lovers—slanted through the trees that lined the river bank, showing them the way as Marcus drew her farther and farther away from her friends. The air was warm and sultry, with tiny insects darting along the surface of the water, the sound of revelry and music growing ever fainter.

They talked of inconsequential things, of Atwood and the people who lived there, until Eve realised how far they had walked and began to panic. Her behaviour was completely irrational and she wondered what her parents would say if they were to find out about this. Their code of behaviour was strict and must be adhered to. She should not be alone with a man who was not her betrothed—and certainly not walking alone along a river bank, half-hidden from everyone by a curtain of trees.

They paused and Marcus let go of the reins to allow his horse to drink from the river. Leaning negligently against a tree he folded his arms across his chest, watching Eve in speculative silence through narrowed eyes. He had removed his coat and loosened his neck cloth, and beneath the soft linen shirt his muscles flexed with any slight movement he made. He exuded a brute strength and posed with leashed sensuality, a hard set to his jaw and a cynicism in his ice-cold eyes. But then he smiled, lazily and devastatingly, his teeth as white as his neckcloth.

The breeze blew Eve's hair across her face and she reached up and absently drew it back, combing her fingers through it and sweeping it behind her ears, unconscious of how seductive the gesture was to Marcus. He stood absolutely still, watching her with a look that was possessive, and, looking at him, something in his expression made Eve flush and catch her breath, dropping her arm self-consciously. The moment was intimate, warm and vibrantly alive. His vitality at such close quarters alarmed her.

'I—I must go back,' she said, thrown into sudden panic, biting her lip nervously and keeping her face averted from his. She wanted to escape, to run away, and yet, at the same time, she could not move. 'My friends will be wondering what has become of me.'

Marcus reached out and placed his fingers under her chin and turned it round to face him.

'Look at me.'

She glanced up at him, breathing rapidly from between parted lips so moist, so soft, her wonderful liquid eyes wide and luminous, her small breasts thrusting against the bodice of her dress. She was the perfect picture of alluring innocence, but Marcus was not to be deceived. To a lustful man those magnificent eyes were proving to be far too alluring and inviting.

'You know it's wrong to be alone with me—that no decent young lady would dream of taking a walk with a total stranger. What makes you think you are safe?'

Eve flushed, her glorious violet eyes mist bright, knowing that now was the time she should tell him who she was, that she had never intended things to go this far, but somehow she couldn't. She found his presence vaguely threatening and just hoped he would allow her to leave and return to the others, and in so doing forget all about her. But his eyes had taken on a whole new look, one she neither recognised nor understood, one which seemed to scorch her with the intensity of his passion, making her wonder if she was strong enough to withstand him. They burned into her, stopping all motion.

'Clearly I am not one of the decent, well-bred young ladies you are acquainted with,' she said, her voice quavering. 'You already know by my forward behaviour when I asked you to dance that my knowledge of protocol is negligible. I—I assumed that because of who you are—your elevated position—I would be safe. This has all been a terrible mistake,' she said lamely, alarm bells beginning to scream through her head. 'I—I must return to my friends. I should never have come. I—I don't know why I did.'

Eve watched in wary alarm as Marcus moved closer, driven by an uncontrollable compulsion to possess her, her behaviour from the very start telling him that the last thing she wanted was to return to her friends just yet. 'Don't you? You're here with me because you want to be. You want what I want. Don't deny it because I will not believe you—and don't be too eager to run away back to your friends.'

Marcus should have seen the panic in her eyes, heard the slight catch in her voice, but all he could think of was her lips and how soft and inviting they looked. Sweeping the tangle of her hair from her face, he took it firmly in both his hands and lowered his head, feeling an explosion of passion the moment he touched her. His mouth clamped down on hers, snatching her breath from between her lips before she could protest, feeling the blood pounding through his veins with the scorching heat of desire.

Eve was too stunned to do anything except let him kiss her, but when he did not feel her respond he raised his head and frowned, puzzled, slipping his hands about her waist and pulling her close, their bodies touching full length.

'I want no chaste kiss, lady,' he said, his voice low and husky. 'I think you know how to do better than that.'

His hand slipped behind her neck as again he lowered his

head, and with tantalising slowness he caressed her lips with his own before kissing her deeply, surprising, but not shocking her. Naïve and inexperienced, she acted purely on instinct, responding naturally to his tender assault on her lips—and it was not just her lips that began to open and respond, but her whole body as they clung to each other, becoming caught up in a wave of pleasure.

Eve was seduced by his mouth, becoming captive to his touch, his caress and the promise of things to come, secret, mysterious things that set her body trembling. She didn't know what was happening to her. No one had told her what happened when men and women were intimate together. An inexperienced girl could not have imagined such a kiss. She had never been kissed by a man in her life, and to be kissed like this for the first time was devastating. The feelings he aroused in her, with his lips, his touch, his eyes, were irrational, nameless. But she was not so overcome with passion to know that what she was doing was wrong, very wrong, and she must put an end to it.

'Please—you must let me go,' she whispered, her lips against his. 'You must not do this.'

Marcus seemed not to hear her plea and continued to seek her lips, his inquisitive fingers caressing the soft swell of her breasts. She pushed her hands against his chest and stood back, breathless, gazing up at him in helpless appeal, while wanting what he had to offer with a physical intensity which was like no other need she had ever known or imagined.

'Please—this is not right—we shouldn't. If anyone should find out that I've been alone with you—the—the proprieties—the conventions...'

Jolted back to his senses, Marcus stared at her. 'What the devil are you talking about? Why should rules of social etiquette affect you—a doxy?'

Eve's cheeks burned at the insult. 'How dare you! I am no doxy.'

'You gave a pretty good imitation of one.'

'I am not,' she flared, trying to still the wild beating of her heart.

'Then who the devil are you?'

For a brief second Eve considered telling a small lie but thought better of it, knowing she would be found out—besides, she did not tell lies, preferring to tell the truth no matter what the situation. She turned as if to walk away but fury and dread at what she might tell him made him reach out and pull her round to face him. She tried to shrink away, but he held her firmly.

'Who are you?' he demanded coldly.

Taking a deep breath, Eve met his gaze squarely, all coquetry gone as her spirit rose to grapple with this unpleasant turn of events. The air between them had become tense and charged with an entirely new kind of emotion.

'I—I am Eve Somerville,' she whispered, forcing herself to look directly into his eyes. 'Sir John Somerville's daughter.'

Marcus stared down at her as though he had been felled. His jawline tightened, his eyes became steady and glacial, his face going as white as his neck cloth. 'Dear Lord! What folly is this? Is this true? Are you Eve Somerville?'

She nodded dumbly, lowering her gaze, flinching before the exasperation in his voice and the cold glitter in his ice blue eyes. Never had she felt such humiliation.

'Look at me,' he demanded.

Unwillingly Eve raised her head and met his eyes, defiance and perturbation on her face. He glared down at her, embracing her in a look that was ice cold.

'I never thought to meet Sir John's daughter in a mad escapade of this kind—but it seems I was wrong. Have you no sense?' he said, thrusting his face close to hers, the line of his mouth cruel. His hands shot out and clamped down hard on her shoulders and he shook her so forcefully that she thought her head would come off. 'Can't you see that it was the height of dangerous folly to embark on such a madcap scheme as this?' he admonished severely.

'It was a mistake,' she said desperately, wishing he would release his vicious hold on her.

'A mistake of your doing. The responsibility for your being here is your own. What made you seek me out?' he demanded. 'Come—don't keep me in suspense.' He fumed with growing impatience, thrusting her away from him and raking his hand in sheer frustration through his hair. 'Why did you not tell me who you were?'

Full of shame and mortification Eve wished the ground would open and swallow her up. Never had she felt so wretched. He watched her with a deadly calm.

'I—I meant to—but somehow—it—it was a hoax, a charade, that is all—my friends dared me to ask you to dance—'

Marcus looked at her as if she had taken leave of her senses. 'A hoax? Do you actually have the impertinence to tell me this was a hoax? My God, are you shameless? Can't you see? Has it not occurred to you that by your foolishness it is not only your own reputation that might be ruined, but also my own? And you are betrothed, are you not—or about to be—to Leslie Stephenson?'

'Yes,' she replied. His face was frightening, but feeling wrath and indignation rising inside her, she tossed back her head and glared at him defiantly.

'Then let us hope he does not hear of this, otherwise any expectations you might have of him asking for your hand in marriage will have been dashed. Now go home to your mother, Miss Somerville, she must be wondering where you are. If I were your father and I heard of this little episode—and you can be assured he will for I intend seeking him out at once— then you could be sure of a sound thrashing.'

His stern rebuke inflamed a smouldering resentment towards him inside Eve. 'Then I can only thank God that you are not my father,' she flared.

'You may, Miss Somerville. You may. In my opinion you are a self-indulgent, spoiled brat—the type I hold in contempt. You behaved like an accomplished flirt. You didn't know what you were doing—what you were asking for when you so out-rageously made sexual overtures to a gentleman of my years and experience with women. Perhaps you will think twice the next time you want to play games—and I strongly advise you to learn the rules.'

Eve stared at him, her mind trying to adjust to his words. No one had ever spoken to her like this before or insulted her so severely. Fury blazed in his eyes as they locked relentlessly on to hers, but she stood before him, full of youthful courage, spirit and pride. Her mind was no longer in control and she had no idea how adorable she looked with her face flushed with ire and her eyes blazing furiously.

'And what of your own conduct? You should have known better than to take advantage of me, regardless of who I might be—unless this is how you normally behave,' she accused him.

'I never take advantage of defenceless young ladies—but you did not give me the impression of being defenceless. If you, Miss Somerville, are under the impression that you may sport with me in any manner you please, then let me tell you that you do not know me.'

'And after your insulting attack on my person I have no wish to know you. It would be interesting to know how much of a gentleman you are, Mr Fitzalan—had you not found out in time who I am.'

'Were I not a gentleman, Miss Somerville, it would not matter a damn who you are. I would behave much worse and take advantage of your delectable charms here and now. And I know by your response that, if I had not released you when I did, with a little gentle persuasion you would have yielded to me completely, flinging all caution to the four winds with no thought of the consequences. Let me tell you that I rarely refuse that which is so flagrantly offered to me, but consid-ering your age and that you are Sir John's daughter—who, as you know, is an extremely good friend of mine—I must de-cline your offer.'

Eve was infuriated. 'Oh—how dare you speak to me like this? I know what you must think—'

'I don't think so, lady. If you did you'd turn and run,' he said with menacing, murderous fury. 'Now return to your friends before they send out a search party and accuse me of compromising you. Having met you, I cannot think of anything that would upset me more than your father insisting that I do the gentlemanly thing and marry you myself.'

Chapter Four

In disagreeable silence Eve turned from Marcus Fitzalan, her heart heavy with shame and helpless misery. Never had she been so shaken and humiliated in her seventeen years as she was then. Hurrying back along the path, she discovered to her mortification that her indiscretion had been witnessed not only by Angela but also by Leslie Stephenson, who was staring at her in absolute incredulity.

Unable to utter a word of explanation in her defence she hurried on, too ashamed, angry and humiliated to speak to anyone—but not before she had glimpsed, through the blur of tears that almost blinded her, Angela's look of triumph and barely concealed smile. Her features were stamped with smugness and a confidence which came from the knowledge that Eve's association with Leslie Stephenson lay in ruins.

Left alone, Marcus was angered beyond words that he had fallen into a pit of his own making. But she was right. Before he knew who she was he'd had every reason to believe by her actions and forward behaviour that she'd had lovers before, despite her youth, and something perverse inside him had refused to call a halt to his assault on what he believed to be a willing body.

He could be forgiven for thinking that her eagerness, her very willingness to have him kiss her, had confused him into believing she was experienced in the ways of seduction, but if this was her general pattern of behaviour when she was not under the watchful eye of her parents, then it was as well they knew about it, and soon.

Marcus Fitzalan did exactly as he said he would and had spoken to Eve's father immediately. Her parents' anger and disbelief at what she had done made the whole thing much worse. Her future looked bleak. Aware that Atwood society neither forgave nor forgot an indiscretion, and to avoid Eve becoming the object of derision, her parents sent her to Cumbria post haste to stay with her grandmother and did not allow her to return until the whole affair had died down.

But sadly Eve never saw her mother again, for she died before Eve returned to Atwood, leaving her with a well of grief and self-reproach. Blaming herself bitterly for not being there when her mother needed her, it was something she did not get over, and she spent her days in self-imposed isolation at Burntwood Hall, ignoring Emma's pleas to accompany her to the local assemblies and soirées in an attempt to cheer her, only venturing abroad for the odd visit to her Aunt Shona in London or her grandmother in Cumbria.

Mr Fitzalan, it would appear, was beyond reproach where her father was concerned. He held him in such high regard that he believed every word he said. It was not the first misdemeanour his high-spirited daughter was guilty of, and he had always said that one day she would go too far. Both he and his wife had been in agreement that her wild spirits were difficult to curb. But Eve was extremely angry that they chose to ignore Mr Fitzalan's part in the affair, making her suspect he might not have told them just how intimate their meeting had been at Atwood Fair.

And as for Leslie Stephenson, at the first whiff of a scandal he abruptly withdrew his suit and married Angela instead, just as she had contrived it.

The sheer malice of Angela's trickery had angered Eve beyond words—all because Angela coveted the man who was considering marriage to her. Angela had made sure Eve was seen with Mr Fitzalan, and was unable to believe her good fortune when he had declined Eve's request to dance and had disappeared into the bushes with her. When it had come out, Leslie had married Angela instead—only to die in a riding accident a year later, leaving Angela an extremely wealthy young widow.

Until that fateful night Eve had believed Angela to be her friend, and the pain of her betrayal hurt more than Leslie's rejection. She had not seen her since, but never would she forgive her unspeakable malice and deceit. She and Emma remained close, but Angela's name was never mentioned between them.

Eve was glad to put the whole sorry affair behind her, hoping she would never have the misfortune to set eyes on Marcus Fitzalan again. He had spared her nothing, making her see herself as fast, a flirt and a spoiled, overindulged, selfish child, but as she agonised over his cruel accusations, reluctantly she had to admit that they were close to the truth.

But no matter how resentful she felt towards him, he had awoken her desire, had left her with a strange ache rising inside her, and a sharp new hunger and need in her heart she could not explain. Looking back, she knew that that was the time when childhood had left her. She would never again be that same carefree, impulsive girl.

It was someone knocking on her door that woke Eve from her fitful sleep. With a deep sigh she opened her eyes, her mind still full of Marcus Fitzalan and that day three years ago as she rose and crossed wearily to the door, surprised to see her grandmother, who had come to speak to her before retiring for the night. Usually her presence had a daunting effect on Eve, but today too much had happened for her to feel intimidated by her grandmother. Whenever she came to visit them the house always became a different place, quiet and subdued, her presence invading every room from the attics to the cellars, and felt by everyone.

There were always the same questions and answers, the same stiff rules to be adhered to. She always demanded much of Eve's time, commanding her to read to her for hours, and she would sit with her to make sure she did her embroidery, a task Eve found tedious at the best of times. In the past her grandmother had constantly reproached her mother for allowing Eve too much freedom to do as she pleased, and the whole household would breathe a sigh of relief when she went back to Cumbria.

'Forgive me for disturbing you, Eve, but I must speak to you,' she said, stepping into the room and seating herself in an armchair by the fire, the very chair Eve herself had occupied until her grandmother had knocked on her door and roused her from her melancholy thoughts.

'Of course, Grandmother,' Eve replied quietly, giving no indication that this was a conversation she would have preferred to defer until another time, feeling in no mood to talk to anyone.

While she waited for her grandmother to speak she moved towards the window, pushing aside the heavy curtains and looking out, aware of a feeling of gloom and despondency. The night was dark now and beyond the church she could see the warm lights of Atwood glimmering in the distance, and also, some considerable distance away from the township, stood the tall, ghostly shape of the engine house of Atwood Mine and its surrounding spoil heaps, indicative of the area and so distinctive a feature of the landscape.

Her thoughts barely penetrated the fog that clouded her mind. She was numb in mind, body and soul, unable to comprehend all that had happened that day and what it would mean to her future. Her father's will had turned her life into an irretrievable disaster. How could he have done this to her—and why? How could he want her to marry Mr Fitzalan? The very idea horrified her.

But the thought of Atwood Mine falling into Gerald's hands brought a great emptiness of heart. He knew nothing about mining—and even though it would still be managed by competent men, if she let it happen he would be in absolute control. It would not be long before he spent the profits and it ran into difficulties. Everything her father had worked to achieve on the estate would be eradicated by Gerald, this she was certain of, and she would hate to see Atwood Mine go the same way.

Not until today had she realised how dear, how important the mine was to her, and she wondered what had possessed her to hold it so lightly all her life. Her father had been so proud of it, so proud of its efficiency, its worth—the lifeblood of the Somervilles, he often said. He had worked hard to make it what it was, and many were the times when he had been there from dawn until dark, causing her mother to gently taunt and tease him, telling him she would find it easier to accept another woman as a rival for his affections, but a coal mine was insupportable.

She sighed deeply. To leave Burntwood Hall would be like being uprooted, but to lose the mine completely and let Gerald have the run of it would tear her heart. She couldn't let it go. For his own reasons her father had bequeathed half of it to her—a half which would become a whole if she were to do as he asked and marry Mr Fitzalan—but that was the stumbling block. Marcus Fitzalan! There must be some other way of keeping the mine out of Gerald's hands other than that. There had to be. She couldn't let it go, she thought desperately. She just couldn't.

Of course Eve knew that as a married woman she couldn't actually be seen as the owner of the mine, in the eyes of the law, but whatever else Marcus Fitzalan was he was a man of his word. Eve felt certain he would stand by her father's legacy to her.

She had given the matter some considerable thought all day, trying to find some way to escape the impossible situation she found herself to be in, anything, so long as she need not marry Mr Fitzalan or go to live with her grandmother in a wild and unfrequented area of Cumbria.

But as her brain had gone round and round in ever confusing circles she could see no escape. If she wanted to hold on to a part of her past—to Atwood Mine, which she was fiercely determined not to let go—then she really had no choice but to marry Mr Fitzalan. But for now she would hold out against making that decision for as long as she could in the hope that a solution to her dilemma would present itself.

'This has all come as a terrible shock to you, Eve,' said her grandmother at length.

'Yes—it has, Grandmother. From my earliest memories my father's devotion was to be relied on unquestionably. I don't understand what has happened—why he has done this. Do you know? Did he discuss this with you? Mr Fitzalan has tried explaining it to me but still I fail to understand any of it.'

'Yes—your father did discuss the matter with me briefly when I visited you twelve months ago.' She looked away, awkward, suddenly.

'So you knew what he intended all along.'

'He wanted my opinion.'

'And you gave it. You approved of what he intended doing—that it would be in my best interests to marry Mr Fitzalan?'

'Yes, I did. I saw no reason not to. He is a good man and you know your father held him in the highest regard. He always admired a man who knew his own mind.'

She didn't tell her how deeply concerned her father had been by Leslie Stephenson's cruel rejection of her almost three years ago, or that it troubled him greatly to see that she showed no interest in marrying anyone since that time. But he loved her dearly and wanted to know she would be well taken care of after his death, and to his mind there was only one man worthy of his beautiful, spirited daughter, a man with a spirit to equal her own, and that man was Marcus Fitzalan.

He knew he had it within his power to bring the two of them together—that Atwood Mine would be used as the bait—and the idea of Eve being in the protective care of Mr Fitzalan when he was gone gave him a great deal of comfort.

'I know this isn't easy for you and you have every right to be angry, Eve. But what do you feel about Mr Fitzalan?' asked her grandmother directly. 'Will you marry him?'

'Oh, Grandmother—how can I? I hardly know him.'

'That will not be difficult to remedy. I would, of course, be happy to accommodate you in Cumbria, Eve, but for your own good I would advise you to accede to your father's wishes and stay here and marry.'

Eve turned slowly and looked at her grandmother, sensing by the tone of her voice and the manner in which she spoke that she didn't want her to go and live with her in Cumbria, which she considered strange, for she had never objected to her visits in the past—in fact, she had always encouraged them.

With her thin fingers coiled around the knob of her cane, her grandmother sat so straight and stiff she might have been armour plated. She was a woman of great dignity and had been beautiful in her time, and despite her grand age of sixty years the signs remained. But there was no emotion of any kind in her expression, no softness or gentle understanding, as she would have seen on her mother's face before her death.

Sensing what she was thinking, her grandmother looked at her severely. 'And you needn't look so put out, Eve. You know how much I look forward to your visits—but that's all they were. Cumbria's no place for a young girl with her whole life before her, and if you were to go and live with your Aunt Shona in London you know you would not endure it for long. After the first few weeks the excitement of city life would have worn off and you would be pining to be back in the West Riding. It always happens.'

Eve sighed. What her grandmother said was true. She always looked forward to visiting London and her Aunt Shona, but the excitement of the parties and balls her aunt and cousins were so fond of attending soon wore off and she could never wait to return home.

'But I don't want to marry Mr Fitzalan, Grandmother. He is practically a stranger to me—which I am sure you find surprising, considering the close friendship that existed between him and my father. From what I have heard of him I do not like him. Besides, he is so old.'

'Rubbish. Thirty is not old. My dear Eve,' her grandmother remonstrated with undue sharpness, 'you have to marry some time, so why not marry Mr Fitzalan? He may not have been blessed with noble blood, as you have fortunately been yourself, but there was nothing unsophisticated about him that I could see.

'Despite his humble origins, the fact remains that through his father's marriage to Mr Henry Woodrow's daughter, a gentleman and wealthy businessman over at Netherley, his present credentials are admirable. He is a man of power and influence, of considerable property and business—and owner of a fine house too, I have been told, built by his grandfather. It is reputed to be very grand indeed. I am sure life would be pleasant for you living there.'

'I dare say it would be—if I agree to marry him. Although it would appear that I am left with little choice, Grandmother,' she said, wondering what her grandmother would say if she knew of the close familiarity Eve and Mr Fitzalan had displayed towards each other three years ago at Atwood Fair.

She spoke harshly, more than was usual when she addressed her grandmother, causing the redoubtable lady to cast an imperious eye over her, but she did not reprimand her as she would have done at any other time, for she put Eve's irritability down to the trauma of the day.

'However, no one seems to have considered the idea that Mr Fitzalan might not want to marry me,' Eve said with an inappropriate lack of seriousness. 'He might surprise everyone and decide that the mine is not so very important to him after all—although, should that be the case, I doubt another will hurry to take his place. The reduced size of my inheritance is hardly large enough to tempt any other man in asking for me.'

'Nonsense. Two thousand pounds a year is a veritable fortune to some young men. And you forget that when I die, Eve, you will be comfortably well off—although not as well off as I should have liked to leave you, as I am the head of a large family and have other dependents scattered throughout the length and breadth of England. But that will not be for some considerable time because I fully intend living a good many years yet.

'But I would still advise you to seriously consider marrying Mr Fitzalan. Despite what you have just said, by all accounts he would dispose of everything he owns to bring Atwood Mine back into his family—so he will not take much persuading to marry you. I am sure if you put your mind to it and do not repeat the performance of this afternoon—when you forgot your manners and accused the poor man so shockingly of contriving to obtain the mine by devious means from your father—you will get on well enough.'

'I said nothing to Mr Fitzalan that he did not deserve.'

'Whatever your opinions might be, they are unjust and ill-founded, Eve. You really should know better than to listen to tittle-tattle. Your outburst was unpardonable and at any other time you could have been sure of my severest reproof.'

'But I don't love him—and I doubt I could ever love such a man as he has been painted,' and as I know him to be, she thought with secret shame.

Her grandmother stared at her askance. 'Love? What has love to do with anything? You are talking nonsense. If it's love you want then I dare say it will come with marriage. Young people of today enjoy a greater independence than was the case in my day, when marriages were arranged for the benefit of families. In situations such as ours it is expected to bring advantage, wealth and status to the prospective partners and their families. If this nation is to remain strong then it is important that distinguished families like our own continue to uphold that tradition.'

'But this is not your day, Grandmother,' cried Eve, unable to keep the bitterness and frustration from her voice, causing her grandmother to draw herself up and look at her severely.

'Maybe not—and I can see that things have not changed for the better. In cases such as this, take my advice and leave your emotions behind. Marriage is too crucial a matter to be determined on such frivolous considerations as romantic love. Call it old-fashioned if you must, but I am of the belief that children should defer to their parents regarding marriage. However, with marriage to Mr Fitzalan in mind, it's a pity your father did not think of introducing the two of you sooner.'

'But I had no wish to meet him.'

As if sensing her wretchedness, her grandmother's expression softened a little. 'Despite the fact that your parents allowed you to do very much as you pleased for most of the time, running about the countryside like a young hoyden, you're a good girl, Eve—and I am pleased to see you have become a sensible young lady at last, with far more about you than Shona's and Mary's girls,' she said, referring to her two remaining daughters, which caused Eve to look at her in surprise, for this was praise indeed coming from her grandmother.

'Listen, Eve,' she went on, leaning slightly forward in her chair and fixing her granddaughter with a hard stare. 'I know you think I am being hard—cruel, even, in asking you to think seriously about marriage to Mr Fitzalan—but like your father I want to see you well secured. If you stubbornly refuse, then apart from the annuity your father has left you—and your mother's jewellery and other possessions, which are already in your possession but not worth a fortune—you will lose everything to Gerald—and there's a wastrel if ever there was. You cannot turn your back on this chance of retaining something of your father's estate—which to my mind is the *best* thing he could have left you.

'Coming from Cumbria I have only a little knowledge of

the mining of coal, but I know enough to realise that it is the lifeblood of the people in this area and one of the most important, profitable commodities in England. Its potential and economic significance is immense. I have seen for myself that mines are being sunk all the way along Atwood Valley, and your father told me himself that Atwood Mine has no rival. Trade is increasing at a rapid rate and explorations have shown there are unexploited deep seams of coal reserves. My dear girl—you would be a fool to let it go.'

For the first time Eve felt a reluctant stirring of admiration for her grandmother. The intensity of feeling in her voice and her eyes told her that she cared, that it did matter to her what became of her, and she was grateful, but she could not suppress a deep sigh. 'You make it sound like an ultimatum, Grandmother—like some necessary evil.'

'I don't mean to—but you *must* think about it,' she said animatedly, thumping her stick, which she was never without, hard on the carpet. 'Let Gerald play at being Lord of the Manor all he likes—but you take control of the mine.'

'Me and Mr Fitzalan, of course.'

'Yes. You know your father would not have set down these conditions had he not your best interests at heart. He always wanted you and Mr Fitzalan to marry and this was his way of bringing it about. Take what is offered, Eve, and ask no questions. Had things been different he would have wanted you to marry a man of your own choosing, but knowing he would not be here to look after you, to protect you, he did what he thought was right and best for you.'

Eve's eyes remained doubtful, but on looking at the situation with cold logic, it was with reluctance that she recognised the sense of her grandmother's words. She was right. If she wanted to hold on to her pride and something she considered to be her birthright, then she really had no choice.

'I promise I shall give the matter serious thought, Grandmother. At this moment I cannot say more than that.'

Gerald left for his home on the day following the funeral,

leaving Eve with the knowledge that he would return to take up residence at Burntwood Hall just as soon as he had put his affairs in order.

She was alone in her father's study, writing letters to people who had been unable to travel to the funeral, when he entered to tell her of his departure and what he intended to do. She had no choice but to speak to him, to see the mockery in his eyes and hear the lust in his voice. She shuddered at the sight of him for she disliked him intensely. The mere thought of him had the power to make her draw her breath in sharply.

If he was aware of it he seemed unconcerned and chose to ignore it. He relaxed at the sight of her, a twisted smile curving his lips, and yet his expression remained hard, his eyes alert, boldly lingering appreciatively, greedily, on the soft swelling mounds of her breasts, insolently taking in every detail. Eve met his gaze coldly. She had known ever since his last visit to Burntwood Hall that he was attracted by her—known it by the way he looked at her—and she hated him—the smile on his slack lips, the glint in his dark eyes.

Sitting in a large winged chair beside the fire, he folded his hands casually across his rapidly expanding stomach and stretched his legs out in front of him with the lazy grace of a big cat, a cold, calculating gleam in his eyes as he looked at her sitting demurely at her father's desk.

'Do forgive me for intruding on your privacy, Eve, but I wanted to speak to you before returning to my home. I waited until I knew your grandmother would be resting, when I would be sure to find you alone. There is much to be done, you understand. Not wishing to appear uncharitable I just wanted to tell you that you must continue to look on Burntwood Hall as your home for just as long as you want to—that I have no intention of "turning you out", so to speak,' he said, with feigned sympathy and generosity in his eyes.

The truth of it was that Gerald had become aware of Eve as a woman several visits ago—an extremely beautiful and desirable woman, and extremely accessible while ever she continued to live at Burntwood Hall—but more importantly he also saw her as a means of retaining Atwood Mine, which would revert to him should she refuse to marry Marcus Fitzalan, and provide him with a much needed constant source of revenue for years to come.

But he was also in the devil of a fix. Having borrowed money after losing heavily at cards at his club in St James's, from men who knew he was Sir John Somerville's heir—a great deal of money, thirty-five thousand pounds to be exact, with an extortionate interest on the amount borrowed—there was no possible way he could repay the loan until he came into his inheritance. Before he left London the moneylenders, having heard of Sir John's death, had begun turning on the pressure for him to repay the loan with a terrible force. They were closing in on him, crushing him like a vice. He had to get the money. He was becoming desperate. The mere thought of what they would do to him if he didn't come up with it made sweat break out on the palms of his hands and his heart pound uncontrollably.

These men were experts at what they did, men who would not be crossed or defied. Gerald had soon learned from their dealings with others that beneath their elegant exteriors they possessed muscles of steel combined with a ruthlessness and cruelty that stopped at nothing—tactics he would not hesitate to employ himself on others to obtain the means to repay the loan and get these men off his back for good, and only the income from Atwood Mine would enable him to obtain the kind of money he needed to do that. Sir John's death had come as an enormous relief. He could not believe his good fortune—but without the mine his inheritance would not be enough to repay what he owed without selling off more land and property.

Everything hung on Eve's decision—on her not marrying Marcus Fitzalan. He was counting on her love for Burntwood Hall being greater than her obligation to her father and his wish that she marry Fitzalan. And if not, then there were other ways of preventing a marriage from taking place between them. So desperate and determined was he to have the mine reverted to him that he would go to any lengths to do so. By fair means or foul—it didn't matter to him. He would win in the end.

'That is extremely generous of you, Gerald,' Eve said stiffly in answer to his offer, breaking in on his thoughts, putting down her pen and folding her hands in her lap, the loss of everything that was familiar to her suddenly becoming more bitter as she looked at him coldly and in silence, calmly and warily waiting for him to continue, shuddering slightly as he continued to watch her with the calculating eyes of a man eager for conquest. Every nerve of her body was tense as she waited for him to continue, fighting a creeping fear.

'I must tell you that I do not intend letting go of Atwood Mine,' Gerald said, sounding very sure of himself. 'I assumed that it would come as part and parcel of my inheritance.'

'My father—and Mr Fitzalan's father and grandfather before that—worked too hard to make it what it is today to be foolish enough to leave it to someone who would not appreciate its worth, Gerald. You are renowned for spending money faster than it can be earned—and I can only hope you appreciate and keep this house in better order than you have your own, which, as I understand it, is soon to be auctioned off to pay your creditors.'

Gerald's eyes narrowed and his voice was calm and full of meaning when he spoke. 'Never fear, Eve—I shall appreciate it and I know *exactly* what Atwood Mine is worth.'

'Yes, I'm sure you do—down to the last penny, I shouldn't wonder. It is rumoured that you are heavily in debt—that you need a great deal of money to pay off a massive loan for a debt you incurred after an unsuccessful card game,' she said scathingly.

He frowned crossly. 'How do you know about that?'

'I know a great many things about you.'

Gerald shrugged carelessly, his instinct telling him she had acquired this information from Marcus Fitzalan, damn the man. 'I don't deny it. Indeed, I have no reason to.'

Eve's lips curled with irony. 'No—somehow I didn't think you would.'

Gerald ignored her sarcasm, knowing nothing was to be gained by showing his anger at present. 'Tell me, Eve—have you decided whether or not to marry Fitzalan?'

'No, not yet. And when I do he will be the first to know.'

'You don't have to marry him, you know. I observed how angry you were yesterday when your father's will was being read—that you were not exactly enamoured by his suggestion that the two of you marry. I can understand the anger you must feel, when I remember how the man almost ruined you three years ago. Small wonder you are still at daggers drawn,' he drawled. 'Forgive me, Eve, but Marcus Fitzalan does seem a trifle dull and on the serious side for such a vivacious, beautiful creature as yourself. You have grown into an exceedingly lovely young woman.'

He rose and moved slowly towards where she was sitting. His lips slackened in a sensuous smile and a sudden fire leapt into his eyes as he devoured her, his eyes dwelling appreciatively on her lovely face.

Eve ignored the unwelcome compliment and stood up quickly, moving away instinctively to avoid getting too close, the thought of any contact with him revolting her. If only she could treat him with icy detachment and appear indifferent to him, but somehow he always managed to slip through her guard. His eyes fastened themselves on hers and he smiled thinly.

'There is an alternative, you know.'

'Oh? And what might that be?'

He shrugged, a callously hard malicious gleam entering his eyes. 'I merely thought you could stay here and take your mother's place.'

His insolent, smiling face angered Eve beyond words and a

wave of sick loathing swept over her. She favoured him with a glance of bitter contempt.

'What! Marry you?'

'Why not? You will find me more appreciative of your charms than Marcus Fitzalan, I do assure you.'

'You flatter yourself if you think that,' she replied drily, eyeing him with distaste, without flinching before his direct gaze, revulsion rising up inside her so that it almost choked her.

'Not only that—if you marry me, it would ensure Atwood Mine will remain in our possession, where it belongs.'

'If you recall the contents of my father's will, Gerald, you will know that it does not require marriage to me to have the mine reverted to you. I merely have to refuse to marry Mr Fitzalan, that is all.'

'*That* I am aware of—but I know Burntwood Hall means a great deal to you, and marriage to me would enable you to live here for the entirety of your life. Surely my suggestion is a far more agreeable prospect than marriage to Marcus Fitzalan. After all, we both stand to gain something—besides the pleasure it would accord me having you here,' he said, exhibiting an inordinate, lascivious interest in her body as his gaze swept over her.

Eve stared at him in stupefaction, rendered speechless by the content of his words and their implication, hearing him savour every word he spoke as he imagined how great his eventual triumph would be over Marcus Fitzalan if Atwood Mine was snatched from under his arrogant nose by her say so. She could not deny that the temptation to do so was great indeed, but fear prickled her spine and a small voice deep inside her told her not to underestimate Gerald. He could be dangerous, and if she chose to remain at Burntwood Hall as his wife feeling as she did about him, life would be one long agony. Her chin came up and she glared at him, quivering with a mixture of anger and fear.

'You are mistaken if you think that. I would not marry you if you were the last man on earth.'

Gerald sighed, pretending not to have noticed the force with which she spoke. 'Why you have such a low opinion of me baffles me, Eve.'

'My opinion of you was decided years ago.'

'Come now,' he coaxed, his voice persuasive and intimate. 'You know the situation and you have so much common sense, which is what I have always admired about you. It occurred to me that it is a solution to both our problems.'

'It is you who has the problem, Gerald. Not I.'

'Nevertheless, it is a generous gesture on my part.'

'Generous, you say!' exclaimed Eve forcefully. 'You have the most astonishing effrontery. Do you take me for a fool? You are only generous in the sense that your proposal of marriage to me is nothing more than a cunning ploy to prevent a marriage from taking place between myself and Mr Fitzalan. It is nothing more than that to get your hands on the mine.'

'I agree there is that, but where my proposal is concerned let me assure you that I am thinking only of you.'

He drew closer to her and took her hand between his, which she quickly snatched away, feeling as if she had been burned. Gerald's eyes narrowed menacingly.

'Don't touch me.' Eve flared with an anger that was all the more violent because it was born of fear. 'Don't touch me or I swear I shall scream for the servants—whatever the consequences. Now please go, Gerald.'

Gerald sighed and took a step back, speaking with a terrifying softness. 'What a little spitfire you are, Eve, but I like it in you. You are so fiery—so adorable. It suits you to be angry. It makes your eyes sparkle and your wonderful bosom to heave. You are like a horse that is unbroken—but one day I shall be the one to rectify that.'

It was not so much a threat as a statement of fact, which made Eve's blood run cold. She saw the fire leap in his eyes and heard the passion rising his voice, and she sensed danger.

'I think you have said quite enough, Gerald. Now please go.' She looked him straight in the face, her eyes blazing. He must have seen the hatred.

Gerald's eyes narrowed, and without warning his attitude changed. His expression convulsed and he seized Eve's wrist in a painful grasp, beginning to speak in a low, angry voice.

'I'll go, Eve, but I shall be back very soon to take your father's place in this house.'

'You! You are not half the man my father was,' Eve said scornfully.

'No, maybe not in your eyes. But know this, Eve,' he said, a warning underlying his words, which told Eve that he spoke in deadly seriousness, 'I am a man who must conquer—must win—whatever the odds against him, and I shall do all in my power to prevent you marrying Marcus Fitzalan in order to obtain the mine.'

'Even if you have to kill me first?' she hissed, wrenching her arm free of his grasp.

'Oh, yes. Even that if necessary. Nothing will stand in my way. I can be very ugly when crossed. You would do well in the future to remember it. So don't be foolish, Eve. Think about what I have said very carefully, because if you do not heed my words you will regret it.'

Eve's face turned ashen, sensing this was no idle threat spoken in the heat of the moment. 'You would not dare.'

Gerald shrugged. 'Why not? On the other hand, if you act sensibly, as I hope you will, then I can promise no harm will come to you.'

She glared at him with pure loathing. 'You are a scoundrel. I hate you.'

'Yes, I know. However, that does not disturb me. With some women, hatred has more allure than love.' He gave her a twisted smile. 'I shall have Atwood Mine, Eve. You can depend on it.'

Eve watched him go, sitting down to steady her nerves and trembling limbs, feeling an icy trickle of fear run down her spine, knowing she could expect no mercy and nothing but violence from him; and he would never be satisfied until he had Atwood Mine in his grasp.

But it was madness to think Gerald would harm her. He would never dare do that. She forced herself to believe this and cast such thoughts from her mind, but she was shaken to the core by what had just passed between them.

Chapter Five

For three weeks Marcus continued with the everyday mundane activities of his mines, the towering engine house at Atwood Mine in the distance a constant reminder of how close he was to owning it once more—providing he married Sir John's daughter. For sentimental reasons the mine was important to him, but he was a businessman and would be lying if he said he did not know of its potential, that it was a veritable gold mine compared to all the other mines in the area.

He continued to work the mines opened by his grandfather, who had speculated every penny to make them successful. As his own interests had expanded further, three years ago he had taken out a lease on a hundred acres of land on an adjacent estate for thirty years to come, for a substantial yearly rent on the two pits he had sunk; through his own determination and dedication, and the financial backing of his partners, they were rapidly increasing their output of coal.

But it was not enough to meet demand, which was why he was concentrating all his efforts on developing another, deeper mine, at Pendle Hill, three miles to the north of Atwood Mine.

He was fortunate to be situated within the marvellous new network of navigational canals that were being cut through the industrial regions. This expansion of inland waterways greatly eased the transportation problems, making it possible to expand into geographically larger markets.

Since the day of Sir John's funeral he was surprised that, hardened though he was, he was once again unable to cast Eve Somerville from his mind. He had made the occasional visit to Burntwood Hall in the past but, apart from their encounter at Atwood Fair, he had never had the pleasure of meeting her again—if it could be called a pleasure now that he had. She was always away staying with friends when he called or visiting her grandmother in Cumbria or her aunt in London.

On the day of the funeral he had watched her with a speculative gaze. Although she had sat docilely beside her grandmother throughout the day, drawing on an inner strength to see her through, he had sensed her restlessness, her impatience for it to be over. She had been like a young, leashed colt, eager to break free.

He admired the way she had conducted herself, sensing she wasn't the type to faint or weep in the company of others—a trait, he suspected, she'd inherited from her formidable grandmother—although witnessing her private grief, when she had thought herself to be alone at her father's graveside later, had touched a hidden chord deep inside him.

Constantly he found himself dwelling on her warm femininity, and for the first time—despite the strong liking and respect he had felt for Sir John and would always feel—anger welled up inside him against the man, and also against himself for being unable to turn his back on what he had offered, possibly at the price of his daughter's happiness.

He was touched by some private scruples. It really was shameful of him and utterly mercenary to consider using her so callously, to intend making her his wife merely to obtain the mine. But when he recollected how lovely and spirited she was, how young and vulnerable, despite her quality of mind to show self-possession, how ripe she was for being initiated along the secret, mysterious paths of womanhood, he smiled, his instinct telling him that, given time, they would both be well satisfied with the arrangement.

Curious to see for herself the object of her inheritance—should she agree to marry Mr Fitzalan—and having cast her meeting with Gerald to the back of her mind, Eve seized the opportunity of doing so one fine, sunny morning four weeks after her father's funeral, taking the road that led up to the mine, accompanied by her grandmother's elderly maid, her grandmother having declined her invitation to go with her.

But it was no easy matter trying to forget Gerald. Ever since her conversation with him on the day after the funeral, when he had reduced her to a frightening, trembling awareness of him, she was determined to leave Burntwood Hall before he returned to take up residence—and she would do everything within her power to keep Atwood Mine out of his hands.

But no matter how hard she tried to dispel his threatening image from her mind, there was an obscure menace about him which unnerved her. He was reluctant to let the mine go, this she knew, but to what desperate lengths would he go to hold on to it? she asked herself, suddenly afraid for her own safety as every sense she possessed screamed out a warning.

Her air of despondency began to recede the closer she got to the mine. The hillside was covered with mounds of black slag and slate, and a pond of thick, black slurry lay at the bottom, still and unmoving and shining like black glass beneath the glare of the sun.

Atwood Mine rose above the dark, metallic line of the canal which threaded its way along the valley bottom—an artificial waterway which had been constructed by her father to cut the cost of carrying coal by road to the larger Aire and Calder Navigation's waterway.

On the other side of the canal stood the town of Atwood, a conglomeration of shops and dwelling places, with a broad main street going through the middle, and on the outskirts was a huddle of colliers' cottages, principally for those colliers employed by the Somervilles to work Atwood Mine and others in the area.

A pall of grey smoke hung over the village, which had begun as a small settlement and was steadily beginning to encroach insidiously on the township of Atwood, as more and more colliers and their families moved into the area to work with the rapid expansion of the coal industry. The mine, large in comparison with other mines in the area, was reached by a swing bridge over the canal.

The closer they got to the mine Eve could hear the clanking and groaning of the pumping engine drawing water up from the pit, the giant contraption nodding its great head like a tired-out old donkey over the cavernous opening of the shaft. She could see the wooden-constructed headgear, winding ropes and pulley wheels, which raised to the surface the cage holding the tubs of hand-hewn coal, operated in the shaft by a steam-driven winding engine.

The carriage pulled into the pit yard, which was bustling with activity. Youths pushed tubs of shining lumps of coal, which was moved from the surface by wagons pulled by sweating horses, down the track to the canal where it was loaded on to the waiting barges. The mine employed men, women and young boys, although the women were not employed to work underground and worked in the sheds with some of the younger boys.

The carriage and its occupants drew the attention of the workers as it pulled up beside a rather magnificent chestnut horse, tethered to a rail outside one of the sheds with a wooden awning, which was used as an office, where Eve hoped to find Gerald's brother, Matthew, the young man who had been employed by her father as one of the mine's agents.

Instructing her grandmother's maid to remain in the carriage, she stepped out just as a young clerk—in a state of nervous agitation owing to the unexpected arrival and importance of the visitor—emerged from the office.

Eve smiled at him. 'I'm here to see Mr Somerville. Would you kindly tell him I'm here?'

'I'm sorry, but both Mr Somerville and the manager are away today, Miss Somerville. They had some business to attend to in Netherley.'

'I see,' she said, feeling a rush of disappointment. 'Oh, well—it's my fault. I should have told him I intended paying him a visit.'

She turned back to the carriage, thinking to come back another time, when her eyes were drawn to a tall, black-suited gentleman who loomed out of the brick engine house. At first she was as startled as if she had seen a ghost, and her stomach did a little somersault when she recognised Marcus Fitzalan.

Immediately he saw her and smiled suavely, his white teeth gleaming startlingly as he walked briskly towards her, as though it were the most natural thing in the world that he should be there. He thought how fetching she looked, despite the sombre black morning dress and bonnet she wore.

'My dear Miss Somerville. You are the last person I expected to see here.'

Eve stiffened her spine and gave him a cold stare. 'I could say the same about you, Mr Fitzalan. Your visit is rather premature, isn't it? Wouldn't it be wiser to wait until you have my answer before eyeing up the merchandise—in a manner of speaking, of course?'

He grinned infuriatingly, giving a dismissive nod to the young clerk, who was glad to escape inside the office. 'I like to be prepared for every eventuality, Miss Somerville. And you? Are you interested in the workings of a coal mine?'

'If I am to become part-owner, Mr Fitzalan, then I intend learning as much as I can in order to understand and protect my inheritance. All I know about the coal industry I have learned from my father over the years—which is very little, considering a large part of my livelihood depends on it.'

'And you suddenly want to know more?'

'Yes, and being a woman will not make any difference. I

hope you do not share the common failing of most men, Mr Fitzalan, and suffer from the masculine illusion that women do not have heads for business, that they should bow and be guided by the superior knowledge of men and have no opinions of their own—and, in particular, have no place at a coal mine.'

'Heaven forbid I should think that,' he answered, his teeth gleaming as his bold dark eyes laughed down into hers, 'and, if I did, I would not dare say so. I like a woman who speaks her mind, Miss Somerville, and I see you're not only beautiful but courageous too.'

Eve flushed, so surprised by the compliment that she was thrown off balance, but then she checked herself. 'Thank you. A compliment from you of all people is to be appreciated,' she said drily. 'But flattery will not get you the mine, Mr Fitzalan. I do not weaken so easily.'

Marcus smiled and gave a sardonic lift to his brows. 'Come now, don't be coy,' he said softly. 'I, more than anyone, know how vulnerable you can be, just how weak you can be—how easy it is to destroy your resistance with just a little tender persuasion.'

He laughed freely, his black eyes dancing in merciless merriment as he seemed to enjoy the confusion his words caused her, seeing her cheeks flush crimson with furious embarrassment and shame at his reference to their amorous encounter three years ago. But he took pity on her.

'Fear not,' he chuckled. 'Your secret is safe with me, and I promise not to repeat my barbaric display to seduce you into marriage.'

Roused to resentment, and conscious that they were being observed by several pairs of curious eyes, Eve tried not to lose her composure to anger, but she was highly incensed by the ungentlemanly manner in which he spoke to her, lightly and infuriatingly referring to matters he knew would cause her embarrassment.

'Your reference to what took place between us three years

ago is highly offensive and insulting, Mr Fitzalan,' she said
with deep indignation, trying to speak with composure. 'And
nothing you can say can excuse your own contemptible conduct that day. However, you are mistaken if you think I am
still the same green girl I was then. Things have changed. I
have changed, and I am not so easily seduced by arrogant,
self-opinionated men. Nothing *you* say will affect my decision
about the mine and my own future.'

With a strong feeling of displeasure Eve saw that Marcus
was watching her with an air which told her he was neither
penitent about his previous behaviour towards her nor moved
by any feeling of remorse.

'There is no need to be so impassioned,' he smiled infuri-
atingly. 'I believe you. Fortunately I have a sensitive heart and
I am not unaware how difficult the decision is for you to make.
But I ask you not to take too long in making up your mind.'

'You do not like being kept waiting, is that it, Mr Fitzalan?'

'It is indeed.'

'Then spare me your sensitive heart. I would find more
compassion in a lump of coal,' she said coldly. 'Have you
seen all you came to see of the mine?' she asked, turning and
beginning to walk back to the carriage.

'No, far from it. Unfortunately the manager is absent.'

'Yes. He's gone into Netherley with Mr Somerville—Matthew, one of the mine's agents. Matthew is Gerald's younger
brother,' she said, pausing and looking up at him, seeing him
grimace. 'No matter what your opinion might be of Gerald, I
have to tell you that Matthew is a fine young man, with a
strong mind and good conscience. The only thing that can be
said against him is that he is the younger son, which does not
allow him to inherit the estate. You will be relieved to know
he is not at all like Gerald,' she said, wondering how he would
react if she told him what had passed between herself and
Gerald on the day he had left Burntwood Hall—of the threats
he had made, and how, on leaving, he had left her a trembling
wreck.

'I'm glad to hear it. Another such as Gerald would be quite intolerable. Your father did mention him on occasion, but I cannot say that we have been introduced.'

'My father was extremely fond of Matthew. He has always shown an eager interest in mining and it was my father's intention to involve him more in the business,' Eve explained. 'He has already learned a great deal and, unlike Gerald, I know it would be safe in his hands. Gerald wouldn't want to soil his hand by getting physically involved in any industry—unless it is to sit back and cream off the profits, of course. I—I hear you are sinking a new shaft at Pendle Hill.'

Marcus's expression became serious, as it always did when he spoke of mining matters. 'Yes, and it is proving to be both expensive and time consuming. I don't mind admitting it is fraught with problems and is a drain on my resources.'

'But you must think it worthwhile to continue.'

'Very much so. The surveys and test bores I had done proved extremely favourable. It is a high-risk venture and will be very deep, but I, and my promoters, are well experienced in colliery matters and keen to proceed. I have two collieries nearing exhaustion, and the way the need for coal is increasing in the Aire and Calder valleys, if I do not speculate, the united output from the other mines will be insufficient to meet the demand.'

'Then I can see why acquiring Atwood Mine would be beneficial to you,' Eve said, with a trace of sarcasm.

Marcus's face hardened. 'My interest in Atwood Mine is more of a personal matter, Miss Somerville,' he answered sharply.

'And if it becomes yours once more, am I to understand that you would not make changes?'

'Yes, I would,' he replied without hesitation. 'The area is well proven and eventually I would sink a new shaft and extend in other directions, which would mean installing a new pumping engine to lift the water.'

'But what is wrong with the old one?'

'It's slow and outdated. I would have it replaced by one of Mr Boulton and Mr Watt's machines, which I am also having installed at Pendle Hill. The greater the power, the deeper the shaft—and because the stocks of shallow coal are running low, I do intend going much, much deeper, with a new engine lifting tons of water out of the mine with every stroke.'

Eve looked at him coolly, her instinct telling her he was man enough to do justice to what seemed to her to be a mammoth task. 'You are ambitious, Mr Fitzalan,' she stated calmly.

'Yes. I admit it. But with the expansion of Atwood Mine and the opening of Pendle Hill, it will attract more industry to the area—iron, brick and glass works and such like, providing employment for many.'

'But surely the deeper the shaft then the miners' work becomes more dangerous.'

'There are risks in any undertaking, but everything will be done to ensure their safety. We do our best to make them secure in their employment—and in the case of my own pits, we put the boys—none under the age of eight—to the easiest places below ground, although it is normal for them to learn their trade with their fathers or another relative.'

'But not all children are so fortunate, Mr Fitzalan. Some children have no family and I hear are treated quite abysmally.'

'Sadly, that is the case. However, I employ a number of children as bound apprentices from the Foundling Hospital at Netherley, and only in a very few instances are they treated so badly as to warrant a case to be brought before the Petty or Quarter Sessions. On the whole they are treated well and have little cause for complaint.'

'But disasters do occur. Atwood Mine has had its share of roof falls and floods over the years,' Eve said with a trace of sadness. 'And, as you will know, it is notorious for its outbursts of gas, resulting in dreadful explosions. Valuable though the coal is, often the colliers pay with their lives—and if not, they are horrendously injured, leaving them incapable of working and supporting their families for the rest of their lives.'

'Which is the case in almost every pit, and extremely tragic. We do our best to help such cases,' Marcus said. 'Like your father and other coalmasters, Miss Somerville, I subscribe to the General Infirmary at Leeds, which means that any bad accident cases from the collieries can be treated immediately.'

'And are women employed in your pits, Mr Fitzalan?'

He frowned, looking at her seriously. 'No—and never will be,' he replied firmly. 'As far as I am aware, there are no females employed below ground in any of the large West Riding collieries, and, personally, I find the very idea of them working alongside men in the kind of conditions that exist below ground quite abhorrent.'

Eve eyed him calmly. He had all her attention. His knowledge about mining she did not doubt, but his sincere concern for the people he employed made her look at him in a different light. His refusal to employ very small children and women down his mines—as was not the case with mine owners in other parts of the country—roused her grudging admiration.

She thought of his importance, of how much power he wielded over those who depended on him for their subsistence, making her realise that what he had just told her was making her think of him with a deeper sentiment than she ever had before. She turned and resumed her walk back to the carriage, just as the cage was bringing the colliers off their shift, their hours of work being from six in the morning until four in the afternoon. She paused and looked with pity at the men and boys clad in dirty rags, their bare legs exposed to above the knees.

Black and weary, they walked with their heads bent, looking neither right nor left, as if they had been driven to the limits of physical endurance. Some were permanently stooped from working in the dark passages below ground, where the roofs were supported by pillars of coal.

Along these passages, clouded with floating coal dust and

bad air, some so steep and others so narrow that the boys would have to crawl on their hands and knees, they would drag or push their laden baskets, filled by the hewers, to the bottom of the shaft where it would be raised to the surface— and there would be the devil to pay if the check weighman found they were not filled to capacity.

Many were aged prematurely with the dust, and older men could be seen with curved and worn backs, concave chests and sickly coughs and tight-lipped grey faces. Many of them found an early grave owing to lung disease or accidents.

'How do they stand it?' she murmured almost to herself.

'I often wonder that myself,' Marcus replied quietly, following her gaze.

'These men exist in a kind of world...living a life that is so far removed from my own that I cannot imagine it.'

'One cannot help but admire their stoic courage and their persistence to endure, for they get little in return for their toil. But mining is their livelihood. They know nothing else.'

Sighing deeply, Eve walked on. 'I wish you every success with Pendle Hill, Mr Fitzalan. What happens to this mine remains to be seen.'

'But it is not a matter to be dismissed lightly,' he said, following her and assisting her into the carriage, where her grandmother's maid was dozing lightly in a corner.

'No, indeed. I have told you that I shall give it my serious consideration. I just wish that in considering the mine I did not have to consider my relationship with you. Goodbye, Mr Fitzalan.'

With the great house around her still and silent, Eve felt nothing inside but a well of emptiness and a profound loneliness that stretched before her like a never-ending road. Anguish was not something she was accustomed to in her life, but now it washed over her like a tidal wave.

Feeling restless and wanting to clear her head early one fine, sunny morning when her grandmother had not yet risen, Eve

had the groom saddle her favourite horse, and for the first time
since her father's death she defied convention and cast decorum to the four winds as she cantered out towards the hills,
curtly dismissing the groom when she saw he intended going
with her, for she had a strong need to be by herself.

Besides, the grounds and surrounding hills where she would
ride were familiar places where she had once ridden with her
father. With long tendrils of early-morning mist curling along
the ground and between the trees, which the hot sun would
soon burn away, her ride took on a strong feeling of nostalgia
when she thought this might be the last time she would be
able to gallop over the estate she was loath to leave.

She rode her milk-white mare hard and as no lady should—
in slim-fitting black breeches and astride, which had brought
a frown of deep displeasure to the groom's features when he
had seen her, and would have brought a stern reprimand from
her grandmother if she knew she was riding about the countryside unaccompanied and dressed for all the world like a
man, having temporarily cast off her black mourning dress.

Eve was unaware of the stir she had created in the stables,
and would care little if she had—the need for privacy and to
taste complete freedom for a little while so intense inside her
that she refused to let anything get in the way of her ride, or
to allow her mind to dwell on her inevitable future.

For an hour she rode along well-known tracks, weaving her
way through the trees towering above her as she passed
through woods which clothed the sides of the hills, giving her
horse its head, exulting in its powerful force beneath her and
its energy, pressing her heels in its flanks and urging it to
greater exertion, before pausing on a grassy hill to admire and
savour the view stretched out beneath her and to let her mare
breathe. The day was hot and brilliant, the trees faded and
limp with the heat and dusty with summer. With her long legs
resting in the stirrups, she sat relaxed, feeling a welcome
breeze waft over her flushed cheeks.

Resuming her ride, she headed for the towpath running

along the side of the canal, following it for some distance away from the village, passing barges laden with coal being drawn by tired horses, and seeing few people until she came to the Navigation Inn on the other side of the canal—not the most select establishment in the area, being a popular ale house for miners where they could slake their thirst after a hard day's toil down the mine. Finding the air heavy and humid by the water she turned back towards the hills.

So lost was she in her thoughts that she didn't realise until it was too late that she had ventured on to a neighbouring estate at Pendle Hill, where Marcus Fitzalan, having leased land from the landowner, was in the process of sinking a new shaft and having a new steam engine built and installed, the one he had told her about when they had met at Atwood Mine.

She paused in a clearing while her horse bent its neck and drank from a stream, having to squint, for the sunlight hurt her eyes as she looked at the untidy sprawl of newly erected pit buildings and the partly built engine house not fifty yards away, seeing several men hurrying quickly away from where the shaft was being sunk. She did not see Mr Fitzalan at first, for her eyes had not consciously sought his presence, but suddenly he was there, and she could not explain why her emotions became bemused or why her breath caught in her throat the way it did.

His breeches and white shirt were dirty and dishevelled from his labours, and he too was striding quickly away from the shaft and in the opposite direction from her, but, turning, as if he sensed her watching him, he saw her. She could not see the expression on his face but he halted in his tracks, as if amazed to see her there, but he made no move to approach her and carried on walking away. Relieved, Eve was about to turn and ride away, but too late.

Totally unprepared, suddenly she realised what was happening, why the men were hurrying away from the shaft, when the ground beneath her shuddered violently and the air became filled with a noise that almost blasted her out of the saddle, making her eardrums vibrate and jolting her senses.

With her knowledge of coal mines she knew the sinking of some shafts often proved to be more difficult than others, when thick beds of iron-stone more difficult to penetrate than flint were encountered and had to be blasted out. That this was in the process of being done occurred to her when, a split second later, the blast was followed by another, so earthshattering that she felt her brain knocking against the inside of her skull, the offending rock and stone being thrown high up into the air.

Immediately her terrified horse rolled its maddened eyes and screamed and reared, thrashing the air frantically with its hooves, and she was unable to prevent it from taking the bit in its teeth and bolting wildly. Being an expert rider, Eve fought to bring her mount under control as it went charging through the woods, knowing that in its maddened state it was useless trying to guide it with the bit, and sitting as balanced in the saddle as she could while she let it run blindly on, knowing it couldn't possibly keep up this pace for long and that it would have to slow down eventually.

But to her horror a fence suddenly loomed ahead of her, much too high for her mare to jump clear. Fearing the worst, the blood pounding in her throat, in desperation she applied her right heel firmly to her horse's side and the mare wheeled obediently to gallop at an angle. With enormous relief Eve felt her beginning to slow down, becoming aware for the first time of the hollow thunder of hooves behind her.

At last she brought her horse under control and managed to bring it to a shuddering halt. White-faced, she turned to see the man on the horse come thundering through the undergrowth towards her, the two almost like one being. She knew immediately that it was Marcus Fitzalan, having recognised the tall chestnut stallion he rode.

He jerked on the reins, drawing his horse to a halt, which must have taken all his strength, for it was a huge beast and he had been riding at full gallop. Jumping down, he didn't hesitate to come to her and, as if to establish his supremacy, reached up and dragged her unceremoniously from the saddle.

Tearing herself from his arms, Eve was trembling with anger brought on by fear.

'Take your hands off me,' she flared indignantly, having had no time to recover her self-possession. She still felt unsteady with shock and the ragged thumping of her heart had not yet slowed to an even beat. Reaching out, she tried to calm her quivering mare with soothing words. She was lathered with sweat and foam dropped in frothy blobs from her bit. But the usually gentle horse picked up her anger and unease and continued to pull away from her.

In exasperation Marcus snatched the reins from her hands and tethered the horse to a sturdy tree before turning to her, his face white with rage, all his muscles tense, and a pulse throbbing at his temple.

'What in hell's name were you trying to do?' he blazed down at her, his eyes like molten ice. 'Kill yourself?'

'Me?' she broke out furiously. 'I thought it was you who was trying to do that? You saw me there. Why did you not warn me what was to happen—that you were blasting?'

'There was no time. I had to make sure the men close to the shaft were well out of the way before the explosion. You were far enough away not to be in any kind of danger.'

'Ha! Try telling *that* to my horse. Look at her. She's terrified.'

'Then you should know how to control your horse.'

'I am perfectly capable of handling my horse, Mr Fitzalan— as you must have judged for yourself, even though it would kill you to admit it,' Eve seethed, the force of his remark increasing her anger.

'Maybe you're right, but in the name of God I have never seen anything like this,' he said, suddenly appalled as he stepped back to take in her appearance, noticing for the first time that she was wearing breeches. 'Do you usually roam about the countryside unaccompanied, riding your horse astride and dressed in breeches?' he demanded.

Eve flung back her head rebelliously. 'No, not normally, but I felt like doing so today.'

'And you grandmother? Is she still staying with you at Burntwood Hall.'

'Yes. She will not be returning to Cumbria until my future is settled.'

'Very wise—taking into account your behaviour today, which is both reckless and irresponsible. Is she aware that you ride unaccompanied—and dressed as you are?'

'My grandmother is not even aware that I have left the house, and I am sure she would agree with you and be quite shocked by my appearance—but my clothes are the least of my worries just now. Besides—I like my freedom, Mr Fitzalan.'

'It would appear you have too much freedom, Miss Somerville,' he accused her harshly, while secretly thinking he had never seen her look more lovely—with her cheeks faintly flushed from the gallop, and some stray locks of glossy black hair that had escaped from its demure coil beneath her hat lying on the red silk collar of her blouse. After a long, hot ride he would have expected most ladies to appear drained and exhausted, whereas Eve radiated vitality, giving no hint of any discomfort she might have suffered when her horse bolted.

'Are you normally indiscreet?' he asked, giving no indication that he thought her a truly amazing young woman. She rode well and he admired the way she had handled her horse, having the presence of mind to bring it quickly under control the way she had.

'I do nothing I am ashamed of—and please do not think I rode this way so that I might chance to bump into you. It was not my intention to stray off Somerville land, and so if you don't mind I will return to it and continue with my ride.'

'Not until your horse—and yourself—have cooled down,'

Marcus said firmly, standing in front of her with his hands on his hips and preventing her from mounting her horse.

Stung to indignation, Eve was fuming. 'Then I shall walk her back.'

'Two miles?'

'Yes—if necessary.'

'Don't be a fool. Wait a while and then she'll be fit to ride.'

Enraged at finding herself held at bay, warm blood flooded her face. 'Do you mean to keep me here?'

'You can leave whenever you wish. You are not my prisoner.'

'Then have the goodness to move aside and let me pass.'

When he didn't do as she asked she eyed him warily, unsure what to do next. To pass him she would have to touch him, and after her last encounter on finding herself alone with him in a wood, she was determined to keep her distance.

'When I saw your horse bolt I came after you at once.'

'How dare you present yourself as my self-proclaimed champion. I'm glad you didn't rescue me, otherwise you would have placed me in the humiliating position of having to be grateful to you. You could have saved yourself the trouble and stayed at the mine—where I am sure your presence would be appreciated more,' replied Eve ungraciously. 'I managed to bring my mount under control myself.'

Marcus glared at her. 'You could easily have been thrown.'

'Well, I wasn't. Go back to your mine, Mr Fitzalan. I'm sure your men will be wondering where you've got to. Heaven help us should they come looking for you and find us alone like this. Imagine how people will talk,' she remarked with a strong hint of sarcasm.

'And that would bother you, would it?'

'No. Not in the slightest. But is it your intention to make me conspicuous—to ruin my reputation as you did once before—by keeping me here? Once is a scandal, but twice is not to be endured. Perhaps it is your belief that in doing so you will be able to force me into marriage—that by using your powers of persuasion you are hoping to rekindle the time you lured me into the woods three years ago?'

Marcus smiled crookedly, his anger of a moment earlier melting as he remembered the time she spoke of—when she had kissed him with such tender passion—with a great deal of pleasure. 'As to that, I was the one being compromised. I did not lure you. You came willingly, as I remember.'

'You remember too much,' she snapped.

'And you were tempted then.'

'I was very young and stupid.'

'And now you are wiser?'

'Yes, and no longer foolish enough to get carried away by you.'

'And despite your statement to the contrary the last time we met, you are sure of that, are you?' he asked, smiling, his eyes gleaming cruelly as he moved towards her.

Seething with anger, Eve tried to move further away. 'Don't you dare come near me. You're a monster, Marcus Fitzalan,' she flared.

'I'm happy to hear you address me in a more familiar manner, Miss Somerville. Marcus Fitzalan is an improvement on Mr Fitzalan.'

Eve ignored his gentle sarcasm. 'You're no better than those worthless fortune hunters my grandmother often refers to—except that with you it's a coal mine you have a mind to seduce from me.'

Marcus stopped then, his mocking smile widening. 'Half a coal mine,' he reminded her coldly.

'I don't care if a hundred coal mines are at stake. I have no intention of meekly accepting my fate. Believe me, Mr Fitzalan, marrying me would not be worth it.'

'Maybe you're right—but I shall never know unless I try it,' he said, as inch by terrifying inch he moved steadily closer until she was pressed up against a tree and there was nowhere she could go to escape him.

Chapter Six

Eve stood perfectly still, unable to look away, knowing that she was very much in danger of becoming overwhelmed by him, his lean, muscular body emanating raw power and his sternly handsome face hovering so very close.

Slowly his eyes moved down from her face and over the rippling silk of her red blouse tucked into her waistband, the sight of her long, slim legs and hips outlined beneath her close-fitting breeches causing a lazy, appreciative smile to twist his lips, and he found himself dwelling with a good deal of pleasure on the tantalising delights underneath.

'And I would be a fool if I thought marriage to you had nothing more to offer than a coal mine,' he murmured, meeting her gaze. Seeing shock mingle with fear in her wonderful eyes, he moved away a little, becoming less threatening to her sensibilities. He grinned infuriatingly. 'Just testing the water, so to speak,' he said softly, but his instinct told him she was no more immune to him now and her own vulnerability than she had been three years ago.

'Then don't venture too deep, Mr Fitzalan, otherwise you might find yourself out of your depth,' she retorted coldly.

His eyebrows arched and his pale blue eyes danced wickedly. 'There's little danger of that, Miss Somerville. I'm an extremely good swimmer. Now come along. If you insist on returning to Burntwood Hall, I'll ride part of the way back with you.'

'No. There's no need. I am perfectly capable of riding back myself.'

'I'm sure you are,' he said, moving towards her horse and making quite sure it was calm enough for her to mount once more, 'but they can do without me at the mine for a while and it will give me great pleasure to accompany you.'

Drawing a long breath Eve could tell he would not be dissuaded. 'Very well. If you insist.'

'I do.' He frowned crossly when she declined his gesture to help her mount, stubbornly preferring to do it herself—which she did, the agility of her movements as she swung one long leg easily over the saddle making his pulses quicken. 'Miss Somerville—Eve,' he said, his expression serious. 'Must there be enmity between us? Must you persist in getting on my wrong side all the time? Can't we call a truce and begin speaking to each other like adults?'

Unwillingly Eve looked down at him, meeting his gaze squarely, finding the warmth in his eyes far more disturbing and disarming than his anger, and making it extremely difficult to regard him as an enemy. She sighed, beginning to relax and soften towards him.

'Yes—you are right,' she conceded, 'and I suppose I should thank you for coming to my rescue so promptly. My horse could easily have thrown me. I do realise that.'

They rode in single file along a narrow track, which made conversation impossible between them for a while. Riding slowly ahead of Marcus, a curious dreaminess pervaded Eve as she let the sun's warmth seep into her. Time seemed to slow and everything around them was lulled in the shimmering heat. Tall grass and bracken grew along the banks on either side of the path, and the merry chirrup of birds in the trees, the buzz of an occasional bee and the snorting of their horses were all that disturbed the quiet. When the path opened out and they rode side by side, Marcus cast her an admiring glance.

'You know, you really should not ride alone,' he said quietly. 'All manner of folk roam these woods around Atwood.'

Lulled into a sense of calm by the gentle movement of the horse and the warm sun on her face, Eve glanced sideways at him, seeing he was in earnest. 'Why, Mr Fitzalan, you amaze me. Is it to protect me that you insisted on accompanying me?'

'Yes.'

She flashed him a bright smile. 'How gallant.'

He responded with a grin. 'There. Now you know I am not all bad, does that improve my character in your eyes?'

'It's too soon to say. There's still a great deal about you that I don't know. You are an opportunist, I believe.'

'If you mean I seize everything that comes my way, you are right. But I am not so mercenary as to do so without regard for principles or consequence.'

'And Atwood Mine? Does that mean more to you than personal relationships?'

'If you had asked me that before your father died I would have said yes. I always believed romantic relationships to be for dreamers and fools.'

'And now? What has changed?'

'You,' he replied bluntly.

Eve looked at him with a newly acquired wisdom, smiling wryly. 'I've already told you not to use false flattery on me, Mr Fitzalan. I am not deceived. I am no fool and know the mine's worth. Come, admit it. You want it badly enough to seduce me into marriage.'

He frowned crossly. 'If you want to know the truth, I'm beginning to curse the wretched mine. No matter what my feelings turn out to be regarding yourself, you will always have reason to be suspicious, to doubt them because of the mine. How much better it would be if I could pay court to you without you forever accusing me of having an ulterior motive.'

His words rendered Eve speechless, and she stared across at him, so surprised that for once she was unsure how to respond.

'You…have given some thought to the matter which is important to us both, I hope?' Marcus asked at length as they continued to amble in the direction of Burntwood Hall.

'Yes, I have—but the matter you speak of means more to you than it does to me, I think, Mr Fitzalan,' she said—which was not entirely true, but she would not give him the satisfaction of letting him know just how much Atwood Mine meant to her.

But Marcus was no fool. He knew by the fierce intensity he had seen in her eyes when Mr Soames had read out the conditions of her father's will exactly how much she wanted to hold on to it.

'You must understand that all this is very difficult for me,' she said.

'I realise that,' he replied, noticing that her tongue had lost none of its edge, despite her agreement to call a truce, 'but it has to be faced some time—and it's no use pretending I don't have a self-interest in the mine.'

'I know that. It's rather like myself. I took it for granted that more of my father's assets, as well as Atwood Mine, would be left to me, you see,' she said with marked irony which was not lost on Marcus.

He gave a wry smile. 'I learned long ago never to take anything for granted.'

Eve was beginning to feel a little uncomfortable and vaguely irritated by his close inspection as he turned his head towards her. She met his gaze, noticing how pale and blue his eyes were—as clear and sharp as the mountain streams that tumbled over the rocks and through the valleys in her grandmother's native Cumbria.

'How are you, really?' he asked, with a gentleness Eve would not have expected from him.

It was only a simple question, but there was so much sincerity in his voice that she looked at him with astonishment and studied him closely, his absolute masculinity stirring some hidden feminine instinct that her innocence and inexperience did not give her the liberty to recognise. She didn't know if it was the unblinking fascination of his eyes or the sensation his nearness evoked in her, but for a split second she was unable to stir, becoming mesmerised as she gazed at him. Then, with a shiver, she immediately looked away.

'I am as well as I can be—considering the unfortunate nature of the circumstances. Still, with time, I'm sure I'll get over it,' she answered with a forced lightness.

Her grieving was evident to Marcus, but he strongly suspected it was not just for her father that she mourned. 'It will be difficult for you, I'm sure, having to leave Burntwood Hall,' he said. 'It must mean a great deal to you.'

Eve's expression became curiously soft, with a yearning quality that touched Marcus. For a moment her face became unguarded and, for the first time in their acquaintance, it showed him something of the lost child behind the deliberately maintained façade of the woman. His heart contracted at the grief he saw etched on her lovely face, her violet eyes so dark with suffering they were almost black. It was clear that losing her father so tragically, plus the shock of his will, had done a great deal of emotional damage.

'Yes,' she confessed, in answer to his question, 'it will. I confess I hadn't thought how much it has come to mean to me until now. It saddens me to think how little Gerald will appreciate it. But it cannot be easy for you, either, knowing you could stand to lose the opportunity of owning Atwood Mine once more,' she remarked matter of factly as their horses fell into step beside each other, walking slowly along the paths that snaked along the hillside, neither of them feeling the need for haste as they conversed easily together for the first time.

'Only if you refuse to agree to become my wife.'

Eve's heart contracted at his words, for they told her that his mind was already made up.

'But I remember you telling me that you don't want a wife any more than I want a husband, Mr Fitzalan. Why—by your persistence, if I didn't know better, I would think that you find me completely irresistible and that you cannot live without me. I may not take kindly to having a coal mine as a rival for my husband's affections—if we marry, that is.'

'Nor I, Miss Somerville,' Marcus replied, smiling thinly and preferring to ignore her sarcasm, but a dangerous light gleamed in his eyes. 'I might say the same about you—seeing that we will be equal partners, don't forget.'

'Nevertheless, you must want it badly—enough to tie yourself down to a woman who is almost a stranger to you. Tell me why Atwood Mine is so important to you? By all accounts you already own several mines, have shares in others and invest your money wisely, enabling you to live like a prince for the rest of your life.'

'That's true, but Atwood Mine is important to me in the sense that it used to belong to my family. I know of its potential—that it's the most profitable mine in the area, with untapped coal reserves way beyond imagination. But it means more to me than that,' he said, speaking wistfully, a yearning, nostalgic quality entering his eyes which Eve saw and was surprised by, for it gave her an insight of the man who spoke, which she had glimpsed once before, when they had met and talked at Atwood Mine just a few days ago; for a moment, they seemed to be encapsulated by a quiet companionship.

'It was started by my grandfather and my own father died in that mine. I was at school at the time and was not aware that my mother—who hated everything to do with coal and felt unable to profit from something that had been the means of causing her untold misery—had sold the lease to your father until it was too late to do anything about it.'

'And if you had known, you would have stopped her?'

'Definitely.'

'I see,' she said, realising what a crushing blow it must have been for him to discover what his mother had done. It wasn't just a mine to him, it was much more than that. It represented everything his grandfather had fought so hard to achieve. It was a symbol of years of physically demanding toil. There was little wonder he wanted it back in his family. 'I knew nothing of this. And you felt no resentment towards my father for taking it from you?'

'Why should I? Apart from my own sense of loss there was nothing wrong with the transaction. He was a businessman and had done nothing wrong. As you know, your father and I became good friends and he was a tremendous help to me when I too went into the mining industry. He taught me a great deal about mining, for which I shall be eternally grateful. I admired him enormously and shall miss him in many ways.'

Eve knew by the depth of feeling with which he spoke those last words that he was speaking from the heart. The feeling between them had been mutual, their friendship firm and enduring, and a force entered Eve that made her own resentment and jealousy, which she had nurtured against Marcus Fitzalan for so long, seem petty in comparison.

She recollected the time when she had first begun to feel this way, when she had been a child and Marcus Fitzalan had started taking an interest in mining after his own father had died. Her father had recognised his natural aptitude for business and taken him under his wing. He had admired the way Marcus had set out to establish himself in the coal industry by being keen to learn and having ambition and drive, which had won admiration from friends and rivals alike.

Eve's resentment and bitterness stemmed from a time long before their encounter at Atwood Fair, when her father had come to look upon him almost as the son he'd never had, which had distanced him from her even further. Her father had talked of him often, constantly referring to things he had said and done, causing her to wonder if he ever spared a thought for anyone else...or for her.

'I regret we never met,' Marcus went on, smiling down at her, having no idea what was passing through her mind—he would have been shocked and surprised if he had. 'Perhaps we might have become friends before now.'

Eve was prompted to say she doubted it, but thought better of it.

'I did see you once—when you came to the house with my father. I was fourteen at the time. My friend Emma Parkinson and I were on the landing, looking down into the hall when you were leaving.'

'Oh!' he said, trying to imagine what she would have looked like then, as a child looking through the banisters. 'And what impression did I make?'

'You didn't,' she replied coldly, the peace of a moment before short-lived as she detected the mocking note in his voice. 'I remember telling Emma that I couldn't see what all the fuss was about. Your reputation for being one for the ladies had preceded you, you see.'

He smiled at that. 'My reputation?'

'Yes. It may surprise you to know that the odd bits of gossip about your liaisons and conquests have filtered through to Atwood from time to time.'

'So—you think you know all about me, do you? I am a notorious womaniser, gambler and anything else that defames my character—is that correct? Come,' he said when he saw her hesitate, one of his dark brows arched and his eyes gleaming with derisive humour, 'we must be frank with each other.'

'Very well—yes. I remember Emma thinking you were quite the handsomest thing on two legs.'

He laughed outright with unfeigned amusement. 'A lady after my own heart. I must remind you to introduce me to your friend Emma some time. And you?' he asked, watching her face closely. 'Tell me what you thought of me.'

She shrugged. 'I'm not as easily flustered as Emma. When she saw I wasn't impressed, she told me you would make a meal out of me in no time at all.'

'And what was your reply to that?'

'Only that I would give you indigestion,' she replied, regarding him with open candour.

Marcus's lips twitched at the corners as he tried to suppress a smile, thinking how very young she was. From his youth he had been favoured by women for his good looks and arrogant ways, and had been more than willing to sample their charms, but Eve Somerville was not at all like any of them, which he found a refreshing change.

'Yes, I think you are probably right,' he said softly, full of secret amusement as he raised his brows and let his eyes travel over her from head to toe, an assessment not devoid of insolence and appreciation, which caused a flush of embarrassment to spring to Eve's cheeks, 'but I think I would have to fatten you up a little first.'

All at once his expression became serious. 'You have made it plain that there is a great deal about me you do not like, but how this can be, when you really know nothing about me at all, leaves me feeling quite intrigued.'

'Why should it? By all accounts—'

'Gossip, you mean.'

'If you like. By all accounts, wherever you go, you have ladies dripping from your arms like bats in a belfry. To you love and relationships are a game, one that you are good at— used to winning and the world's worst loser. Forgive me if I appear outspoken, Mr Fitzalan,' she said in a matter-of-fact way when she saw his eyes open wide with surprise that she should speak with such candour, 'but you did ask that I should be frank—and, if we are to marry, then it's as well that I know all there is to know about you. Does it disappoint you to know what others say and think of you?'

He cocked a sleek black brow, speaking ironically. 'I long since ceased to worry about other people's opinions of me. However,' he said on a softer note, a warm intimacy creeping into his voice, and his incredible gaze passing over her in a manner which caused her stomach to quiver despite her resolve to stand firm against him, 'I am flattered to know I have kindled so much interest in you over the years.'

Eve flushed, bristling at his tone. 'Why—you conceited—'

'So others were fond of pointing out when I was a boy,' he said quickly, smiling infuriatingly and his eyes flashing wickedly.

'A trait which has continued.'

He was watching her, his expression unfathomable. 'So, you do not care for my arrogance and conceit?'

'No—not much.'

'But then—you know so little about me.'

'As much as I want to know. The knowledge I have of you does not inspire me to want to know more.'

'Pity. Only…a little knowledge can be dangerous,' he said softly, meaningfully.

'Oh, I'm perfectly capable of avoiding danger.'

'And you're sure of that, are you?'

'Naturally.'

Marcus smiled, mocking. 'Tell me, Miss Somerville, are you afraid to marry me?'

Looking into his intense, pale blue eyes Eve rose to the challenge. 'No, Mr Fitzalan. I'm afraid of no man.'

'You may protest all you like, but I get the distinct feeling that I unsettle you in some way.'

'You do not unsettle me in the slightest,' she replied with a slight quiver in her voice, beginning to feel exceedingly discomposed by the content of the conversation—and by his gaze and crooked smile which drenched her in its sensuality.

'Yes, I do. You're blushing.'

'No, I am not,' she protested, knowing she was and feeling the colour intensify under his frank scrutiny.

'Yes, you are. But don't worry, you look quite charming and your cheeks are as deliciously pink as those roses,' he said, indicating a wonderful array of dog roses rampantly blooming along the edge of the path, his voice stroking her like a caress.

Her gaze trapped in his, Eve regarded him in silence. He was riding far too close, she thought, and his potent maleness was making her feel too vulnerable by far.

Marcus smiled, his pale blue eyes dazzlingly clear and full of mischievous delight, well satisfied, knowing full well exactly how much havoc he was presenting to her sensibilities.

They paused for a moment, facing each other. Marcus looked into Eve's bold, fiery eyes, letting his gaze dwell appreciatively on her perfect features. He was a man of power and pride who always walked a straight line. He had always known what he wanted and usually got it—and he had already made up his mind that he wanted Eve Somerville…with or without the mine.

Given time he would cure her of her rebellious nature and mould her into the kind of woman he wanted his wife to be. A task he would enjoy. He intended to launch an assault on her that would have her weak at the knees and begging for him to make theirs a marriage in every sense of the word.

'Let me assure you that what you have just accused me of being—a philanderer of the worst possible kind, I believe—is exceedingly exaggerated. You really shouldn't listen to gossip. I am sorry to disappoint you and shatter the misguided illusion you appear to have of me, but I must tell you that it is with some regret that I find I have little time for the kind of pleasures you speak of. Much of my time is taken up with the more important matters of business.'

'And how can I be sure of that?'

'You'll have to take my word for it. But why it should appear to matter so much to you puzzles me.'

'It matters only in the sense that, if I agree to become your wife, I will be the butt of no one's joke.'

'And I would not have it so, Miss Somerville. However,' he said on a more serious note, 'this is a matter far too important for us to be sidetracked into light discussion. We have something much more important to occupy us. If we marry, we benefit considerably. If we don't, we stand to lose everything. It's a dilemma—don't you agree?'

'Yes.'

'I admit I have a lot to lose if we do not marry—and why shouldn't I avail myself of your father's generous offer in order to obtain the mine?'

'Half the mine,' Eve reminded him sharply.

Marcus bowed his head in acquiescence. Once again Eve met his glacier gaze. 'Of course. I stand corrected. Come, don't tell me you find the prospect of living in Cumbria with your grandmother appealing. Even marriage to me would be better than that.'

'Would it? I'm not so sure about that.' Eve sighed as they began to ride on, deflated, suddenly, for in truth she was unable to disagree with him. 'Nevertheless, you are right,' she conceded. 'My grandmother is not the easiest of women to get on with. She has ruled her family for many years, acting in accordance to the way she herself was brought up, and has little understanding for human frailties. The whole family stands in awe of her. My mother always became a different person in her presence. She always put off as long as she could Grandmother's visits.'

'And what is her opinion of all this? Is she in favour of a marriage taking place between us?'

'Yes. My grandmother is happy enough for me to marry you. She wants to see me settled. But she belongs to the old school, where a young lady should marry the man of her parents' choosing for advantage, wealth and title. Debilitating emotions such as romantic love she sees as a weakness which does not enter into the scheme of things.'

'And is that how you would like to enter marriage?'

'Of course,' she said frankly. 'What woman would not?'

He smiled. 'You make your grandmother sound like a tyrant—but I'm sure you exaggerate. Until the funeral we had not met, but I found her company pleasant enough.'

'She always gives that impression to strangers, but don't be fooled by it. If you become better acquainted with her, you'll soon share the opinion of everyone else.'

Marcus arched his black brows and looked down at her quizzically. 'Oh? And is there a chance of that—that we'll become better acquainted, I mean?'

'Why—I—I—'

'Come, now,' he said, smiling crookedly at her confusion. 'Am I to understand that you might agree to become my wife? Forgive me, but do you find me so repulsive?' he asked when he saw a look of distaste cross her face.

'I would prefer to choose my own husband—that is all.'

'Don't young ladies in your position usually have husbands found for them?'

'Yes—but not with conditions such as we have been presented with. The prospect my father has laid before me is one I feel loath to accept.'

'I can understand that. Is there anyone else you are contemplating marrying?'

Eve gave him a level gaze. 'No. But I think it is only fair to tell you that Gerald has asked me to marry him.'

Marcus looked at her in astonishment. His face became a stone mask, devoid of all expression. Gerald was a complication he could do without. 'He has what?' His voice was like ice, hard and implacable. The thought that Gerald Somerville would do his utmost to obtain the mine had crawled into his mind when he had been made aware of the conditions of Sir John's will, and it gave him no joy to discover that his worst fear had been realised.

'Gerald has asked me to—'

'I heard you the first time,' he exploded, causing Eve to start and tremble slightly at the anger her announcement had aroused in him. 'And what did you say?' he demanded. 'What was your answer? Because you know it was not what your father would have wished.'

'I said no,' she answered quietly. 'I do not reciprocate his attention.' She shuddered, recalling her last emotive encounter with Gerald, which still had the power to evoke fear and create unease within her. 'Nothing could ever tempt me to marry Gerald.'

Swamped with relief Marcus studied her thoughtfully, concerned to see how, when speaking, she avoided his eyes and how her voice trembled, which was suspicious in itself. He looked at her for a long moment, as if he debated some problem in his mind but could only determine an answer in the expression of her face.

'But it would appear I am a valuable commodity in the marriage market suddenly,' Eve continued quietly, 'and whoever I choose will profit enormously—except myself. But what of you? Is there no lady you would rather marry?'

'No,' he replied—too quickly, Eve thought, watching him closely. He radiated an unshakable calm and she was unable to read his well-schooled features, but her instinct told her he might not be telling her the truth. Did he want the mine so much that he was prepared to jeopardise a relationship he might already have with someone else? And, if so, was a man who would go to such drastic lengths to obtain what he wanted the kind of man she wanted to spend the rest of her life with?

'Let me make a suggestion—make it easier for you,' he went on. 'If you agree to become my wife, we will make it a marriage in name only—a marriage of convenience—until we want it otherwise. Come—what do you say?'

Eve looked at him sharply. 'A purely platonic relationship, you mean? A relationship in which we could each lead our own lives.'

'Up to a point.' He smiled slightly when he saw her relief.

'Do you mean it?' she asked. This was better than she had expected.

'Of course. But only until the time comes when there is better understanding between us—when we are no longer strangers. Could you agree to those terms?'

Their eyes met and held, and for some reason Eve could not explain, his words caused a faint stirring of disappointment inside her, causing her to question it and ask herself why this should be, unless it was that she wanted more of a commitment from him.

'It would be a private matter and would be between us and no one else. Let's face it,' he said, 'the situation is distasteful to us both, but whatever resentments we feel it is important to give the impression that all is well between us.'

'Pretend, you mean.'

'Precisely. We could announce our betrothal now and be married as soon as the required term of mourning for your father has been honoured—providing it is within the six months he stipulated in his will.'

'You do not waste much time, do you, Mr Fitzalan?' Eve said drily, having always hoped that when the time came for her to marry the moment of proposal would come from the heart, not as some cold and impersonal business proposition.

'Not when there's something I want.'

'And you want the mine—or half of it. Even if you have to take me as part of the package.'

'Yes. But it is a package I am not displeased with,' he replied softly, his eyes holding hers, causing a crimson flush to spring once more to her cheeks.

Marcus saw so many conflicting emotions chase across her face, which was far too expressive, and he realised she was not nearly as hard and in control as she would like him to think.

They had reached Burntwood Hall and to Eve's surprise Marcus dismounted, indicating that she should do the same. Taking her by the shoulders, he turned her towards him, his eyes serious and surprisingly understanding.

'Whatever your decision, Eve,' he said softly, speaking her name for the first time with an intimacy that already had them attached, his eyes penetrating as they held hers, 'I am on your side. Please believe that. No matter what harsh, misguided opinion you have of me—I am not your enemy. So what do you say? Will you consent to be my wife?'

As Eve returned his gaze, her expression was serious. The quality of his voice was smooth and it seemed to her that he had suddenly ironed all the difficulties facing them away—as if he had mesmerised them both by the quietness of his voice. The pressure of his fingers on her shoulders made her heart begin to beat in an unpredictable manner and his gaze held her spellbound, weaving some magic web around her from which there was no escape.

'I don't know. Every instinct is telling me I should know more about you, Mr Fitzalan, and your home and family, before I make up my mind.'

'Of course. That is what I would expect. Let me begin by telling you that my family consists of two brothers, both younger than myself, who have made their careers in the Navy. William, the middle one, is married with two children and lives in London—when not at sea, that is. Michael, who is just twenty, comes home to Brooklands when he can— which is where I live with my mother.'

'I see. And your mother? Will she accept me under these circumstances, do you think?'

'If she likes you and knows it is what I want, then she will not oppose you. I wonder—would you consider coming to Brooklands, to see for yourself what it's like? Take a look, see the house and find out all you need to know about me before you decide?'

Eve looked at him steadily. 'With no strings attached?'

'No strings.'

'Then—yes.' She smiled. 'I would like that.'

'Good. My mother is entertaining a few friends to dinner next Wednesday. Would you care to come along—if you have no other engagement, that is?'

'Yes, thank you,' she replied, relieved she would not be alone with him. 'I have no other engagement. But I cannot possibly come by myself.'

'I realise that. The invitation extends to your grandmother also. Do you have any objections to that?'

'No. I shall look forward to it.'

'Good. I shall look forward to showing you my home. Brooklands was built by my grandfather and may not be as old or as grand as Burntwood Hall, but it is lovely all the same. I am sure you will not be disappointed.'

He looked at her seriously for a long moment, reaching up and brushing her cheek slowly and gently with the back of his fingers, sending a disconcerting tremor of warm pleasure coursing through her and causing her heart to skip a beat, knowing full well that she was in danger of succumbing to his fatal charm—as no doubt he was certain she would.

Eve made no effort to move away, and as Marcus looked deeply into her eyes his own were tender, and she trembled once more, unable to control it. His fingers were warm, soft and strong, gently massaging her cheek, and she felt a sudden urge to turn her head and kiss the palm of his hand.

'You are under no obligation to marry me, Eve, but I sincerely hope you will. I want to marry you. I want to make you my wife. If you say yes, you will make me an extremely happy man. I believe I could make you love me.'

His voice was deep and incredibly sincere. Eve was deeply moved by his words, spoken seriously and without arrogance. His eyes continued to hold hers and his lips curved in a quiet smile. She gazed up at him, and a long moment passed before she replied.

'Yes,' she whispered. 'Perhaps you could.' She stepped back from him, afraid of the turmoil inside her, afraid of the weakening effect he was having on her emotions.

Marcus sensed what she was thinking. 'You are an extremely beautiful and desirable young woman—and please do not accuse me of flattering you in order to seduce you into marriage. The statement is completely true and spoken from the heart. Don't fight me, Eve. Don't be afraid to come close.'

'Afraid?'

'Yes. Because of the past you are wary and wish to avoid

being hurt. I don't blame you, but I assure you that the last thing I want to do is to hurt or distress you in any way.'

'You seem to know me well, Mr Fitzalan.'

'Well enough to deduce certain things, and well enough to know I want to marry you with or without your half of Atwood Mine.'

Eve stared at him—bemused and tranquillised by his soft words, knowing she was in danger of falling completely beneath his spell. In the past he had caused her nothing but grief. He had hurt her and aroused her resentment and jealousy by holding a special place in her father's affections—a place she had childishly wanted all to herself—and, knowing all this, still she was attracted to him. She didn't seem to be able to help it.

She took another step back, trying to shake off the effect he was having on her, knowing she should listen to the warning bell ringing inside her head—and yet why was she hoping…wanting him to kiss her?

'I—I must go,' she murmured, avoiding his penetrating gaze, unable to think clearly with him looking at her like that. 'Thank you for seeing me home.'

'The pleasure was all mine.'

It was as he was leaving, mounted on his horse in the driveway, that he paused and looked down at her. His expression was grave, his eyes still penetrating, but she could not see what lay behind them.

'The last thing I want to do is alarm you, but promise me you will take care.'

'Why? What are you saying?'

'It worries me that you are alone here—with Gerald in such close proximity. I am not unaware that he covets the mine, that he feels cheated. He is well aware that if we do not marry the mine will revert to him—and, from what I know of him, he is ruthless enough to try anything to hold on to it. He has already taken the first step by asking you to become his wife.

If he should approach you and threaten you in any way—you will let me know?'

Eve was touched by his concern. There was so much warmth and sincerity in his voice that she was quite disarmed. She smiled softly, giving him no indication that Gerald had already threatened her. Not wishing to cause trouble and hoping that Gerald's threats had been empty and that she would not have to face him in the future, she fully intended leaving Burntwood Hall before he arrived to take up residence.

'Yes. I will.'

Chapter Seven

Marcus left Eve an extremely confused young woman. That night, as sleep eluded her, she continued to think of the things he had said to her, things she could not believe he had said—especially the part when he had told her that he wanted to marry her with or without her half of Atwood Mine. That she found difficult to believe. It was too preposterous for words.

She had vowed never again to let him make her lose her composure as she had that time when he had made a fool of her in front of her friends, a time when he had got her so bewildered she hardly knew right from wrong—when his kisses had robbed her of the ability to think clearly.

She had been a silly, stupid girl, so inexperienced and unqualified to deal with a man of the world like Marcus Fitzalan that she had been wide open to seduction. He had attempted to seduce her for his own amusement, his improper behaviour towards her both inexcusable and unforgivable, and she told herself that she must not allow herself to weaken, to give in to his forceful personality a second time.

But no matter how she railed against him, telling herself that she disliked him intensely, that she would rather be consigned to hell than consider marriage to him, she could not deny that on finding herself alone with him once again, she had wanted him to repeat the same offence he had perpetrated against her person three years ago.

In fact, she was so confused she found it difficult—if not impossible—to analyse her feelings. There was that same fierce tug to her senses in being near him as there had been when he had drawn her away from her friends at Atwood Fair. For a long while after that encounter thoughts of him had persisted on intruding into her everyday life. In spite of her determination not to be similarly affected, she feared that resolve was lost, and found herself looking forward to her visit to Brooklands and to meeting his mother.

Eve's grandmother was delighted at the prospect of visiting Brooklands, and glad to see that Eve was being sensible at last now that the initial shock of the contents of her father's will had lessened slightly, after tilting her world sideways and flinging her life into total confusion. She suspected that her granddaughter's easy acceptance of the invitation to visit Brooklands and to meet Mrs Fitzalan was because she was softening towards Marcus Fitzalan, despite her earlier avowal to the contrary.

'I shall look forward to seeing Brooklands, Eve. I am honoured to have been invited—although you could hardly go without a chaperon,' she said as she walked slowly beside her granddaughter in the garden, enjoying the late afternoon sunshine. It was the day after Marcus had issued the invitation. Lady Pemberton cast Eve a shrewd glance. 'Does this mean that you are seriously considering marriage to Mr Fitzalan after all?'

'Yes,' Eve admitted. 'I realise that I must.'

'Good. I like him. He is a charming man and I am sure he is the one for you,' she said firmly. 'Although what a pity you're in mourning, Eve. It would have been so nice if you could have worn something of a more cheerful colour to make you look your best. I never did like black on young ladies. It's too severe for my liking.'

'I'm sure Mr Fitzalan will not notice what I'm wearing, Grandmother,' she smiled.

'Nevertheless, it's time you were introduced to his mother if you two are to marry.'

'Yes, I know. But I would also like to know Mr Fitzalan a little better before I decide.'

'That is sensible. You are bemused by him, I can see that— which is natural with a man of his character. But I know a good man when I see one. He will make a good husband.'

Eve stared at her grandmother, looking slightly forlorn. 'Will he? Do you really think so, Grandmother?'

Lady Pemberton reached out and patted her arm gently. 'Oh, yes.'

'But will a man who is respected, important, rich and powerful, owner of not one but several coal mines, and who lives in a splendid house, make a good husband in every other sense?'

Her grandmother smiled with understanding, remembering they'd had a similar conversation before. 'It helps. Money is an extremely useful commodity, Eve. As for the rest—the matters of the heart which I know are so important to you—they will come later. Now, stop frowning. It spoils your face. You must look forward to going to Brooklands and your meeting with Mrs Fitzalan.'

Ruth Fitzalan was the mother of three sons: Marcus, the eldest, because of his passion for mining and being his father's heir, was the only one left at home—unlike William and Michael, who had both sought careers in the Navy. Ruth was a tall, slender woman with a strong personality, not unlike Marcus in features, but, unlike him, her hair was light brown and liberally streaked with grey. She was a woman highly thought of and respected in the area, the only daughter of a man of considerable standing, socially and financially, and a leader in local government affairs.

She was proud of the way Marcus had taken over the reins

when her husband had died. Everywhere he went people courted his favour. Sir John Somerville had taught him how to select the right ventures in which to invest his money—and success had brought him notoriety and more wealth. But there was a price to pay—his right to privacy in Netherley—which was why he went further afield to partake of his pleasures— usually to London, where he combined business with pleasure.

But invariably he was seen and the lady on his arm at the time would be discussed at length by the gossips who longed to know more about him, until the affair had been grossly exaggerated, giving him the reputation of a rake. In and around Netherley he declined to accept invitations to balls and soirées, with matchmaking mothers trying to pair him off with their daughters, but he was aware of how they whispered and speculated among themselves.

Ruth was not at all enamoured over the affair between her son and Eve Somerville and had made her opinion known immediately she learned of the unusual conditions of John Somerville's will. Granted, the girl was eminently suitable to be Marcus's wife, and she had nothing against her or her family, for Sir John had been a good friend and business partner of both her late husband and Marcus, but—having no knowledge of what had happened between them at Atwood Fair three years earlier, the gossip it had created in Atwood at the time not having reached her ears—as far as she was aware, Marcus and Eve had not been introduced before the day of the funeral.

The haste and enthusiasm with which he wanted to marry Eve Somerville had come as a surprise and something of a shock to her, for until then Marcus had shown no sign of wanting to settle down, despite his amours in London and the eligible daughters of marriageable age of friends and acquaintance she had brought to the house and paraded before him in the hope that one of them would catch his eye.

And now, just when she thought she had found him the right girl in Angela Stephenson—a beautiful, strong-minded young widow who was the daughter of a close friend—he had casually shattered any expectations she had that the two of them would eventually marry.

Having spent some considerable time both in London and on her late husband's estate a little further north, which had been inherited by his brother after his death, Angela had recently come to spend some time with her parents at their home in Little Bolton, almost three miles from Netherley.

And who could blame her for beginning to hope for the match, for it had been plain for everyone to see that when they were in London Angela was strongly attracted by Marcus from the start, although it had not gone unnoticed by her keen eye that Marcus did not appear to be enthusiastic about forming a close relationship with Angela, and did not go out of his way to seek her company. She had thought that, when they returned to Netherley, something might develop between them and give both families reason to hope that a marriage just might be hovering blissfully on the horizon.

'I've invited Miss Somerville to Brooklands next Wednesday, Mother,' Marcus told her on returning from the mine, having returned there after his parting with Eve. He was still wearing his soiled and sweaty clothes, his black hair falling untidily over his handsome face as he strode into his mother's sitting room, where she was always to be found in the late afternoon, either reading or industriously employed at her needlework, seated before a long window where the light was good and where she could gaze out over the well laid-out rose gardens beyond.

Closing her book and placing it on an occasional table beside her chair, his mother looked up at him and her lips thinned, her grey eyes surveying her son reprovingly. 'But you can't have,' she said with a note of alarm. 'You know very well there will be quite a gathering here on Wednesday.'

'That is precisely the reason why I suggested that she come that particular day. She will be among people she knows and will not feel so uncomfortable. Her grandmother will be accompanying her.'

'But what about Angela?'

Marcus frowned with annoyance. 'Angela? What about Angela?'

'Marcus! You cannot have forgotten that she will be here with her parents.'

'No, I have not forgotten, but I fail to see why that should make any difference to my inviting Eve Somerville.' He sighed in exasperation, perfectly aware what was passing through his mother's mind. 'Mother—please. Will you stop trying to run my life?'

'Surely I am to be allowed to express an opinion.'

'Of course you are—but I have not made any commitment to Angela or given her any reason to think I am likely to, for that matter.'

'Nevertheless, there is an understanding—'

'No, Mother,' he said sharply. 'Only in your own mind.'

'Is it so unreasonable of me to want to see you settled with a wife—the *right* wife?' his mother said with slight emphasis on the last words.

'No. It is not unreasonable.'

'But Angela is so right for you,' she persisted fervently.

'No,' said Marcus sharply, trying to hold on to his patience. 'Angela is right for you, Mother. Angela Stephenson means absolutely nothing to me. I am always polite and courteous towards her because of the close friendship that exists between you and her mother. That is all. In fact, if you want the absolute truth, I do not care for her in the slightest. You must allow me to choose my own wife—to my own satisfaction.'

'Choose! If you are contemplating marrying Eve Somerville, then it is hardly by choice, is it? You would not give her a second glance if it were not for the mine,' she said crossly, observing the implacable lines of determination on her son's face, which told her he would not be dissuaded on this.

He was showing the same kind of stubborn resistance he'd shown ever since he was a little boy.

Fully aware of the conditions of Sir John's will, she had left Marcus in no doubt of her disapproval. It was not that she had anything against Eve Somerville—in fact, she had got to know Sir John quite well through the business transactions he and Marcus had made together over the years, coming to like and respect him for his integrity and sound common sense. It was Atwood Mine that was anathema to her, the mine she had sold to Sir John, the mine that had taken the life of her beloved husband. Because of that, she never wanted to see it back in her family again.

'You must want the mine pretty badly, Marcus, to consider marrying Eve Somerville in order to get it. Why—you had never met her until the day of the funeral. The next thing you'll be telling me is that you've named the day.'

'It's too soon for that. If she does agree to become my wife, we will become betrothed immediately. One of the conditions in Sir John's will is that we marry within six months.'

'When Atwood Mine will become yours,' Ruth said drily. 'I cannot help thinking that you will be marrying her for all the wrong reasons. But why is it so important to you? We are not paupers and certainly have no need of it. Do not forget it was in that mine that your father was killed.'

'I know that, Mother—but I also know how much Atwood Mine meant to him, and how hard my grandfather had to work to get it established, sinking every penny he had into making it succeed. That is the reason why I want it back in this family—where it belongs.'

'Despite the pain you know it will cause me?'

'Yes,' he replied gently. 'And for what it's worth, I'm sorry. I would not hurt you for the world, Mother, you know that—but this is something I must do.'

'And you are prepared to marry Eve Somerville to get it?'

'Yes. The lease has another fifteen years to run and I shudder to think what state it will be in by that time if it is handed over to Gerald Somerville.'

'I find it strange that Sir John did not leave you the mine outright without imposing these harsh conditions on you. Why did he not leave you the mine without you having to take his daughter? Good heavens, Marcus, what is wrong with the girl?'

'There is nothing wrong with her. In fact, she is extremely beautiful and quite charming. I think it was his way of making sure she would be well taken care of.'

'And you truly believe you can be happy within a marriage based on conditions such as these?'

'I see no reason why not. I know of marriages that have been made on rockier foundations and, given time, have turned out to the satisfaction of both parties. You must try to understand just how difficult all this is for Eve. She's had a lot to contend with, losing first her mother two years ago and now her father in such tragic circumstances. Please meet her—welcome her here. I know you'll like her. No one meeting her could fail to do that.'

His mother sighed, knowing by the tone of his voice and the look in his eye that he was determined to marry her regardless of anything she had to say. She looked at him, at his tall, lean figure, noticing how clear and compelling his pale blue eyes were as they gazed down into her own, and, as she never failed to do, she warmed to him, knowing as only a mother can how important it was for him to know he had her blessing and support on a matter such as this—regardless of any misgivings she might have.

As she relented, a softness entered her eyes as it never failed to do for, like his father before him, he always succeeded in breaking through her reserve. Marcus was a man of many complexities, who went through life with amusement and a cool recklessness, prepared to go along with most things providing none interfered with him. Sighing, she reached up and took his hand.

'Very well, Marcus. You need have no worries on my account. If she is all you say she is, then how can I fail to like her?'

'She is—and more besides. She has warm, velvety-soft violet eyes that would melt even the coldest stone,' he said with a teasing note to his voice, bending down and placing a kiss lightly on his mother's cheek, satisfied that she would come to terms, with no further argument, with what he intended doing.

'Dear me,' she murmured, receiving his kiss with a smile, 'if you begin speaking like this then I shall believe you are already halfway to being in love with her.'

'Yes—I believe I am. I have never met anyone quite like her. I am determined to marry her—and when I do, you may rest assured that it will be for all the right reasons,' Marcus smiled, straightening up and gently tweaking her cheek with his finger and thumb.

Eve was in no way disappointed when she saw Brooklands for the first time, which surprised her, for long ago, when she had made up her mind to dislike everything about Marcus Fitzalan, Brooklands had not been excluded.

The house, which was situated about a mile north of Netherley, nestled in a fold between the hills which protected it from wind and weather. There was something stately about the tall beeches that lined either side of the long winding drive leading to the house, their branches meeting overhead and virtually shutting out the sunlight.

Her first glimpse of the stately house, built of brick which had mellowed over the years, did not disappoint her in the least. It was a fine, long-fronted house with a columned porch and stables at the rear. Long French windows opened on to a rose-strewn balustraded terrace, overlooking well-maintained gardens and with lawns stretched out like thick velvet.

Eve was impressed and thought it quite remarkable that Marcus's grandfather had managed to make his way into the ranks of the landed gentry, buying land and building this great house, all from the production of coal.

The carriage came to a halt at the bottom of a short flight of steps and immediately, as if he had been waiting behind the door, Marcus came out of the house to meet them, his thick black hair glossy and brushed back from his face. He was immaculately dressed in a well-cut black suit. White silk stockings encased his muscular calves and a white cravat at his throat enhanced his dark good looks.

Stepping towards the carriage, he opened the door himself and reached inside, taking Eve's hand to help her alight after one of the servants had pulled down the steps. Despite the fact that she was in mourning she had taken particular care over her appearance, wanting so much to look her best when she was introduced to Mrs Fitzalan. Her black dress was made of silk gauze and was very simple, with a tight bodice and full skirt, the severity of it softened by a white lace collar at her throat.

On seeing her Marcus drew in a deep breath, his eyes glittering as they flicked over her with undisguised approval, from the tips of her pretty velvet slippers to her wealth of thick black hair coiled expertly about her head, making her appear older and more seductively alluring.

After greeting Lady Pemberton politely, sensing Eve's nervousness Marcus took hold of her hand, feeling her fingers tremble slightly.

'You look lovely,' he murmured in a gentle tone as he lifted her fingers to his lips, his gaze searching her face. 'I trust you suffered no ill effects from the other day when your horse bolted?'

'No. None, thank you. It would take more than that to unnerve me, Mr Fitzalan.' She smiled.

'Come and meet my mother. You can be assured of a welcome. She's looking forward to meeting you. Some of the other guests have arrived—some you are already acquainted with. Try not to be nervous.'

Eve quivered beneath his touch, thinking he looked breath-takingly handsome. She felt the force, the vital, physical power within him, and the warm grasp of his hand reassured her and she was strengthened by it. It was comforting to know there would be a large gathering. Glancing up at him, she saw he was smiling crookedly down at her.

Marcus conducted Eve and her grandmother into a large square hall with tall doorways and marble pillars. An elegant blue-carpeted staircase rose up from the centre to form a gallery. Eve's first impression of the house was one of elegance, but so intent was she on her meeting with Mrs Fitzalan that she paid little attention to her surroundings.

Mrs Fitzalan was happily conversing with her other guests but became silent when she saw Marcus. She glanced at the lovely young woman by his side and, after making a quick assessment, a feeling of relief washed over her. She liked what she saw and smiled, moving forward to welcome her and Lady Pemberton, determined they would feel in no way ill at ease during their visit to Brooklands.

'Mother, allow me to present Lady Pemberton and Miss Eve Somerville. Lady Pemberton, Miss Somerville, this is my mother.'

After her grandmother had been introduced, Eve smiled a little shyly at Marcus's mother. 'How do you do, Mrs Fitzalan,' she said politely, her first impression of Mrs Fitzalan was of her presence. Dressed in a wonderful shade of jade green, with diamonds at her throat and dripping from her ears, she looked younger than Eve had expected, a slim, elegant lady radiating calm and confidence who was completely at ease.

She had expected coldness and stiffness and was relieved to see there was neither—in fact, there were no reservations at all in the welcome. However, she did wonder how Mrs Fitzalan had reacted when her son had told her of the conditions of Eve's father's will.

'I am well, thank you, and happy to welcome you and Lady

Pemberton to Brooklands. I have heard so much about you, my dear—both from your father and Marcus—that I am glad to meet you at last. Your father was a frequent visitor—but, unfortunately, his visits were always on matters of business. Now you are here you must relax and enjoy yourself, but first you must meet our other guests, although some of them you will already know. As you see, we have quite a large gathering. After that, seeing that dinner will be a little late this evening, owing to some crisis or other in the kitchen which I hope Cook will sort out eventually—' she laughed '—I will show you the house.'

Eve and her grandmother were drawn forward and introduced to the other guests gathered in groups in the large pillared hall and in the adjacent drawing room, where servants flitted about balancing trays of drinks, offering them to the guests in order to make the time spent waiting for the meal to begin more pleasurable.

Immediately her grandmother was claimed by an acquaintance. Those unknown to Eve gave her a curious glance while others said how nice it was to see her, complimenting her on how well she looked. The fact that Marcus had casually informed them of her expected arrival earlier had already caused some arched eyebrows and given rise to speculation.

With a certain amount of indolence Marcus stood back while Eve was taken in hand by his mother. His pale blue eyes smiled as he observed, but his expression gave away nothing of his thoughts.

'You don't mind, do you, Marcus, if I take Miss Somerville away and show her the house—and perhaps take a quick look at the garden while there is still enough daylight left?'

'Of course not.' He smiled. 'Although I was hoping to do that myself.'

'Thank you. I would like that,' said Eve. 'But I should hate to take either of you away from your guests.'

'Don't worry about that,' smiled Mrs Fitzalan. 'The evening

is very informal. There are still one or two guests to arrive, but Marcus will receive them.'

Marcus raised his eyebrows, but before he could reply his mother said, 'Rest assured that I shall not neglect our other guests for too long. You can stay and entertain them, Marcus, while I get to know Miss Somerville a little better. We can gossip as we go along. No doubt the gentlemen will converse about that which is closest to their hearts—such as coal mines, how much coal they are producing and the latest in pumping engines—but I will not tolerate any discourse on the subject at the dinner table. By that time I hope it will have been exhausted and you can concentrate on more pleasant topics of conversation.'

'Very well, Mother,' Marcus said, knowing there was no irresistible argument he could raise that would have any effect on her and allow him to show Miss Somerville the house instead, 'but do not deprive us of your company for too long. All the guests have not yet arrived and I am sure they will want to be introduced to Miss Somerville before dinner.'

As Mrs Fitzalan gave her a quick tour of the house Eve took an interest in everything she saw, listening to her hostess as she chatted animatedly, clearly proud of the house her husband's father had built.

It lacked the feeling of antiquity and history that one was aware of when entering Burntwood Hall, but Brooklands had a wonderful, refreshing elegance in its modern furnishings. The decorations added lightness to the rooms—pastel shades, striped and floral wallpapers, with long windows and mirrors reflecting the light.

Eve admired the fine paintings that adorned the walls of every room, some being family portraits. She paused to examine one in particular that had pride of place on a long landing on the first floor. It was of a man in his prime, and not unlike Marcus in features.

Mrs Fitzalan paused beside her when she saw Eve's interest.

'The gentleman is my husband's father—Marcus's grandfather, founder of Atwood Mine.'

'Yes, I thought it might be. The resemblance to Mr Fitzalan is striking. What was he like, Mrs Fitzalan? Did you know him long?'

She smiled. 'Yes. He was an excellent man—of good character. He was respected by all who knew him and he worked hard all his life to achieve success, devoting all his time to his work and the affairs of the neighbourhood. When I married Marcus's father I lived here for a number of years before he died. We got on well—and I fell in love with Brooklands the minute I laid eyes on it.'

'Who would not? I think it's a wonderful house, Mrs Fitzalan. It's so different from Burntwood Hall, which is steeped in antiquity.'

'Ah—but no worse for that, my dear. A house as old as Burntwood Hall I am sure will have some fascinating stories to tell—they enrich a house, I always think, and make it much more interesting for the inhabitants. But I'm so glad you like Brooklands. Perhaps it will make your decision as to whether or not you marry Marcus a little easier.'

Eve flushed. 'Yes—perhaps.'

Eventually they came out on to the terrace where the seductive scent of roses wafted about them. Up until then their conversation had been of matters in general and about the house, but now Mrs Fitzalan looked at Eve intently, saying unexpectedly, 'Marcus has a habit of springing surprises on me, Miss Somerville—and I was never more surprised than when he told me of your father's will, of the conditions he imposed on you both. How do you feel about it?'

Eve was startled and unprepared for the question. 'Why, I confess I was as surprised as you, Mrs Fitzalan—at the time.'

'And have you had time to consider what you will do?' She smiled when she saw the confusion in Eve's eyes, for it was clear she had not expected her to broach the subject quite so soon, if at all. 'I'm sorry, my dear,' she said. 'You'd be quite within your rights to tell me to mind my own business. I do tend to let my tongue run away with me which frequently gets me into trouble. But it is a matter that is important to all of us.'

'Of—of course,' Eve found herself stammering. 'There's no need to apologise, Mrs Fitzalan.'

'It's just that Marcus can be so serious at times—and I see so little of him. I do try to keep abreast of what's going on, but it's so difficult. He's either supervising the running of the mines, away on some business or other, or dining with friends.'

'I do understand, but, in truth, neither of us has had the opportunity to discuss the matter properly. But we both agree that it would be as well to get to know each other a little better before we commit ourselves to anything. It might turn out that we are incompatible.'

'That's very sensible. But Atwood Mine is important to you, is it not?'

'Yes,' she replied, her eyes meeting those of the older woman's steadily. 'I would be lying if I said otherwise—and I know it means a great deal to Mr Fitzalan. He is loath to let the opportunity of being part-owner of his father's mine slip through his fingers—but I only hope he considers carefully what marriage to me will entail—should I agree to marry him, of course.'

'He does tend to let his enthusiasm run away with him— like his obsession for a new shaft he is sinking at the moment at Pendle Hill. He is trying to do it as quickly as possible in order to get the mine producing before two of the old pits are exhausted—which, I have to say, is proving extremely difficult and takes up nearly all his time. But he never does anything without careful thought.'

Mention of the new mine Marcus was sinking brought to mind the day she had witnessed just how difficult it was proving to be at first hand, causing her to remember the explosions as he was trying to blast his way through the rock and how terrified her horse had been, which had caused it to bolt. She also remembered their ride back to Burntwood Hall and their long conversation, which had enabled her to understand him a little better, and to make her think of him a little less severely, but she said none of this to Mrs Fitzalan.

'This matter between the two of you is important to him,' Mrs Fitzalan continued, 'but no matter how important Atwood Mine is to him—and I must tell you that he never forgave me for selling the lease to your father all those years ago after the death of my dear husband—I know he will put it aside while he thinks of that.'

'I sincerely hope so, Mrs Fitzalan.'

'Marcus is marked with the same proud arrogance and indomitable will as his father and grandfather before him. He is like a whirlwind, my dear. Anyone meeting him for the first time cannot help but be swept along with him—so, if you will allow me to give you some advice,' she said kindly and persuasively, 'do not let him pressure you into making a decision before you have thought it through very carefully, will you? This is not just about Atwood Mine. It's about you and Marcus—and your future happiness together. It is imperative to you both that you make the right decision.'

'I know and I don't intend to.'

'Good girl.'

At that moment one of the servants came out on to the terrace. Mrs Fitzalan had a quiet word with her before turning back to Eve, a look of exasperation on her face.

'You must excuse me, my dear. It would seem the crisis in the kitchen has yet to be resolved and needs my intervention. Would you like to return to the others?'

Eve smiled. 'No, not just yet. It's such a lovely evening I think I'll stay here for a while longer, if that's all right, Mrs Fitzalan, and probably take a walk in the garden.'

'Of course. I'll be back shortly.'

As Ruth Fitzalan went to sort out the domestic crisis in the kitchen she felt better for having met Eve Somerville and could see why Marcus had spoken so highly of her. Any doubts she had felt prior to meeting her had been quashed the moment they had been introduced—and when she had seen the way Marcus had looked at her. His eyes had held an open admiration and something else, something she had never seen in his eyes before, and it gladdened her heart. There was an open honesty about Eve that she found refreshing and she found herself intensely curious to know her better.

She appeared sensitive and reserved, and yet she suspected Eve was no stupid innocent who would only open her mouth to say yes and no. She recognised a strong will, someone who would not be bullied—which would do Marcus good. Yes, she approved, and if they decided to marry, then bringing Atwood Mine back into the family was just something she would have to come to terms with. However, there was still the problem of Angela to be surmounted, she thought, having no idea that the two were acquaintances of long standing.

Angela, who would no doubt have arrived by now with her parents, was a young woman different in temperament to Eve. It would be interesting to see what her reaction would be when she was introduced to Miss Somerville and realised she had a rival for her son's affections—not only in the shape of a lovely young woman, she thought with considerable amusement, but also a coal mine.

Eve watched Mrs Fitzalan go before perching on the edge of the stone balustrade that fronted the terrace, sighing deeply as she tried to picture herself living there, of being the wife of Marcus Fitzalan. She tried to think of him dispassionately, not to let her emotions become involved, because if she did she was afraid she was in danger of being overwhelmed by him. He had a way of intruding into her thoughts when for so long her desire had been to keep him out.

He was different to any man she had ever met, and somehow the resentment she had built up against him over the years no longer seemed important now that she had got to know him a little. Despite their differences he had made a deep impression on her, this she could not deny, but she could not say that she really liked him—at least, not in the way one should when contemplating marriage. He was arrogant and accustomed to obedience from those about him, a man who set himself above others—all traits she did not admire.

But then, never had she met a man who was so alive, so full of confidence, a man who both stimulated and excited her, and he had a sensuous way of regarding her that made her physically aware of herself as a woman. He was certainly attractive, and seeing his home and meeting his mother presented some temptation.

With these thoughts occupying her mind, she breathed deeply of the sweet-scented air and let her eyes wander in the gathering dusk, looking with appreciation at the flower-filled gardens spread out before her, and a line of dark yews that marched down to the river beyond. The garden was laid out in formal flower beds forming a circle, the centre piece being a fountain where water spouted from a cornucopia held by three exquisitely carved cherubs, the fine mist of its spray drifting on the slight breeze.

She was about to step off the terrace into the garden when her attention was caught by a woman who emerged from a door of the house, trailing her shawl carelessly behind her as she walked aimlessly towards the fountain where she sat on its rim, gazing down and drawing her fingers over the surface of the water. She wore an oyster-coloured silk dress, and despite the chill of the evening her shoulders were bare, but she seemed oblivious to it.

Eve stood watching her in fascination, wondering who she could be, but then, as the woman turned slightly, she froze in recognition. It was Angela Stephenson. Her mouth went suddenly dry and clammy; sweat broke out on her brow on seeing Angela again after all this time, and the bitterness over the way Angela had tricked and deceived her, then claimed Leslie for herself, had not lessened and went searing through Eve like a knife.

Numb with shock, she watched as Angela threw back her head and looked up at the moon, closing her eyes, a beatific, dreaming smile on her face. Suddenly a man appeared out of the house and stood looking around the garden, as if he was searching for someone. He was about to turn and go back inside, but on seeing Angela he walked towards her.

Angela watched his approach without moving her position, and when he stood close, looking down into her upturned face, he smiled and sat beside her. The man was Marcus and Eve stared at them fixedly, feeling a searing stab of jealousy pierce her heart. She clenched her teeth and dug her fingernails into the palms of her hands to stop herself from crying out.

They seemed relaxed together, close, even, and when he rose he took her hand and she stood beside him, handing him her shawl which he slowly draped around her shoulders. They were in profile so Eve was unable to see the expressions on their faces, but she sensed it was intimate. With a familiarity that seemed to be born of long acquaintance, Angela tucked her hand possessively into the crook of Marcus's arm and the two strolled leisurely back towards the house, mounting a flight of stone steps and going inside.

But before they did so Angela seemed to sense Eve's gaze and turned her head to where Eve stood observing them. For a moment their eyes collided and they stared at each other, and then Eve saw her smile, not in the least put out about being observed, but there was something smug, almost a complacent self-satisfaction, in that smile, a smile that sent her a message of possession. She shivered suddenly, as if a cold hand had reached out and gripped her heart. Seeing Marcus and Angela together was like a stone being thrown into a quiet pool.

Chapter Eight

Just when Eve thought she was beginning to relax there was a tension inside her when she returned to the others and came face to face with Angela. She felt sick and trembling inside at the mere thought of confronting this woman who had caused her so much misery in the past. She had already decided to keep the fact that she had been a silent observer of the intimate little scene from Marcus, considering it had nothing to do with her and that she did not know him well enough to speculate on what his relationship with Angela might be.

Angela did not seem surprised to see her at Brooklands, giving Eve the distinct impression that she already knew all about the situation that existed between herself and Marcus. Her sharp, woman's instinct told her that she had a rival in her old adversary, which made her determined to be on her guard.

Close to, she saw Angela was still quite exquisite, her auburn hair arranged superbly in soft curls with ringlets on either side of her face, her mouth full and pouting, her cheek bones angular, causing her hazel eyes to slant a little. Eve could see that she was all woman and very much aware of the fact. Angela exuded a sultry sensuality that men would find impossible to resist—even Marcus Fitzalan, it would seem. She was very cool and fixed Eve with a hard stare, and then she smiled, a tight, carefully controlled smile, her eyes glittering, hard and ruthless as of old, and full of triumph.

Unaware that there was any animosity between them, Marcus introduced them, surprised to discover they already knew each other—he had taken little notice of Eve's companions on the day they had met at Atwood Fair and that Angela had been one of them. But it quickly became plain to him that the two were far from being friends when he heard the soft, sharp intake of Eve's breath and felt her stiffen beside him, and saw her fingers close tightly round her fan, her knuckles straining sharply beneath her white skin. The atmosphere between them was charged with something so palpable he could almost feel it, touch it, and he was at once puzzled by it and curious as to the reason. Seeing the initial look that passed between the two ladies, with the instinct of a seafaring man he feared a squall approaching, albeit a mild one.

Instead of turning her back and walking away, which was what Eve was tempted to do, courageously she stayed and faced Angela and forced a smile to her lips, giving no indication to either Marcus or Angela how painful this meeting was for her.

'Hello, Angela,' she said, her voice surprisingly level, telling herself she had nothing to fear from her, but her heart was palpitating nevertheless and she felt stifled. 'You are well, I hope.'

Angela inclined her head slightly and showed her pearl white teeth in a simulated smile, resentment and jealousy beginning to rise in her eyes which seemed to narrow a little, shining and as hard as a cat's, her look conveying to Eve that nothing was changed between them and that she was displeased by the attention Marcus was showing her.

'Perfectly. How long is it since we last saw each other? It must be ages,' she said, speaking in a cold and controlled voice—and lightly contemptuous, Eve's sharp ears detected, which made her hackles rise.

'Three years, I believe,' she answered, steeling herself,

equally as cold, feeling as though she were encased in ice, refusing to feel intimidated by Angela.

'Of course. It was on the day of Atwood Fair...if my memory serves me correctly.'

If Angela intended to embarrass Eve by referring to that day she was mistaken, for Eve did not look in the least put out. 'There was never anything wrong with your memory, as I remember, Angela,' she replied with a touch of humour. She turned to Marcus who was watching them in puzzlement. 'Angela and I were together at the fair that day—you remember, don't you, Mr Fitzalan? The day you so shamefully ruined my reputation,' she said pointedly, with a soft smile curving her lips.

With the eyes of both ladies upon him Marcus smiled down at Eve wickedly. 'How could I ever forget it? That day will remain imprinted on my mind for all time. But I do not remember seeing you there, Angela.'

'You wouldn't,' said Eve quickly on a teasing note, trying to make light of the humiliation she had felt three years ago, while trembling inside. 'It wasn't Angela who approached you.'

The byplay between Eve and Marcus caused Angela's eyes to flare with sudden anger. She lifted her chin a little in annoyance, trying not to show it as she gazed at Marcus. 'I was not acquainted with you at the time, Marcus,' she purred, her voice deep and provocative when she addressed him, throwing him a dazzlingly provocative smile.

'No,' Eve said, her beautiful brows rising slightly, the look she cast Angela making it clear that she remembered all Angela was guilty of where Eve was concerned that day, and that she was made of sterner stuff than Angela gave her credit for. 'We were just foolish young girls intent on mischief, as I remember, when the watchful eyes of our chaperon happened to wander for a while. But this is not the time to reminisce, Angela, and what occurred is ancient history now. Is that not so, Mr Fitzalan?'

Marcus's eyes twinkled and he smiled down at her with easy good humour. 'Oh—not all that ancient. I still reflect on what occurred with a certain amount of pleasure,' he murmured with a rueful, conspiratorial smile.

Sensing the tension inside Eve and feeling her tremble beside him, Marcus didn't need to be told that she and Angela were no longer friends; in fact, he was sure that if they were to find themselves together in an empty room their claws would come out and there would be all-out war. He knew Eve was finding it extremely difficult to maintain her calm demeanor and quickly rescued her from the situation.

'Please excuse us, Angela. I have to introduce Miss Somerville to one or two guests before we go into dinner.'

'Of course,' she replied, her voice stilted.

Eve shot Marcus a grateful smile when they moved on, ignoring the sudden noise of Angela's fan snapping shut behind them.

'You look pale—you were trembling,' he said softly when they were out of earshot and Angela had turned away, keeping his eyes on Eve with uncomfortable steadiness.

'Was I? I wasn't aware of it,' Eve replied, sounding terse, trying to hold on to her composure but her anger getting the better of her, making her want to lash out at someone, and pretending that she couldn't feel Marcus's eyes on her, querying, trying to probe, gently.

'I get the distinct impression that you and Angela are no longer the best of friends,' he said quietly lest they be overheard, steering her away from the groups of people gathered around, some sitting, some standing, conversing animatedly while waiting to be summoned into dinner, his mother flitting from group to group like a firefly, laughing and talking to friends of long standing.

'Friends? The fact of having lost the man I was to marry to a woman who contrived it to happen does not constitute the greatest bond of affection between us,' Eve confessed bitterly. 'Angela is adept at manipulating and controlling people—in fact, there is no one better, no one more subtle. People become like putty in her fingers. She tried very hard to destroy me, and almost succeeded. She was not my true friend. She never was—although she always pretended to be when it suited her. She betrayed me in the worst possible way.'

'By marrying Leslie Stephenson, the man you hoped to marry yourself?'

'Yes. And I don't think you need me to tell you how it came about,' she said cuttingly, accusingly, turning to look up at Marcus and fixing him with a hard stare, remembering the part he had played in her fall from grace. Her anger was now all aimed at him. 'Despite the lightness of my tone and touch of humour when I spoke to Angela, I hold you both equally responsible for what I suffered as a consequence of that day.'

Before Marcus could utter a word in his defence she had turned abruptly to speak to one of the guests, hearing him draw a sudden breath as she did so, knowing her thrust had gone home.

The dining room was elegantly furnished, lit by a huge crystal chandelier suspended above the exquisitely arrayed table that glittered and sparkled, the room becoming a kaleidoscope of colours when everyone was assembled. A variety of dishes of different flavours and delicacies was served, all equally delicious. Everyone seemed in high spirits, with laughter and conversation animated and of general topics of the day.

The meal passed pleasantly enough and Eve, still recovering from her confrontation with Angela, was relieved that she was seated at the opposite end of the long table, just far enough away to avoid any discourse. Although even when Angela wasn't looking at her, Eve felt herself undergoing her scrutiny, and when their eyes did meet Angela would flash one of her smug, knowing smiles, leaving Eve silently fuming.

She realised that getting angry accomplished nothing, and that was exactly what Angela had set out to do—and succeeded, she thought, reproaching herself when she recalled the harsh words she had directed at Marcus. She took several deep breaths in an attempt to calm her nerves, but there was no room for anything in her heart other than anger and a vast disappointment, for no matter how polite and persuasive Marcus might be towards her, she realised that she meant no more to him than a means to an end. When he had accompanied her on her ride he had told her that he would be happy to marry her without the mine—and fool that she had been to believe him.

Later, the gentlemen joined the ladies in the drawing room, having remained behind to partake of the customary after-dinner port and brandy. Every so often Marcus would meet Eve's gaze but he was in no hurry to speak to her as she mingled easily with the other guests, then sat for a while companionably with her grandmother, taking great care to avoid coming into contact with Angela again. He watched her absorb the atmosphere of the house, confident that she could not fail to be impressed by Brooklands—and by his mother who was, as always, charm and graciousness personified.

Eventually he managed to draw her away from the others, determined to speak to her alone, sensitive to the fact that she was still smarting over her meeting with Angela. They stood on the terrace—on the very spot where Eve had witnessed the intimate scene between himself and Angela earlier.

Eve was unable to cast thoughts of Angela from her mind, for she had acted like a pall on the whole evening. But she did experience a feeling of anticipation on finding herself alone with Marcus on the rose-scented terrace on a starlit night—alone, and yet not alone, for they were within sound of the others in the drawing room, their voices and the tinkling notes of the pianoforte in the background...and the image of Angela with her sly, insolent smile standing between them.

Marcus's manner was misleadingly indolent, his expression giving nothing away of his thoughts, but his eyes were questioning and forever watchful. Among so many people and seated apart at the dining table, they'd had no opportunity to converse, but his concentrated gaze had watched Eve carefully all evening, glad to see she looked relaxed, and that she showed no sign of the tension and anger created in her by her encounter with Angela earlier, but he was not deceived and knew it was still there, simmering away below the surface.

But whatever it was that caused so much animosity between Eve and Angela, Marcus did not feel as tolerant of Angela as he had. However, he was determined not to let it interfere with what was important to himself and Eve or allow either of them to forget the purpose of her visit to Brooklands this evening. He was impatient to have the matter that was uppermost in both their minds resolved between them, and seeing how perfectly she blended in with her surroundings, he was certain he almost had his quarry and was determined to pin her down before the evening was over.

Moving a little away from her, he leaned casually against the balustrade and looked to where she stood, her profile etched against the star-strewn sky, her face gleaming like alabaster in the white glow of the moon which bathed the garden in an incandescent light. She was proud and fine, and he wanted her. He suddenly realised that he wanted her more now than he had in the beginning. He wanted the challenge of her, to experience her goodness, and to see how she would come to terms with her passion when she was roused, to understand it.

He savoured the soft ivory tones of her face and the long gracious lines of her body, which were evident beneath the black silk of her dress. He liked the way her neck rose graceful and stem-like from her slender shoulders, and the way she moved, her steps light, with an unconscious swing to her body. Apart from her face and the white lace of the collar at her throat she was all black, as black as a blackthorn—and just as prickly if she was touched on the raw.

But beneath it all she was an innocent, which was such a rarity in the circles in which he moved when in London, where almost every woman of marriageable age he came into contact

with possessed the same grasping, immoral drive that moti-
vated women like Angela Stephenson, who, he was just beginning to realise, had all the trappings of a troublemaker.

Eve sighed and met the intensity of Marcus's wintry blue
gaze, beginning to relax as she became lulled by the quiet and
privacy of the terrace and the enveloping dim light, becoming
impelled by the sensations he roused in her, which became
stronger each time they met. She smiled softly.

'I feel that I must apologise for my harsh words earlier. I—
I did not intend allowing Angela to provoke me so easily. I
knew what she was like. I should be inured to her by now,
don't you think. I—it's just that I always swore that when we
met—which was inevitable that we would one day at just such
an occasion as this—I would never let her know how much
she hurt me when she married Leslie.'

'I understand,' Marcus murmured gently. 'Taking into account that I knew you hoped to marry him, and knowing that
Angela did become his wife—I confess that I did not know
the two of you were already acquainted. I realise now that I
should not have been so insensitive as to introduce you. Am
I forgiven?'

Eve smiled, beginning to melt beneath the warmth of his
gaze as he studied her closely. 'Of course.'

'Thank you. And so, Miss Somerville,' Marcus said, having
no desire to talk about Angela or Leslie Stephenson at this
moment, and wanting them both cast down into oblivion,
'what is your opinion of Brooklands? Is it to your liking?'

'Yes. I have to say it's a lovely house,' she replied, unable
to keep the admiration she felt for his home out of her voice,
while at the same time wanting so much to ask him about his
relationship with Angela, but was too proud to do so.

'I'm happy you think so,' he said, speaking softly, and looking at him Eve thought he sounded genuinely pleased.

'I remember you telling me you have two brothers,' she
said by way of conversation. 'I do not imagine they get home
very often if they are in the Navy.'

'No, which is unfortunate for my mother. She misses them both dreadfully.'

'Didn't either of them consider joining you in the mining industry?'

'No. They both take after my mother's family in that. Two of her uncles and one of her brothers were naval people.'

'And did the sea not appeal to you?'

A smile touched his lips. 'No. I take after my father and grandfather—which is fortunate, for I do have a position to uphold in the house.'

'And were you close to your father?'

'Very, until he was killed so tragically in Atwood Mine. But what of you, Miss Somerville? You were close to your father, were you not?'

A look of desolation entered Eve's eyes as she felt the pain of memory. 'Yes, I was.'

Marcus looked at her searchingly. 'He always spoke of you with affection.'

'Both my parents were exemplary. My only regret is that before my father died I saw so little of him. He chose to spend so much of his time away from home—as you will know, Mr Fitzalan,' she said with a faint hint of accusation, unable to conceal the bitterness she still felt, aware as she spoke that a constraint had come between them.

Marcus's eyes narrowed. 'Away from you, I think you mean,' he said quietly.

'Yes. That is what I mean,' she admitted, having subdued her feelings for so long that she was unable to prevent them bubbling to the surface. 'He was always at the mine—or with you. I missed so many precious weeks before he died—and when he did come home I would have to sit and listen to him talking about the mine, about you—of your attributes, of which there were so many—and I would feel such pain. Tell me, have you ever been jealous?' she asked softly.

'Jealous? No. I do not believe so.'

'Well, I was jealous of you. Silly, isn't it?' she said, giving a bitter, quivering little laugh. 'But I was. I was so jealous I wanted to scream every time my father spoke your name. He would listen to no wrong said about you—and even after that unfortunate incident at Atwood Fair you still remained above reproach in his eyes. He refused to consider defending my honour by insisting that you account for *your* actions. He said the fault was all mine.'

As she spoke, remembering, her eyes became stormy and malevolent. Her face was like an icon, her eyes luminous with unshed tears and exaggeratedly large in her heart-shaped face as she looked at him.

Marcus nodded slightly. So that was it. Now he understood the reason for her coldness, her hostility. It wasn't just the humiliation she had suffered at his hands on the day of Atwood Fair that had brought about her strong resentment. She had resented the time her father had spent with him.

'What can I say? Forgive me. I never knew.'

'Would it have made any difference if you had?'

'That I cannot answer.'

'I know. But how could you have known? Apart from the unfortunate circumstances of our first encounter you hardly knew I existed. And why should you?'

'But I did. I continued to think of you for a long time afterwards.'

'Really! You surprise me. After accusing me to my face of being an overindulged spoiled child—the type you hold in contempt, I believe you said—you cannot have thought of me with favour.'

'Forgive me. I was very angry.'

'Yes, you were—and with good reason,' she admitted on a sigh. 'You did not say anything I did not deserve.' She cast him a thin smile. 'My father would have agreed with you.'

'Perhaps—but it is clear to me that his absence from Burntwood Hall for the last months of his life continues to trouble you a great deal.'

She shook her head a little sadly, a whimsical smile breaking through. 'No. It did, but not any more. I learned to come to terms with it a long time ago.'

'Have you? Forgive me, but I am not convinced—and contrary to what you may believe, we were not always together. I have many business concerns which did not involve your father and which required a great deal of my time.'

'Yes—I know that now. I am being very foolish. I should not be speaking like this.'

Marcus sighed deeply, sorry for the anguish she must have felt for so long. 'You must have realised how difficult those last weeks were for your father—that his work kept him going, kept his mind occupied and off his illness. You, more than anyone, will know there were times when his pain was too hard for him to bear. He knew it could only get worse and that eventually he would become confined to his bed—something he looked on with absolute dread.'

'I know.'

'Do not blame him for paying too much attention to his work instead of remaining at home—he would have had too much time on his hands to brood about what was to happen to him. It was not intentional and was not done to hurt you. In fact—hard though it is to accept—perhaps the carriage accident was a blessing in disguise. It saved him a great deal of suffering.'

They both fell silent for several moments until Marcus said at length, determined to discuss the subject uppermost in his mind, 'Tell me, do you feel drawn to Brooklands—enough to make it your home?'

Eve hesitated, her expression becoming tight once more, for she realised he was about to ask her the question she had been dreading, but one she knew she must face sooner or later.

'I have already told you that I like it very much.'

'That is no answer. You are being evasive.'

'No. I know what you are suggesting,' she said coolly.

'Then what is your answer?'

Their eyes met and held and, for some reason Eve could

not explain, she knew she did not want to refuse. But then, how could she? she asked herself with bitter irony. What else could she do? What else was she fit for except going to live with her grandmother or her Aunt Shona? Whereas marriage to Marcus Fitzalan would ensure her a lifetime of security—and she would inherit half of Atwood Mine and in so doing hold on to a part of her past.

But she had no illusions. The kind of love that should exist between a husband and wife did not come into her decision, for it was the kind of love that had once existed between her parents—the kind of love she had never experienced and could never hope to if she was to enter into a cold and impersonal marriage of convenience with a man who would marry her for one reason only. Despite his words to the contrary when he had escorted her from Pendle Hill back to Burntwood Hall the previous week, Marcus Fitzalan had no more interest in her beyond the mine that marriage to her would bring him.

Eve looked at him, her face surprisingly calm as she prepared to tell him her decision, but her voice was strained, leaving Marcus in no doubt of the difficulty she had found in reaching her conclusion.

'It is a strange situation, is it not? We had only ever met once in our lives before the day of the funeral, and yet we find ourselves drawn together by my father. Normally I would scorn such a union and despise my father for placing the necessity before me.'

'Necessity?' Marcus asked suddenly.

'Yes. There is no other word for it. We each recognise the advantages of the conditions he laid down. We both want Atwood Mine. About that we are very definite. Short of marrying Gerald—which I have already told you is out of the question—the cards are stacked heavily against me. If I do not agree to marry you, you may not gain anything but you do not lose anything either, whereas I stand to lose a great deal. The way I see it, I really have no choice. I am between the

FREE GIFTS! FREE BOOKS!

— PLAY —
L♥VE HEARTS
Scratch 'n' Match Game

Peel off label & place inside

MATCH 'N' CLAIM
UP TO 4 <u>FREE</u> BOOKS
PLUS A <u>FREE</u> MYSTERY GIFT

See Inside...

— PLAY —
L♥VE HEARTS

Scratch 'n' Match Game to see what you can claim

HERE'S HOW TO PLAY:

1. Peel off the "TRUE LOVE" label from the front cover. Place it in the space provided opposite. Then with a coin carefully scratch away the silver circle. Reveal a matching love heart and you'll be eligible to receive 4 free books and a free mystery gift!

2. Complete and return this card and we'll send you specially selected Mills & Boon® novels from the Historical Romance™ series. These books are yours to keep absolutely FREE.

3. There's no catch. You're under no obligation to buy anything. We charge nothing for your first shipment. And you don't have to make any minimum number of purchases - not even one!

4. The fact is thousands of readers enjoy receiving books by mail from the Reader Service™, at least a month before they are available in the shops. They like the convenience of home delivery, and of course postage and packing is completely FREE!

5. We hope that after receiving your free books you'll want to remain a subscriber. But the choice is yours - to continue or cancel, any time at all! So why not take up our invitation, with no risk of any kind. You'll be glad you did!

Scratch 'n' Match your love hearts and claim today
You've got nothing to lose and everything to gain

— PLAY —
L♥VE HEARTS
Scratch 'n' Match Game...

> Place sticker here and scratch off silver circle opposite

How many FREE GIFTS can you claim with your LOVE HEART?

Scratch 'n' Match Claim Chart

  CLAIM 4 FREE BOOKS & A FREE MYSTERY GIFT

  CLAIM 4 FREE BOOKS

  CLAIM 2 FREE BOOKS

YES! I have placed my label from the front cover in the space provided above and scratched away the silver circle. Please send me all the free gifts for which I qualify, as shown on the claim chart above. I understand that I am under no obligation to purchase any books, as explained overleaf. I am over 18 years of age.

H8II

MS/MRS/MISS/MR   INITIALS

BLOCK CAPITALS PLEASE

SURNAME

ADDRESS

POSTCODE

THE READER SERVICE™
FREEPOST SEA3794
CROYDON
Surrey
CR9 3AQ

DETACH AND RETURN THIS CARD TODAY, NO STAMP NEEDED! ◀

devil and the deep blue sea. Beggars can't be choosers, Mr Fitzalan, so—what can I say other than, yes, I will marry you.'

In the dim light Marcus's face was suddenly grim, his dark eyebrows drawn together in a straight line.

'You are extremely forthright, Miss Somerville.'

'That is a natural characteristic of mine.'

'Do you always speak your mind?'

'Yes. Why? Does it offend you?'

'Not at all. Plain speaking is a quality I admire—providing it is tempered with tact and one knows when to keep one's opinions to oneself so as not to give offence.'

Eve looked at him sharply. 'Are you criticising me, Mr Fitzalan?'

Marcus's jaw tightened and his eyes glittered, his lips curving in slight scorn as he regarded her coolly, having hoped that when she finally agreed to become his wife she would have done so with a little more enthusiasm instead of the frigid politeness of a stranger.

'I would not presume. However, you are right—and I accept I have nothing to lose and much to gain. You are not obliged to marry me, so the choice is yours entirely. But I had hoped that, in making up your mind to become my wife, you would make your decision to do so sound less like you were going to your execution,' he said, his tone biting and angry.

'I cannot help how I feel,' she flared, an angry pink flush staining her cheeks. 'You can hardly expect me to be over the moon at the prospect. Dear Lord! I don't want to marry you. I don't want to marry anyone—but I am determined to make the best of it.'

'Then for *that* I suppose I must be thankful,' Marcus replied with cutting scorn. 'I know you must have tried to find a way out of this, but unless you are prepared to leave Atwood altogether and go and live in Cumbria, then there isn't one that I can see.'

'I know that. I have almost turned myself inside out trying to find some way of avoiding this, but it is truly impossible.'

'So it is settled, then?'

Eve took a deep, shuddering breath. 'Yes.'

'Then since we have reached an understanding we will announce our betrothal at once and be married just as soon as
you are out of mourning.'

'Oh, no,' she said quickly. 'I do not wish to wait. The
sooner the better.' She smiled with slight irony when she saw
him arch his eyebrows in questionable surprise. 'Not because
of any romantic inclinations I might feel towards yourself, you
understand, but because I have no wish to be at Burntwood
Hall when Gerald arrives to take up residence.'

This was better than Marcus had hoped for. 'And when do
you expect him to arrive?'

'In about a month, I think.'

'Very well. We will be married within the month—just as
soon as it can be arranged. However, no matter what our feelings are for each other, I must insist that we make it appear
to the world that we live amicably together. Is that understood?'

There was a warning underlying the lightness to his words
that Eve was fully aware of. 'Yes, I understand perfectly.'

'And you have no objections to this?'

'No. Providing you abide by the bargain we made.'

His eyes narrowed. 'Bargain? Please—refresh my memory.
What bargain was that?'

'That ours will be a marriage in name only.'

'Yes, I remember saying that—and I meant it. But I will
make it clear here and now, Eve, that it is not a situation I
will allow to persist indefinitely. Do you really expect me to
live with you in marriage and not complete our union?'

He rose from where he was sitting perched on the edge of
the balustrade, intimidating Eve with his imposing height. His
eyes glittered in the dim light like steel flints and she eyed
him warily, aware of the tension between them.

'No—but—I—I hoped—'

'Then don't,' he said sharply. 'I shall keep the bargain I

made until there is better understanding between us—but it will be only a temporary situation of short duration; a situation, as your husband, I shall feel at liberty to remedy any time I choose, and there is not a law in the land that will say I do not have the right.'

His jibe, savage and taunting, flicked over Eve like a whiplash, and his eyes glittered with a fire that burned her raw. For a moment she stared at him in horror and shrank back into the shadows, her eyes darkening, both frightened and fascinated by his anger, but then she seemed to burst into life as her chin came up and her lips tightened, her eyes blazing in defiance at what he implied.

'You mean you would force me?'

The smile that broke across his white teeth was infuriating. 'I have never forced my attentions on a woman who didn't want me—and I feel no temptation to do so now. Despite your hostile manner and waspish tongue—which, I might tell you, I will not endure when we are married—I have seen in your eyes and felt on your lips that which gives me hope for better things. I do not think, when you become my wife, I shall have too long to wait before things change.'

Temper flared in Eve's eyes as hot, angry words bubbled to her lips. 'Then I think I should make it plain here and now that I have no intention of changing—and if I do not live up to your expectations then you can go to the devil and be damned.'

She was so angry that she turned abruptly and moved across the terrace, intending to return to the drawing room, but before she realised what was happening Marcus had quickly crossed the short space that divided them with the speed of a cat and she found herself pinned against the cold stone wall of the house, his fingers biting cruelly into her shoulders, too tightly for either propriety or comfort.

For the first time sheer terror gripped Eve when she saw the blazing fury in his eyes. They were so compelling that she was unable to look away, and his face was so close to hers that she could smell the brandy on his breath, feel the heat of it wafting her flesh.

'Take your hands off me, you—you brute,' she hissed. 'If you don't I shall scream.'

He smiled, ignoring her plea, his eyes becoming focused on her lips as he lowered his mouth closer to hers. 'I don't think you'll do that,' he murmured, his lips finding hers at last, happy to discover they were every bit as soft and sweet as he remembered them to be, when he had first sampled their delights three years ago at Atwood Fair.

When he placed his mouth on hers Eve felt her stomach plunge. She panicked, raising her hand to push him away, but instead she found herself pushing herself closer, feeling the hardness of his body pressed close to hers. Suddenly his arms slackened a little and one hand began caressing the back of her neck, causing a strange, warm feeling to begin sweeping over her, a feeling that was new and exciting. His lips, which were hard and demanding at first, began to soften and he kissed her deeply, slowly and deliberately, and Eve felt fire shoot through her veins followed by a melting sweetness as her own lips began to respond and open under his, allowing him to drink his fill, satisfying the thirst that had tormented him for so long.

It was a kiss that seemed to last forever, and for one mad, glorious moment Eve wanted it to. For the first time in her life she felt an unknown joy awaking inside her as she was carried along on a wave of pleasure and exciting sensations began to stir inside her, sensations she had experienced only once before in her life, and he had been the one to bring them to her awareness then—so long ago, now it seemed. She felt bereft when his lips left hers, only to sigh with unbelievable bliss as they proceeded to travel ever so slowly down her neck, burying themselves in the soft curve of her throat where a pulse was beating just beneath the surface of her skin. Feeling his mouth pass over her naked flesh was like a flutter of wings, causing the blood to pound through her veins with the heat of desire.

Realising at last what was happening, that his tender assault on her body was succeeding in breaking down all her resistance, Eve was shocked to her core. She half-opened her eyes, as she forced herself out of her rapturous state, only to find his already fixed on hers.

'Please, Marcus—don't do this,' she begged softly, visibly shaken by what he had done.

But he ignored her plea and folded her in his arms once more, tasting her unresisting, willing lips, moist, fragrant, as sweet as honey, feeling her body pressed close to his, so firm, yet soft and yielding, her rounded breasts taut against him.

Eve purred like a kitten to his touch, which was incredibly sensual, feeling a quiver build up in the pit of her stomach, not knowing what she wanted from him, only that she was engulfed with an unfulfilled, aching need, having nothing but imaginings with which to compare the sweet agony of passion that rolled over her in huge waves.

When Marcus broke their embrace and lifted his head, his body throbbing uncontrollably, his senses reeling, he found himself wanting her with a fierceness that took his breath away. Never had he seen anyone so lovely.

'If I could have my way, I would take my pleasure of you here and now,' he murmured looking deep into her eyes, his lips hovering over hers, warm and dangerous, 'and awaken all the passion I sense you are capable of feeling.'

Still reeling from his devastating kiss, Eve stared up at him helplessly, wanting nothing more than for him to carry her away and make love to her, knowing the ecstasy of their union would bring her a wondering awe, but she was ashamed of her thoughts, ashamed that she was behaving in exactly the same manner as she had three years ago at Atwood Fair.

Looking down at her, Marcus saw how her lips suddenly trembled and that her face was chalk white beneath the mass of her black hair. Her eyes shone with bravely held tears, causing something inside him to melt. The sight of her aroused every protective instinct in him. She looked so young, so innocent, that it would be easy to take advantage of her, but he couldn't. He did not release her, but they stood and looked deep into each other's eyes, and for a moment something passed between them and each knew what the other was thinking.

Eve gazed up at him, mesmerised by his eyes that burned like twin, blue-white flames. She saw a softening in their depths as a solitary tear ran slowly down her cheek, which he wiped away gently with his finger.

'You are not as opposed to me as you would like me to believe,' he said, having read her response with his instinctive sensitivity, his smile one of satisfaction that he had just proved his point. 'However, I apologise, Eve. I did not mean this to happen. Please don't worry. I meant what I said and promise you will go unmolested after we are married, until the time comes when you want it otherwise.'

He let his hands fall to his sides and stepped back, leaving her trembling so badly she had to lean against the wall for support. Her heart was thumping so hard. The cold rationality in her head was telling her not to get involved with him, that it was sheer madness to marry a man who could render her so defenceless, and yet the emotional upheaval he had brought to her heart made her crave for more of what he wanted to give. Everything in her body had responded, shamelessly, wantonly.

'Please compose yourself. I think it is time we went back inside. I also think now is as good a time as any to announce our betrothal, don't you—after I have had a quiet word with my mother and your grandmother, of course. I will call on you at Burntwood Hall in a day or so to discuss the matter further.'

'I—I may not be there,' she said stiffly, still trembling slightly from what had happened between them.

'Oh?'

'I—I am going to stay with my friend Emma Parkinson—

she lives just outside Atwood on the Leeds road. Her mother has kindly invited me to stay with them for a few days. She thinks the change will be good for me.'

Marcus nodded. 'I'm sure she's right. I'll call on you there if need be,' he replied and, taking her arm, guided her into the drawing room.

Chapter Nine

Travelling back to Burntwood Hall, it was hard for Eve to think of herself as being betrothed to Marcus Fitzalan. The very idea of becoming his wife filled her with an excited dread. Whenever they met he made her feel defensive and there was a tension between them that was palpable. She was always in control when in the company of anyone else—but this was not the case when she was with him. She was far too aware of him and he disturbed her in a way she found uncomfortable and difficult to deal with. No one had ever had this effect on her before.

She told herself that marriage to him would be a disaster and it was not too late to call it off—to raise the drawbridge and exist in a state of siege, to retreat to the sanity she had known before she had been made aware of his existence—but remembering his kiss and the things he had said to her brought a wave of crimson to her cheeks.

Every nerve ending in her body had screamed out to her and all he had done was kiss her. What would it be like when he made love to her? This thought caused her heart to race and her eyes to open wide in alarm, realising that already she was thinking along those lines. He had told her he would not attempt to consummate their marriage until she was ready— but how long would she be able to hold out, seeing him day after day and knowing he was sleeping close by night after night. How long would she want to?

Sitting beside her grandmother—who was delighted with the outcome of the evening—she felt peculiar, warm stirrings deep inside her and her tongue passed over her lips. She could still taste the brandy Marcus had been drinking earlier, and they continued to tingle, feeling soft after his kiss. She drew in a deep breath which she released as a shuddering sigh, causing her grandmother to turn and look at her curiously.

'Are you all right, Eve?'

'Yes—yes. Perfectly, thank you.' She smiled, laying her head back on the upholstery and closing her eyes as so many conflicting and chaotic emotions chased round and round inside her head—bewilderment, anger and humiliation, and yet one thing rose clear and certain. She had not wanted Marcus to stop kissing her. She could not begin to fathom what her feelings were for him—but one thing she did know was that she couldn't stop thinking about him.

All through the following day Eve reflected on her evening at Brooklands—and not least on her meeting with Angela. She recalled the moment when she had returned to the drawing room with Marcus, when he had drawn her to his side and announced that she had done him the honour of agreeing to become his wife. Involuntarily her eyes had sought out Angela, and apart from a narrowing of her eyes her expression had not changed.

Their decision to marry was greeted with ill-disguised approval and they were showered with warm congratulations.

But just what did Angela mean to Marcus? She was puzzled for there had been something contradictory in Marcus and Angela's attitudes towards each other all evening.

Having observed them display a certain intimacy when they had been together in the garden, and then seeing them in the company of others when they rarely spoke or acknowledged each other—which she thought might have been deliberate—

appeared strange to her and opened her mind to suspicion, which began making progress at a rapid pace the more she thought about it.

But why should it matter? she asked herself. Why did it rouse in her such a host of perplexing emotions that gave rise to so much confusion within herself? She had already made up her mind that she would marry Marcus Fitzalan for her own advantage, and had he not suggested that their marriage was to be a marriage in name only until they wanted it otherwise? A suggestion she had welcomed wholeheartedly until he had weakened her by kissing her so passionately, so deliberately, in an attempt to break down her resolve.

But this still did not change anything and she did not flatter herself that he felt any attachment to her. If there was something going on between himself and Mrs Stephenson, then he must want Atwood Mine very badly indeed to enter into such a marriage whilst being in love with another woman. But no matter how cold and impersonal an arrangement their marriage would be, she would not be made a fool of or humiliated, and would not take lightly to his carrying on an attachment under her very nose when she was his wife.

A few days after her visit to Brooklands, with her grandmother's permission—Lady Pemberton was to remain at Burntwood Hall until after Eve's wedding to Marcus—Eve went to stay with her close friend Emma Parkinson, who lived not far away in a fine manor house with her family. Her father was the local squire and, although the family did not possess a fortune, they were reasonably well off.

Eve and Emma had met as children and had been best friends ever since. The Parkinson household was such a contrast to her own; whereas she was an only child, Emma was the eldest of seven sisters and one brother, ranging from herself at nineteen to the twins at five years old.

Two days into her visit, they took a picnic to the river that flowed through the meadows half a mile from the house. It was a Sunday and the afternoon was hot and sultry, the children with their faces aglow playing happily and noisily on the river bank, with nursemaids and Nanny looking on from beneath the welcome shade of some trees, gossiping and industriously laying out the picnic on the grass.

With her feet bare after paddling in the cool, shallow water and hugging her knees in front of her, from where she sat beside Emma, who was half lying on the grass beside her, Eve looked on enviously, always happy to be a part of this charmed circle, content to watch and listen to the sound of the children's laughter.

'You're so lucky, Em,' she sighed wistfully, calling her by the shortened form of her name as she always did.

'Lucky?' said Emma squinting up at her, her fingers plucking idly at the grass.

'Mmm. To have a large family around you all the time. I'd give anything to have at least one brother or sister—but not to have any…'

'Don't go on,' laughed Emma lightly, glad that Eve had come to stay for a few days, and hoping that the summer activities they never failed to indulge in—picnics and riding and bathing in the river—might alleviate some of the sadness and grief that stared out of her eyes.

'There are times when they drive us to distraction. The twins are impossible and lead poor Nanny a merry dance. Mind you—Jonathan always winds them up and they are invariably punished for his misdeeds. He's a menace,' she said, smiling fondly as she watched her seven-year-old brother torment the twins unmercifully, with jovial, tousled-haired twenty-one-year-old Matthew Somerville, Gerald's younger brother, trying his best to maintain some semblance of order among the children, but with little success.

Matthew, of whom Eve's father had been extremely fond, did not resemble Gerald in any way, being of a gentle, often serious disposition. He was employed at Atwood Mine as an agent, responsible for the hiring of colliers, whilst learning as much about the mining industry as he could. It being Sunday and a day of rest, he had come along to share their picnic—although whether or not he would have done so had Emma not been present remained open to speculation.

'My parents tend to spoil Jonathan abominably,' Emma went on, 'because he's the only son and everyone thinks he's so special. But if you like children so much, Eve, you'll be able to have some of your own soon,' she said, rolling on to her stomach and resting her face on her hand, looking up at Eve sideways, her lips curling in a teasing smile, well aware that she was seriously considering marriage to the handsome and quite delectable Marcus Fitzalan. She knew of the conditions of her father's will and couldn't for the life of her think why Eve was being so reticent about it. Had it been her she would have jumped at it like a shot.

Eve flushed and bit her lip. 'I doubt it—at least not for a long time yet. Oh, Em,' she murmured, a yearning quality to her voice. 'I had long since made up my mind that I was going to meet the man of my dreams, fall in love and live happily ever after.'

'Sadly, life isn't like that.'

'I know. Marcus must think I'm awfully young—a child, even, in his eyes, but these last weeks have made me grow up very quickly. I feel as though I've aged twenty years and have a distinct feeling that I've been cheated somewhere along the way.'

'Cheated! I wouldn't say that. Not when you're about to marry the most eligible man in the West Riding. There are plenty of women who would give their eye teeth to be in your position—and you can count me as one of them.' She laughed lightly. 'You do intend marrying him, don't you?'

'I have told him I will. Although the fact of the matter is that I really have no choice,' she said with bitter regret.

'Well, my advice is not to change your mind. You must look on this as a golden opportunity. Don't let it slip through your fingers. If you do and you go to live with your grandmother with nothing to look at day in and day out but hills and sheep, then mark my words, you'll live to regret it.'

'It's just that I want to make quite sure I'm doing the right thing, Em. Now I am my own mistress I'm reluctant to change that. Why should I marry anyone if I don't want to? The truth is I'm frightened. I'm frightened of marrying this man and having him control my life. And that makes me angry.'

'If you don't marry Marcus Fitzalan then you're a fool,' Emma replied bluntly. 'Not only will you lose the opportunity of becoming the wife of the most handsome, sought-after bachelor in the district, but you'll also lose Atwood Mine—and considering all *that* entails, it is not something you should pass over lightly.'

'I don't have to marry him to retain Atwood Mine, Em,' she said quietly. 'I could remain at Burntwood Hall for the rest of my life if I so wished, and let the Somervilles keep the mine—at least for the remaining fifteen years of the lease—if I marry Gerald.'

Emma's eyes opened wide with astonishment. 'What?' she gasped. 'Eve—you wouldn't—you couldn't.'

Unsmiling, Eve shook her head. 'No—not in a million years. But he has asked me. I cannot say that I like Gerald very much, if at all. There's a side to him that's decidedly unpleasant. He—he frightens me sometimes. It's a pity Matthew wasn't the elder of the two.' She sighed. 'How much easier everything would be if he had inherited the estate instead of Gerald.'

Emma's eyes clouded over and her face became serious as she quietly contemplated Eve's words—and Eve would not have been surprised to know that Emma was saying a silent prayer of thankfulness that Matthew was not the elder of the two brothers, for she was well and truly smitten by him herself.

'Don't worry, Em—' Eve smiled reassuringly, having read her thoughts '—I know just how close you and Matthew have become of late. Anyone would have to be blind not to see.

But do you think obtaining Atwood Mine will make Marcus Fitzalan like me any better?' she asked, wistfully watching a small white butterfly as it flitted among a carpet of forget-me-nots close to the river bank. 'The seeds of discord have already been sown, Em—when I foolishly took up Angela's challenge that day at Atwood Fair.'

'That's rubbish, Eve,' Emma admonished forcefully. 'That's all forgotten now—over and done with. It must be, otherwise he would not be marrying you.' Sighing in exasperation at Eve's stubborn reluctance to fall victim to Mr Fitzalan's charms, Emma sat up, brushing pieces of dried grass from her skirts as she straightened them over her outstretched legs.

'Tell me, Eve. When you're with Mr Fitzalan, feeling like this, how do you manage to conceal your hostility? Does it not make him angry?'

'I'm sure it does—but I do find it difficult at times. He is so proud and arrogant—so full of his own importance.'

'It is scarcely to be wondered at. A man as rich as Mr Fitzalan, and with everything in his favour, can afford to be. I have heard that among his friends he is an agreeable, good-humoured man—but I have also heard he has the most violent temper. You would do well not to aggravate him before you are married, otherwise he might change his mind and marry someone else instead.'

Eve gave her a sharply suspicious look. 'I doubt it. Atwood Mine is too important for him to do that. But I dare say he would not be aware of my existence if my father had not made it over to the both of us on condition that we marry. But, Em,' she said, with slight reticence, knowing how her friend with her lively disposition loved to socialise—more often than not at the assembly rooms in both Atwood and Netherley, where she loved to gossip and contrived to learn what news she could about people in the area—and that if anyone knew anything about what was going on it was Emma, 'have you heard anything regarding Mr Fitzalan—gossip, I mean, and a certain person who is known to us both?'

Emma's eyes opened wide at the possibility of a scandal. 'No. Should I have?'

Eve shrugged. 'No. I don't suppose so. I—I just thought that—perhaps—seeing as you rarely miss any of the assemblies either in Atwood or Netherley, you might have heard something, that's all.'

'No, I can't say that I have. Mr Fitzalan's name frequently crops up in conversation, and everyone knows he has been romantically linked to several ladies in the past, but considering he has never shown the smallest interest in attending any of the local assemblies, nothing is known for certain. But what lady do you have in mind? Oh, Eve,' she begged when she saw Eve look away, as if she was reluctant to enlarge on what it was that had prompted her to ask the question in the first place. 'You have to tell me. What lady? What's her name?'

Sighing, Eve looked at her and said, 'Angela Lambert—or Stephenson, as she became after marrying Leslie.'

Emma was momentarily stunned. 'Angela? Angela and Mr Fitzalan? No—that is the most ridiculous thing I have heard in a long while. I do not believe it—and neither must you. What I do know about her is that, after Leslie died, by all accounts she did not resemble a grieving widow. She spent some considerable time in London where, according to Matthew, she became well acquainted with Gerald and his friends. She returned to the north four months ago. I cannot say that I have heard of her being involved in any way with Mr Fitzalan—not romantically, anyway, which is what I think you are implying. What gives you reason to think she is?'

'Oh—no reason, really,' Eve replied, forcing herself to smile. It came as no surprise that she was acquainted with Gerald, mixing as they did in the same social circles, both in the north and in London. 'Forget I said anything. I'm just being silly, that's all.'

Frowning, Emma cast her a serious glance, knowing Eve was not given to making idle statements without good reason, and that she had been deeply hurt by Angela's duplicity three years ago over the affair with Leslie Stephenson. She had every reason to be suspicious and on her guard where Angela was concerned.

'I'm sure you are, Eve. But why ask?'

'Only because I met her when I went to Brooklands. I—I chanced to see her in the garden with Marcus and they displayed a familiarity that gave me reason to suspect she might be more to him than a mere acquaintance. She—she made me feel like an intruder.'

'Well, if she did it was probably because she was jealous. We both know how malicious and conniving she can be when the mood takes her. Good heavens, it's you Mr Fitzalan's marrying, not her. If I were you I'd think no more about it.' Emma cocked her head sideways, looking at Eve with a gentle, teasing, whimsical smile. 'But if it concerns you so much, would I be right in thinking your feelings for Mr Fitzalan are not entirely hostile after all?'

Lowering her eyes Eve sighed deeply, the pink flush that suddenly sprung to her cheeks telling Emma all she needed to know. 'Yes, you would,' she admitted softly. 'He has a way of confusing me to such an extent that I do not know what I'm doing or saying half the time.' She looked up to find Emma watching her.

'It sounds to me as though you are already halfway to being in love with him,' she said softly.

'Yes,' she replied, meeting Emma's gaze, finding it impossible to give a different answer. 'It certainly looks that way. His treatment of me that day at Atwood Fair showed him to be a man without reserve or scruples, and I had every reason in the world to dislike him. I have always turned a deaf ear to those who esteemed and valued him, who spoke of him with affection and merit.'

'And now?'

'Now I am astonished and apprehensively perturbed that I no longer find it easy to discredit him. I have carried a strong prejudice against him for so long—but now I am getting to know him a little better, I am beginning to suspect I may have done him an injustice as I begin to see a different side to his nature, the side my father so admired. It would seem I might have to change my opinion of his worth.'

Emma smiled softly. 'Then I am glad to hear it. To begin a life together with so much bitterness and resentment between you would not make for a happy marriage. Now come along,' she said, getting to her feet. 'Nanny's beckoning to us. All the children are sitting down so I think it must be time to eat.'

Eve followed her, surprised by her revelation as to what her feelings were for Marcus, and how easy it had been to admit her true feelings to Emma. But having been the recipient of Angela's vindictiveness and knowing just what she was capable of, it was no easy matter dismissing her from her mind or the threat she posed to her future happiness with Marcus.

As Emma helped clear away the remains of the picnic, the children, along with Matthew and Eve, took to the river and in no time at all the voices of shrill childish laughter rose and fell in paroxysms of uncontrollable mirth as they splashed hilariously in the warm, shallow water, uncaring that their clothes were getting hopelessly wet as they tried to drench Matthew. He had a riotous sense of fun and they loved him unashamedly.

Having decided to ride over to the Parkinsons to see Eve, it was into this setting that Marcus headed, being drawn to it by the ringing tones of laughter. Just missing the playful interlude Eve and Matthew had been indulging in with the children, who had left them and scampered back to their nursemaids to be rubbed dry—an interlude which had left them happily exhausted—Marcus came quietly into the small clearing surrounded by trees, the thick, purple-shadowed undergrowth beyond consisting of blackberry and honeysuckle and a carpet of blue forget-me-nots. The trees were arranged in such a way as to allow the benign warmth of the sun to enter and become entrapped.

Marcus stared in astonishment to see Eve stretched out on the grassy bank. She lay quite still looking up at the small clouds that floated across the vast, untroubled sky, breathing deeply. He allowed his eyes to drink their fill. She looked as he imagined her namesake must have looked in the Garden of Eden—womanly, utterly female and at one with her surroundings, bewitching, completely unprepossessing and enchanting.

But he felt the joy of seeing her drain from him when his eyes strayed to the young man lying by her side. Panic and anger seized him. He told himself that the situation could not be as it looked, that this precious being he had only just found had been stolen from him before he'd had the chance to analyse the extent of the emotions she had aroused in him. But when his mind flashed back to the day he had first laid eyes on her three years ago, when he had accused her of being a promiscuous little flirt, perhaps he had not been so far from the truth after all.

When the lone horseman rode into the clearing, his horse's hooves muddying the crystal-clear water close to the bank, and his long shadow stretching menacingly over them both and blocking out the light of the sun, Matthew sat bolt upright, startled out of his reverie and frozen into stillness as he gaped wordlessly at the man who had come upon them so unexpectedly.

Marcus lounged indolently in the saddle while his large, sleek chestnut horse bent its head to drink the water. Matthew shrank visibly beneath his seniority and his withering glacier gaze, sensing his anger and deep displeasure. Having seen him on occasion when he had come to the mine to see Sir John, he knew him to be Eve's intended.

Aware of how the situation must look to Marcus—with Matthew's breeches wet and rolled up above his knees, his shirt hanging loose and his face flushed from his recent antics in the river as he had happily accompanied the children at their play—he wished he could disappear into thin air. His face became blood red with embarrassment.

Having had a moment to observe them, Marcus felt his stomach churn. Seeing Eve like this, dishevelled, with her rich curtain of hair, long and silky and glossy black, hanging loose, almost took his breath away and he could not take his eyes from her. She was magnificent. She held her head proudly, her violet eyes burning up into his, showing neither alarm at his appearance or caring much for modesty. He was disturbed by the sight of her, feeling a stirring of warmth in his loins.

She was laid out on the grass with her shoes and stockings strewn beside her, her face flushed from the sun's rays and her recent laughter, and the lower half of her legs exposed— long, white, slim and perfect—causing anger to shoot through Marcus like molten fire. How dare she let this callow youth see her like this, making no attempt to cover herself. Having seen the familiarity they displayed together a moment earlier caused his mouth to tighten ominously.

Matthew looked somewhat shamefaced and bemused but Eve, slowly sitting up, stared at her betrothed in defiance, in silent challenge to his authority, but his eyes were compelling and flashing with that particular pale blue that heralded trouble.

'I sincerely hope this is not how it looks,' said Marcus with an icy calm, his gaze, flicking from one to the other, coming to rest on Matthew, whom he vaguely recognised but could not place just then. 'I don't believe we've met. Be so good as to introduce us will you, Eve?'

'Gladly. Although considering you are already acquainted with his elder brother, I am surprised to find you have not met before. Matthew, may I present Mr Fitzalan. This is Matthew Somerville, Marcus. Gerald's brother. He is employed as an agent at Atwood Mine.'

Marcus's dark brows drew together in deep displeasure, certain that anyone who had the misfortune to be related to Gerald Somerville must be lacking in moral restraint.

Matthew scrambled to his feet, clearly flustered, having no idea of the deep hatred Mr Fitzalan felt for his elder brother.

'Yes—I—I know who you are, sir—you're—'

'Miss Somerville's betrothed,' Marcus said cuttingly. 'Is that not right, Eve?'

'Yes,' she replied, knowing by the cold severity on Marcus's handsome face that the fragile unity they had shared so briefly at Brooklands had begun to disappear.

'Then may I take this opportunity to congratulate you, sir,' said Matthew politely and hurriedly. Bending down he grasped his shoes, eager to extricate himself from the embarrassment of the unpleasant situation as quickly as possible. 'Excuse me. I must see what the children are up to.'

Coolly Marcus watched him go before fixing his hard gaze on Eve. Seeing his gaze flick coldly and contemptuously over the length of her body, and how his eyes came to rest on her bare legs, she modestly covered them with her skirts, but her toes peeped out in a continued act of defiance. The gesture angered him. It mattered not one jot to her that she had allowed the youth to look his fill while denying the same right to her betrothed. When they were married all that would change. He would show her from the start that she could not play the imperious young madam with him. Unflustered, she looked up at him boldly.

Marcus dismounted. His forbearance, never strong, was about to crack under her defiance. He stood looking down at her without speaking, but the tautness of his body, his brilliant eyes and the curl of his firm lips, told Eve everything she needed to know. He loomed over her like an angry, avenging god—but why he should be so incensed with anger baffled her. She sighed. Why couldn't it be someone like Matthew her father had left half of Atwood Mine to—someone she could relate to, someone uncomplicated? How much easier it would have been for her to decide.

With a sigh she got to her feet, trying to brush the creases out of her dress with her hands. 'I am surprised to see you, Marcus. I thought you were a busy man—too busy to ride about the countryside paying social calls.'

'Not too busy to call on my betrothed,' he replied coldly, ignoring her faint sarcasm.

'I am flattered. How did you know where to find me?'

'I did call at the house in the hope of seeing you,' he confessed. 'Mrs Parkinson told me where you could be found. It's fortunate I came when I did—otherwise there's no telling what you and Mr Somerville would have been up to. Have you nothing to say for yourself?'

'No. I don't feel that I have to defend myself to you,' she said looking at him calmly, ignoring the danger signals in his eyes, realising that the proud arrogance and indomitable will his mother had spoken of was set on a collision course with her own. 'I care nothing for your anger or your bullying. I do not fear you, Marcus.'

Marcus seethed inwardly, trying hard to control his anger. He took a menacing step towards her. 'The last thing I want is for you to fear me, Eve, but I am asking you to explain yourself. After all, there is only one thing that comes to mind when I see you behaving like a strumpet.'

Eve gasped with indignation. 'Don't be ridiculous. Because I was indiscreet once you think me capable of anything. Perhaps if you did not go creeping around and spying on me you would have seen the situation for what it was. You cannot possibly be angry at the friendly playfulness we were indulging in with the children a moment ago. It is commonplace when we are all together and, besides, Matthew and I have known each other from children.'

'Even children grow up,' Marcus said with scorn. 'Don't pretend to be so naïve. You know as well as I what must pass through his mind when you are alone together—and half undressed.'

Eve stared at him in defiance, enraged by the implication of his words. 'For heaven's sake, Marcus Fitzalan—you are behaving like a jealous husband already. I have only removed my shoes and stockings so that I might play in the river with the children—and do not judge everyone by your own questionable standards. I am sure that what you imply has never crossed Matthew's mind—and besides, Emma is the object of his affections, not I. Perhaps you object to people enjoying themselves, is that it?'

'Not at all. I like enjoying myself as much as the next man—but what I do object to is watching my future wife make a ridiculous spectacle of herself.'

'Oh! This is too much,' Eve expostulated. 'There is nothing ridiculous about playing with children.' She gave him a look of furious loathing. 'Perhaps you object to children, too.'

'I like children very much as it happens—and I intend filling the nursery at Brooklands with them in the not-too-distant future.'

'Don't you think you should consult me first?'

'Oh, I will. When the time is right. The kind of behaviour I found you indulging in today goes beyond the bounds of propriety, and when we are married I shall expect you to uphold the respectable position in society as befitting my wife. I shall feel happier when you concern yourself with your own household and children instead of other peoples'.'

'And I was brought up to understand that ladies are treated with courtesy and respect.'

Marcus smiled thinly. 'One must act like a lady if she wishes to be treated as such,' he said scathingly.

Eve flushed, lifting her head and glaring at him haughtily. 'I resent that. How dare you address me in this manner?'

Marcus stepped closer to her, feeling the blood pounding in his temples at her proud defiance to stand firm against him. 'Oh, I do dare—when I find the woman I am to marry carousing in the bushes unashamedly with an adolescent youth.'

'We were not carousing in the bushes and Matthew is not an adolescent youth. He is a responsible, caring adult, a relative and a man my father was extremely fond of. And what I do does not concern you,' she spat, her own eyes blazing as hot as his.

'Oh, yes it does, lady,' he snarled, his metallic eyes glittering with a fire that burned her raw. 'I will not stand by and be denied by my own wife that which she would give freely to another.'

Eve's own eyes narrowed furiously. 'I am not your wife yet, Marcus—and nor am I likely to be if you carry on in this aggressive manner. You told me you would not touch me until I was ready? Do you go back on your word so soon?'

'I never go back on my word. But you will not deny me indefinitely. I am not a patient man and abstinence is a heavy penance. However—I do not intend abstaining for life.'

'Then don't waste your time waiting for me.'

'I won't—but let it be understood that there will be no little amours behind my back. If you think you can carry on an affair, then you do not know me.'

'And if you can address me in this manner then let me tell you that I have no wish to know you,' Eve flared.

'Damn your insolence,' he hissed.

'Then tell me, Marcus,' she said, throwing back her head, taunting him with her words, 'does what you have just said apply to you also?'

'What do you mean?'

'Angela Stephenson,' she said coldly, accusingly, her voice straining itself between her taut lips.

Amazement registered in Marcus's eyes and to her chagrin, instead of looking guilty or abashed, he threw back his head and laughed, a razor-edged laugh, the sound of it going soaring and ringing through the trees. Seeing red, Eve was infuriated—more with herself than she was with him, since she had not intended mentioning the incident she had witnessed in the gardens at Brooklands.

The last thing she wanted was to give him the satisfaction of knowing it troubled her, which would no doubt give rise to considerable amusement and give him reason to accuse her of jealousy. She wanted to lash out at him, to hurt him, and she glared up at him, her hair rippling in the soft breeze as their eyes became locked together.

'Angela!' he laughed, his eyes warm with his humour. 'That is ridiculous. Angela is a acquaintance and nothing more—and she is only that because her mother and my own happen to be close friends.' His smile suddenly broadened and his eyes narrowed suddenly. 'Oh! Jealous, are we?'

Eve's eyes snapped and her chin came up. 'No more than you were just now of Matthew,' she replied primly.

'Only because of the impropriety of the situation.'

'Come now—' she laughed, unable to resist a little sarcastic teasing '—you looked fit to throw him into the river—and don't deny it.'

'I don't. But believe me, Angela Stephenson is an acquaintance and nothing more.'

'After seeing the two you together in the garden at Brooklands, that is not the impression you gave me—and by her manner I suspect she is of the same opinion.'

Marcus's eyes narrowed and he became thoughtful as he tried to think what she could be referring to. 'I did meet Angela in the garden shortly after she arrived—quite by chance, I assure you. As a matter of fact, it may surprise you to know that I was looking for you at the time and was disappointed not to find you. I came upon Angela sitting by the fountain instead. That's all it was. But how you can accuse me of spying on *you* when you are guilty of the same offence, I confess puzzles me. If you were watching, then you should have made your presence known.'

Eve was seething and she found his mocking smile intolerable. How dared he put her in the wrong in this manner. 'It was way beyond me to interrupt such an intimate tête-à-tête. But I do not have to put up with this. It's not too late. I don't have to marry you,' she fumed, struggling to keep her voice under control.

'Oh, yes, you do,' he growled, his anger returning, the grinding resolve which always kept him in complete control with those with whom he dealt rising to the fore. 'If you want to hold on to Atwood Mine you do and you know it. You need me just as much as I need you and there's not a damned thing you can to about it. Now—put on your shoes and come and introduce me to your friends. The sooner that young pup realises you really are to be my wife the better I shall feel.'

'Put your stamp on me—is that what you mean?'

'If you like.'

'Then if you are to meet everyone I would be obliged if you would alter your expression.'

Marcus threw her a questioning look.

'You are likely to frighten the children,' she said tartly, tossing her hair out of her eyes and beginning to walk on ahead of him carrying her shoes and stockings, uncaring whether he followed her or not.

Marcus watched her go and then, grasping his horse's bridle, he chuckled softly to himself. With the flicker of a smile at the corners of his lips he began to follow, regarding her with admiration. Doubtless there would be many more skirmishes ahead he could look forward to.

Chapter Ten

If Eve thought Marcus would frighten the children he soon proved her wrong, and from the mischievous glances he kept throwing her way he seemed to delight in doing so. At first they were in awe of him, fixing him with dubious, uneasy glances, but he soon captivated their attention, possessing a natural ability to control them in a way that left their nurse-maids and Nanny more than a little amazed. They were enchanted.

Eve observed him with puzzlement, especially as she had just accused him of not liking children. He seemed to have a natural rapport with them and it was quite a novelty to see him in his shirt sleeves entertaining them, sending them into gales of laughter as they rolled about the grass.

'Well, who would have thought it?' said Emma, coming to sit beside Eve on the grass.

'Who indeed?' murmured Eve.

'Shall we rescue him, do you think?'

'No, let's leave him. It would be a shame to spoil his enjoyment.'

'Mr Fitzalan is so different from what I expected. I'm astonished. Clearly he has a fondness for children.'

'I'm as astonished as you are, Em. He is so much altered I hardly know him.'

'After your harsh description of him earlier he is not at all what I expected. There is nothing disagreeable about his character at all.'

Eve had to agree that Emma was right, but she suspected that it might just be a temporary measure to placate her for some mischievous reason of his own. Never had she seen him so unreserved, so eager to please as he sought to gain the good opinion of Emma and to put Matthew at his ease. The change in him was so great she could not restrain her amazement.

She looked at him as though for the first time and saw that with his hair lightly ruffled he looked much younger and less formidable, and for a moment she had the impression that he was little more than a boy himself. He did seem genuinely fond of children, and they of him. When she managed to catch his eye she saw so much laughter on his face that he seemed a long way removed from the proud, arrogant man she had come to know. It gave her an insight of a different side to him she was looking forward to knowing better.

After a while Marcus came to join Eve where she sat on the grass with her arms around her drawn-up knees watching him. Slipping into his coat, his black hair shining and falling over his brow, he sat beside her, and she felt a tingling of exhilaration, feeling drawn to him against her will by a compelling magnetism that radiated from his very presence.

'Really, Marcus, I am quite impressed. Never would I have believed you to be so good with children. I am pleased to see you do not view them as an encumbrance after all.'

'I told you, I like children.'

'You seem to be such an expert at controlling them that, should we have children in the future, I think we will be able to dispense with the services of a nanny.'

He smiled into her eyes. 'I'm not such an expert—or so patient.' He sighed, stretching out his long booted legs. Leaning on his elbow, he lay sideways looking up at her. 'I have yet to tell you the purpose for my coming here today.'

'Oh?'

'I have arranged for the wedding to take place at Atwood Church in just over three weeks' time—after the banns have been called. I hope that is agreeable to you.'

'Yes. I told you—the sooner the better. I have no wish to be at Burntwood Hall when Gerald arrives.'

On returning to Burntwood Hall after her visit to Emma, to her absolute dismay Eve found Gerald had arrived to take up residence. A terrible coldness gripped her as she entered the house. The violence of their last encounter, when he had uttered such menacing, ugly threats against her, leaving her in no doubt as to his determination to obtain Atwood Mine, crowded in on her mind. He had arrived unannounced, throwing the servants into utter confusion, and her grandmother was nowhere to be seen.

Steeling herself for her meeting with her father's cousin, she crossed the hall to the drawing room, finding not only Gerald but also Matthew, who looked awkward and apologetic as he watched Eve enter, aware of the dislike she felt for Gerald and how painful it was for her having to leave her home.

Having discarded his coat, carelessly at ease, Gerald was lounging in a large chair by the window, one of his elegantly shod feet resting on an upholstered foot stool. Already he had a proprietorial air about him. With a little shiver of dislike Eve was at once repelled, a pain in the region of her heart reminding her he was now the owner of Burntwood Hall, that she was the visitor, and there was not a thing she could do about it.

A decanter of claret stood on a green baize table beside him, and his slender hand idly turned his full glass to catch the light. He saw Eve come in but didn't bother to get up, his only movement being to raise a lazy eyebrow and throw her a mocking smile.

'Well, here's a strange turnout. I arrive to claim my inheritance and you were not here to welcome me, Eve. Imagine my disappointment.'

Mastering her surprise and disappointment, she said coldly, 'I'm sure you'll soon get over it, Gerald. Forgive me if I seem surprised. I did not expect you quite so soon.'

'Clearly,' he said, sipping at his claret and licking his lips, which made his mouth look like a vivid slash across his face.

'I—I hope you don't mind us being here,' said Matthew, stepping forward.

'Mind? Why should she mind?' Gerald expostulated before Eve could reply, momentarily roused out of quiet contemplation of his half-filled glass. 'A man does not need permission to enter his own home—is that not right, Eve?'

'Yes—of course,' she replied stiffly, trying hard to ignore his insolently smiling face. 'And will you be living here, Matthew?' she asked, favouring him with a warm smile, trying to put him at ease, for she knew how much Gerald's presence always intimidated him.

'Yes—I'm afraid so,' he said with a quick glance at his elder brother. 'It—it is necessary, you understand.'

Yes, Eve understood only too well. No doubt their own home would have to be sold to pay Gerald's creditors. How long would it be, she wondered sadly, before Burntwood Hall went down the same rotten, corrupt road now it was in his incapable hands?

'To be sure, you did not stay long at the Parkinsons,' Gerald commented.

'I did not wish to leave my grandmother alone for too long, that is why.'

'And when is the eminent lady to relieve us of her irksome presence?' he asked, speaking facetiously, for he had no liking for Lady Pemberton, but Eve paid no attention.

'Just as soon as I am married to Mr Fitzalan,' she replied coolly.

On hearing this Gerald's body became taut and he sat up in the chair, placing his glass beside the decanter on the table beside him. He was aware of this disagreeable fact, for it was common knowledge all over the West Riding that Eve had accepted Marcus Fitzalan's suit, and he did not approve. His eyes snapped open, alert, glittering with menace.

'So I hear,' he said, the quietness of his voice and the way his eyes fixed themselves on Eve's face having an unnerving effect. 'So—you have decided to marry our illustrious neighbour—a man without background or breeding, although I suppose his wealth can make amends for that.'

'It is no business of yours whom I marry—and insulting him will not help either. Mr Fitzalan is a gentleman and highly respected.'

'Then if the gossips were to be believed at the time, a true gentleman would not have taken advantage of your innocence and naïvety and attempted to seduce you before casting you aside so lightly—which, if my memory serves me correctly, is precisely what he did to you three years ago, and in so doing ruined any hopes you might have had of making a prestigious marriage.'

'As you say, that was a long time ago and best forgotten. I refuse to discuss the matter with you. All I ask is that you permit my grandmother and myself to remain here at Burntwood Hall until I marry Mr Fitzalan. It will only be for a matter of a few weeks. A month at the most.'

'I told you after your father's funeral that you don't have to leave. It is not unavoidable. I shall be happy to accommodate you for as long as you wish to stay. My offer of marriage still stands.'

'Which I still reject.'

'Come now, Eve, my offer is extremely generous. Marriage to me would not lack advantage. You would be mistress of this place—and wealthy beyond most people's imagination if we retain Atwood Mine. What more do you want?'

'What more indeed, Gerald?' she said scathingly. 'It is the choice of husband that is in question.'

All trace of blandness was wiped from Gerald's face and

Eve saw violence quiver in every inch of his frame. Two high spots of colour stained his cheeks and his mouth twisted in bitter scorn. 'Then you're a fool if you think you will be happy married to Marcus Fitzalan.'

'His intentions are honourable.'

'Pretentions, more like,' he sneered, his lips drawn back over his teeth. 'If I remember your words correctly when you first became aware of the terms of your father's will, you said that the day you marry Marcus Fitzalan will be the day when hell freezes over—that you would never agree to the conditions he laid down. The depth of your hatred and contempt for Fitzalan was plain for all to see. It's amazing to see how quickly he has brought you to heel.'

Eve's eyes glittered with rage. 'At the reading of my father's will I was upset and naturally angry when I discovered what he asked of me. But things change—I have changed, and after giving the matter of my future a great deal of consideration—and getting to know Mr Fitzalan better than I did—I know what I am doing is right. But whatever I do is not your concern, Gerald. It has nothing whatsoever to do with you.'

Gerald gave her a contemptuous smile. 'Perhaps not, but do not delude yourself into believing it's you he wants, Eve, because it isn't. It's the mine—but,' he said, being a consummate actor and looking completely at ease once more as he prepared to throw a spoke in the wheel, crossing one satin-clad leg over the other and regarding her with disdain, his devious mind reminding him that there was someone else who courted Fitzalan's favour, someone else who had her sights firmly set on becoming Mrs Fitzalan, 'I dare say that when the novelty of marriage to you wears off, the woman he might have married will continue to warm his bed as she has before.'

The remark was thrown carelessly, deliberately, causing Eve's eyes to flash with indignation and colour to flare in her face. 'I do not care for your words, Gerald. I have no idea what you're talking about—and nor do I care to. How dare you speak to me like this?'

He shrugged, his features marked by nonchalance. 'I merely state the obvious.' Suddenly Gerald's smile became one of malignant pleasure, knowing women and their eternal curiosity and was sure she wanted to know more, despite what she said.

'It's Angela Stephenson he's been carrying on an intrigue with, Angela whom he would prefer to marry him, but unfortunately she does not have the advantage of possessing a certain coal mine he is so desirous to obtain. He's probably with her this very minute.'

Gerald was taunting her, but Eve was determined not to let him get under her skin and arouse her to an expression of her personal feelings. Although she felt like she'd been felled and was frozen to a slender sliver of steel, she merely smiled and lifted her eyebrows in pretended surprise.

'Your sarcasm and cutting remarks are wasted, Gerald. They will neither destroy me or my intention to marry Mr Fitzalan, so you might as well save your breath. Besides, I do not believe you. But—if what you say is true—then I'm afraid Angela is going to be disappointed.' She smiled with irony. 'However, if she is so desirous to obtain another husband, she need not look very far. Perhaps with just a little persuasion she can be tempted to transfer her affections to you.

'After all, now you have come into your inheritance, women like Angela will find you an extremely desirable prospect. I know she was financially well taken care of when Leslie died, but his brother inherited his estate. No doubt she is looking for somewhere to settle, and who would be well pleased with all this.'

Gerald frowned, watching her closely. 'Angela and I are just good friends. I've told you,' he said, his eyes penetrating as he continued to watch her closely, 'she has other fish to fry in the form of Marcus Fitzalan. All men are lamentably weak, my dear, where women are concerned, and a woman as beautiful as Angela can exert an inordinate power over them.'

'Marcus cannot be accused of being weak, Gerald.'

'Don't be naïve,' he said sharply. 'He is marrying you to

get his hands on Atwood Mine and you're a fool if you think otherwise.'

Gerald's narrowed eyes conveyed a threat and he did not care that his tone was openly menacing. 'Angela is vengeful and you will do well not to underestimate her. As you know to your cost, my dear, she is no simple little sugar-mop who will stand by and watch you take what she wants without a fight.'

The colour had left Eve's face, having become white with anger. 'Is that a threat?'

'I would not presume. Say, rather, that I am warning you.'

Eve's hands clenched by her sides as she fought to retain her composure. 'Please excuse me, Gerald. I have no wish to stay and listen to this. I must go and see my grandmother.'

Trying to hold on to her dignity, she turned from him, moving towards the door.

'Oh—and by the way,' he said carelessly, halting her momentarily. 'I've invited some people to stay. There will be a large party arriving at the weekend. Instruct the servants to see that things are made ready. This place is like a mausoleum,' he commented, replenishing his empty glass. 'It could do with some life injected into it.'

Matthew followed Eve out of the room.

'Eve—please wait. I am so sorry about this. I tried to stop Gerald arriving unannounced, but you know what he's like. He just wouldn't listen.'

Eve smiled, swallowing back the lump that had risen in her throat. 'When did he ever?' She sighed when she saw the unhappiness on Matthew's face, feeling some sympathy for him. Gerald was hardly an ideal role model for a younger brother. 'But you need not apologise. It's not your fault, Matthew. But how much easier all this would be if you had been born before Gerald. Forgive me. I know he is your brother and that you are fond of him in your own way—but I have to say that he is the most unpleasant man I have ever come across.'

As she climbed the stairs to go in search of her grandmother, if she had looked back she would have seen, through the open door of the drawing room, that Gerald's face was no longer mocking, but had become purposeful. It was the face of a man who has been struck a hard blow—and whose mind was already reorganising and planning what steps to take next. He was determined to obtain Atwood Mine, which was a sure and continuous source of wealth, ensuring that once he had settled his loan from the moneylenders, who were becoming aggressively persistent, he could live in the lap of luxury for at least fifteen years—and the only thing he had to do to obtain it was to prevent a marriage from taking place between Eve and Marcus Fitzalan.

Eve felt as if the breath had been knocked out of her after her meeting with Gerald. She went to her own room to compose herself before presenting herself to her grandmother, extremely disturbed by what Gerald had told her about Marcus and Angela. But it was a lie. It had to be a lie concocted by Gerald with no other reason than to stop her marrying Marcus and therefore prevent him from obtaining Atwood Mine.

It did not surprise her that women would find Marcus attractive. Who would not? He was so strikingly handsome. To her cost, she already knew Angela was potential trouble. She was beautiful, in a provocative sense, voluptuous and alluring—hardly the kind of woman any woman would like to find interested in the man she was to marry.

But Marcus had denied there was anything of a romantic nature between them, and she had believed him; having learned to trust him after getting to know him better, she knew him to be a man of truth and integrity, and that the use of any form of deception was beneath him.

But she recalled Angela's past trickery and the barely concealed challenge she had seen in her eyes at Brooklands, and the possessive manner with which she had clung to Marcus's arm when they had left the garden together. She also recalled the intimacy of the scene, the familiarity they had shown towards each other. If she had not known that Angela was aware of her watching them together from the terrace and had characteristically played on this—and if Marcus had not told her he had come out into the garden in search of her and to his disappointment had found Angela there instead—she would have reason to believe there just might be some element of truth in what Gerald had told her.

The house became a hive of industrious activity as rooms were got ready and the kitchen worked at full stretch to prepare food for Gerald's guests and accompanying servants. Knowing full well the sort of people they would be, for Gerald was not the type of person who would keep the company of anyone who did not share his own enthusiasm for high living, Eve was determined to keep a low profile during the visit.

The guests arrived in a succession of fine carriages, the wide driveway in front of the house a picture of gaiety and confusion as they alighted. They were flamboyant and colourful, a dozen in all, three of the gentlemen having brought their wives, who, to Eve's mind, were rather giddy, empty-headed creatures, with whom she had very little in common.

Gerald's friends could not be accused of being dull or dowdy, and she was quite certain her mother and father would not have approved. They belonged to London's social world, which Gerald enjoyed to excess. Having seen many like them on her trips to London, it took Eve no more than a quick glance to see that they were a raucous, disreputable bunch and completely superficial.

They were to stay a week before travelling on to Harrogate to partake of someone else's hospitality. Like Gerald, the gentlemen suffered from a surfeit of idleness. When they grew tired of London they visited friends in the provinces, expecting them to provide a multitude of diversions, with a continuous play of variety and amusement.

Eve made a great impression on them all—despite being

unable to say the same for them. The gentlemen looked at her with undisguised admiration, although there was something insolent and insulting in the way their eyes openly devoured her—especially one gentleman called Timothy Harding, who had a long, prominent nose and deep-set blue eyes. He was nearing thirty and his head and body seemed too large for his spindly legs. He made a great deal of being introduced to her, bowing and almost slobbering over her small hand, seeming not to notice how she flinched when his lips touched her fingers.

'This is a long-awaited pleasure, Miss Somerville,' he said in a curiously falsetto voice, which seemed incongruous to his heavy features. 'Gerald has told us so much about you and I am pleased to see his praise has not been exaggerated. I compliment you on your magnificent house. Gerald is indeed fortunate in his inheritance.'

'Thank you,' she said coolly, her eyes sweeping critically over his person, finding him extremely distasteful and becoming eager to make her escape, 'although Burntwood Hall is no longer my home. However, I am sure it will give Gerald great pleasure to show you around later.'

'I would much rather see it with you,' he said, smiling lewdly to reveal yellowing teeth, his voice low with seduction.

Eve winced, sharply indignant at his sheer effrontery. However, she forced herself to smile sweetly. 'I'm sure you would, but unfortunately I shall be otherwise engaged.'

When they had been shown into the drawing room and were taking refreshment, she left them to return to her grandmother, taking every eye with her as she swept out of the room. She paused as one paralysed outside the door on hearing one of the gentlemen make an unpleasant remark. Her body went tense, for it had to be herself they were talking about.

'My God—pretty little piece, isn't she?' Timothy Harding remarked. 'Plucky, too. Good thing you can't read my mind.'

'Maybe not,' said Gerald drolly, 'but you have a distorted

mind, Timothy, and, knowing you have the manners and behaviour of a sewer rat, I can well imagine.'

'Sight too prim and proper for me,' said another unattached gentleman called David Blenkinsop.

'You lucky devil, Gerald. You always did have a penchant for beautiful women. Does she come with your inheritance?'

Eve heard Gerald laugh lightly with salacious undertones.

'You've got the wrong idea about her, Timothy. David was nearer the truth. Unlike the women you usually keep company with, she will not be tempted by the lure of flattery—to the regret of every red-blooded male in the West Riding.'

'My suspicion tells me she can be a spitfire when roused—still waters and all that. I have a fancy to ask her for an assignation. You won't be offended, will you, Gerald?' Timothy persisted. 'What I'd give to possess *her* maidenhead. And you can't complain, old boy. I have it on good authority you were lying with my latest whore while you were in London recently. Unless you have a mind to lie with Miss Somerville yourself?'

Gerald laughed, and there was something horrible and malicious in its tone, but he was not to be so obliging to his friend. 'There is a difference. Miss Somerville is not a whore, Timothy, and I would be obliged if you would keep your hands off her. I have my own plans for little Miss Somerville.'

This light-hearted conversation caused much amusement among them all, but Eve did not find being the object of such callous and open discussion at all amusing. They might be aristocrats, but there was nothing distinguished about their behaviour. Their very crudeness offended her. With her cheeks burning with anger and indignation she went to her room.

Gerald's guests spent the next two days riding, fishing and shooting on the estate, taking advantage of all that was offered. Eve painstakingly avoided them, but she could not ignore them, and after much persuasion she did partake in the occasional game of cards after dinner.

On the third day it rained, forcing everyone to remain in-

doors. Tired of keeping to her room or keeping her grandmother company, Eve went downstairs to find a book to read
in the library. Familiar feminine laughter greeted her when she
reached the hall; peering into the drawing room, her stomach
plummeted on seeing Angela, her gold taffeta skirts rustling
like a gentle breeze as she swept among the company strewn
lazily about the room, pleased by the interest she had aroused
in the form of open admiration in the men and envy in the
plainer-looking ladies.

She was arrestingly beautiful, but her eyes became as hard
and ruthless as a cat's watching a mouse before it pounces as
she observed Eve from across the room, her gaze passing over
her with a sliding contempt.

Eve merely inclined her head politely in greeting, having
realised that because of her close friendship with Gerald
Angela was bound to turn up at Burntwood Hall sooner or
later, but having no wish to stay and have to speak to her she
turned and went into the library adjacent to the drawing room.
She was about to pick a book off the shelves and browse
through it, but at that moment Angela entered, leaving the door
slightly ajar behind her.

The two stood gazing at each other for a moment in silence
and then Angela gave Eve a smug, superior smile, her eyes
resting on her with a deadly coldness, but, unfazed, Eve sighed
and moved towards the window, knowing she hadn't come to
reconcile their differences.

'Please do not insult me with simpering compliments and
insincere smiles, Angela. If it won't pain you too much I
would be obliged if you would tell me why you have followed
me in here. I do not think you can have anything to say to me
that I want to listen to—unless, of course, it is to offer an
apology for your diabolical conduct towards me, which, I
might tell you, is three years too late.'

Angela's eyes glittered, growing steady with anger, taking
in every detail of Eve's face and perfect figure with a rage
born of jealousy. 'No, it won't pain me to tell you why I have

followed you in here, Eve—and it is not to offer you an apology since I do not consider I have anything to apologise for. Despite what happened between you and Marcus on the day of Atwood Fair, Leslie would have married me in the end. It is just that I should hate to see you get hurt a second time and thought to offer you a word of advice before you make a fool of yourself yet again.'

Eve's eyes opened wide in mock surprise. 'Excuse me if I seem surprised, Angela, but consideration for my well-being coming from you takes some believing. What are you talking about?'

Angela's lips curled. 'You know what I am talking about.'

Eve gave a delicate lift to her eyebrows. Her pride rose, ready to do combat. 'I'm afraid not. Please—enlighten me.'

'I hear you are to marry Marcus Fitzalan.'

'Yes. But I cannot for the life of me think what that has to do with you—unless, of course, you wish to congratulate me.'

'That I will never do. I've told you. I am here to try and stop you making a fool of yourself.'

Eve looked at her with distaste, wondering how she had ever been so stupid as to consider this malicious, vituperative woman her friend.

'And how am I likely to do that?'

Her hazel eyes gleaming with calculated malice, Angela studied her with unhidden scorn, and when she spoke her voice was low and intense. 'I think I know Marcus better than you do. How will you endure it being married to him, knowing it is me he loves—me he will always love?'

Eve raised her eyebrows in mock surprise. 'Love! You must know him well, Angela?'

'Yes. We became friends in London—*good friends*,' she informed her, placing strong emphasis on the last two words. 'Here—look at this,' she said, holding her fan out to her, a beautiful pale blue and silver fan inlaid with diamonds, which told Eve it was extremely valuable. 'This was Marcus's most recent gift. He gave it to me on my birthday—one of several

gifts he bought me over the months since we were first introduced. He is always so thoughtful—so generous.'

Swallowing painfully Eve blanched, becoming prey to a
gnawing uncertainty. Her heart wrenched. Oh, did ever a fool
greater than herself draw breath, she chided herself, with anger
and admonishment at her own stupidity. Angela had mali-
ciously and wantonly deceived and betrayed her in the past
by destroying any hope of happiness she might have had with
Leslie—and, after doing it once, who was to say she would
not do so a second time? Had she been duped yet again? She
stared at the fan, unable to believe that such a little thing as
this could be about to change her whole life.

'How do I know he gave you this?'

'Because he had it inscribed. See,' Angela said smugly,
opening it and showing her the inscription.

The inscription was simple and Eve read 'With all my love.
Happy Birthday. Marcus', but it left Eve in no doubt that
Marcus had given it to her. Eve looked at her.

'You always were skilful at throwing fuel on the fire,
weren't you, Angela?'

Angela's face was transfigured with a fearful joy as she took
savage pleasure in flinging searing hurtful words in the teeth
of her rival. Everything she uttered was calculated to provoke
Eve's anger to greater heights, an anger she fondly hoped
would provoke her into changing her mind about marrying
Marcus.

'When I returned to the north he continued to see me. But
for you and that wretched mine, it is me he would be marrying.'

Eve was looking at her with a repugnant horror, wanting to
slap the sneering, triumphant smile from her lips, but she held
on to her control.

Angela moved menacingly closer, snapping the offending
fan shut, her whole body tense and purposeful. 'I know how
persuasive Marcus can be when there is something he wants—
and I do not doubt for one minute that he has used that same

persuasion on you to tempt you into marriage, convincing you it is you he wants. But he is considering marriage to you with the same dispassionate logic with which he approaches his business transactions—and with Atwood Mine to mark his decision it is all the more exciting and challenging for him. Do you imagine for one minute it is you he wants?'

'I don't know, Angela. You tell me. I am not practised in the subtle arts of conniving and scheming the way you are.' Eve's lips curled with scorn, but she was stung by Angela's remark, particularly since she now knew it to be true. 'But I think I please Marcus as well as you—although my methods may not be quite the same. Tell me, Angela—do you always have to have that which is mine? Perhaps it gives it a special value. I think you are trying to tell me not to marry Marcus— am I right?'

Clearly angry, Angela turned from her sharply and moved quickly towards the door. 'Think what you like,' she flung the words back over her shoulder, 'but take care, Eve,' she said, turning back to her, her eyes narrowed and gleaming viciously. 'You're not married yet and I mean to have him. I intend to be his wife and I will not let you stand in my way.'

'And what will you do to achieve that short of killing me?' demanded Eve.

Angela smiled thinly, a vicious glitter in her eyes. 'Oh, I'll think of something, you can be sure of that. I can be a mighty dangerous enemy if I choose.'

When she had gone Eve was trembling with anger and apprehension, more disturbed by their conversation than she cared to admit. Angela might be beautiful, but she was also as venomous as sin, a woman who would use her feminine wiles like a weapon, selfishly and ruthlessly, to gain her own ends.

She would be a fool to deny that Angela posed a threat, and yet she felt more threatened by Gerald. But she did not trust either of them and between them they were proving to be a lethal combination.

* * *

From a distance Eve observed Angela with Gerald the following day when she called, having travelled in the carriage from her parents' home in Little Bolton. When they looked at her and each other there were secrets in their eyes, and she knew neither of them would have any compunction in destroying her.

Having seen the fan which Marcus had given Angela, having it flaunted before her very eyes, had upset her more than she realised, bringing tears of misery and disappointment to her eyes. She swallowed against the constriction in her throat and her heart twisted with pain as resentment against Angela tore through her, fighting with her rage and her jealousy. Just when she thought she and Marcus were becoming close, by knowing this, he had been removed to a great distance.

In the beginning, because their marriage was to be one of convenience, when emotions were not involved, she might have turned a blind eye to his transgressions—but even then she would have wanted it to be anyone rather than Angela he was involved with. Oh, yes, he would marry her, but he would never love her, not as she loved him, which, after looking into her heart and examining her thoughts and feelings, she had come to realise with astounding clarity—but he must never know.

Love had crept up on her—she had admitted as much to Emma. Her feelings and emotions when she was with Marcus were always so confused that she hadn't realised what was happening to her, and now it was too late. But she must never give in to her feelings—to the hopes and sentiments she had cherished and indulged since her visit to Brooklands. Ever since he had kissed her three years ago, no other man had been able to stir her heart the way he had—to anger and passion and every emotion known to man, which was the reason why she had lived in self-imposed isolation since.

It was ironic to know she was in love with a man she had unwillingly accepted to be her husband, and it would be no easy matter knowing that while he was marrying her he was thinking of someone else.

But, she thought bitterly, she knew the score, that she would not have his full attention. That would be elsewhere. She would be entering into the marriage with her eyes wide open, knowing what to expect, so why should she feel so disappointed and let down? If she went ahead knowing this, it was a situation she would have to learn to live with and make the best of.

Chapter Eleven

Later, just before everyone retired for the night, several of the gentlemen, having imbibed too much liquor, were behaving in a rowdy and unruly fashion. Returning from her grandmother's room where she had been to bid her goodnight, Eve encountered Gerald in the shadows on the top of the stairs, watching her. She had to pass him, and as she moved closer she saw there was something in his eyes which made her throat tighten and a thrill of fear to course through her veins.

It was plain that he had been drinking heavily but his gait was not unsteady. His eyes shone with an unusual glassy brilliance and his hair fell dishevelled over his forehead. His cravat was unfastened and hung untidily, and his white crumpled shirt was stained with wine and flopped open to reveal the upper part of his chest. He was terrifying when he was like this, his sneering, his sarcasm more cutting, more cruel, more precise. She was about to turn and go back to her room, but his voice halted her and he sauntered to where she stood.

'Where are you going?' he asked, his voice low, menacing.

'To my room,' she said, trying to still her wildly beating heart.

His hand shot out and gripped her arm as she was about to move away, which she tried to pull from his grasp, but without success.

'Will you not join us downstairs in a nightcap before you do? My friends—especially Timothy—are most offended that you have not allowed them to become better acquainted with you during their visit.'

Eve glared at him. 'If they are offended then they have only themselves to blame. Had they behaved more like gentlemen I might have been more amenable towards them. You're drunk. All of you. Now please let me go. Don't touch me, Gerald.'

'Why—it is not the first time you have been touched,' he drawled, undiscouraged by her anger. Bringing his evil, smiling face close to hers, his lust-filled eyes held a frightening glitter and travelled insolently over her body. Instinctively Eve tried to break free but he held her harder, hurting her. His other hand reached up and gripped her chin relentlessly, and he pulled her close, holding her captive body firmly against his. His breath was warm on her face, the heavy fumes of spirits making her stomach heave.

'I know a great deal about you, more than you think—about what happened between you and Marcus Fitzalan at Atwood Fair. How you threw yourself at him—and how it went a good deal further than a kiss, which he duped your father into believing was all that happened between you.'

'And I do not have to guess who told you this. Could it be Angela, I wonder?' She struggled within his grasp. 'Let me go, Gerald. Release me this instant.'

'And if I don't? What will you do?'

'I will see that Marcus hears of this.'

'But he is not here now to save you, is he?' said Gerald, who would not allow the close proximity of Marcus Fitzalan to deter his interest in Eve. 'And how do you think he will react when he realises I have dared lay hands on what he intends to be his? Somehow I do not think he will care about that, providing you bring him that which is dearer to his heart than any woman—Atwood Mine. So, if you thought to rekindle the liaison which took place between you three years ago—don't hold out too many hopes.'

'And isn't that the most important thing to you, also?'

'Yes. I admit it freely. But you would come as an added bonus. You attract me—your very resistance excites me to distraction.'

'If that is meant to be a compliment, then please save your breath. I hold you in contempt.'

'I care nothing for your opinion of me. I could break you if I so desired.' He laughed harshly, his eyes dilated and blood-shot as he thrust his face closer. 'What a firebrand you are. I'll conquer you—and the harder you fight the sweeter will be the ultimate pleasure. One day I shall have you at my mercy. I swear I shall.'

'Never. You will have to kill me first.'

'That I shall do, if necessary—especially if you do not heed my warning and call off your wedding to Marcus Fitzalan. I mean to have Atwood Mine, Eve, and I shall go to any lengths to do so.'

Eve was rendered speechless by the content of his words and listened with horror to the implication. His arms became slack and she thrust herself away, turning from him and going blindly back to her room, locking the door in her terror that he would come after her, shivering with a revulsion that rocked her whole body, her breath coming brokenly between her lips, unable to think of anything other than the man who had brought her to this state of weakness, a man whom she hated and feared.

That night she slept badly, nervously, her subconscious un-usually active. She no longer felt safe at Burntwood Hall, but she had no choice but to endure the crisis until it went away. Gerald had threatened her, but she had no reason to believe he would make good his threats as long as she kept her dis-tance.

But shortly after midnight a sudden sense of suffocating

danger brought her to a trembling awareness that something was about to happen when she heard a step outside her room. Moonlight streamed in through the half-open drapes and, rising, she went quickly to the door and stood there listening, straining her ears in the pregnant, terrifying silence that gripped the house, and then, starting with terror, she saw the handle slowly begin to turn. If she had not had the presence of mind to lock her door it would have opened—and she could not bear to dwell on what might have happened then.

She stood there, her heart thumping so badly she had to fight the inexplicable impulse to scream, certain that it was Gerald, and equally certain she could hear him breathing behind the door. Trembling violently, she did not move until she heard his footsteps die away. It was a long time before she crawled back to bed, taking long, steadying breaths to bring herself under control. Pulling the covers up under her chin, not even their soft warmth could still the chill in her trembling limbs, and try as she might, she could not sleep.

Staring blankly into the dark, her mind would give her no peace. It was in turmoil as she tried to forget about Gerald and think rationally about her relationship with Marcus. The problem Angela had presented her with would not go away. It was distasteful, which she would rather not confront, but she had no choice. She had truly wanted to make her ill-fated marriage to Marcus work, but with cold logic she knew she must reflect on her options yet again in the light of the problem Angela had presented her with, since she did not believe she would be able to deal with having a reluctant husband with equanimity.

Could she live with a man who was in love with another woman? she asked herself. No, she thought decisively, not even to hold on to Atwood Mine. Every time she looked into his eyes she would see him with Angela and torture herself when she imagined what they did together, what they talked about. But how could she bear to part from him now, loving him as she did? It would be like tearing the heart out of her breast, a heart on which he had put his hands and would never let go.

Suddenly she saw all her hopes and dreams begin to disintegrate before her eyes. An agonising, overwhelming awareness of what she must do brought a sudden deadening of her mind, a mind in which ardour and love for the man her father had wanted her to marry had been born, despite her antagonism towards him at the beginning. He was a man in possession of a steel-tempered strength, a man with an indomitable will who could not be manipulated, who had moved in on her, catching, twisting and moulding her into the shape of the woman he wanted his wife to be.

And now she was going to have to match his steel-tempered strength and prepare herself to face and absorb his anger when she told him she could not marry him, knowing his rage would be unconquerable when he discovered he was to be denied access to what had once been his family's dearest possession—Atwood Mine.

Having made her decision she felt empty and drained of life. Turning and burying her face in the pillow she wept hard, weeping until there were no more tears left in her.

When Marcus rode over to Burntwood Hall the afternoon after Gerald's assault on Eve, which had left her shaken and acutely afraid for her safety, he was surprised to see so much activity—and he was both horrified and alarmed for Eve's well-being when he saw Gerald had arrived to take up residence sooner than anyone had expected.

The large assembly of visitors had spent the morning riding about the estate and had just consumed a heavy luncheon when he was admitted to the house. They all turned simultaneously and watched as he walked purposefully into the centre of the room, his eye sweeping over them with disdain. He was coolly polite to Gerald, who regarded him with studied indifference, and he curtly acknowledged his disreputable bunch of friends before going out into the garden, where, on enquiring of one of the servants, he was told Eve could be found.

On seeing her he paused for a moment, his eyes held by her pale, graceful figure as she walked aimlessly along the paths in the formal garden that stretched down to a low stone wall, giving way to open fields and copses beyond. Her figure was slightly stooped and she looked so young, still very much a girl, her modest apparel and demure manner showing no resemblance to the fiery young woman he had encountered at the Parkinsons just a few days earlier.

He advanced towards her calmly, supremely unaware of the tumult raging within her breast or the clouds of apprehension hanging heavy on her shoulders. Beset by fear she was still deeply shaken by Gerald's violent assault of the previous evening, and certain he had been the one who had come to her room later.

Tired and bewildered, having fallen into a black hole of despondency and desolation that was so deep she felt she would never be able to clamber out and, having reached the painful decision that she could no longer consider herself betrothed to Marcus, sensing someone behind her she whirled round like a frightened rabbit.

A lock of hair had fallen over her face, and Marcus noticed how her hand trembled slightly when she smoothed it hastily into place. He saw that her face was very pale, her eyes wide and dark with a look of fear.

'Oh—Marcus! You gave me a frightful turn,' she gasped, having sought the quiet of the garden to escape the lewd and lustful, menacing eyes of Gerald and his male guests.

'And since when have you been the nervous type?' he murmured softly. 'Since Gerald arrived at Burntwood Hall with his associates, I don't doubt,' he said in answer to his own question, his expression grave and serious and at the same time enquiring. 'Why did you not inform me of his arrival?'

'Why—I—I saw no need,' she answered hesitantly, avoiding his direct, penetrating gaze, forcing herself to try and speak naturally, while part of her brain was agitated by what she had to tell him, knowing it could not be put off.

'And his friends. They have lost no time in paying him a visit.'

'It is no longer up to me to say who can and cannot stay at Burntwood Hall,' she said sharply.

'I realise that.' He frowned. 'Are they giving you a difficult time?'

'Nothing I cannot handle,' she replied, with far more conviction than she felt in her attempt to convince him that everything was all right, refusing to give in to the attraction that was making her heart race and her legs go weak.

Unconvinced by her statement Marcus frowned deeply and anger flared in his eyes. 'Eve, you are telling me the truth—because if Gerald has threatened you in any way, by God—I'll—'

'No—no,' she said quickly, lowering her eyes to cover her confusion, afraid that if he looked too close he would see she was lying. But his concern for her well-being warmed her heart.

'Nevertheless, there is quite a gathering. How long do they intend staying?'

'A week, I think. This is their fourth day.'

'Then let us hope they are not so overwhelmed by Gerald's generous hospitality that they decide to increase their length of stay. I must say he is looking rather smug and pleased with himself.'

'He has good reason—considering.'

'How is your grandmother?'

'Quite well—but she refuses to venture from her rooms at present.'

'I cannot say that I blame her,' he said, slowly walking beside her along the narrow paths that meandered between the blooming flower beds. 'Eve—I want you and your grandmother to come to Brooklands. The reason for my invitation is obvious. Besides, my mother would love to have you.

Naturally, she is eager to get to know you better and to discuss the wedding.'

He spoke quietly, but hearing the sound of laughter coming from the open windows of the house, Eve had the impression that he was alert and tense. There was no mistaking that he was in earnest and she felt a warmth in her heart for his consideration, tempted to accept his offer and go and live at Brooklands—to turn to him for the safety and security she craved.

Yet at that moment her conversation with Angela and his gift to her was still painfully clear in her mind, and she felt he was more dangerous to her than Gerald. She must have the courage to tell him that she had decided not to marry him after all and put an end to the whole sorry situation. She would rather get it over and done with than put it off and have the dread of doing it another time.

'That is very amiable of you, Marcus—but I must refuse.'

Pausing, he took her shoulders in his hands and forced her to look at him, the sweet, wild essence of her vulnerability staring out of her eyes. She was acting strangely, and he sensed something was wrong, very wrong. If only she would tell him what it was.

'Eve—why will you not let me help you? I am not blind. I can see how things are here. Do you feel yourself to be in any danger from Gerald?'

His eyes were warm with consideration and his voice was gentle, which surprised her, because whenever they met their conversation was like a fencing match. Feeling close to tears by the hopelessness of her situation, she swallowed down a hard lump that had risen in her throat, shaking her head slowly. 'No,' she lied, feeling the danger all around her, but her heart refusing to credit it while she was with Marcus. With him she was not afraid, thinking it was all a figment of her imagination and that Gerald would not harm her.

'Then will you promise me one thing?'

'What is it?'

'That if you are threatened or feel in any kind of danger—you will come to me at Brooklands—or send me word? I will come immediately.'

Taking the bit between her teeth, unable to go on pretending any longer, she took a step back from him, her face becoming hard, her expression closed, her violet eyes fixed steadily on his. Never had she felt more wretched, for what she was about to do was the worst thing she had ever had to do in her life.

'You may not want me at Brooklands when I tell you what I have been meaning to tell you ever since your arrival.'

He looked at her, his face impassive as he waited for her to continue. He did not have too much difficulty reading her expression and he could see her features were tense with some kind of emotional struggle.

'Marcus—I—I have decided not to marry you after all.'

His face changed as her words and their implication hit him, but if he was startled by her statement he did not show it. His eyes became fixed to her face and gleamed like molten fire. 'And may I ask what has brought about this decision?'

'I simply cannot go through with it. I have decided to go and live in Cumbria with my grandmother after all.'

Marcus's expression became pale with anger, which gradually became visible in every feature. He did not speak as he turned away from her, straight and proud, and Eve could almost feel the effort he was exerting to keep his anger under control.

'I see,' he said at length, turning suddenly to face her, with violence, on the verge of losing the struggle within himself. His pale blue eyes had gone hard between the narrowed lids, his face like granite, and he spoke with chill precision.

'And have you no sense of obligation—to me as well as to your father? We made a bargain, if you remember, and I fully intended keeping my side of that bargain.'

'Then I apologise for any inconvenience I may have caused you,' she said, trying to maintain the frozen stillness that held her in its grip. 'I know you will hate me for this, if you do not already, and I cannot blame you, but in all conscience I cannot marry you.'

'And the mine?'

'This is me I am talking about—not the mine,' she said quietly. 'The mine no longer seems important to me. I won't marry you, Marcus. I can't.'

There was so much finality in those two simple words that Marcus was momentarily at a loss to know what to say. He looked at her, thinking of arguments that might move her to reconsider. But he could see by the implacable set of her chin and the way her face was set against him, that this was not a decision she had taken lightly and he must respect that. But something had happened, something she was not telling him, and he strongly suspected it had something to do with Gerald's arrival.

His face hardened into an expressionless mask, his eyes probing hers like dagger thrusts, searching for answers as to why she was doing this. 'Don't you think you owe me an explanation?' he said tightly. 'Can't you tell me why, all of a sudden, I have become repugnant to you?'

'You—you haven't.'

'No? Then do you know what a man thinks when the woman he is betrothed to suddenly backs out of the agreement?'

Eve shook her head, quaking in front of his granite features.

'That perhaps there is someone else who has taken his place in her affections—if he was ever there in the first place,' he said with biting scorn. 'Who is it? Is it Gerald—or one of his dandified friends who has caught your eye?'

'Please, credit me with a little more taste. There is no one—and I have given you no reason to accuse me so abominably,' she flared, wanting to ask him about Angela, to beg him to tell her that what she had said were all lies, that he had never bought her gifts, and that nothing had ever happened between them—but her pride, and fearing he would confirm what Angela had so smugly told her was true, prevented her from doing so. Unable to look into his burning eyes she lowered her gaze, tears clogging in her throat. He might be a philanderer, but her heart refused to let go of the burning love it carried. 'I—I think you should leave.'

'No. I will not leave until this is settled between us.'

'It is settled. I am sorry. There is nothing else I can say.'

She tried to walk past him but his hand reached out and stopped her.

'Damn you—you cannot do this.'

'Yes, I can,' she replied wretchedly, trying not to look at him, at his blazing eyes. He was too powerful, too close and far too masculine. She was fighting tears, struggling to keep her voice under control, longing for him to take her in his arms, to feel his mouth on hers, setting her body on fire. But the image of Angela, with her sly, insolent smile, stood between them.

Their attention was caught by the clattering sound of horses' hooves and carriage wheels in the drive. Glancing towards it, Eve saw an elegant carriage drawn by a pair of sprightly white horses. It pulled up in front of the house and the lone occupant stepped out. Even from that distance she recognised Angela. As if recovering from a shock she experienced a fierce stab of jealousy and a coldness swept over her as she watched her walk towards the house, the sunlight catching the shining blue folds of her dress. She averted her face, having no wish to become embroiled in another argument with her.

'You have another guest, it seems,' said Marcus, with little interest, failing to recognise the carriage or its occupant, annoyed that it had arrived at that moment, diverting Eve's attention.

'No. It is Angela Stephenson,' she said with a brittle sound to her voice, her eyes glittering with hate. 'What an opportune moment for her to arrive. It is Gerald she has come to see— but I am sure she will be highly delighted to see you, and being aware of your interest for passionate affairs, Marcus, your delight will be just as great—and her presence will no doubt help soften the blow I have just dealt you,' she retorted with biting sarcasm, causing him to look at her sharply. Her anger on seeing Angela had revived her spirit. 'Please, excuse me,' she said quickly, her expression clouded, as though she were a thousand miles away. 'I must go and see if my grandmother is in need of anything.'

She turned from him but Marcus reached out and gripped her arm, moving closer, his mouth tightening as he stared at her gently heaving bosom and the tantalising mouth, determined not to let the matter end like this. He towered over her, his face dark and threatening, his overpowering physical presence and his intention catching Eve off guard. 'Before you go, tell me that this is what you really want—for our ways to part—never to see each other again?' he said, his voice softened to almost a whisper as he lowered his face to hers.

'Yes, it is,' she replied, her heart beginning to beat frantically as she tried avoiding his penetrating eyes.

'Then dare to look me in the eye and tell me,' he demanded, looking at her, the sunlight bathing her in light, her heavy mass of black hair surrounding her pale face accentuating its almost transparent whiteness.

'Yes,' she said at last, reluctantly. 'It is what I want.'

'And tell me that you don't want me to touch you, to kiss you. Despite the fact that you were raised to exhibit restraint and behave with proper decorum as befits a lady, I know how easy it is to make you forget all that, to make you behave with such wanton abandon.'

Before Eve, who was quite unprepared, could protest Marcus had hauled her against his chest, his hands unyielding as his mouth swooped down on hers. A fierce, silent, merciless struggle went on inside Eve as she fought to free herself, but Marcus was in full possession of his strength and she felt herself weakening slowly, knowing she could not hold out against him as a blaze of excitement leapt through her, her reaction a purely primitive one.

Avidly, like a man starving, Marcus crushed his lips over

hers, a kiss that devoured them, setting them both aflame, and he felt her trembling with innocence and helpless surrender against him, the heat from her scented body acting like a drug to his senses. He tasted her sweet breath, as her mouth responded, opening against his, and with a long, shuddering sigh their bodies became fused together as he determinedly pursued his course of sensual persuasion.

Eve could feel the heat and vibrancy of his body, with every sinew pressed against hers. She couldn't breathe and felt herself going soft, unable to resist temptation, forgetting everything as his hand left her waist to cup the gentle fullness of her breast, before rising and caressing the back of her neck, sweeping her whole body in one long, shuddering caress.

As quickly as Marcus had swept her into his arms just as quickly did he release her, thrusting her away from him with an abruptness that left her senses reeling. After their intimate contact he felt fire streaking through his loins and was almost overwhelmed with a mixture of pain and pleasure, finding her slender, supple young body more than capable of arousing him. His strategic attempt to weaken her into submission had rebounded with a vengeance. He had only succeeded in driving himself almost insane as he came close to losing the battle for control.

Wide-eyed and trembling with vulnerability Eve stared at him, so breathtakingly lovely he was almost blinded by the sight of her. Making a fierce effort to dominate and restrain himself his expression was grim, his eyebrows drawn together in anger as he glared at her, wanting her with a fierceness that left him breathless.

Dumbfounded, Eve stood there looking at him, shock holding her motionless. How weak she seemed suddenly, how helpless before him. She had not meant this to happen. It had only resulted in complicating matters further, making her love him all the more and regretting the decision she had made.

'I apologise for my barbaric behaviour, but when you remember during your long, lonely nights how it felt to have me hold you—to kiss you—and how willing your body was to respond, your desire will be sharpened with remorse. You may deny me until you are blue in the face, but the speed with which your body is aroused whenever I touch you proclaims stronger than any words how much you want to be with me.'

Helplessly Eve stared at him, her cheeks flushed and her lips soft and trembling, feeling an unfulfilled need inside her that made it impossible for her to deny that what he said was true.

'This is not the end, Eve,' Marcus went on, his voice low and soft in the silence that surrounded them. 'When you have calmed down we will discuss this further. You cannot put me from your life so easily. I shall not allow you to.'

'You must,' she whispered, her voice quivering slightly as she tried to bring her body under control. 'I have made up my mind. Please do not make it more difficult for me than it is already. There is nothing more to be said. Goodbye, Marcus.'

Dragging herself away she ran from him, entering the house through a side entrance, not wishing to come face to face with Angela. She was glad to escape Marcus's presence, glad she had told him, wanting nothing more at that moment than to soothe her head and compose her nerves that were in shreds after her meeting with him and the savagery of his kiss.

Marcus watched her go, bewildered and angry, trying to fathom out the reason for her change of heart; the only thing he could think of was that she had become infatuated by some-one else. Despite her denial it was the only thing that made sense, but if this were the case then he doubted she would have yielded to his embrace quite so willingly. But when he thought this might indeed be so, he was unprepared for the searing pain of jealousy and hurt that overwhelmed him, which was beyond anything he had imagined existed.

In tight-lipped, rigid silence, biting back his fury and clamping his teeth together, he glared after her, tempted to go after her and demand an explanation to give him a chance to defend himself, but deciding against it. Setting his jaw he turned on his heel and stalked away. He'd be damned if he would plead with her further.

He intended to leave at once, knowing there was no longer any reason to remain, until he saw Angela walking towards him.

On reaching her room Eve swilled her burning cheeks with cold water, knowing Angela would have sought him out. Looking out of the window, which faced the gardens where she had left Marcus, she saw to her dismay that Angela had indeed found him and sauntered by his side.

Eve felt the world tremble beneath her and hot anger sear through her as she watched them together. Marcus gave the impression that nothing untoward had happened, seeming friendly towards Angela, gracious as he bowed his head and listened to what she had to say, considerately holding her arm when they descended a short flight of steps to prevent her from falling. With lingering looks—always a professional when it came to coquetry—Angela gazed up at him from beneath half-closed lids, laughter bubbling to her smiling lips at something he said.

Eve's grandmother was shocked and deeply disappointed by Eve's decision not to marry Marcus.

'You cannot mean this, Eve,' she said in disbelief.

'Yes, I do, Grandmother. I cannot marry him. I have told him so and there is an end to the matter.'

'How can it be an end? Too much is at stake.'

'No. Only Atwood Mine. As far as I am concerned Gerald can have it.'

'I can well imagine the extent of Mr Fitzalan's anger when you told him of this.'

'Yes, but his disappointment stems from losing the mine, not from any sentiments he might feel for myself. I was merely a means to an end, that is all—and I will not be a party to this any longer. I believe I have acted in a manner which will constitute my future happiness.'

Unconvinced, her grandmother looked at her closely, curious to know what had brought all this about. Her shrewd eyes observed her trembling lips and scanned the angry young face, seeing hurt and anguish mirrored in her lovely eyes.

'And might I ask what has happened to bring about this change of heart? I thought you and Mr Fitzalan were getting on rather well.'

'I thought so too. But it would seem Marcus has deceived us both. He has used me ill,' she said fiercely. 'He has been indulging in an affair with a woman I once deemed to call my friend, for some considerable time—a woman he would have married were it not for my father's will. The affair continues and will do so after we are married. I cannot accept that—and how do I know that if he tires of her he wouldn't soon be off on his next pursuit?

'Knowing your views on marriage, Grandmother, you probably think I am being very silly and foolish. But how dare he treat me so abominably? I will not be humiliated. I will not marry him simply to oblige my father, Marcus or you.'

'And has he told you he is in love with this other woman?'

'No. And he is not likely to. But I know it to be true. The woman in question has told me so herself—and so has Gerald.'

'I would take little notice of what he has to say, Eve, but it is evident you believe them—without giving Mr Fitzalan the chance to explain things to you himself. That's extremely harsh, don't you think?'

'Maybe. But I do believe them. I have every reason to after seeing them together with my own eyes, seen the beautiful gift he has given her—one of many, I was told. I will not be made a fool of.'

'I see. Then what can I say? I am deeply disappointed. I always thought Mr Fitzalan to be the one for you.'

Eve sighed. 'I'm sorry, Grandmother. Do not blame me for rejecting him.'

'I do not blame you. But what is to be done?'

'I shall return with you to Cumbria—if you will let me. And I would like to be out of this house as soon as possible. I cannot remain in it any longer now Gerald has arrived.'

'Very well. If you are resolved then we will not dwell on it. We will leave tomorrow—and I have to say I shall not be sorry to see the back of Gerald myself.'

Eve was desperately unhappy as she ordered her maid to begin packing her trunks for her departure for Cumbria. No matter how far away from Marcus she went, she would never forget him. Nothing would ever be the same again.

Chapter Twelve

On receiving a note from Eve informing her of her imminent departure, a stunned Emma came to say goodbye the following morning, believing Gerald to be the reason for her leaving.

'Oh, Eve!' she exclaimed on entering her room, staring in disbelief as her maid bustled about packing the trunks with her clothes and other possessions she was to take with her to Cumbria. 'Has Gerald made life so difficult for you that you have to leave? Well, you don't have to. You and your grandmother must come and stay with us until the wedding.'

'I cannot lie to you, Emma. Gerald is determined to obtain Atwood Mine and has issued savage threats against me concerning this. I have to admit that I am terrified and have reason to fear him—and it is one of the reasons why I am leaving Atwood.'

'Come and tell me,' said Emma, drawing her towards the bed where they sat facing each other. She was shocked to see how changed her friend was since the last time she had seen her on the day of the picnic. Then she had radiated vitality, but now her face was stricken and as white as the lace collar at her throat, and her dark circled eyes looked very tired.

'I am going to Cumbria with my grandmother.'

'But you can't. You are to be married in little more than two weeks. There is so much to do in preparation.'

'I won't be getting married, Emma,' Eve said quietly.

'But why? What has happened?'

'I am not marrying Marcus. I—I cannot.'

Seeing how distraught Eve was, Emma took her cold hand in her own. 'Tell me what's wrong. It's not just Gerald and his threats, is it? I can see that something else is wrong. Has something happened to Mr Fitzalan—is that it?' she asked, alarm entering her voice when she thought this might be the reason.

Eve shook her head sadly, haltingly relating the conversation she had had with Angela. Emma listened in stunned disbelief.

'I do not know when I have been more shocked,' she said when Eve fell silent. 'It is almost beyond belief that she would do it to you again. Who would think that so much wickedness could exist in one woman? And you believed her? Oh, Eve. We both know what Angela is capable of, but I strongly suspect she is just jealous of your relationship with Mr Fitzalan. If you run off to Cumbria now she will have triumphed over you yet again.'

'I have seen the proof of his affection for her, Em,' she said quietly.

'What kind of proof?'

'A fan, which Angela said was a gift from him. It was beautiful—pale blue and silver, and inlaid with diamonds. It was inscribed most lovingly, Em, and I saw his name with my own eyes. What more damning evidence could I have than that?'

Emma was shocked to hear this but, being acquainted with Angela's cunning and conniving ways, she was not utterly convinced and still thought Eve should give Marcus the benefit of the doubt.

Eve sighed, shaking her head in utter dejection. 'Oh, Em, I don't know anything any more. I told you on the day of the picnic that when they were together their behaviour was suspicious, leading me to believe their relationship was closer than that of mere acquaintance.'

'But you told me Mr Fitzalan denied it.'

'It is hardly something he would admit to. They have been very clever. I've been duped. Like Gerald, the mine is so important he will go to any lengths to obtain it.'

'It may not be as bad as it seems. Forgive me, Eve, but I cannot believe Mr Fitzalan would behave so dreadfully. In all fairness to him, you really ought to give him the benefit of the doubt until you have asked him outright as to the truth of it, instead of going off at half-cock.'

'I can't help it,' Eve said with angry confusion, trying desperately to keep her emotions under control. 'I could not bear to hear him lie to me again—but nor could I bear to hear him confirm what Angela told me to be the truth.'

'Then it is a dilemma that cannot be resolved unless you ask him outright. Do you intend to remain in ignorance?'

'Yes. I know the mine drew us together in the beginning, but Marcus has disappointed me. While he was paying court to me was it so very wrong of me to expect him to be faithful? Three years ago I was deeply hurt and humiliated by them both—equally. I will not go through all that again. I couldn't stand it, Em.'

Emma fell silent for a moment, studying her friend, touched by the grief she glimpsed there. She squeezed her hand in understanding, for what Eve said was true. She had been hurt, deeply. In fact it was a wonder she had managed to get over the indignities and ultimate heartbreak that had resulted from that silly, malicious challenge Angela had thrown down. It had been an affair in which Mr Fitzalan had been unfairly exonerated from all blame.

'As I recall, after confronting your father with his account of the affair—an account which I suspect did not cover the whole truth, otherwise he would not have been so lenient towards him and would have called him out and shot him at dawn—and after being absolved of any blame, he went directly to London for a considerable period of time. Maybe he would be more concerned and understanding if he knew that because of your encounter with him at Atwood Fair, it seriously damaged your reputation almost beyond recall. I doubt he has any idea how much you suffered because of it—or that it was contrived by Angela to secure Leslie Stephenson for herself.'

'Perhaps you're right. But you know, Em, my mother spent all the years of my life teaching me how to behave in a proper and ladylike manner, but I flouted all the rules. I should not have gone off alone with Marcus the way I did. After behaving so outrageously, I suppose my parents' anger and the harsh treatment I received from the people of Atwood was no less than I deserved.'

'Nevertheless, Mr Fitzalan cannot be acquitted of blame.'

'I don't exonerate him—at least, not entirely.'

Emma sighed, looking compassionately into the pale, pensive face of her friend. 'You love him very much, don't you, Eve?' she said quietly.

'Yes,' she whispered, blinking back her tears. 'I didn't realise just how much until today. But I stupidly forgot that his interests went no further than Atwood Mine. I am a fool to have let my feelings become involved—to dream dreams which have no foundation in reality.'

Gerald found it almost impossible to hide his jubilation when he knew Eve was to leave for Cumbria with her grandmother. After she had said goodbye to the servants, most of whom would be staying on at Burntwood Hall when she had gone, he managed to get her alone just before her departure.

'Running scared, Eve?' he taunted coldly.

'I do not run scared from you, Gerald.'

'Nevertheless, I am pleased to see you heeded my warning,' he said softly. 'Am I to take it that you are not to wed our illustrious neighbour after all?'

Eve looked at him with icy contempt, refusing to give him the satisfaction of knowing her decision. Let him speculate.

'Don't look so smug, Gerald. I am merely going to Cumbria for a short while. I have almost five months left in which to marry Mr Fitzalan, don't forget.'

And on that note Eve left Burntwood Hall, wondering if she would ever return.

On the journey to Cumbria with her grandmother, putting Gerald and his threats behind her, her spirits rose a little, but she was possessed of a curious apathy where Marcus was concerned. It had been hard for her to leave Burntwood Hall and Atwood, and her eyes were bleak with anguish, her heart numb with pain when she thought she might never see Marcus again. A man of his implacable character would never forgive her for the way she had rebuffed him. There would be no reconciliation, past differences forgotten.

It was the day after Eve had left for Cumbria with Lady Pemberton when Emma travelled to Brooklands to see Marcus. She could not have explained the impulse that made her act as she did, for she had no sympathy for him, considering him to be harsh, sardonic and pitiless. She only knew that she had to do something to help Eve.

She was not well acquainted with Marcus Fitzalan, only having spoken to him casually on the odd occasion. He was so formidable and excessively male, radiating a force and vitality that always made her feel shy and awkward when in his company. When she was shown into his presence she tried to focus her mind on how she had seen him at the picnic, because then he had not seemed quite so awe-inspiring as he had unashamedly amused the children; on doing so, her embarrassment and confusion began to fade.

On returning to Brooklands after leaving Burntwood Hall two days earlier, frustration was exploding inside Marcus as he tried to regain some semblance of control over his damaged pride and to marshal his scattered thoughts. He was both furious and confused by Eve's behaviour, craving an explanation to it all and having to suppress the urge to return and plead or persuade her to reconsider her decision, but his angry male pride prevented him from doing so.

Like a man possessed he threw himself into his busy work schedule to still his anger and frustration—anger that the mere thought of her left him throbbing for her like a lovesick youth. Only when night came did the terrible pain of her rejection, and what it would mean to his future to be without her, return, bringing with it an unthinkable, unbearable hurt.

At these times his mind gave way to long, slow thoughts of her, and he would dwell on how much she had come to mean to him, how much he had come to love her. He had known many women in the past—beautiful and amusing women, women he had loved and forgotten—but none of them touching his heart, not in the way Eve had done. It was as if his heart had been reserved for her and her alone, and even though she could drive him to the brink of anger and despair, nothing she could say or do would ever change that.

When Emma was shown into his study he rose from behind his desk, coming forward to offer her a seat, his face cold and indifferent and yet polite.

'Do sit down, Miss Parkinson. I have to say that I am surprised to see you here. Am I correct in thinking your visit is connected with Eve?'

'Yes,' she replied, sitting down while he remained standing. His tone was abrupt and stripped of compassion, and at any other time she would have turned and fled, for he bore no resemblance to the man who had amused her brother and sisters without restraint on the day of the picnic, but, nervous though she was, she faced him bravely. 'I—I came because I am worried about her. There are certain things I think you should know, Mr Fitzalan.'

'About Eve?'

'Yes.'

'Then why did she not come herself instead of sending her friend?' he asked sharply.

'She did not send me and would be extremely angry if she knew I had come here. However, I have to tell you that she has left Atwood and gone to Cumbria with her grandmother.'

Marcus froze, staring at her hard, and in that instant the austere control vanished from his sharp-edged, handsome face. Even though she had told him she would go with her grandmother to Cumbria, not for one moment had he believed she would leave, and not so soon. Renewed anger and a curious sense of desolation washed over him as he tried to keep his feelings under control.

'I see. When?'

'Yesterday.'

'Then what is the purpose of your visit? What have you to tell me that she did not see fit to tell me herself?'

'Have you really no idea why she told you she could not marry you, Mr Fitzalan?' Emma asked quietly, wishing he would sit down since his sheer height and forcefulness made her feel intimidated.

'No. I assumed that with the arrival of Gerald and his friends one of them had caught her eye. It's the only thing that makes sense.'

'Then you do her a grave injustice, sir,' said Emma sharply, ready to spring to Eve's defence, unwilling to hear any wrong said about her. 'Ever since you took advantage of her innocence three years ago—almost ruining her reputation beyond repair, there has been no other man in her life—and—after this, I doubt there ever will be unless it can be put right.'

'Ruin?' Marcus's lips tightened, then he gave a half-angry laugh. 'Miss Parkinson—what are you talking about?'

'That because of a silly, stupid prank that went terribly wrong, Eve has suffered because of it ever since. What happened between you and Eve soon became common knowledge. Angela Stephenson saw to that. But when you left for London the following day, had you no conscience?' she dared to say accusingly, for she too had been angered by the indifference and inconsideration he had shown towards Eve at the time.

'She was just seventeen years old, Mr Fitzalan, and her future looked bleak. To avoid her becoming an object of derision her parents sent her to Cumbria to stay with her grandmother—but the people of Atwood neither forgave not forgot her indiscretion. As you know, Leslie Stephenson withdrew his suit and married Angela—just as she had contrived it.'

'That I do know—and I remember Eve telling me that the whole thing was devised by Angela, but I regret to say I thought little of it at the time. I did not believe her to be capable of such vindictiveness.'

'Forgive me, Mr Fitzalan, but there appears to be a great deal you do not know about Angela,' Emma said with harsh criticism. 'Do you know that Eve did not return to Atwood for several months and never saw her mother again? She died of consumption—but, being a friend of Sir John Somerville, you will know that,' she said, with a trace of irony to her soft voice. 'Can you imagine how Eve has tortured herself over this? She should have been there. Her mother needed her and should not have died without seeing her.

'Eve never got over it and blamed herself. This tragedy kindled the sympathies of the people of Atwood and they welcomed Eve back. But the harm was done. Apart from visiting her Aunt Shona in London and her grandmother in Cumbria, she remained at Burntwood Hall in self-imposed seclusion.'

Marcus was clearly extremely shocked to hear this. 'Dear Lord—I knew nothing of this.'

'Of course not. Netherley is five miles from Atwood—but it might just as well be fifty. Eve told me of your anger on finding out who she was. Perhaps you thought to teach her a lesson—and you did—a harsh lesson, Mr Fitzalan. A lesson she did not deserve. It's rather cruel, don't you think, that whereas you treated the affair so lightly—and that you were beyond reproach where her father was concerned—Eve was treated so severely?'

Marcus did not move. He was like a cold, marble statue. Emma's revelations tore through him like a white-hot blade of anguish, searing and burning, unaware that he had inflicted so much pain, so much torment on Eve. He'd had no idea how much she had suffered because of his callous treatment of her. Sir John had never given him any indication of her distress, and he had been too thoughtless and too busy with other matters to enquire.

There had been no emotional ties between himself and Eve, and he had pompously believed he had taught her a harsh lesson in life, his only remembrance being when he left her of how it had felt to hold her supple young body close to his own, and how she had kissed him with such tender passion. He could not think without flinching of the things he had said to her—a flirt, promiscuous, a doxy—and how he had treated her. He now knew her to be none of these things.

He was choked with remorse. His conduct had been both wicked and unforgivable, and there was little wonder she had been hostile towards him when they'd met again at her father's funeral. He'd deserved all of it.

Anger and rage at his own blind stupidity overwhelmed him. How could he have treated someone as pure and sweet as she was so dastardly? Being a young, inexperienced girl, she'd had no defences against life to protect her. She had been the innocent victim of a prank that had gone hopelessly wrong—that had inadvertently placed her in the path of a man who could only be described as a libertine. There was no excuse for his conduct that day. Being an experienced man of the world he should have known better.

'What can I say? At the time I could not have foreseen the profound effect the incident—not nearly so insignificant as I had imagined it to be—would have on Eve's life…or my own. I knew she had gone to Cumbria and that Leslie Stephenson had dropped his suit and married Angela—and that her mother had died—but I was absent at the time and did not hear of it until I returned. Believe me when I say I had no idea Eve was not with her. But I still do not understand why she left—why she rejected me. Unless it was out of revenge for what I did to her.'

'Eve is not vengeful, Mr Fitzalan. She changed her mind about marrying you when Angela told her the two of you were in love and having an affair. Gerald lost no time, either, in confirming this.'

'Naturally! He would be only too happy to encourage a relationship between Angela and myself—for it would be to his advantage,' Marcus said fiercely.

'Perhaps if she had not fallen in love with you herself—and had it been anyone other that Angela,' Emma said quietly, 'it would not have hurt so much. Being the type of person she is, she was too proud to ask if this was true, too afraid that you would confirm what Angela had told her—especially when Angela flaunted a fan, a gift from you to her, under Eve's nose.'

Marcus stared at her in genuine astonishment. 'But that's ridiculous. A fan, you say? A gift from me to her?'

'Yes.'

'But I never gave Angela a gift.'

'That was not what Angela told Eve. Apparently if was affectionately inscribed.'

Becoming thoughtful, Marcus shook his head slowly. 'The only fan I have given to anyone was to my mother two years ago on her birthday—a very fine one of blue and silver, inlaid with diamonds.'

Emma sighed, beginning to see all too clearly what Angela had tried to do. 'That sounds like the one.'

'Then I can only surmise that my mother lent it to Angela or her mother on some occasion and they failed to return it. Please believe me when I tell you that Angela means nothing to me and never has—and I told Eve this when she broached the matter to me only last week. I had hoped I'd convinced her, but it seems I was wrong.'

'You did at the time, but when confronted by Angela—and when she produced such damning evidence—you cannot blame Eve for doubting you. When Angela called to see her at Burntwood Hall a few days ago, and after hearing what she had to say, Eve was not wholly convinced you were telling the truth—and Angela can be very convincing, Mr Fitzalan.'

'And what has Eve done to her to make her so vindictive towards her?'

'She has done nothing. Angela is of an extremely jealous disposition and it was enough when they were children that Eve's family were rich and titled—that she was beautiful and popular with everyone she came into contact with—and that she attracted the attention of Leslie Stephenson, which ultimately played on Angela's jealousy. She begrudged his attentions towards Eve. Her scheme was designed to alienate his affections away from Eve in the hope that he would turn to her. She was determined to secure him for herself whether she wanted him or not—merely to spite Eve.'

'And my arrival at Atwood Fair that day provided her with an opportunity to shame her, to manipulate her into a situation that would embarrass her.'

'Yes. The challenge was that Eve had to succeed in getting you to dance with her in the hope that Leslie would see you together and become jealous and increase his desire to marry her. He had been dithering for weeks about asking her father's consent to marry her, and Angela convinced her it was just what he needed to sharpen him up. When you disappeared into the trees with her it was more than Angela could have hoped for. She soon found Leslie and made quite sure he saw the two of you together.'

Marcus sighed when she fell silent. 'And I know the rest.'

Emma nodded. 'Being friends of long standing, I was well acquainted with Angela and her ways. I knew perfectly well what she was up to and tried reasoning with her when Eve had gone, but in moments like those she is deaf and blind to everything save her own satisfaction and needs. And despite what Eve told you, Gerald was making her life extremely unpleasant for her at Burntwood Hall—in a way that only Gerald can.'

Marcus paled visibly. 'My God, I should have known. I should have insisted she came here to Brooklands. But when she rejected me so firmly, I have to admit that I was so furious that all thoughts of Gerald went out of my head. What did he do to her?'

'He did not touch her, if that is what you mean,' Emma said quickly, wanting to reassure him of that. 'Eve knows that Gerald hides a streak of savagery that gives her reason to fear him. His rages are rare but dangerous. He has made it absolutely clear to her that he will go to any lengths to obtain Atwood Mine, and the threatening quality of his behaviour has terrified her. She is dreadfully afraid that if she were to go ahead and marry you, before the wedding could take place Gerald would contrive for her to meet with some well-organised accident, taking care that suspicions do not fall on him.'

A cold anger gleamed in Marcus's eyes. 'He would not dare.'

'I think he would, and Eve is right to fear him. She is afraid of both Gerald and Angela, Mr Fitzalan. Gerald wants the mine—Angela wants you. Together they could be a force to be reckoned with—a deadly combination, don't you agree?'

'Indeed.'

'However, Angela may be jealous and vindictive, but I do not believe she would do Eve any physical harm.'

'But knowing how spirited Eve is, I am surprised she gave in to Gerald's threats so submissively.'

'She would not have done once, but her fear finally obliterated her courage.' Emma rose and moved to stand close to Marcus, her face serious, the worry she so clearly felt for Eve mirrored in her eyes as she looked with gravity into his. 'I have spent three years picking up the pieces of my closest friend, Mr Fitzalan—and just when I thought she was beginning to put all the heartache and unpleasantness behind her, it starts up again. I doubt she can take much more.'

'But why did she not ask me about Angela? Why go to such extremes?'

'Both Lady Pemberton and myself tried persuading her to confront you with this, but she would not hear of it. She is so headstrong, like a wilful child at times. What will you do now?'

'You don't have to worry about Eve any longer, Miss Parkinson,' he said softly. 'I shall leave for Cumbria first thing in the morning—just as soon as I have paid a visit to Little Bolton to see Angela and put a few things straight. And then I think Eve and I must have a serious talk.'

'But what if she is too afraid of Gerald and his threats to risk returning?'

'I guarantee she will be safe with me. Once I have found her nothing—*no one*—will ever part me from her.'

Emma smiled, relieved. It was as though a great weight had been lifted from her mind. He spoke with such fervour that she was convinced he would take care of Eve and see she came to no harm.

'Forgive me, Mr Fitzalan, but I have to tell you that ever since that unfortunate day three years ago, I have silently wondered whether God was wise for placing you in her path. I see now that he was.'

Marcus looked at Emma, his face still. 'No one could have made me a more wonderful gift. I can't thank you enough for coming here today, Miss Parkinson. I owe you a great deal.'

'I did it for Eve, Mr Fitzalan. After all she has been through, her happiness is my sole concern. And if you can persuade her to reconsider her decision and to return to Atwood, then you must bring her to stay with us until the wedding. I can speak for my parents for they are extremely fond of her and love having her to stay. It's impossible for her to return to Burntwood Hall the way things are.'

Emma left after taking refreshment and having a friendly chat with Mrs Fitzalan, who confirmed that she had indeed lent Angela's mother her fan. It was on the night of the dinner party, when Eve had come to Brooklands with her grandmother. Mrs Lambert, having misplaced her own fan, had found the evening excessively warm and asked if she might borrow one of her own. Of course, she had been only too happy to oblige. No doubt she would return it when next she came.

Mrs Fitzalan knew of Eve's departure for Cumbria but had no idea she had ended her betrothal to Marcus, so Emma did not enlighten her. Not wishing to worry his mother unduly Marcus had not told her, hoping Eve would come to her senses and see the error of her decision.

Emma's coming to Brooklands had brought Marcus to a frame of mind which, if not exactly easy, was less tortured than before. He could think more calmly about Eve, realising how, with the malicious knowledge Angela had implanted in her mind, she had become swamped with doubt and mistrust.

He became filled with a dark rage when he thought of Angela, and that she had made Eve suffer untold misery for some spiteful reason of her own. He understood that what Angela had told her must have resurrected all the torments she had suffered three years ago, and that it had been the final blow that had broken her spirit so that she could no longer remain at Burntwood Hall. His attitude became sympathetic. After all, he could not blame her for acting as she had, and how could he possibly expect her to trust him after what he had done to her?

He would never know the depth of suspicion and hatred that had driven Eve to reject him and escape to Cumbria with her grandmother, but what he did know with absolute clarity was that he could not give her up. She was unlike any other woman he had ever known and he could not face the pain of losing her. He dwelt with something akin to wonder on what Emma had told him—that Eve was in love with him—and he wanted to know the extent of her love and when her feelings had changed towards him.

Intent on paying Angela a visit, he had to resist the urge to go to Eve at once, for more than anything else he wanted to justify himself to her, for her to know she had been wrong to believe Angela and her scheming lies. He was prepared to expend all his patience in breaking down the barriers between them, to bare his soul and hers, to tell her nothing in the world mattered except her.

But one thing troubled him deeply. While ever Atwood Mine remained at the centre of their marriage agreement it would forever remain a barrier that separated them, and she would always have an element of doubt about his love for her. He wanted the mine, but not without Eve.

Angela's surprise on seeing Marcus was evident, for it was the first time he had visited her parents' home, which was modest compared to the magnificence of Brooklands and Burntwood Hall, and had always been the cause of much of her resentment towards Eve. This had increased a thousandfold when she had become aware of Sir John Somerville's will— that he wanted Eve to marry Marcus, the man she herself had become infatuated with when they had been properly introduced by their mothers in London some months ago.

She had fawned and simpered before him to attract his attention, and he had always been polite and solicitous towards her, but it rankled that he was no more attracted to her than he was to all the other women who flocked around him, eager for his attentions. Always used to having her own way in everything, with men falling at her feet wherever she went, it annoyed her when Marcus made it plain that he was quite oblivious to her charms.

But already tired of being a widow, and desperate to marry

a man who would keep her in the style she had become accustomed to in the short time she had been married to Lesley—although not even the well-off Stephensons could compete with the wealth of Marcus Fitzalan—she was fiercely determined to capture him. She thought she might succeed when they returned to the West Riding, without the competition of other ambitious women flitting around him, and when they were in each other's company more—which proved to be often, their mothers being such close friends.

Then Sir John Somerville had died and laid down conditions in his will that threatened her own chances of marrying Marcus. This had infuriated her. Having set her own sights on him, she could not bear to be beaten and embarrassed by Eve. Her resentment against her was great indeed. Eve had always had too much, always been popular and sought after because of who she was, and in the past she, Angela, had pretended friendship, while secretly having no misgivings of wanting her downfall. It seemed that nothing else in her life had ever been so important. Any defeat of hers would give her immense satisfaction.

She received Marcus alone, becoming quietly alert and suspicious, noticing the obvious tension lining his sternly handsome features, knowing with a shattering certainty a moment later that he had been told of her conversation with Eve.

Marcus gave her an unsmiling nod, finding it virtually impossible to restrain his anger. 'This is not a social visit, Angela,' he said, the tone of his voice direct and as hard as steel, his expression the same. 'It is unappealing but necessary and I do not have much time. I am on my way to Cumbria to try and persuade Eve to return. You do know she has left Atwood, don't you?'

Angela blanched at the unwelcome news that he was to fetch her back but remained silent, waiting patiently for him to continue.

'What have you been saying to Eve?' he demanded harshly. 'What have you to say for yourself, Angela?'

'Me? Why—nothing that is not true, Marcus.'

'Don't insult my intelligence with your simpering denials. How dare you go to Burntwood Hall and pour your lies into Eve's ears—and in so threatening a manner?' he accused her angrily. 'And how dare you have the audacity to do something so base as to show her a fan you told her was a gift from me to you? You know perfectly well it was a gift from me to my mother, which she kindly let your own mother borrow on the night of the dinner party when you both came to Brooklands— the night when Eve was there also. Do you deny it?'

Angela allowed a scornful smile to play on her lips. 'No. The fan was an innocent fabrication on my part, I do confess, but what I told her were not lies. I told her nothing but the truth.'

'The truth? I never realised you could be so deceitful or conniving, or that you could be so talkative.' He moved to stand in front of her, looking down into her hazel eyes with a hard, murderous gleam, his lips curled over his teeth. 'How soft and persuasive you can be at times, Angela—how soothing and seductive your voice, but your caressing tones and beguiling smile do not cancel out the hard, calculating gleam in your eyes. Until now I did not guess what a weight of hatred and treachery you concealed, but at last I am beginning to understand you—and also to understand why, with such damning evidence, Eve believed your lies.'

Marcus's sharp tone stung Angela to awareness, and when she realised what he was saying her face became contorted with rage, her eyes as hard as ice and her fists clenched by her sides.

'You have deceived me into believing I was the one you cared for—the one whom you would marry,' she hissed.

'If that is what you think, you deceive yourself. I have never given you reason to believe that you are anything more than an acquaintance and you know it. I do not want you—not now—not ever. Is that clear? Eve was never your friend, was she? But what you have done to her—causing her unnecessary suffering—I cannot and shall not forget.'

'*You* are not entirely blameless,' Angela accused him scathingly.

'No, I am not, but I did not realise it until yesterday and will reproach myself for ever more.' His face was white with anger and his voice became icy calm as his eyes glittered and held hers. 'I love Eve—and I will say no more because I do not have to justify my feelings to you of all people. But I will say this—that you, Angela, are an evil-minded witch and the dirtiest fighter I have ever met…and believe me, I've met some dirty fighters in my time. You will stoop to any depths to get what you want.'

A deadly smile twisted Angela's distorted features and her voice became dangerously soft. 'You are right, Marcus. I do hate Eve. I hated her long before that day at Atwood Fair. But I won that time, and whether or not I do so again remains to be seen. I won't say I hope you'll be very happy together. We both know I would be lying.'

Marcus stared at her. Rarely had he seen such hatred in a human face. His anger was pitiless and so powerful he had to clench his hands by his sides to prevent them reaching out and throttling her for all the pain Eve had suffered because of her jealousy and hatred.

His eyes narrowed. 'For some malicious reason of your own, you are hellbent on destroying her, but I shall tell you this. Take care, for if any harm comes to Eve by your hand I shall have my revenge. There is no hole deep and dark enough for you to hide from me. I shall find you—that I swear.'

Marcus left Angela then, and if he had raised his voice or struck her she would have borne it better. Instead he kept his tone temperate, but his eyes were like slivers of ice, showing the depth of his anger. As Angela watched him go there was an all-too-evident hunger for revenge burning in her heart—but this time it was not only directed at Eve, but at Marcus also.

Chapter Thirteen

Eve's horse followed a grassy track almost of its own volition, where it stretched and wound on and upwards through a cool forest, between tall trees—ancient English oaks and lofty beeches, shivering aspen and silver birch, their leaves, soon to cover the ground, shimmering and trembling in the slight breeze that rustled through them, the green of their summer glory giving way to the onset of autumn, turning them to burnished copper, russet and gold. She rode slowly for almost an hour, until she came out of the trees and paused on the summit of a grassy hill.

Dismounting, she tethered her horse to a tree, where it began to graze while she sat on the grass in solitude, seeing once again the familiar character of the pastoral landscape spread out below her, beautiful and dramatic, and her heart was still. All around her was loneliness and emptiness, the majesty of the jagged expanse of the Cumbrian mountains separated by high passes and deep lakes beyond her, fell and dale scenery at its most impressive, the wind breathing low in the trees.

To the north she could see the dramatic Langdale Pikes, and to the east she recognised the remote Dunnerdale village of Seathwaite, and beyond that the grey slate houses of Ambleside near the northern end of the silvery waters of Lake Windermere. She allowed her eyes to drink their fill, the apathy which had cloaked her since leaving Atwood beginning to lift as her spirits rose.

For the first time since coming to Ruston House, her grandmother's Cumbrian home, three days ago, she allowed her thoughts to turn wholly to Marcus. His betrayal with Angela lived and breathed inside her mind, torturing her. Because he had betrayed her love with the woman who had once pretended friendship while being bent on destroying her, it was like a double profanation in itself. When he had left her, she had thought her heart would break, crushed with despair, but she had refused to give in to her anguish, unable to cry any more tears, for they had all been shed before she had left Burntwood Hall.

Already she missed him, missed the joy the sound of his voice brought her, his nearness, for it seemed like a thousand years since she had last laid eyes on his face, but she had to go on, to survive. Her grandmother had told her that she would, that time heals all things—but she knew it never would. Nothing but death could take away the love she carried within her heart. Nothing would ever heal the sense of desolation that covered her like a shroud. Her heart twisted with anguish when she realised what she had done to him, knowing how angry he must be and that he would never want to set eyes on her again.

But at that moment, as Marcus rode up the steep path and emerged into the open sunlight, she didn't know how far from the truth that was. He paused, insensible to the wonderful scenery all around him, every sense he possessed becoming riveted on Eve's still figure. She was dressed in a sensible black woollen skirt and crisp white blouse buttoned up to her throat, having removed her jacket and bonnet and placed them on the grass beside where she sat.

Her hair, coiled in the nape of her neck, shone and was as smooth and black as a raven's wing, and her face was serene and curiously soft, with a yearning, nostalgic quality as she gazed at the fells laid out far below. It was as if she was stifled by some emotion, as if her inner peace had been crushed and she had come to this peaceful hilltop to gain some quiet relief. Her expression was so calm, so open, that his breath almost ceased and his blood congealed, for it was as if her soul lay bare. Never had he seen her look more lovely, more desirable—darkly, beautifully perfect.

His love for her was more alive than he had imagined and his pulses leapt to the knowledge. It was so discernible that he could almost reach out and touch it, see it, and smell its sweet, intense aroma. Mesmerised, he became lost in thought as he silently watched the play of sunlight and shadow upon her lovely face, the rise and fall of her chest as she gently breathed, content to stand and gaze at her, but she turned her head, as if the compulsion of his intent gaze was strong enough to tell her he was there.

Eve stared at him, at his well-known features, so deeply buried in her heart. Her attention became riveted, a world of feelings for an instant flashing across her face, her eyes recognising his presence but her brain telling her he must be a figment of her imagination. For just a moment she thought she must be suffering from some kind of delusion, brought on by a wish of her own. She became still, her eyes brimming with love, disbelieving that he had come to her.

How long had he been standing there watching her? she asked herself, with his black hair blowing in the breeze, his bearing stamped with noble pride and emanating so much strength and naked power that he seemed as hard and invincible as Scafell and Langdale Pikes soaring in the distance.

Emotion rendered her speechless, her wide violet eyes imploring and devouring him all at once, and for one brief, marvellous moment her heart went soaring as high as the hills and she forgot everything save the immense joy that he had come to her after so much suffering.

She stood up and for a long moment they looked at each other with love and longing, until, relieved from the shock of his unexpected appearance, and unable to forget that she had broken their betrothal which was the reason why she had come to Cumbria, Eve managed to speak.

'Marcus! You! You here!'

He looked at her with inexpressible tenderness, moving towards her, his eyes narrowing in the bright sunshine, wanting to reach out and draw her into his arms, but all he could do was gaze at her.

'Did you honestly think I would dismiss you so lightly from my life? When we parted at Burntwood Hall I told you that I would not allow you to dismiss me so easily. I arrived at Ruston House shortly after you left on your ride. Your grandmother told me the direction you had taken.'

'Did she? I often come up here when I'm staying with her. The view is quite magnificent.'

Marcus frowned. 'Please—you might look pleased to see me.'

'I—I am so surprised,' she murmured, feeling her heart give a leap of consternation and, she had to admit, a certain excitement.

'I apologise if I frightened you.'

'You didn't frighten me. I—I cannot imagine why you have followed me here—after our conversation at Burntwood Hall,' she said, flushing as the memory of that day and the harsh words they had exchanged—and his savage kiss that had rendered her helpless—came flooding back to her, praying she would be strong enough to withstand the fatal attraction which never failed to draw her towards him, like metal filings to a magnet.

'When you rejected me so firmly—so decisively,' he reminded her, watching her closely. 'I haven't forgotten. But we have matters to discuss which are important to us both.'

'You could have written and saved yourself the journey,' Eve suggested.

'I daresay I could. But what I wanted to say could not be put down in a letter. I wanted to see you—to put things right between us, and persuade you to return with me.'

'That is not possible. Nothing you can say can possibly tempt me to return to Atwood.'

'No, not to Atwood. To Netherley—to Brooklands, as my wife.'

Eve stared at him aghast, unable to believe he had the effrontery to expect her to still marry him after all he was guilty of. All the hot, angry words that had festered inside her since she had last seen him bubbled to her lips, for no longer could she remain silent on his affair with Angela.

'Surely not even *you* would have the impudence to expect me to marry you while you are indulging in an affair with someone else? The fact that it is Angela—after all she is guilty of where I am concerned—is too much to be borne. Perhaps I should have been less eaten up with anger if it had been someone else.'

'Please explain what you are talking about. I am quite astonished.'

'Are you? When you asked me why I had broken our betrothal I did not tell you the reason then—but now you have it. It needs no further explanation from me. I saw the proof of your feelings for Angela with my own eyes when she flaunted the fan you gave her before me—affectionately and so very touchingly inscribed by you. One of several gifts you have given her over the months of your acquaintance, she told me. I will not be played false, Marcus. And when she called at Burntwood Hall after I had left you that day, how dare you be so attentive towards her—almost loverlike—in front of me.'

Eve waited expectantly, watching him, wanting desperately for him to explain about his relationship with Angela—to set her mind at rest by reassuring her there was nothing to substantiate her jealous imaginings. But she was disappointed to see neither surprise or guilt register in his eyes; in fact, he remained infuriatingly cool and implacable.

'Was I? I was not aware that I was being,' he said at last, 'and I was certainly not being any more attentive towards Angela than I would have been had it been anyone else.'

'Angela is not just anyone else, Marcus,' Eve argued heatedly. 'You were being excessively attentive. I saw you. Are you her lover?'

He stared at her with some element of amusement, glad to see her spirit had not been defeated after all by Gerald's threatening behaviour.

'Are you?' she demanded.

A smile moved across Marcus's face, slowly, infuriatingly, his eyes becoming gently teasing as he moved closer, speaking softly. 'Well now, considering how matters stand between us—that you disapprove of me and have rejected me so completely—that is something I refuse to divulge.'

'Oh! You beast!'

'Am I?' He was mocking her with a wry sort of humour. 'I was wounded, Eve, deeply. Surely you cannot blame me for finding solace and forgetfulness in the arms of someone else.'

'There are other, worthier ways of finding solace and forgetfulness than to abandon yourself in the arms of another woman. But then, no doubt there have been many times in the past when you have sought pleasure in Angela's arms.'

'I find it strange that you should take me to task over this. After all—you can hardly blame me for seeking affection elsewhere when you rejected me so firmly now, can you?' His eyes darkened and he smiled slightly, mocking her, playing a subtle game with her emotions. 'Unless your excessive anger has been roused by my attentions towards Angela because you care a little after all.'

'Care? Care for you?' she flared furiously. 'You are arrogant in your assumptions.'

'I don't believe so. Perhaps you should look into your heart and ask yourself the reason for your anger. Has it taken the devotions I apparently show to another woman to make you aware of the true nature of your feelings?'

'No. I already know how I feel—I— Oh...' Flustered, Eve

turned from him sharply in embarrassment, having said too much.

Marcus smiled, lifting one eyebrow quizzically. 'Pray continue. You have my avid attention,' he murmured over her shoulder, so close that Eve could feel his warm breath caressing her ear, and the heat from his body. 'Don't stop now— not when you were about to divulge the depth of your feelings. Would I be correct in thinking that because you believe I am involved in an affair with Angela is why you called off our betrothal?'

Sighing dejectedly Eve nodded, turning to face him. 'Yes. It took me a long time to get over what happened between us that day at Atwood Fair—to put some semblance of order back into my life. I am not prepared to jeopardise that by entering into a marriage that cannot fail to end in tragedy because my husband is in love with another woman.'

Marcus's expression became serious, the gentle teasing he had indulged in disappearing from his eyes.

'But I am not. Eve—listen to me,' he said, taking her hand and drawing her towards him. 'I am not having—and never have had—an affair with Angela. I have never thought of her as anything other than an acquaintance. You have to believe that.'

'Then why did you have to be so attentive, so loverlike towards her? And how can you explain your gift to her? And you have just said—'

'Forget what I just said. I was teasing—which was cruel of me and I apologise. The fan can be explained quite simply. It was my mother's fan you saw—a fan I gave to her on her birthday two years ago. My mother lent it to Angela's mother on the night you came to Brooklands. It was a warm night, as you will remember, and Mrs Lambert had misplaced hers. She must have taken it home with her, and it is clear that for her own malicious reasons Angela set out to cause you further distress by pretending I had given it to her.'

Eve stared at him. His explanation was so simple that she

was beginning to feel very foolish. She remembered that the fan had been inscribed but it had not been dedicated to anyone in particular, so Angela had thought to use it out of sheer deviousness.

'I—I see,' she said softly. 'From past experience I should have seen through Angela's ploy—that it was just a typical touch of cruelty on her part to make me believe you saw marriage to me as nothing more than a business deal. In moments like those—when she sees something she wants being taken from her—she is deaf and blind to everything save her own hatred. But to go to such lengths—it is clear she must feel something for you, Marcus.'

'Perhaps—but it is entirely one-sided. You must believe that, Eve. The day you saw me strolling with her in the garden at Burntwood Hall—after you had so firmly rejected me—I behaved in a manner for which I am deeply ashamed. If I had known then the extent of Angela's malice towards you, how deeply her lies have hurt you, both now and in the past, I would not have been so attentive, but at the time I did it to goad you because you had driven me to such anger.

'I did it in an attempt to break through your indifference. I knew you were watching as we walked in the garden. I glimpsed you at the window of your room, and thought if I could raise your anger you would show some positive feeling—and I am pleased to see I succeeded.'

'You put on a good act,' Eve smiled, her lips trembling.

'I did, didn't I? But I'm tired of acting. I shall do what I should have done at the very beginning,' he murmured, moving closer, a slow smile curving his handsome lips as his smouldering gaze dropped to her breasts, softening, lingering, as if he could well imagine what lay beneath her high-necked blouse. 'You, my darling, are going to discover how dominant, how primitive a man I can be.'

'Am I?' Eve asked, feeling her cheeks burn crimson beneath his scorching look, that same arousing look she remembered from that fateful day three years ago, and the occasions after when he had kissed her, weakening her and arousing sensations and images that reminded her how quickly and wantonly she had yielded to him, how his arms had held her close, and how it had felt to have his mouth close over hers and to feel her body shuddering with awakened passion.

'Yes—and very soon. But for now I will have to content myself with a kiss.'

Drenched in the sun's warmth Marcus placed his hands on her shoulders and looked deep into her eyes, soft, swimming, velvety and glowing with an inner light. Eve trembled, unable to control it. His hands were strong and warm; lifting one of them up he caressed her cheek with a featherlight touch, and lowering his head he drew her against him and held her tightly, causing a ripple of intense pleasure to go soaring through her as she melted against him. Covering her mouth with his own, his parted lips were warm and moist, pressing, gently probing, firm and growing more and more insistent, his kiss long and urgent.

After a moment, with a sigh Marcus raised his head and looked down into Eve's upturned face, keeping her pressed close to him as he drank in her beauty, feeling the graceful swell of her breasts against his chest. He was unable to believe he was holding her in his arms when so recently she had told him she wanted nothing more to do with him. She was tantalising, bewitching him so that he thought she must be some kind of sorceress. Only a man with ice instead of blood in his veins could have resisted her looking as she did at that moment.

Lowering his head, with expert slowness he trailed his lips across her cheek, kissing and gently gnawing with his teeth at the soft, fleshy lobe of her ear, hearing her sharp intake of breath as he gently tugged. Raising his head he smiled slowly, but she moved away a little as his face descended to hers once more.

'Please do not try to distract my mind by trying to seduce me, Marcus,' Eve said breathlessly, while gazing up at him with silent yearning, wanting nothing more than to lie on the grass with him and let him make love to her. 'The time has come when there must be truth between us. We have still much to discuss. I have so much to tell you.'

Marcus pulled her back, this time circling her with his arms to prevent her escape, longing to repeat the kiss but having to content himself for now with holding her. 'I know all I need to know for now,' he murmured, his voice husky with seduction that both thrilled and excited her. 'Your dear friend Emma Parkinson saw to that.'

'Emma?'

'Yes. She came to see me when you left with your grandmother—and I must say she can be quite forceful when she has a mind. I made no effort to defend myself when she accused me so severely of ungentlemanly conduct towards you three years ago at Atwood Fair—but did you know you made quite an impression on me that day? It certainly showed me you were no prim and proper cold-blooded female. I never forgot you.'

A thousand memories came flooding back to Eve of that day; in fact, they had never left her, but her foolish, wanton behaviour had made it impossible for her to look back with joy. She changed colour and brusquely pulled away from him, but secretly his words gave her reason to rejoice, for it was the closest he had come to saying he cared for her.

'Marcus,' she said quietly, 'please do not mention that day again. I have always retained a strange, unreal and at the same time uneasy memory of the time when I unashamedly threw myself at you. I cannot bear to think of it. I want to forget the whole of it.'

He smiled. 'My memory is not so accommodating—and nor do I want to forget how it was to kiss you, to feel your response, which makes me want to repeat the offence.'

He became serious. 'But I did exert unwarranted force on you. I was so full of my own conceit that in my arrogance I lost sight of what I might have done to you. I sincerely regret my actions, and I am truly sorry for any hurt and humiliation I may have caused you. I had no idea you suffered so much distress owing to my ignoble behaviour. How you must have hated me and blamed me for being the cause of your absence from Burntwood Hall when your mother died.'

Pain filled Eve's eyes and sadness wrenched her heart at the mention of her mother, for she still reproached herself for not being with her when she had needed her.

'I cannot deny that it was a terrible time and I deeply regret not being with her. But it would seem Emma has let her tongue run away with her. You must have had an extremely long and interesting conversation. What else did she tell you, Marcus?'

'She told me about Angela's visit to you at Burntwood Hall and her lies—and she also told me of your fear of Gerald and the threats he made, which he will answer for when I return to Netherley,' he said, his voice low with anger and his expression becoming grim.

'No,' said Eve quickly in alarm. 'I would rather you leave things as they are. He did me no physical harm so I would prefer to forget what he said. But tell me more about your relationship with Angela,' she said in an attempt to divert his thoughts from Gerald, not wishing to recall his menacing behaviour towards her or his threats, which worried her far more than she was prepared to admit.

Marcus sighed, his eyes fastening on the delectability of her soft lips. 'I am tired of talking about Angela.'

'Do not tell me you were blind to her charms, Marcus,' Eve breathed, trying to ignore the look in his eyes. 'Whatever else she is, Angela is an extremely beautiful woman,' she said, determined not to let him fudge and escape the issue. If she was to reassess her decision about marriage to him it was important to her that she knew everything there was to know.

'But not as beautiful as you,' Marcus murmured gallantly. 'You will be happy when I tell you that I have severed all connections with Angela. I have made plain what my feelings are for her and I doubt very much that she will bother us in the future.'

'You went to see her?'

'After Miss Parkinson's revelations, I could not ignore what she had done to you.'

'How long have you known Angela?'

'We met briefly in London, and when she returned to the West Riding she began calling at Brooklands with her parents—who, as you know, are friends of my mother.'

'Yes, I do know that. But did you not see the venom—the spite behind Angel's smile?'

'No. I confess I didn't.' He smiled. 'I never looked close enough for that. I have to say, my love, I was not as well acquainted with Angela as you—clearly an unfortunate acquaintance which has taught you to read her schemes and venomous insinuations.' He sighed, sitting down on the soft grass and drawing her down beside him.

'Caprice born of indifference and my mother's gentle coaxing drew us together and nothing more—and even if your father had not laid down conditions in his will, and if I had never met you, my darling,' he said, gathering her into his arms and planting a kiss on her lips, 'I could never have married Angela—not in a million years. What I felt for her was a poor emotion compared with the joy and blinding love I feel in just looking at you.'

He looked down at Eve's enchanting face, gazing at her with so much tenderness that happiness and joy went soaring through her and she allowed herself to hope in a way she never had before.

'There—now I've told you. Without realising it, you, my darling Eve, have become an immeasurably important part of my life. If you refuse to renew your promise to become my wife then I shall be the most miserable of men. I shall never be free of you. I would give you the world to make you happy.'

The quiet words did nothing to dispel the doubt hovering

at the back of Eve's mind that sprang cruelly to the fore to torment her, refusing to go away as she wanted it to—to enable her to drift along in the knowledge that he would be marrying her for no other reason than that he loved her.

She sighed. 'I will be more than happy to renew my promise to become your wife—but I don't want the world, Marcus. Titles and wealth mean nothing to me—and the one thing that seems to matter so much to you is no longer important to me.'

Marcus looked down at her, frowning. 'I take it that you are referring to Atwood Mine?'

'Yes,' she said quietly, averting her gaze.

Marcus was serious. 'Eve, look at me.'

Slowly she raised her eyes to his once more.

'Ever since your friend Miss Parkinson came to see me, I have given the matter a great deal of serious thought. What I have to suggest may shock and surprise you, but, with your agreement, I have decided to put the mine in trust for our children.'

Eve stared at him in disbelief, rendered speechless by his announcement, knowing just how much it had cost him to make that decision.

'If you are in agreement, that is what I will do.'

'Why—I—yes, yes, of course,' Eve uttered—what else could she say? She was extremely surprised by the unexpectedness of his suggestion and pleased. It was like being thrown a life line, something to cling on to. 'But—are you absolutely certain about this, Marcus?'

'I am as certain as I can be.'

'Then—then what can I say?' she stammered.

Marcus looked at her steadily, frowning a little. 'You seem a little confused.'

'No—no.' She smiled. 'I think it's a good idea. It's just that I do not want you to do something you will have cause to regret later.'

'I shan't regret it, and our children will benefit in the future—God grant we are so blessed.'

'And—and you will do this for me?' she asked quietly, genuinely moved by his decision, a decision which told her she meant more to him than she had ever dared to hope.

'For you, my darling, I would do anything.'

'But it doesn't seem fair. You are entitled to it. No one can question your right. Atwood Mine is what you've wanted for so long—to work it as your father did, and your grandfather before that. Consigning it to trustees will be painful for you, having to watch it being administered by others.'

Marcus smiled wryly. 'Sometimes getting what you want doesn't always seem fair, Eve. Owning Atwood Mine will always make you doubt my love—and that is the last thing I want. I do not want it. It would be the worst kind of punishment. I am doing the right thing. I am certain of it. Besides, I shall ensure that I have the utmost confidence in the trustees in whose care it is placed.'

With a rapidly beating heart, Eve was looking at him as she had never dared to look at him before, unable to believe he would do this enormous thing for her. He had abolished in one fell swoop any doubt she had that he loved her. His eyes burned down into hers with all the love and passion she had despaired of ever seeing there, and her own were brilliant with happiness.

'Then what can I say?'

'Only that you will renew your promise to become my wife.'

'Yes,' she whispered. 'There is nothing I want more than that.'

'When you left Burntwood Hall in such a hurry, Gerald must have questioned your reason for doing so. Did you by any chance tell him we were not to be married?'

'No.'

He smiled slowly, arching one sleek black brow, the teasing note returning to his voice. 'I see. Then that leaves me wondering that you may not have been so certain of your decision not to marry me after all.'

Eve looked up at him impishly. 'No. I know you would like me to admit that was the reason, but it wasn't. I merely wanted Gerald to sweat a little longer. Was that so very wrong of me?'

'Considering his harsh treatment of you—no, it was not. However, until we are married I would like you to come and live at Brooklands.'

'No—I think it would be best if I stayed with Emma, Marcus—until the wedding, that is.'

He frowned. 'I'd prefer having you at Brooklands where I can keep an eye on you.'

A cold hand seemed to clutch at Eve's heart, knowing what had prompted him to say this. 'Do you think Gerald will issue more threats, Marcus?'

Marcus thought Gerald was desperate and evil enough to go further than to utter threats against her, but kept his thoughts to himself, not wishing to worry her unduly.

'I sincerely hope not.'

'Then if you take me directly to Mr and Mrs Parkinson's, Gerald need not know I have returned until the wedding.'

Marcus frowned, uncomfortable about this, but he could see this was what she wanted. 'Very well. I have to go to Leeds as soon as we return, on business, and I shall also proceed with setting up the trust for the mine, which will be controlled by a board of trustees until one or more of our children are of an age to take control themselves.'

'But what if there are no children?' Eve asked, trying not to sound too pessimistic. 'It is not uncommon.'

'I know. If that is the case I shall see that my brothers' children benefit. But,' he said, looking deep into her eyes, 'I sincerely hope we have a nursery full of children, and,' he murmured, his voice thickened by desire, his lips nuzzling her cheek, so soft they were like wings on her flesh, 'I aim to set about making babies the moment we are married. I shall teach you how to make love, my darling, and I hope you will prove to be a willing and enthusiastic pupil.'

Eve gave him an incandescent smile. 'I really can't think of anything I would like doing better.' She sighed against him. 'I do love you, Marcus. I can't find the words to say how much.'

His arms tightened around her. 'I know. I love you in the same way. I want you to promise me you will not venture away from the Parkinsons' house while I am in Leeds—in case Gerald should discover where you are and come calling,' he said, his gaze once again becoming fastened to her lips as a soft breeze scented with pine caressed them. His eyes darkened. 'But at this moment I have no wish to discuss Gerald. I have other, much more important things on my mind to consider.'

'Oh? Such as?'

'Whether or not you will object if I kiss you again.'

'I did not object when you kissed me before.'

'Very well,' he murmured, proceeding to kiss her once more, unable to sit so close and not do so. He paused for a moment, fanning her lips with his warm breath. 'I can see you don't mind, but considering the bargain we made some time ago—that ours will be a marriage in name only until we want it otherwise—I shall abide by that and stop whenever you want me to.'

Eve sighed breathlessly against him as he tenderly assaulted her lips once more. She didn't want him to stop. She couldn't. She was powerless. She wanted him to go on and on.

'Do you mind if I break the bargain?' she breathed.

'No, I suppose not,' he smiled, smoothing a finger across her cheek. 'I welcome it. I am feeling extremely relieved to realise that Atwood Mine is no longer the most important thing in the world to me,' he said, 'now that I have been caught up in emotions over which I have no control.'

'No?' she whispered, placing small, tantalising kisses on his lips.

'No,' he admitted. 'It is now a close second—not the most important.'

'Then please tell me—what would be the first?'

'Do you really have to ask?'

'I think so.'

'Do I really have to show you?'

'Yes,' she sighed provocatively. 'It might be rather enlightening.'

'You are insatiable, Miss Somerville,' he said, his lips against hers, enchanted by her.

'If I am it is your fault,' she murmured, smiling in a tantalising way that swelled his heart.

And with that he proceeded to show her, laying her down on the grass and leaning over her.

Marcus's hands were gently caressing, arousing Eve to undreamed-of delights as he kissed her deeply, his breath fanning her lips warmly. She melted willingly in his arms, responding with such exquisite pleasure and causing Marcus to almost lose control. He was overcome with desire for her, and felt the heat rising inside him. His tender persuasiveness vanished, becoming replaced by a scorching demand, his hands clasping her face between them, his lips grinding on to hers, stifling her, but she welcomed his kiss and he felt her respond. Wrapping his arms about her, he crushed her as she moaned against him, filled with pleasure.

They were both far away, absorbed with each other, knowing now for certain that they loved each other desperately, that they had been created for each other through all time, and in their joy they forgot everything and everyone who had threatened to destroy their happiness.

When they could tear themselves apart and leave their pillow of grass, they rode at a leisurely pace back to Ruston House where Lady Pemberton was waiting with eager anticipation, knowing by the happiness she saw radiated on her granddaughter's face that all had been happily resolved between her and Mr Fitzalan.

Chapter Fourteen

Mr and Mrs Parkinson were delighted to have Eve stay with them until the wedding, and Eve was secure in the knowledge that her return to Atwood would remain unknown to Gerald until the wedding, a week hence, and despite the distinction of the two people involved, and the pomp and ceremony that would have accompanied such a wedding, it was to be the quietest wedding Atwood had seen for many a year.

But unbeknown to either Marcus or Eve, Angela saw them taking the road that bypassed Atwood and heading for the Parkinsons' house whilst she was out riding. On observing them together, jealousy and anger flared anew within her, reminding her of Marcus's angry and humiliating visit to her home, when he had rejected her and berated her so severely over her despicable treatment of Eve.

Determined to make things as unpleasant as possible between them, with a slow, malicious smile of triumph curving her lips, she turned her horse in the direction of Burntwood Hall, knowing she would experience a deep sense of satisfaction when Eve got her comeuppance.

After making sure she was settled with the Parkinsons, Marcus took his leave of her, an expression of immense concern clouding his face, for he was seriously anxious for her safety.

'Promise me not to venture out alone—that you will remain in the house and await my return from Leeds, when I shall fetch you over to Brooklands to see my mother. She is most anxious to discuss with you matters concerning the wedding and your position at Brooklands as my wife.'

Eve smiled up at him, strangely pleased by his solicitude. 'Of course I promise. I shall do exactly as you say.'

'Good,' he said, wanting to sweep her into his arms and kiss her full on her lips, but owing to the fact that there seemed to be a hundred pairs of smiling, inquisitive eyes observing his departure, it was with some annoyance that he had to content himself with giving her a light peck on the cheek.

Eve watched him go, exhilarated and deliriously happy in her love, his kiss still warm on her cheek as she impatiently began counting the days to their wedding, but the sweet drift of happiness was soon shattered when a letter was delivered to her from Burntwood Hall shortly after Marcus had left for Netherley.

Eve was in the parlour with Emma and she went cold on recognising Gerald's sprawling handwriting, staring at it with dread, reluctant to open it.

Seeing her dilemma and unease, Emma came to stand beside her. 'You'll have to open it, Eve—read what he has to say.'

Eve swallowed hard, a sudden fear clutching her heart. 'But how does he know I've returned to Atwood—and so soon? Someone must have seen me and told him. I must say he's lost no time in contacting me so the letter must have been written with some urgency.'

With trembling fingers she opened it, reading how he wished to apologise for his conduct before she had left Burntwood Hall and inviting her to dine with him the following day, stressing they had matters to discuss which were important to them both and could not be ignored.

Sensing her worry, Emma asked if she might read it, staring at Eve in incredulity when she had finished.

'Why, the man is impertinent,' she gasped. 'After all he is guilty of where you are concerned—threatening you so abominably, which was so upsetting to you at the time. You cannot go, Eve. You must show the letter to Mr Fitzalan and stay clear of Burntwood Hall—at least until after you are married. I fear Gerald is a reckless libertine with evil intent. He is known to be of an erratic temperament and I am sure you would not be safe.'

'Yes, you are right, Em. I shall answer his letter declining his invitation, of course, and let him know I do not welcome his attentions.'

Which she did. However, after Gerald's past, despicable conduct towards her, it came as no surprise that her refusal did not end his interest, for another letter arrived the following day repeating his invitation, which Eve ignored, although his audacity and persistence aroused all Emma's anger.

Eve tried to reassure her that she was not worried unduly by Gerald's behaviour, but deep inside she was terrified of him, becoming plagued by tension and impatient to see Marcus. Two days later when no further letter came from Gerald, her spirits were uplifted when another letter came, this time from Mrs Fitzalan, inviting her to Brooklands two days hence, by which time Marcus would have returned from Leeds. Eve began to feel much less alarmed, and being surrounded by boisterous children, it was hard not to feel light hearted.

The day before she was to go to Brooklands, Emma was to accompany her parents on a visit to friends on the other side of Atwood. They were to take the children, all except Jonathan, who hated visiting and declared he wasn't feeling very well. With some concern Mrs Parkinson felt his brow, but in the absence of a temperature she decided he was not so ill as to justify putting off her visit. However, she still thought it best to leave him at home where he must remain in bed until she returned. If he was no better she would send for the doctor.

Eve declined their offer that she accompany them, insisting

Emma went with them when she offered to remain at home with Eve for company.

'You're certain you don't mind me leaving you, Eve? I'll stay with you if you want me to.'

Eve smiled. 'I don't mind, Em—truly. I shall read a book to occupy my time, and have a look in at Jonathan later.'

'Are you sure you'll be all right?'

'What possible harm can come to me here?' she laughed.

They had not been gone an hour when the childrens' nurse-maid sought her out in the parlour where she was sitting on the window seat quietly reading a book. On looking up, she saw the young woman looked extremely worried and was wringing her hands in agitation.

'Why, what is it, Maggie?'

'It's Master Jonathan, miss. I left him sleeping—or so I thought at the time—but when I went to his room ten minutes since he wasn't there. His bed is empty and he's not in his room.'

'But I thought he wasn't feeling well.'

'So he said, miss. But Master Jonathan has a habit of putting it on when he wants to get out of things—and pretty good he is at it too. He's done it often enough in the past.'

'Well—have you searched the house?'

'Yes, miss, but he's not to be found anywhere. Nanny's searching the attics but he's not thought to be up there.'

Eve frowned. 'Oh, dear,' she said, putting her book down and getting up. 'We'd better look for him. He can't be far.'

'Yes, miss. He'll have gone off somewhere.'

At first Eve was unperturbed, but when Jonathan did not return after half an hour she grew alarmed and ordered what servants there were—six, all told—to extend their search beyond the grounds, to divide and go off in separate ways. Watching them go, she turned to Maggie.

'Have you any idea where he might have gone, Maggie? Think very hard. Where does he like to go—to play? Does he have friends close by he might have gone to visit?'

'He does have friends at the Fairchilds who live close by—and there is a boy his age at the Simpsons down the road he visits now and then. He also likes to go fishing to the river or the pond—but he knows never to go alone.'

Eve went cold and felt dread quicken within her. The river! Why hadn't she thought of that? Jonathan loved to fish; in fact, it was his favourite pastime, but he never went to the river unless he was accompanied by his father or another adult member of the household. Besides, it was half a mile away and too close to the quarry for comfort. Surely he could not have gone there. The dangers were too great, and when she glanced out of the window and saw dark storm clouds gathering overhead, her alarm for Jonathan's safety grew.

'Dear Lord, Maggie—with the weather about to take a turn for the worse, let's hope he hasn't gone to the river. It's extremely naughty of him if he has. Run to the stables and instruct one of the grooms to enquire at any of the houses in the neighbourhood he might have gone to—the Fairchilds and the Simpsons in particular. Meanwhile I'll go to the river. When the others return—and if he still isn't found—have them follow me.'

Without thought for her own safety, and all the promises she had made to Marcus that she would not leave the house under any circumstances, thinking only of Jonathan, Eve immediately set off on foot in the direction of the river, unaware as she entered a wood some distance from the house that she was being followed. Eventually she came to a fork in the path, praying that Jonathan hadn't taken the steep path to the right, which was a shortcut past the deep, disused quarry to the river. The path was treacherous, especially after heavy rain, which made the edge crumble. One wrong foot could prove fatal.

Snagging her clothes on loose briars, she hurried along a twisting track, her heart hammering inside her chest. Emerging from the wood she breathed a huge sigh of relief on seeing the shining, tumbling water of the river ahead of her. It ran into a pond a quarter of a mile away, constructed to feed the canal further along. As she ran she tried to ignore the ever-darkening sky as her eyes scoured the river bank for Jonathan's small figure, fully expecting to see him sitting contentedly with his fishing rod dangling into the water, but as yet there was no sign of anyone.

Standing at the water's edge she stared in desolation at the water tumbling over its rocky bed, too shallow at this part to be of danger should Jonathan have found his way here and fallen in—but the pond was another matter. Quickly she ran towards it, knowing that if he wasn't there she would have to return by way of the quarry.

Hoping and praying nothing dreadful had befallen him, she was unable to believe her good fortune when she saw his golden head beneath some trees, where he sat on his bright red coat, just as she had imagined him, calmly placing something small and wriggling on to his fishing hook before casting his line into the water.

Eve's relief was enormous. She laughed out loud, calling his name as she lifted her skirts and ran towards him, not knowing whether to scold him or hug him with the sheer joy and relief she felt on finding him safe.

He looked up and grinned sheepishly at her when he saw her, but then his young face became transfigured with terror and he stood up quickly, screaming something at her and pointing at something behind her, as his fishing rod fell into the water and drifted away.

Instinctively Eve stopped, unable to hear what it was he screamed at her, and before she could turn and see what had so alarmed him, she felt her arms grasped roughly by hands from behind. Taken completely by surprise she struggled desperately to free herself, calling to Jonathan to run back to the house, but then she stumbled forward, uttering a cry of alarm as she plunged forward, hitting her head on something hard.

Her senses reeling, Eve was aware of two dark shapes bending over her. She wanted to call out to Jonathan, whom she could still hear screaming, to tell him again to run back to the house and fetch help, but as she felt herself seized by strong arms and brutally lifted off the ground, she was swallowed up by a suffocating darkness.

Quite by chance when Marcus was riding from one of his mines towards Netherley, he happened to run into Mr and Mrs Parkinson and almost their entire brood, travelling out to visit friends on the other side of Atwood. After pausing in the roadway to have a few words with them, a soft smile played on his lips as he watched them go on their way.

Having been told in a meaningful way by a smiling Emma that Eve had been left all alone in the house, he turned his horse round and spurred it on in the direction of Atwood, intending to surprise her. He was to collect her the following day to take her to Brooklands, but he hadn't seen her since his departure for Leeds four days ago and already he was missing her like hell.

Inside his pocket he had a gift for her, the first of many he hoped to give her throughout their lives together. It was an engagement ring, a cluster of rubies and diamonds he had purchased the day before in Leeds. It was the most expensive gift he had ever bought, but where Eve was concerned he would spare no expense.

As he rode up the drive towards the house he was aware of a strange quietness all around him, and he smiled, for with so many children normally running about the place it wouldn't always be as peaceful as this. Not until he dismounted did he become aware of the commotion coming from inside the house. Without waiting for someone to let him in he pushed the door open and stepped inside, seeing an extremely anxious-looking Matthew Somerville trying his best to calm the distraught servants.

There was an immediate, penetrating silence when they became aware of Marcus's tall, still figure observing them from the doorway, his presence dominating the scene. He stepped inside the hall, his eyes fixed on Matthew in stern enquiry, all his senses telling him something was very wrong.

'What is it? Has something happened?' Marcus demanded.

Relief that he had come flooded Matthew's eyes and he moved towards him. 'Thank God you're here, sir. I'm afraid something is wrong. I called on my way to the mine to see Emma, only to find the family are all away from home except Jonathan and Eve. According to the servants Jonathan—who had stayed home because he said he wasn't feeling well—went missing shortly after the family left the house, and Eve went to look for him.'

All Marcus's senses became alert. 'Where? Where did she go?'

'To the river. It was suspected that Jonathan might have gone fishing.'

'And what has been done? Has anyone gone after them?'

'Yes—but neither of them are to be found.'

'Then perhaps they are elsewhere.'

Matthew shook his head, reaching out and picking a small boy's red coat up out of a chair and a fishing rod. 'These are Jonathan's. The coat was found beside the river by two of the servants. The rod was found close by in the river where it had become snagged between the rocks. Unfortunately there was no sign of Jonathan or Eve.'

Marcus took the coat and fishing rod from him, holding them in his hands and looking at them hard, as if willing them to tell him what had happened, but he wasn't seeing anything. Something black and formless and terrifying in its secrecy had come alive inside him, almost stopping his breath and wrapping itself around his pounding heart.

'Who found them?' he demanded, looking round the circle of silent, anxious faces, his piercing, blazing eyes glaring at them one by one.

A groom and Maggie stepped forward. 'We did, sir,' said the groom. 'We searched all over for them—even down in the quarry to see if some mishap might have befallen them there—

but there was no sign of them or anyone else. There were signs on the ground close to where we found Master Jonathan's coat that there might have been a struggle, but it was hard to tell. I'm sorry but we had to come back. We didn't know what else to do.'

'You were right to come back. At least now we know where to begin looking. How long is it since Eve left the house?' he asked Matthew.

'Two hours ago.'

Marcus turned away towards the window, his eyes springing fiercely to life and his uncompromising jaw set as hard as granite as he looked in the direction of the river, seeing the first flash of lightning fork across the sky in the distance, followed by a hollow roll of thunder heralding the storm. He knew what had happened, knew without being told, and he became like a man in the grip of a nightmare, cursing himself for having let her out of his sight.

That Gerald had abducted Eve he did not doubt, and the thought of her, bewildered and terrified in the hands of a man who would go to any lengths to get his hands on a piece of property, caused a violent rage to fill his being, which increased with each passing moment. The cold look of black fury on his face when he turned rendered everyone mute.

'Two hours, you say.' His voice vibrated itself round the room, hurtling itself violently against the walls. 'It might just as well be two days. I told her not to leave the house—not to go wandering off by herself. I feared this might happen. I have every reason to believe she has been abducted.'

Ashen-faced, Matthew came to stand beside him. 'This has crossed my own mind but I can think of no reason why anyone would want to abduct Eve and Jonathan.'

Marcus's expression was hard, his eyes cold. 'Can't you? There is one person who springs to mind, Matthew. One person who wants Eve out of the way—one person who is desperate and demented enough—who will go to any lengths to prevent us marrying.'

Matthew blanched, swallowing hard, knowing after one devastating, heartstopping moment who he was referring to. But he could not accept it. 'You think it is Gerald, don't you?'

'Yes. I know it.'

'My brother may be accused of many things, Mr Fitzalan, but he would not resort to this.'

'Your loyalty to your brother is to be commended, Matthew, but he has made threats towards Eve several times since the death of her father. I firmly suspect he is behind this. However, the fact that he has Jonathan as well might save her.'

'Save her?' Matthew gasped, horrified by what he was implying. 'Surely you do not believe Gerald would harm her?'

'Yes. I have no doubt of it. Your brother is devious enough to resort to anything to prevent our marriage in order to retain Atwood Mine. He owes money hand over fist, and even though he is in possession of the estate, without the mine his situation remains desperate.' He looked at the groom. 'Come. We must hurry. Take me to the river where you found Jonathan's coat—and you, Matthew, ride into Atwood and get as many men as can be got to assist with the search. Mr and Mrs Parkinson must also be contacted at their friends' house and told to return at once.'

Matthew followed him out of the house just as the first heavy drops of rain began to fall.

'I do not believe Gerald will harm her, Mr Fitzalan,' he said, knowing better than anybody what his brother was capable of and trying to convince himself he would not stoop to murder.

Marcus looked at him and their eyes locked in fervent prayer to God that he was right.

When Eve regained consciousness she realised with a terrifying reality that her worst nightmare had come true—that Gerald's threats had become reality. She was stiff and sore and lying on a hard soil floor. Hearing a soft whimpering close to her she opened her eyes, looking around without moving her head, for it ached abominably.

Jonathan's white face and frightened eyes were the first things she saw. Crouching between herself and the wall he was like a captive bird, visibly trembling. His cheeks were wet with tears and his eyes filled with fear as, bending over her, he tried to shake her into wakefulness.

Despite her throbbing head and bruised and aching body, Eve set her teeth, determined not to give in to despair, and to thrust the growing, insidious fear away from her. She could not afford to weaken, to think of the dangers, not when she had Jonathan to protect. It was imperative that she kept a clear head and cool brain for when Gerald made his appearance— as he must some time.

Struggling to sit up, she leaned against the wall and gathered Jonathan to her. His body was cold but she was relieved to see there was no evidence that he had been physically abused. Taking comfort from the security of her arms, his trembling lessened.

'It's all right, Jonathan,' she whispered, her lips against his hair, wishing they had on more clothes to keep out the dank cold of the shed. 'Don't be frightened. No one is going to harm us.'

She could hear the storm raging with full force, with rain lashing through the trees, pounding against the walls of the building and on the ground outside. Quickly her eyes took in the comfortless dilapidation of their restricted domain, seeing they were in a small, disused shed, dirty and with huge cobwebs hanging from the walls, and with several broken implements and other useless objects scattered about the floor. A dim light filtered in through some rent sacking covering a small window high up in the wall, and through a hole in the roof where a slate was missing rain dripped through on to the floor.

The window was set too high in the wall for her to reach and there was nothing large enough for her to stand on to enable her to look out, and she knew without getting up and trying it that the stout door would be fastened securely to prevent their escape. On seeing there was no way out her spirits sank. There were so many worked-out pits in the area with disused buildings like this one that they could be almost anywhere.

She tried to remember what had happened. Someone had come at her and grasped her arms roughly from behind. Filled with alarm she had panicked and screamed to Jonathan to run, to go back to the house for help, but he had just stood there, too frightened to move. In a struggle to free herself from the vicious hold of her captor, she had stumbled and hit her head hard on a rock or something, but whatever it was the blow had been sufficient to render her senseless. Before she had lost consciousness she was sure she had seen two men. But what now? she wondered. What would happen next and how long would they have to remain in the shed?

Shuddering from the cold she drew her knees up, unable to believe this was happening to her. She thought it must be a dream and that she would wake up soon, but the damp permeating the walls of the shed and seeping through her clothes and into her body told her it was no dream.

She suspected the men who had brought her to this place—men who had been paid by Gerald—might still be outside somewhere, and if they weren't and she shouted no one would hear her. Anyone with any sense would not be out in this storm.

It wasn't until then that she realised how desperate, how determined Gerald was to obtain Atwood Mine, what lengths he would go to. She had no doubt he was prepared to kill her to do so, but she felt fury against him for daring to perpetrate such terror on a child.

'Jonathan, listen to me. Do you know where we are? Did you see where the men brought us?'

He shook his head, pressing his little body closer. 'No,' he whispered. 'They covered my eyes so I couldn't see.'

'Did you recognise them?'

'No.'

'How many men were there?'

'Two.'

'Did they hurt you?'

'No, but they frightened me.'

'How long do you think it was before we reached this shed?'

'Don't know. Not very long.'

'And did they have horses?'

'Yes. Two of them.'

So, thought Eve despairingly, if their persecutors had brought them here on horseback they could be further away from Atwood than she had at first thought. Closing her eyes, she tightened her arms around Jonathan. 'Don't worry. We'll get out of here. We'll have been missed by now and everyone will be searching for us.' She spoke with more confidence than she felt, but hearing Jonathan sigh she could sense she had won his trust.

Knowing they would have been missed and that everyone would be searching for them was the only thing she had to hold on to. Everyone would be so worried and Mr and Mrs Parkinson and Marcus would be informed immediately. He would suspect Gerald had abducted them and go to see him, forcing him to divulge where they were. He would come soon. He had to.

But suppose no one came? Suppose Gerald refused to disclose their whereabouts and denied all knowledge of their disappearance? She went to the door and hammered on the thick, unresisting wood in fear and frustration, calling for help, but the noise of the storm drowned the sound of her voice. After a while she stopped, knowing it was useless. It was stupid. No one would hear her.

Time dragged on and after what seemed to be an eternity she heard sounds of voices raised in anger outside the door, hearing something about a child and that everything had gone wrong. She sprang to her feet and clutched a terrified Jonathan to her, almost frightened out of her wits and having to suppress a scream when the door was suddenly thrown open and Gerald stepped inside, the two men she assumed had been involved in their abduction standing back. In the first wild, unreasoning panic, she almost threw herself at him, wanting to hurt him for causing herself and Jonathan so much distress.

Gerald stared around the shed, straining his eyes in the dim light, his face twisted by nervous spasms, his nostrils pinched as he realised his scheme had been botched by the two imbeciles he had hired to abduct Eve.

'So I was right,' Eve flared, unable to shake off the intense dislike she felt for this man that covered her like a foul odour. 'It was you who had us brought us here. How dare you? You are loathsome. How could you do such a wicked thing? Jonathan is a child and you have terrified him.'

Gerald's glance merely flicked over the small figure of the boy clinging to Eve's side. 'That part of your abduction was not intended. However, I intend doing all in my power to prevent your marriage to Marcus Fitzalan. When I have finished with you he will hardly appreciate being the recipient of spoiled goods. I doubt he will want a scandal, and I shouldn't think even he wants Atwood Mine so badly as to take you then.'

'Don't count on it, Gerald,' she scorned with an unmasked bitterness in her tone alongside an obvious contempt, unable to control the shaft of hatred that twisted through her, so savage that it must have been felt by Gerald himself. 'He will call you out—and I've heard he's a deadly duellist, with pistols or rapier.'

Gerald laughed, a cold unnatural sound, before his slack lips formed themselves into a malevolent smile. 'I'm a fair shot myself. But I doubt it will get that far. In his eyes you will be a shameless wanton, soiled, used and unfit to be his wife. It will take a miracle to survive the scandal.'

Eve went cold, for what he said was true. In no time at all

lurid versions of her involvement with Gerald would spread like wildfire throughout Atwood and Netherley, and the more people gossiped and speculated the whole sordid, damning episode would have been blown out of all proportion—just like it had been the last time, only then it had been Marcus her name had been linked to, not Gerald, and she would be too humiliated to protest her innocence. But she stood her ground, refusing to be cowed by him.

'And was it your intention to bring me here all along, to this shed, where you could carry out your wicked, sordid act?'

'Oh, no. Had we not been saddled with the boy I had somewhere much more pleasant than this in mind—a place where we would have been comfortable, to be seen enjoying each other's company enormously.'

'And you really expected me to be docile and go along with all this tomfoolery, did you?'

'There are methods I could have adopted to bring about your submission.'

'Drugs, you mean.'

'If necessary.'

Eve looked at him contemptuously, her voice trembling with unsuppressed hatred and anger when she spoke. 'What a loathsome, despicable creature you are, Gerald. I find it impossible to believe we are of the same blood. You are mad, for only a madman could have thought up this diabolical plan to abduct me in order to obtain the mine.'

Gerald's lips twisted in a cruel sneer. 'I am no more bad or loathsome than Fitzalan. And don't be fooled by his soft words, my dear, Eve. I have told you—it's the mine he wants. You come as an extra. Nothing more.'

'You are mistaken,' Eve retorted heatedly, determined to use all her wiles to try and bluff her way out of the ugly, desperate situation. 'I have to tell you, Gerald, that you really could have saved yourself the time and trouble of going to such extreme lengths as to have me abducted.'

His eyes narrowed, glittering like coals from between narrowed lids. 'What are you saying?'

Taking a deep breath Eve met his gaze, prepared to lie, to go to any lengths, to have him release them. Normally she could not get her tongue round a lie, but at this moment she had no such qualms in these desperate circumstances. But the way she felt left her in no doubt of her own uncertainty that she would succeed in what she was about to tell him.

'As you know, I have just returned from Cumbria where Marcus joined me. Perhaps you should ask yourself why.'

'No, but I will ask you—if it is important.'

'Oh, I think it is. You see, Marcus and I were married there.'

Gerald stared at her hard with eyes cold and lifeless. His face grew red and Eve felt herself begin to shake.

'You lie,' he hissed. 'You're trying to fool me. There was no time.'

'There is such a thing as a special licence,' Eve said with a touch of smugness, hoping and praying that she would succeed in convincing him that what she said was true. 'On our return Marcus went to Leeds. You see, Gerald, we intend putting Atwood Mine in trust for our children, and he thought it best to set the wheels in motion right away.'

Gerald was staring at her, his face no longer red but white and mute, and Eve had the satisfaction of seeing him tremble as realisation that what she said might be true sent him to the far reaches beyond his control. He looked like a man possessed of the devil. 'Is this true?' he demanded with a note of hysteria.

'Yes.'

He roared his anger, his frustration, madness filling his eyes as his arms thrust out and he grasped her shoulders in a ferocious grip, shaking her forcibly, savagely, snapping her head back and forth. Jonathan screamed in terror, his cry echoing about the shed as he continued to cling to Eve's skirts.

'You witch,' Gerald screamed, releasing her as suddenly as

he had grasped her, throwing her away from him where she fell against the wall, and, supporting herself, Eve watched him crumble. It was with immense satisfaction that she watched him suffer.

Beginning to realise that there might be some element of truth in what she had told him, that what he had wanted for so long had been finally and irretrievably snatched away, Gerald received it with pain and disbelief. It was too much to be borne. He moaned bestially and seemed to disintegrate into agonising torment before Eve's eyes. She knew she should feel sorry for him, but his menacing threats had instilled so much fear inside her, encapsulating her in an ice-cold, venomous rage that gave her no grounds for pity.

Gerald turned his wretched, demented face from her and moved to the door, breathing heavily.

'Where are you going?' she asked, moving forward in alarm. 'You cannot mean to leave us here.'

'You will remain here until I have decided what to do with you,' he hissed, turning his ravaged face to her once more. 'And don't look so smug. This is not over. You haven't won yet.'

'Come to your senses, Gerald,' she cried, beginning to panic. 'At least take Jonathan home. Have you thought what the consequences of your actions might be? Do you suppose no one will wonder where we are—that they will come look-ing for us?'

'They will never find you here,' he cried savagely. 'It will be hard to prove that I am involved in your disappearance— and should I think of disposing of you it will be no problem. It will be thought you wandered off in search of the boy. There are several uncapped mine shafts in the area and, as you know, accidents happen. At least if you are dead you will unable to accuse me of abduction.'

Eve began to panic as terror swept through her. He seemed to have thought of everything. 'Better that than to be accused of murder—which Marcus will prove. That you can be sure of.'

'Not even he will be clever enough to do that,' Gerald snapped, turning from her.

Alarmed that he was going to leave them there, Eve ran to him and appealed to him to let them go, but a ferocious glance and a violent shove that sent her crashing against the wall once more, showed her the futility of such arguments and he went out, making sure the door was well secured behind him. In desperation she sprang towards it, hammering on the solid wood with her fists, begging him to release them, but all she could hear was the still-driving rain and Gerald and his associates riding away from the shed.

Once again Eve found herself alone with Jonathan, who was whimpering softly with his face buried in her skirts. Utterly dejected and chilled to the bone she sat on the floor, pulling the terrified little boy down into her arms whilst trying to calm her own quivering nerves, her imagination beginning to work feverishly as their waiting began anew.

Chapter Fifteen

With almost the entire neighbourhood out searching for Eve and Jonathan, after making a fruitless search along the river and the pond, Marcus headed for Burntwood Hall, intent on confronting Gerald face to face.

He was shown into the drawing room where Gerald, reclining in front of a huge fire, was feeling utterly deflated in the light of what Eve had told him, his instinct—which was unreliable at the best of times—telling him she might not have been lying in an attempt to secure her release. After all, on recollection, he had thought it odd at the time that both she and Fitzalan had suddenly gone to Cumbria. Already he was bitterly regretting his actions and cursing himself for a fool. By abducting Eve he had seriously jeopardised his newly found status, and after much contemplation he could think of no honourable way of extricating himself without being arrested.

Opposite him sat Angela. For a long time she and Gerald had shared a dubious kind of friendship, being too much alike for it to be close—each holding a certain amount of mistrust for the other. But Angela knew from his past dealings with some of his associates that he could make a dangerous enemy and considered it to her disadvantage to have him as such. She had only just arrived at Burntwood Hall and was unaware that anything untoward had happened to Eve or the boy.

Surprise registered in Gerald's eyes when Marcus strode in, which, Marcus assumed, was feigned for his benefit, for he was certain he was expected. He also detected an underlying sense of nervousness and agitation behind Gerald's tense features.

Marcus was wet through, his clothes and coal-black hair clinging to his flesh, but there was no mistaking the imposing, angry man who glared at Gerald with fierce, pale blue eyes as cold as South Atlantic ice floes. His uncompromising face was set as hard as granite, his body powerful beneath his clothes, and it was all he could do to stop himself pouncing on Gerald and beating him to a bloody pulp but, not wishing to jeopardise either Eve's or Jonathan's safety, he behaved with ominous coolness.

Gerald watched him approach, making no attempt to hide his dislike. His tread had a measured, almost sinister steadiness. He rose casually and faced him. 'Why, Mr Fitzalan! To what do I owe this rather dubious pleasure?'

No matter how much he tried Marcus could not control his seething anger on meeting Gerald's insolent, somewhat smug stare. 'This is not a social call. Were it up to me I would never have set foot in this house again now Eve has left. You know why I am here so I shall be brief and to the point. You do not need me to tell you that Eve and the Parkinson boy have gone missing. I know you are responsible. Where are they? Where are you holding them?'

Gerald stiffened at the abruptness of the question and his eyes narrowed as they locked on those of his visitor. 'I don't know what you're talking about. The charge is ridiculous. Why should you think I am responsible for their disappearance?'

'We both know why.' Marcus pitched his voice low, the delivery of his words cold and lethal, his ice blue eyes gleaming with a deadly purpose. 'When it comes to the matter of

Atwood Mine, if you believe threats and bullying will achieve your purpose you are mistaken. Eve told me of your threats towards her, and when I would have come and confronted you she begged me not to. I now have good reason to regret not doing so.

'You made a serious error in threatening her, and you made an even more serious error when you chose to abduct her—which, I might remind you, is a serious criminal offence. You can be assured that the law will come down heavy on you and you will be committed to prison for a very long time—if they don't hang you.'

Sweat began to glisten on Gerald's forehead and he seemed to lose a little of his confidence as he shrank before the cold fury in Marcus's eyes. But with his own safety at stake he refused to surrender.

'I told you. I know nothing about her disappearance. Whatever she has told you was untrue—and if you believe I would harm a relative of mine you are mistaken,' Gerald lied, Eve's connection to him making no difference in his desire to gain Atwood Mine.

'So you would like me to believe. But you showed little sign of surprise when I told you she was missing. I feel sickened at the thought of someone as sweet and decent as Eve in your cruel and unscrupulous hands. You dared,' he said through clenched teeth, 'you dared to abduct her, thinking that by this means you would bring her to agree to cancel her marriage to me. Well, mark my words, I shall find her.'

Gerald shrugged, trying to look unconcerned while hanging on to Marcus's words in the sudden hope that Eve had been bluffing about a marriage taking place between them in Cumbria after all. His mind worked with sharp cunning, for there might still be a chance that he could succeed with his plan. If a marriage had not occurred between them then there was a possibility that he could still acquire the mine—if Eve were dead.

But to dispose of Eve he would have the unpleasant task of

disposing of the boy too. He would have to, otherwise Jonathan would condemn him, for he could not expect the boy to remain silent once he was set free. He cursed afresh the bungling idiots he had employed to abduct Eve. They should have separated the boy and Eve. He should never have let the boy see him. But it was too late now for self-recriminations

'I hope you do,' Gerald retorted coolly, speaking callously, 'and I hope she is not harmed and you do not find a corpse.'

'You would not dare,' growled Marcus, his expression murderous. His eyes flashed dangerously and he restrained himself with effort. With his fists clenched he held back and gained control of himself, and the hot rage that had possessed him since he had left the river where Eve had been abducted slowly cooled down to an icy anger. The air between them was charged with friction.

Gerald's smug expression began to disappear and he shifted with unease as the ice blue eyes continued to accuse. 'I've told you. Her disappearance has nothing to do with me.'

'And I've told you that I do not believe you. You are a scoundrel, Somerville, who can hold his own with the worst of them. I swear that if you harm one hair on Eve's head, or the boy's, there will be no hiding place safe enough to keep you from my vengeance. I shall settle my account the way you settle yours. You may be a Somerville and have inherited the title, but I am a powerful man and I have powerful friends, and I will destroy you if you so much as touch Eve. I swear by all that is holy that I will kill you with my own hands.'

'Even if you hang for it?'

'It will be a pleasure to pay the consequences afterwards to rid the earth of scum of your sort,' Marcus growled.

Angela stepped forward, and Marcus, having given her scant attention, acknowledged her presence with eyes that had never seen her before. His voice spoke to a stranger.

'As you will have gathered I am in no mood for social niceties, Angela. I am hardly surprised to see you here,' he mocked, casting a condescending, well-meaning glance over them both. 'Birds of a feather, and all that. It would not surprise me to learn that you are involved in this.'

Angela shivered beneath his cold, emotionless eyes, feeling slightly nonplussed. Having listened to the angry interchange between the two men she had gathered the gist of their conversation but, contrary to what Marcus might think, she had taken no part in Eve's abduction. Knowing Gerald's malice and determination to stop a marriage from taking place between Marcus and Eve—which had been as strong as her own but for different reasons—no matter what crime he was guilty of, if he went down she would make certain he did not drag her down with him.

'I know nothing about any of this. You must believe that.'

Strangely Marcus did. She might be guilty of malice and jealousy towards Eve, but he did not believe she would cause her any physical harm. 'Not only has Eve disappeared but also Jonathan Parkinson. His parents will be out of their minds with worry.' He looked at Gerald sharply. 'Where are they, damn you?' he demanded, his fists bunched by his sides as he restrained the urge to lash out at him, his patience almost worn out.

'I've told you, I do not know.' Gerald glowered at him. 'And now I suggest you leave quickly—before I summon the servants and have you thrown out.'

'I'm going, but this is not the end of the matter. I shall return with the law, Somerville, and then we'll see how eager you are to remain silent.'

When Marcus had walked out Gerald's face was as white as his shirt, for he knew with a shattering certainty that he had got himself into a situation from which he was beginning to see there was no way out. If he set off for the Kettlewell Mine now he would be followed, for he strongly suspected Marcus would be having his movements watched. Angela's eyes bored into his, seeing panic and a desperate fear staring out of their depths, knowing exactly what he was guilty of and eager to learn the whole of it.

'Dear Lord! It's incredible. You stupid, mindless fool,' she rasped. 'What have you done? Marcus was right. You will go to any lengths to obtain that damned mine. But no matter what you have in mind for Eve, you cannot harm the boy. Surely not even you would stoop so low as to hurt a child.'

Gerald began pacing up and down the room, becoming more agitated by the moment as he frantically tried to think of a way out. He stopped pacing long enough to look at Angela, suddenly thinking that she might be able to offer a solution to the dilemma he was in, although discretion was hardly her stock in trade.

'Very well—I admit it. I did have Eve abducted with the intention of compromising her sufficently so that she would have no choice but to marry me instead of Fitzalan. But it all went hopelessly wrong. Whatever I had planned for Eve, I had not bargained on the boy. He appeared when the men I employed were in the process of carrying her off, and they had no choice but to take him along.'

'Then where are they now?'

'If I tell you, can I rely on your entire confidence?'

'Only if you promise not to harm them.'

'I can't do that. Don't you see? I stand to lose everything.'

Angela moved closer, reaching out and grabbing his arm, her fingers clenching it so hard that he winced and tried to jerk away. She bent her face close to his, her eyes steadfastly burning into his own. 'You will lose everything anyway, Gerald. Marcus will find her—and when he does, if it is too late, you will hang. So, answer me. Where are they?'

Gerald seemed to sag, sensing all was lost. 'In one of the disused sheds at the worked-out Kettlewell Mine—a mile inland off the Leeds road.'

Angela stared at him for just a moment before turning and rushing out of the room, hoping she would be in time to catch Marcus before he left.

Having left the house, Marcus felt the dire need for fresh air to fill his lungs, to clear his head so that he might think, for his fruitless meeting with Gerald had affected him more than he realised. He paused to have a word with the groom who had taken charge of his horse, questioning him about the buildings in and on the estate, intending not to leave any stone unturned if he was to find Eve and the boy.

It came as a surprise when Angela appeared from the house, running quickly towards him, disregarding the rain as it soaked her clothes. Marcus looked at her coldly.

'Well?'

'You must believe that I had no part in this, Marcus. I can be accused of many things, but I am not a murderess. Gerald has told me that Eve is at the old Kettlewell Mine off the Leeds Road. Do you know how to get there?'

Marcus paled visibly. 'Yes. There isn't a mine in the area I don't know about—but I have reason to be alarmed that he has taken her there. The mine hasn't been worked for some time, but as yet I believe the shaft remains uncapped. I'll go directly. Have someone follow with a carriage and tell them to hurry. There's no telling what state they'll be in when I get there.'

Consumed with an acute sense of urgency, without wasting another moment Marcus had hoisted himself into the saddle and disappeared in a curtain of rain, unaware as he did so that Gerald, overcome with panic, and determined to make one last desperate attempt to save himself, had fled from the house by a back way, regretting having told Angela where Eve and the boy could be found. In no time at all he too was riding towards the Kettlewell Mine, hoping to get there before Marcus and remove any evidence of them having been there.

It would be growing dark soon and the very thought of spending the night in the shed horrified Eve. She was tired and exhausted by fear and anger, by despair that there was no reprieve—and even by hunger. She could not remember when they had last eaten. Jonathan, his tender lips set in a grim line and fear filling his eyes, was miserable and terrified and beginning to shiver in his damp clothes. It was turning extremely cold inside the shed, and she knew if they were there much longer he would catch a chill and could become very ill.

In sheer frustration and frozen to the marrow, after the first aftermath of shock wore off, rage began to burn inside Eve at Gerald's wickedness, growing so intense that she ceased to feel the cold. Her rage generated a peculiar kind of strength and she became infuriated that she might fail to escape. Never had she believe one person could be so evil—the evil side to his nature being robust, no doubt well developed by the wild and wicked ways he lived by whilst in London.

She was unprepared to sit and wait for Gerald to return, having decided their fate, without making some attempt to obtain their freedom. In the gloom she feverishly went and tried the door, seeing the wood was beginning to rot in places, but to her disappointment it wouldn't budge. No doubt it was chained and padlocked on the outside.

With a frenzied urgency she gathered everything she thought might be of use to try and prise the door from its rusty hinges—three in all—hoping the screws holding them in place might be forced out of the wooden jamb or that the hinges might break with some persuasion.

Taking an old broken pick she found on the floor of the shed along with other broken implements, she forced the long steel-curved head between the door and the jamb to use as a lever, grasping the broken shaft and gathering all her strength as she put her entire weight behind it, regardless of the damage the splintered shaft was doing to the tender palms of her hands. There was a slight splintering of the wood around the hinge but the door was stout and stubborn and resisted all her efforts.

Seeing what she was trying to do Jonathan willingly came to help, and together their strength—made five times greater by the spur of freedom—caused one of the hinges to snap. Jonathan gave a whoop of triumph, seeming to recover some of his spirits as he became eager to begin on the second hinge.

Eve's heart was beating wildly and her jaw was set as they

set about it, repeating the same process as for the first, pulling and pushing together, with Eve uttering gentle words of encouragement to Jonathan all the while. Concerned about his tender hands gripping the splintered shaft, she tore a strip of fabric from her dress and wrapped it round.

When the second hinge finally snapped, with freedom so close, sweating and gasping for breath, they lost no time in attacking the last hinge at the bottom of the door, such was their determination to be free of their prison before Gerald came back. Very slowly it yielded to the pressure, and using their last ounce of strength they pulled the door inwards and together stepped outside, their spirits soaring. They were free at last.

It was warmer outside than it had been inside the shed. The storm had passed and the rain had stopped and a cool, refreshing breeze stirred the shining, dripping trees around the disused mine. In the crystalline clarity that had been left in the storm's wake, Eve glanced at her surroundings, recognising the Kettlewell Mine, closed for the past eighteen months, its situation not so convenient and advantageous as the larger Atwood Mine. It was approximately two miles as the crow flies from the river where they had been abducted, and not a soul was about.

The mine had an air of neglect and abandonment, with a motley collection of sheds, all in an advanced state of dereliction except the one in which they had been imprisoned. Some old tubs were full of water and the ground was strewn with old haulage ropes and the remains of a rotting horse gin, gradually becoming buried beneath a wild tangle of ivy and weeds, the wood surrounding it encroaching on the pit yard. Her blood froze at the sight of the black gaping hole of the uncapped mine shaft, with nothing to protect the passer-by from falling into the gaping chasm but a crumbling, low stone wall surrounding it.

The area around Atwood had numerous exhausted pits, their shafts, under the conditions of the lease, carefully filled in and the ground left as it was before. Why this mine had been neglected she had no idea, but it was convenient for Gerald that it had been if he had a mind to dispose of her and Jonathan.

Eve paused for a moment, undecided which way to go, but then she took Jonathan's hand tightly in her own. 'Come along, Jonathan. It's growing dark so we must hurry. I know where we are, having ridden this way many times, so we won't get lost.'

Taking an old overgrown wagon track through the trees that led down a slight incline, they set off hopefully in the direction of Jonathan's home. Having taken a different route from Marcus to the Kettlewell Mine, Gerald was the first to arrive at the shed, becoming overcome with fury when he realised his prisoners had escaped. Aware that everything he had recently gained was about to be destroyed, he set off in pursuit like a man possessed, in the direction he knew they would be heading.

Marcus came upon the shed minutes later, but he feared they might have been taken elsewhere by men Gerald might have left to guard them. He paused, undecided which direction to take, but on seeing the muddy ground churned up by horses' hooves and human footprints, and seeing some of them belonged to a child, he realised they were heading in the direction of Atwood.

It was a relief when Eve saw the open fields and the river in the distance through a break in the trees, for the light was fading quickly and she had no wish to be in the woods after dark—the time when one's imagination began to play strange tricks, when everything became weird and uncanny, when the tall trees became awesome and took on the appearance of giants, and one imagined skulking figures could be seen in the shifting shadows among the undergrowth.

She shivered, hearing the yelp and bark of a dog in the distance, but so raw and tense were her nerves, and such was her sense of weariness, that she was convinced it was a wolf that would emerge from the dark, secret world of the undergrowth at any minute and set upon them both with teeth gleaming in a gaping mouth and claws bare.

Quickly she pulled herself together, rebuking herself severely, knowing nothing could be achieved by surrendering to her silly imaginings. Secure in the knowledge that they would soon be home, Eve and Jonathan were unprepared when suddenly a rider, mounted on a tall grey horse, came riding out of the trees like some kind of spectre, bearing down on them at a terrific speed. They became petrified, staring with terrified eyes as he came closer.

Eve recognised Gerald immediately. He was fearsome to look at, with something wild about him, in no way resembling the Gerald of old who was always calm and utterly in control. His face was ravaged by hatred and bitterness, and there was a cold, demonic look in his eyes, his lips drawn tight over his teeth as he bore down on them.

Quickly Eve recovered her presence of mind, and her instinct to protect Jonathan became paramount to all else. She pushed him behind her, unable to get out of the way of the oncoming threat. Knocked sideways by Gerald's horse they fell heavily to the ground, momentarily stunned by the shock of the fall rather than injury. Powerless, they could not move as Gerald began to bear down on them again.

It was the high-pitched scream of a woman that alerted Marcus to their whereabouts and he headed quickly towards the sound. In a few moments he burst upon the scene just as Gerald was about to dismount beside the huddled figures of Eve and Jonathan, but on seeing Marcus's powerful silhouette against the trees, Gerald let out a howl of outrage and frustration, resembling an enduring, hissing spirit of hatred, before digging his heels viciously into his horse's flanks and riding off at breakneck speed, as if all the demons in hell were chasing him.

Eve struggled to her feet, pulling Jonathan with her, and Marcus saw that she was barely able to stand. She had evidently reached the limits of her strength. Her face was as white as alabaster and pinched as if with cold, but her wonderful violet eyes shone with an unearthly brilliance and were fastened on his as she moved towards him. There was a trembling smile on her lips and her magnificent mane of black hair flowed about her shoulders.

'Marcus!' she said, speaking his name again as he seemed not to hear, dwelling on it with wonder, her legs taking on an added strength as she moved towards him, unable to believe he had come to her in time, saved her and Jonathan from the dreadful fate that Gerald had in store for them.

The palms of her hands were scraped raw and bleeding from her efforts to free herself and Jonathan, which she held out to him, tumbling headlong into his arms as they went around her, clasping her fiercely to him at last, where she immediately felt warm, secure and protected—at one with this man she loved above all else. It was as if she had come home.

At that moment Eve felt more tired than she had ever felt in her whole life. It was as if the last few hours had been days and had drained her of every particle of strength. For a long moment they clung to each other in silence, too relieved and deeply moved by the depth of their feelings for speech.

'Eve—my darling girl,' Marcus said at length. 'It's all right now. Everything is all right. You are safe,' he whispered, overcome with a profound relief that he had found them in time. 'What a time I have had trying to find you. That madman of a Somerville planned his stroke with evil cunning.'

'Yes,' Eve murmured against his neck, a great unbelievable joy overwhelming her. 'I'm safe—free. Oh, Marcus, I can't believe it's really you. Thank God you came in time.'

'When I think of you shut up in that place, knowing of your ordeal, of your terror—of the damage a man of Gerald's nature might have done to you—I could kill him.'

'Hush,' said Eve, raising her head and looking into his tormented eyes. 'I am all right, Marcus. Truly. He did not touch me in the way I know you mean, and for that I am thankful.'

'You look quite worn out. Are either of you hurt?' he asked, holding Eve at arm's length and looking with concern at them both. He was relieved to see that Jonathan looked surprisingly well as he looked up at him in wide-eyed wonder, but Marcus was alarmed when he saw a thin trickle of crusted blood on the side of Eve's face. Murderous fury filled his eyes and reaching up he touched it gently with the tips of his fingers, seeing her wince slightly. 'How did this happen?'

'I took a tumble—hitting my head when the men Gerald employed to abduct me came upon me unawares. But don't worry. I am exhausted but quite unharmed.'

Other people out searching for them, also having been alerted by Eve's scream, suddenly appeared on the scene, taking charge of Jonathan and allowing Marcus to go in pursuit of Gerald.

'Take them to the house,' he ordered. 'Quickly. I'll go after Gerald. If I don't go now it will soon be too dark.'

Eve looked at him in alarm as Jonathan was being lifted up on to a horse in front of one of the rescuers, his little face smiling now, for the whole thing had turned into one big adventure he couldn't wait to tell his sisters about.

'You will be careful, Marcus,' she begged as he swung himself effortlessly into the saddle. 'I couldn't bear it if anything should happen to you.'

Bending down he kissed her upturned lips. 'I will,' he said hoarsely. 'After what Gerald has done this day he has much to answer for. I do not intend letting him escape.'

Eve watched him go, and as she did so she glanced up automatically at the sky, seeing that all the stars were out, shining brightly in a clear, darkening sky, with no evidence of the storm that had raged throughout the day.

Chapter Sixteen

Losing no more time Marcus gave chase, relieved when he had Gerald within his sights once more, and as he gave his horse its head, plunging through the thick woods that cloaked the low hills, he was possessed of a grim determination not to let Gerald escape.

They were heading in the direction of Atwood, and it was a relief when he emerged from the trees and was able to see him clearly as he rode at breakneck speed towards the river, splashing through it and riding over ground that became uneven, broken and treacherous the closer he got to the quarry.

Aware that Marcus was in pursuit and gaining on him, without checking his horse's stride Gerald thrashed its sweating flanks hard with his whip. The terrified horse bolted from the pain cruelly inflicted on it, riding closer to the precarious, crumbling perimeter of the quarry, the recent rain having formed a pond at the bottom that was littered with piles of rocks and boulders which had become dislodged over the years.

Hawthorn and brambles grew thickly along the upper edge to deceive the eye, partly covering the slippery path which was in danger of crumbling down the steep precipice after the recent heavy rain. Marcus could see Gerald getting ever closer to the edge and shouted a warning, but he ignored Marcus. It wasn't until Gerald felt the ground beneath him shudder and he saw loosened earth and rocks tumbling down to the bottom of the quarry, that he tried to draw his horse away, but it was too late.

With a high-pitched, maddened squeal the horse reared up, losing its footing and thrashing its legs wildly at the empty air as it toppled over the edge. Gerald's face registered horror and surprise as he fought to regain control, but there was nothing he could do. Pulling his own horse to a halt, Marcus watched helplessly as horse and rider were somersaulted through the air, seeming to hover for a brief second like a bird, before becoming separated and bouncing off the rocky side of the quarry, finally reaching the bottom where they both lay still.

By this time some of the other riders out with the search party had caught up, and seeing what had happened immediately dismounted and accompanied Marcus down an overgrown track, once used by countless wagons and horses to shift the stone hewn out of the giant hole. Gerald was lying on his back, his limbs flung out grotesquely. His brown eyes were wide open and staring, a thin trickle of blood forming at his mouth. Marcus did not need to place his head on his chest to listen for a heartbeat that did not exist to know that Gerald was dead.

Relief was clearly felt in the Parkinson household when Eve and Jonathan returned, mercifully unharmed. Mrs Parkinson swept the little boy into her arms, refusing to let him out of her sight ever again. On hearing of the events leading up to their abduction, after scolding him severely for going off and causing so much trouble, she hugged him again.

After removing his clothes and placing him in a hot mustard bath, she put him to bed with a bowl of soup, where he was cosseted by all his sisters and his mother. Being a robust child he suffered no aftereffects from the ordeal, not even a chill after his soaking. But the story of how they had escaped from the shed would be an adventure he would never tire of telling.

* * *

The day of Eve's abduction and her imprisonment in the shed at the old Kettlewell Mine was like a grotesque nightmare in her memory. The hour was late but she refused to go to bed until she had seen Marcus. It was as though all the energy she had concentrated on getting out of that shed, of escaping Gerald's evil and protecting Jonathan, had drained out of her, and her spirits sank to such a low ebb that she almost ceased to function.

When she heard the news of Gerald's death in the quarry from one of the searchers, who called at the house with the news, she was overcome with shock—as was Matthew, who left immediately to go to him, even though it was too late.

When Gerald's body had been removed from the quarry, Marcus came straight to her. The house was quiet now, everyone having retired to their room after the worry and excitement of the day's events. Eve came down from her room where she had been resting, waiting for him to come to her.

As she came towards him, her hands outstretched, rage rose inside Marcus when he saw how deeply her ordeal at Gerald's hands had affected her. She was pitiful to look at. Her violet eyes were enormous in her pale face, the dark circles of pain and terror making them look even larger.

He opened his arms and she walked into them like a child seeking succour, but before she laid her head against his chest he saw her chin tremble and tears she could no longer hold back brimming in her eyes and spilling over.

'Oh, Marcus,' she wept, over and over again, with her face against his chest, letting the violence of all the raw emotions that would not come before now flow uncontrollably out of her. He held her a long time, rocking her and kissing her hair, murmuring sweet, gentle words of comfort while she sobbed, quietly and wretchedly, waiting patiently until she had mastered her tears, aching with a love for her that was like a deep, physical pain.

He cradled her in his arms, holding her close while she poured out all her anguish and misery. Everything that had happened to her that day came out in a torrent of words and he listened, knowing that it was good for her to talk like this, that it would help cleanse her of the evil Gerald had perpetrated against her, that it would help with the healing process later.

When Eve became still and quiet in his arms, feeling an unbelievable comfort of knowing he was holding her, that she was safe, she sighed, wiping her tears with her hands.

'My poor darling,' Marcus murmured, his lips against her hair. 'What has he done to you?'

'Nothing that won't heal,' she whispered bravely.

'How is the boy?'

'Jonathan is all right. He—he survived it well—better than I have myself, it would seem,' she said, smiling up at him through her wet lashes.

'Thank God.'

'We—we were told what happened to Gerald. Where is he?' she asked. 'Where has he been taken?'

'Burntwood Hall. It was his home,' he said gently. 'Matthew is there.'

'I know. He—he is taking it very badly. Did he suffer, Marcus?'

'I don't think so. I should think he died instantly. His neck was broken.'

Eve leaned back in his arms and looked up at him, her eyes luminous with tears. 'Gerald tried to destroy me, Marcus. If I hadn't got out of that shed I am certain he would have returned and killed me—and Jonathan, who just happened to be there when the men he paid to abduct me seized their chance by the river.'

Marcus's arms tightened around her. 'If he had then he would not have escaped with his life. I would have found him and exacted my revenge,' he said hoarsely, his voice shaking with angry emotion. 'Come,' he said, taking her hand and leading her into the empty parlour, where they sat close together on a high-backed settle beside the dying embers of the fire, Marcus's arm holding her close, reluctant to let her go ever again. 'How are you feeling now?'

'Overwhelmed by a turmoil of emotions. Oh—it's a combination of relief, gladness, and at the same time a feeling of horror, mingled with some element of surprise—knowing that the man who intended destroying my own life is dead himself. Oh, Marcus, I was so frightened.'

Marcus held her tighter. 'So was I. When Matthew told me you had disappeared, you have no idea how my thoughts tormented me—what I went through.' Sighing, he kissed the top of her head where it rested on his shoulder. 'When I imagined what he might be doing to you—that he might already have killed you—I went through hell. Dear God, how I wish I had never gone to Leeds—that I had insisted on you staying at Brooklands. If I had, none of this would have happened. I should have foreseen what he would do.'

'Don't blame yourself. It wasn't your fault. Neither of us were to know he would go to such drastic lengths.'

'You are very generous but I cannot be acquitted so lightly, my love.'

Eve stirred against him, raising her head and meeting his fierce gaze, seeing just how much he had suffered on her behalf. 'Yes, you can. When Gerald came to see me in the hut where he had Jonathan and me imprisoned, in my desperation I tried to bluff my way out by telling him we had been married by special licence in Cumbria, and that no matter what he did to me it was too late, that he could never get his hands on the mine.'

There was incredulity and admiration in Marcus's eyes. 'And he believed you?'

'At first he was suspicious and uncertain—but I tried to sound so convincing that I think he did in the end. He was so angry I wasn't certain what he would do. He became demented. I begged him to release us but he wouldn't listen. He left us there. I had no way of knowing what he would do next. By the way, there is one thing I do not understand. How did you know where to look for us? When you came upon us in the wood you were coming from the direction of the Kettle-well Mine. Someone must have told you we were there.'

Marcus smiled tenderly down at her. 'It will surprise you to learn that you have Angela to thank for that. She was the one who told me where I could find you.'

Eve stared at him aghast. 'Angela? Are you telling me that *she* had something to do with my abduction?'

'No. She knew nothing about it—not until I went to Burntwood Hall and confronted Gerald. She was there at the time and was clearly horrified that Gerald might be involved in some way. It would seem he told her where you could be found after I'd left, although I do not doubt she managed to force the truth out of him—by whatever means I know not, and nor do I wish to, but I'm grateful to her that she did. She may be jealous of you, my love, but I do not believe she would wish you any physical harm. I do not believe her to be vin-dictive enough for that.'

'I'm glad you think so,' Eve whispered, surprised by Angela's behaviour. 'Acting alone Gerald was bad enough—but Angela and Gerald together would have been a lethal com-bination. How he must have longed for you to confirm that what I had told him about a marriage taking place between us was true or false.'

'He couldn't very well ask me outright. If he had he would have been forced to confess his part in your abduction—and been too afraid of the consequences. I would have had no compunction about killing him.'

Eve drew back and looked up at him, shuddering slightly on observing his taut features and the steely gleam in his eyes, knowing he spoke the truth. 'You would have done that for me?' she asked.

'I would do anything for you, Eve' he said achingly, unable to restrain himself, pulling her back into his arms. 'Never doubt it. I love you and cannot imagine my life without you. I adore you and very soon the whole world will know it.'

'There is one thing that troubles me greatly, Marcus.'

'What is that?'

'These people Gerald owed money to. Are they likely to approach Matthew—being Gerald's brother?'

'I don't think so. If they try I doubt they will get anything. The loan had nothing to do with him. The people who lent Gerald the money are scoundrels of the worst kind. No doubt it's the unfortunate people in the future—people who find themselves in the same desperate situation as Gerald—who will end up paying. The interest on such loans is extortionate. Oh—I almost forgot,' he said, changing the subject. 'I bought you something in Leeds.'

Taking the ring he had bought for her out of his pocket, he placed it on her finger. Eve sighed, dazzled by its beauty, content to wallow in Marcus's doting gaze, having no doubts that he loved her—genuinely loved her—and that that love would grow with time and supplant everything else in importance. She could see that in his eyes and it made her ecstatically happy.

The following morning when Marcus was taking it into his own hands to see that the uncapped shaft at the Kettlewell Mine was securely sealed off, Matthew came to see Eve.

On seeing his deep distress over the death of his brother, her heart went out to him. He was distraught, almost demolished by it, knowing what it would mean to him and that drastic changes would take place and affect his life. He was panicked, and at one fell swoop his youthful air had vanished.

'You know what this means, don't you, Matthew?' Eve said when they were alone walking in the garden, feeling the sun cocooning them in its warmth. 'Gerald's death makes you the heir to the Somerville estate.'

'Yes, I know. But it is not the way I wished to inherit Burntwood Hall.'

'It is more than the truth when I say you are eminently

worthy of taking my father's place, Matthew. It makes me very happy to know the estate will be in capable hands.'

'Thank you, Eve. I shall do my best to always be worthy of it. I promise you that. But I never wanted this. I never thought I would inherit the estate at all. It was always Gerald's right, to pass on to his sons.'

'None of us could have foreseen this happening, Matthew,' Eve said sympathetically.

'I know. I knew what Gerald was—and I also knew he would never reform and give up his wild ways and settle down and take a sincere interest in the estate. But despite what he did to you, Eve—which was quite outrageous and unforgivable and has shocked me deeply—he was always civilised with me. Being so much younger than he was, he always looked out for me—especially after our parents died—and there were times when we were close.'

Eve let him talk, calmly listening to him defending the man who would have had no qualms in getting rid of her in order to retain Atwood Mine. She knew how difficult it had been for Matthew, growing up in Gerald's shadow, and she was sad for him, fighting the compassion welling up inside her, and the urge to argue and tell him he was a fool to be so generous towards a man whom she believed to have been capable of murder. She resisted the urge to vent her own bitterness, for all the raw emotions Gerald had awakened inside her were as strong as ever.

But she could not be so cruel. She would be immediately sorry. Let Matthew keep his illusions. In his own way he had loved Gerald, and Gerald had always treated Matthew well, regardless of what he was guilty of where everyone else was concerned. No matter how hard it was for her to come to terms with what Gerald had done to her, they had been brothers, and she must respect that.

'He wasn't really wicked,' Matthew went on, his eyes filled with pain and grief as he tried to make Eve see a side to his brother only he knew, one she had never seen and had no wish

to. 'As a boy, and later as a youth, our mother and grandmother doted on him, making him spoiled and unprincipled.
He always had too much of everything and thought the world
owed him obeisance. He was too good looking by far—more
so than I was,' he said with admirable humility.

'You are generous towards your brother, Matthew. More
than he deserves,' Eve said gently. 'Your loyalty is to be commended. But do not underestimate yourself. I cannot think
kindly of Gerald, but I do understand that he was your brother
and he did not deserve you. If he had been half the man you
are, my father and I would have been content knowing the
estate was to pass to him—but his character made that impossible.'

'I know, and I do understand, Eve. But,' he sighed, 'I am
a simple man and life has suddenly become extremely com-
plex.'

'I think you'll cope admirably,' she smiled, linking her arm
through his as they continued to walk companionably around
the garden. 'My father would have been a happy man,
Matthew, knowing you were to move into Burntwood Hall—
especially if Emma is to share it with you.'

Matthew stared at her in shocked amazement. 'Emma?
Why—I—I had not thought—'

'You are going to marry her, aren't you, Matthew?'

'Why—yes,' he said, smiling with embarrassment, awkward
suddenly. 'I suppose I am—if she will have me, of course. I
haven't asked her.'

'Then when the time is right I think you should,' Eve said
softly, teasingly, her eyes eloquent and her lips smiling encouragement. 'You are a good man, Matthew. No one knowing you could fail to love you. Whatever happens, no one can
ever doubt you are worthy to fall into my father's footsteps.'

Eve returned to Burntwood Hall and the servants welcomed
her back warmly and tearfully, knowing her return was only
temporary and that she would leave very soon when she mar-

ried Mr Fitzalan. But they were happy knowing Matthew Somerville was next in line and would shortly be taking up residence.

Eve had them all assembled in the hall, telling them Matthew would undoubtedly want them all to stay on, that he would be depending on them, and she knew they would give him all the help and consideration due to him.

Gerald's funeral was as small and quiet an affair as Eve's marriage to Marcus one week later. Eve, having cast off the gloom of mourning, was a vision of loveliness in a dress of cream silk, as slender as a wand as she moved beside Marcus Fitzalan, tall and powerful, looking extremely handsome in his black suit beneath which he wore a white satin waistcoat, his ebony hair brushed smoothly back from his brow.

The wedding was attended by just a few close friends, followed afterwards by a wedding breakfast at Burntwood Hall, where the atmosphere was light-hearted, and Eve would catch her husband's eye and a smile would move across his lean face, his eyes becoming more vividly blue over the rim of his champagne glass, silently informing her of his impatience for the night to come.

'Marriage obviously agrees with you,' he told her softly when he managed to get her to himself for a brief moment. 'I have never seen you look more delectable than you do at this moment.'

'Don't all brides?' she murmured.

'I only have eyes for the one,' he replied.

Emma was almost as radiant as the bride, losing no time in telling Eve that there would be another wedding in the spring of the following year, that Matthew had asked her to marry him.

Eve hugged her happily. 'I am so thrilled for you, Em. Things couldn't have turned out better.'

'I never thought this would happen to me. Can you imagine it? Me! Lady Somerville! Oh—I'll never get used to it.'

'Yes, you will,' laughed Eve, 'and the title could not have

gone to a nicer person. Now I shall be able to come back to Burntwood Hall whenever I like.'

Emma became serious. 'We've both been fortunate, Eve—but Matthew is nervous about his inheritance. It's such an enormous responsibility.'

'He needn't be. He has you by his side and he is by far a worthier heir to the estate than Gerald ever was.'

Mr Soames was present for the wedding, clearly satisfied and highly delighted that things had been resolved between Eve and Marcus Fitzalan in the way her father would have wished. The love they felt for each other was plain to see; in fact, it was difficult to believe they were the same two people who had faced each other with so much rancour at the reading of Sir John's will.

'With Gerald dead and Matthew in charge of the estate, Eve,' he said when they were alone, 'your father would have been well pleased. His main reason for the conditions laid down in his will was to see you taken care of by someone he could trust. Knowing your reasons for doing so, I think you made a wise decision putting Atwood Mine in trust for your children. I know your father would not have objected to this.'

Eve had no regrets when she left Burntwood Hall with Marcus and his mother for her new home.

Ruth Fitzalan, who had been deeply upset by Eve's ordeal at the hands of her father's cousin, could not be happier at the way everything had turned out. She was also enormously relieved that both Eve and Marcus were in agreement about Atwood Mine, having put it in the hands of trustees until any children they might have came of age and were in a position themselves to decide what was to be done with it. Not wishing to be in the way at Brooklands, she had decided to travel to London the following day to stay with her son William, his wife Daisy and their two children.

'Please don't feel that you have to leave Brooklands,' said Eve, aware of her mother-in-law's intent.

'I don't, my dear,' she smiled. 'But it is important that you and Marcus should be alone. I want you to get to know each other and familiarise yourself with Brooklands without me breathing down your neck. I had hoped to travel to London with Angela, but I hear she left last week.'

Marcus and Eve exchanged knowing, secretive glances, having decided not to tell her of Angela's conniving and malicious behaviour towards Eve. It would solve no purpose and would sour the close friendship she had with Angela's parents—and besides, had it not been for Angela telling Marcus where Gerald had taken her, everything might have turned out much different.

'Now you're married, I am hoping to spend more time in London—visiting friends and so forth,' Ruth went on. 'And I am so looking forward to seeing William and Daisy and the children again. There is also a strong possibility that Michael may pay them a visit. His ship is due to dock at Plymouth shortly and he has written that he will try and get up to London.'

She looked fondly at her new daughter-in-law sitting close to Marcus, knowing that if she had not been present they would be in each other's arms. Never had she seen two people look more in love than these two and it gladdened her heart.

'I hope you will like living at Brooklands, Eve. I remember when I first came as a bride I was filled with trepidation—but I soon settled down and grew to love the place.'

'Then I am sure I shall,' Eve smiled.

Marcus looked at her, his eyes warm and full of affection. 'And she will love it all the more because I am there,' he teased softly. He arched a brow, amused when Eve gave him a feigned look of exasperation.

'Why, I see your conceit has not diminished now you are a married man, Marcus,' she chided playfully.

'You're not impressed?'

'Not in the least. You're a complete rogue.'

Marcus gazed at her, his eyes amused. 'I do not deny it. But it cannot bother you too much, otherwise you wouldn't have fallen so readily for my irresistible charm,' he teased and he smiled, the kind of smile that would melt any woman's heart.

Eve returned his smile a little shyly. 'I am beginning to see that I was a complete fool to get involved with you. You're quite outrageous.'

'Absolutely,' he grinned.

'He always was,' commented his mother in complete agreement, wishing the carriage would hurry and reach Brooklands so she could leave the two of them alone.

That night as they got to know each other, neither had any complaints. Marcus was a strong, superlatively aggressive, masterful lover, which was an aspect Eve had suspected of him, but he also knew when to be exquisitely tender and polite. How could either of them have believed that theirs could ever be a marriage of convenience? The attraction between them was too powerful, too consuming for either of them to resist.

On finding themselves alone in the room they were to share, unable to keep his hands off Eve a moment longer, Marcus had immediately encircled her with his arms.

'Have I told you you make the most beautiful bride?' he whispered, catching her ear lobe between his teeth and biting it gently before finding her lips, silently informing her of his love as she felt the hot breath in his throat, the hammering in his chest.

Eve smiled, loving him, wanting him. 'Several times,' she breathed, her lips close to his.

'And you look so delectable in your cream dress—but I am impatient to see what you're wearing under it. I suspect it conceals a body destined to stir the lusty instincts of any man.'

Eve laughed up into his face, flushing delightfully. 'Marcus Fitzalan, you are incorrigible. You will see soon enough,' she said, but she soon saw that all form of resistance was futile for already he was expertly fumbling with her buttons. She gasped. 'Marcus! This is not how a gentleman should behave. I have my maid to undress me.'

'And I have dismissed her. I can assure you I make a rather good lady's maid when the occasion requires it.'

'I am sure you do—but I would thank you not to regale me with the lurid details of your past amours. Kindly keep them to yourself,' she laughed breathlessly as he went on to remove her dress completely, leaving her standing before him in her white, soft shift, which was soon removed along with the rest of her clothes.

She stood tall and slender, lithe-limbed and graceful, watching him calmly as his eyes travelled from the top of her dark head to her slender feet, with incredulity and disbelief, before meeting her eyes. They looked at each other for a long moment that stretched into eternity.

'What can I say?' he murmured at length, moving to stand in front of her. 'You look quite incredible. Exquisite.'

Eve trembled, looking up into his blue, brooding eyes, her face full of passion and her moist lips parted and quivering, longing for the kiss she expected but did not come. Instead he brushed her lips with the tips of his fingers, sensing her mood.

'I intend to make love to you until you beg for mercy.' His lips curled into a smile at the warm glow that shone in her wonderful violet eyes, which told him he would be welcome.

Marcus proceeded to do what his fingers had ached to do all evening. Slowly and methodically he unbound her hair, spreading it like a soft, shimmering cloud over her gleaming shoulders before gathering her up into his arms and carrying her to the bed.

As he leant over her his warm, moist lips began to kiss every inch of her naked body and, touching, lingeringly tracing the line of her hip, her thigh, he felt the curl of her body towards his, the inevitable longing stirring his own. Overwhelmed by the intensity of his passion, Eve yielded herself to his soft, caressing touch willingly, clutching and clinging as he covered her quivering body with his own, and he felt her flow into him with a lavish generosity that left him astounded as they came together as easily as night follows day.

Afterwards Marcus gathered her into his arms and sighed, looking down at her upturned face. 'Happy?'

'Ecstatically.'

'You look wonderful. Your eyes are sparkling and your cheeks are pink. In fact, you look radiant and I cannot wait to make love to you again,' he murmured, his wonderful eyes devouring her, and then they were silent, each anticipating and savouring the sensations building up anew inside them.

'You are lovely, Eve—and you were lovely three years ago—the most captivating young lady I had ever seen. You were gentle, innocent, totally unaware of the effect you had on me.'

'And now?'

'Now you are even more beautiful.'

She smiled. 'I think you flatter me to tempt me, Mr Fitzalan,' she teased.

'You are quite right,' he murmured, his eyes glowing with love and adoration as he gazed down at her. 'Are you complaining, Mrs Fitzalan?' he asked, with his lips nuzzling her neck, persistent, soft, passionate.

'Not when I have such a passionate, attentive husband.'

'Then stop resisting and give in to the magic of the moment, my darling,' he murmured.

And she did as she was told, happy to do so now she was his wife, revelling in the sweet anticipation of the rest of the night—and the rest of their lives to come. They loved and slept and towards morning there was more love, and by the time the sun rose Marcus knew that the wonderful temptress who had tried to seduce him three years ago had returned to him. She had not vanished, after all. She was there, just waiting to be resurrected.

* * * * *

MILLS & BOON®

Historical Romance™

Coming next month

THE PASSIONATE FRIENDS
by Meg Alexander

Book 3 of this exciting Regency trilogy: Dan's story

Dan was back. Judith hadn't seen him since she had
refused his proposal and now she was betrothed to
someone else. Dan clearly couldn't forget the past but
then, neither could Judith.

THE WAYWARD HEART
by Paula Marshall

Book 5 in Paula Marshall's Schuyler Family Chronicles

Nicholas had forsaken his family name and fortune to
pursue a career as an author and had fallen in love with
Verena Marlowe. But how could he convince her family
that he was good enough to marry without relying on
his family name?

On sale from 9th October 1998

Available from WH Smith, John Menzies and Volume One

4 FREE
books and a surprise gift!

We would like to take this opportunity to thank you for reading this Mills & Boon® book by offering you the chance to take FOUR more specially selected titles from the Historical Romance™ series absolutely FREE! We're also making this offer to introduce you to the benefits of the Reader Service™—

- ★ FREE home delivery
- ★ FREE gifts and competitions
- ★ FREE monthly newsletter
- ★ Books available before they're in the shops
- ★ Exclusive Reader Service discounts

Accepting these FREE books and gift places you under no obligation to buy, you may cancel at any time, even after receiving your free shipment. Simply complete your details below and return the entire page to the address below. *You don't even need a stamp!*

YES! Please send me 4 free Historical Romance books and a surprise gift. I understand that unless you hear from me, I will receive 4 superb new titles every month for just £2.99 each, postage and packing free. I am under no obligation to purchase any books and may cancel my subscription at any time. The free books and gift will be mine to keep in any case.

H8YE

Ms/Mrs/Miss/Mr...................Initials ....
BLOCK CAPITALS PLEASE

Surname ....

Address ....

....

..........................Postcode..................................

Send this whole page to:
THE READER SERVICE, FREEPOST, CROYDON, CR9 3WZ
(Eire readers please send coupon to: P.O. BOX 4546, DUBLIN 24.)

Historical Romance is being used as a trademark.

JASMINE CRESSWELL

THE DAUGHTER

Maggie Slade's been on the run for seven years now.
Seven years of living without a life or a future because
she's a woman with a past. And then she meets Sean
McLeod. Maggie has two choices. She can either run,
or learn to trust again and prove her innocence.

"Romantic suspense at its finest."

—Affaire de Coeur

1-55166-425-9
**AVAILABLE IN PAPERBACK
FROM SEPTEMBER, 1998**